Through the
Eyes of Blue

Through the Eyes of Blue

by
Catherine Matsalla

eBooks2go
Your Author Journey Begins Here

Quantity Purchases:
Companies, professional groups, clubs, and other organizations may qualify
for special terms when ordering quantities of this title.
For information, email info@ebooks2go.net,
or call (847) 598-1150 ext. 4141.
www.ebooks2go.net

Published in the United States by eBooks2go, Inc. 1827 Walden
Office Square, Suite 260, Schaumburg, IL 60173

ISBN: 978-1-5457-5386-6

Library of Congress Cataloging in Publication

For Nicolette and Austin – I love you forever and beyond.
And for Blue – thank you for inspiring me.

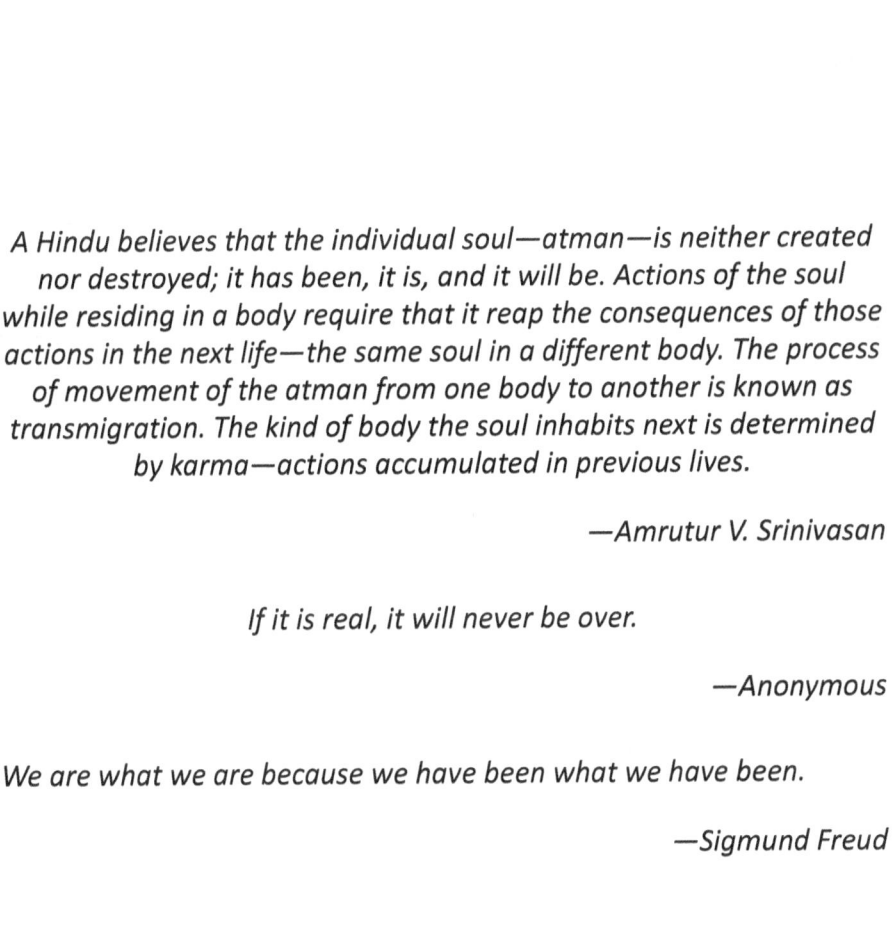

A Hindu believes that the individual soul—atman—is neither created nor destroyed; it has been, it is, and it will be. Actions of the soul while residing in a body require that it reap the consequences of those actions in the next life—the same soul in a different body. The process of movement of the atman from one body to another is known as transmigration. The kind of body the soul inhabits next is determined by karma—actions accumulated in previous lives.

—Amrutur V. Srinivasan

If it is real, it will never be over.

—Anonymous

We are what we are because we have been what we have been.

—Sigmund Freud

Table of Contents

Prologue

Do we truly comprehend how complex love can be? It can be so many things: inimitable, precious, idolized, fleeting, stolen, given, taken away, enduring, and even tragic. Sanskrit legends speak of destined love. It is a karmic connection of two souls who are fated to meet, to collide, and to explode into each other. The legend says that the loved one is instantly recognized because she is loved in every gesture, expression, and word she speaks—every sound she makes and every emotion she holds in her eyes. We know our karmic love by her wings—wings only we can see and that destroy all other desires for love.

So it was in a small village in India long, long ago. This was a destined love described by those who witnessed it—as fierce and as hot as the sun. Perhaps this was the reason for its earthly demise and cosmic immortality. No ordinary person could gaze upon them without being blinded by the intensity of the love they showed each other.

Despite the tradition of arranged marriages, it was determined this couple, Kashi and Amar, were meant to be together from the moment they had laid their spirited eyes upon each other at the apparent naive age of four. The village witnessed their love grow deeper as their bodies grew in age. Each year they became more inseparable, running through the village holding hands, swimming, studying under a tree, or winking at each other during royal ceremonies. The village believed they were extraordinary creatures not only in their physical appearance but also that they must have been sent from the gods to earth as an example of what true love was supposed to be. The talk of the village was this was an arrangement made before this lifetime, and no one should interfere with its destiny. But who are we to presume destiny?

Kashi and Amar said their wedding vows to each other at the age of thirteen in a Vivaha. The celebrations carried on for seven days. The villagers nodded in approval when they saw the tattooed symbols of devotion. Despite their age, Kashi and Amar appeared to hold a lifetime of wisdom, which they demonstrated and shared with whomever they met. Neither cared about earthly possessions or that they were royalty, as they worked together in the fields and ate with the poor no matter how their parents protested. It was forbidden to commune with people of a lower caste, but the villagers protected them from their parents' ridicule through relentless devotion. They fought fiercely and died willingly to protect and grow the kingdom because of their intense devotion to Amar before and especially after the cursed tragedy.

What does a young army commander know about how to handle the devastating loss of his soul mate? How does he handle the guilt? How can he grow old when her life halted in time? Kashi's tragic death silenced a village from believing the gods had blessed this love. It became a new legend that when you become too joyous in your life, too full of happiness and pride, and also too powerful, the gods would strike you down to a life and even an afterlife full of humility and suffering. The gods erase your good karma.

Amar would never forgive himself for Kashi's death. The unanswered questions of ways he could have saved her would haunt him for the rest of his life. He did not take his own life, as some forlorn and tortured lovers do, but he took his suffering as penance and loved no other for the rest of his ninety years.

As a king with no heirs, he was forced by his enemies to relinquish all he and his loyal subjects had conquered in their many years of ruthless battle. On his deathbed, when others had long forgotten the reason for his self-deprecation, he vowed he would make amends to the one irreplaceable reason for his existence. He had tucked deeply in the corners of his memory, yet rehearsed daily, so he would never forget the sound of her voice, the scent of her hair and skin, the caress of her fingers against his face, and the sparkle in her eyes. When he closed his eyes for the very last time, his soul transmigrated into the next pathetic life, and it would continue into another and another. This was his soul's choice. Maybe we *can* control destiny. This would continue until he found her again—to be redeemed by her soul so he could finally forgive himself.

Chapter 1

Parents

I realize now, if it weren't for my parents' divorce, they wouldn't have relented to the idea I get a dog as a companion. I was in those awful awkward preteen years and they worried I was becoming more of a loner than I had always been. I think it was really out of guilt for not spending adequate—for textbook human development—time with me back then. Quite frankly, I got used to being alone because I didn't have much of a choice. We had lived on a rented farm that boarded horses about five miles from the nearest town, and my mother hated to drive me anywhere there were other humans my age, and I was too embarrassed to invite friends over to our old worn and ugly farmhouse. I was fine with not having friends nearby to hang out with. It was not that I didn't like people. I did, and still do, of course. It was just a lot easier to be alone than to try to fit in. I simply preferred my own company to that of my classmates.

My parents were concerned I was being teased or bullied at school, but honestly, my school friends knew me as shy, quiet, smart Giselle, who could run forever. They were OK with that. I was OK with that. My parents were not. They were worriers. So they paid a shrink to psychoanalyze me. He told them I was completely normal and for them not to overanalyze things. He told me he thought I was surprisingly normal despite my parents. I took the opportunity to use my subliminal manipulation to impress upon the psychologist that he suggest to my parents they give me a dog as a way of trying to pull me out of my shell. It would be their idea. I had wanted a dog for so long, but they couldn't be bothered. They didn't have the time.

"Oh my God, this dude thinks I am a sociopath just because I like being alone," I had whined and threw up my arms in rebellion as I circled our small farmhouse kitchen, playing the role with the flare of a turbulent, messed-up, lonely ten-year-old in need of a companion.

"Are you?" she had replied. That was my mom, Mariella Hill-D'Angelo, all in-your-face harshness packaged up in a beautiful body with all the best features from her father, an American Indian, and her mother, who was Irish until she died. Now I think, do we continue to be ourselves after we die? Does nationality matter when we become one with the earth?

My mom inherited the beautiful physical and the not so beautiful character traits from both races, and I won't admit which is which. She had black horsetail thick hair, brilliant green eyes, strong bones, long legs, and slim hips. Yep, she pretty well had it all, including boobs, which I never got from the gene pool. She made all kinds of weird twists, poofs, and braids with her hair. Most of which had annoyed me. I again lost the gene pool with curly, unruly hair that always matted at the nape of my neck. To prevent spiders from nesting, as my mother put it, she would brush it so tightly into a ponytail that my eyebrows ended halfway up my forehead. She refused to let me cut it. She tried to convince me the reason the horses loved me so much was they thought I was one of them, except my tail was on my front end.

My mother was "full of piss and vinegar." She took me through "hell and high water," to quote my father when he was talking about the high-strung stallion we boarded at the farm. During most of my life, our house consisted of a tumultuous blend of "piss and vinegar" mixed with "psycho lonely girl". I recognize now that I was a moody mosaic of Irish feistiness with a small amount of American Indian penchant for placidness, but it all came out through the mouth of an Italian mobster, while my mom was always experiencing some sort of premenstrual syndrome. Then there was the peacemaker, the Italian crooner, my father.

Frank D'Angelo. "Wit da apostrophe, do ya hear me? Wit da apostrophe," he would yell into the phone when ordering something or when at the post office looking for a lost package. He looked like a street fighter off the docks of New York with a Dean Martin face. I think that was why he adored Dean Martin, because they looked so much alike.

"He never drank, you know, Ellie. That was his character on television. But people believed he was an alcoholic in real life. Just goes to show what face you show people in public is not necessarily the face you show yourself in the mirror every morning. Sometimes we have to pretend to be somebody else to get the job done."

My dad was a consummate philosopher, which added to his talent at characterizations to find ways to influence people, including me. He'd pull his shoulders back, stick out his chest, and talk with a New York accent, pretending he was some sort of famous boxer. He always had a way of pacifying my refractory teen attitude. "Whatchoo lookin' at?" he teased me if I threw him a snide curl of my lip while in one of my brooding moods as he danced around on his toes, fists circling in front of his chest. I'd take the same stance, breaking me out of my funk, and he'd throw a roundhouse punch right over my head to start our play boxing until I gave in with a hug around his waist.

"Dad, Mom says you went to college, so why are you driving a truck when you could have been a professor?" I asked when I was at an age to believe any education beyond high school meant you must be brilliantly smart.

My dad would start to pontificate. "Because, Ellie, and listen to me—this is very important. Don't look down on me because of what I chose to do. I love what I do, and it took me a few years to figure that out. When I met your mother, I was in college because it was what my parents wanted. I love learning, but I love the freedom of the road more. I didn't want to work at a desk inside four walls with a boss, jump to a bell, or meet a deadline. Sure, I have deadlines when hauling, but I have freedom too. I found out early what I love to do. You need to find the same. Keep track in your young little head of what makes you happy," he'd say as he tapped gently on top of my head with its tightly pulled-back hair.

I had a comfortable relationship with my dad, but my mother was another story. She never took too much interest in me other than the fame I brought her by the time I got to high school and ranked top in the nation in cross-country running, and later I ranked number one worldwide for ultraendurance running. Before their divorce, I was mostly an inconvenience to her lifestyle.

The reason I figured my parents bickered all the time when my dad was not on the road was my mom didn't like him at home. She didn't like him hanging around, because it cramped her style, and that style was having multiple affairs. Her self-worth was based on how men paid attention to her—too beautiful to be kept in a farmhouse, bored with mundane chores, a husband on the road all the time, and no motivation to hold a job. She invited the attention-giving men to her.

I was an inconvenient pair of eyes and ears in her secret world. She didn't mind when I was out running in the hills or hanging around with the horses. It was the perfect opportunity to sneak in a little male diversion for herself, especially when I was at school. If she needed more time for dalliances—say, on a weekend—she would dare me to run to town with the promise of picking me up later. Soon I figured out I had better run back because she wasn't going to show up. I would take some money from her purse, run to town, eat half a pie at the bakery, and run back.

Back then I felt responsible for my parents' divorce. I felt I started it all. My father had returned home one night and asked my mom what she did with her time while he was away. It was a typical question. She replied with the same typical story, and he didn't listen as usual, as his eyes were glued to reruns of Dean's TV show. But this time I had had enough. My thoughts went back to the day before he got home.

I was miffed for some reason. Probably hadn't done something right in my mom's eyes, so I would get even with her by not going to school. Not sure why I picked that day to play hooky. I never played hooky, because I loved getting away from home. Some would say it was fate. I watched from the barn as a car drove up and a man got out. Nothing too unusual to me, because people came to see their horses all the time. But this guy walked into the house and didn't come out for quite a while, so I sneaked up to peer in through a window, somehow knowing, with an aching gut, that I would see something to validate my suspicions and increase my animosity toward my mother. I stared just long enough, then I turned to run. That was how I dealt with things. I ran.

4

During this typical conversation upon my dad's first night back home, my quiet, deep-seated rebellious side surprisingly piped up behind the protection of my dad sitting in his TV recliner. Before I could stop my vengeful mouth, I asked her, "Who was that man who came to visit inside the house for a few hours?"

I'll never forget her glaring down at me with a mix of shock and anger through narrowed eyes and a furrowed brow. Her eyes shifted toward my father, her eyebrows arched in desperation. Her chin started to tremble. I saw her irises turn dark green, set off by the slight wet, red glow encasing them. I finally outed my mom, but it didn't feel as satisfying as I thought it would. It backfired, hit my dad, ricocheted off him, and hit me. I threw it back at her, hitting her squarely between the eyes. She never saw it coming. How could she have imagined I didn't know what was going on? She expected I was that naive. She assumed I was engulfed in my own little world, as the psychologist had explained. Maybe I was.

My malicious tattling caused a burning chasm between my mother and me. I also broke the tenuous bond in their defective marriage, yet I hated myself for changing the only world I knew. The intense pain I felt in my stomach when my father packed up all his clothes never went away. The pain bounced around my body, depending on which memory triggered it. At times my heart ached to have two parents together again, remembering the laughter and fun times. Other times my head hurt when remembering how I should have thought things out before I instigated the dismantling of my family. I could have kept her secret.

Most of the stuff in our house was a collection of things he didn't care about, except me. The agony of watching him pack and walk out the door while not being able to go with him left me empty. The only reprieve I had was when I got far away from any reminder that he no longer lived with us. I ran to get away from my parents' arguments, and then I ran to get away from the silence. The burden of emotions I carried disappeared when I ran. But my running started way before I understood the need to feel free.

I realize now their unhappiness was not only my mother's fault. It started when I was still in early elementary school. They always started to fight after the usual one happy night of reunion. When the bickering and mean words started up, I would head outside, even in the winter, to try to get as far away as possible. I would run to find peace, until I no longer heard their voices echo in the woods. The forest around the farm brought me solace and became my replacement family. It raised me. The horses we boarded became my siblings in my make-believe adventures as an explorer, cowgirl, or Indian princess. They would watch me with their particular equine mix of big-eyed nervousness and snorting arrogance, oblivious to the role I gave them to play.

Out in the forest, each of us respected each other. The trees only whispered when they talked. Even in a windstorm, despite the audible complaints of their creaking bodies, they made me feel welcome. I felt safe and at home in their world. I felt a primal strength grow within me in the middle of a dark forest while watching a storm brewing in the distance, with winds picking up their strength, chaotically whipping my long hair against my face and whistling whispers in my ear. I felt if the trees could bend to survive storms, so could I. I became a warrior against the winds. The increase of static electricity made me test the limits of time I could remain outside while guessing how long it would take me to sprint back to the house before the hail or rain would sting my exposed skin. I would arrive safely in the back entrance, laughing at my private race against the rain, toweling off before being chastised for wetting the kitchen floor. Those days I was always running from something, and I never wanted to run back.

My parents' divorce gave me a bit of hope for relief from the tension and loud arguments, until I realized I was only going to be staying with my mother. It was not like my mother and I hated each other. I connected much more with my father's free-roaming spirit. I thought we would be together on the road, living one thrilling adventure after another. Having a father who worked away meant he wasn't the disciplinarian. He was the parent who played. He hated laying down the law. But again, I never wanted to misbehave around my father. On the other hand, my mother and I were like two cats in a bag.

My mother did care about me. At least, she tried in her weird ways. She loved me, but caring is a different thing. She wanted to connect with me on the feminine level, even though I was obviously a tomboy.

It made her happy to show me how to dress up to accentuate my femininity, which I didn't think existed. Sometimes I stepped out of my self-centeredness to make her happy, or maybe I felt sorry for her. She was easier to be around when she was happy. She wouldn't nag me to do something, even though I had already done it. Whatever it was, it was never good enough. I was never good enough for some reason. I let her show me how a proper lady would sit, walk, eat, and make conversation. She said a woman should be polite and agreeable, and let the man lead the way. I didn't realize that being obsequious was the last thing I should do.

People always flattered her by saying we looked like sisters. She would roll her eyes in false denial, reaching over to press my shoulders into her against my resistance. Really? I was teensomething, and she was thirtysomething. We had similar features, but they appeared so much better on her than on me. We were both tall and lean, with shoulders that were too wide and hips that were too narrow and not ideal for childbearing, which was why I was an only child. She almost died giving birth to me. We were more like women in male bodies with breasts. That is why I came from a long line of one-child families on her side. Rotten luck.

She had nothing else she could do but flaunt her beauty until alone, divorced, and broke. She discovered she did have some hidden talents. She could recognize every herb, flower, shrub, and tree in the forest. Her estranged father taught her everything he knew about nature when he was around. That was the only place they had spent time together. She never talked much about my grandfather when I was growing up, trying to deny her upbringing. Much later she accepted this unique education, and with a little more research and experimentation, she would brew up aromatic natural healing concoctions in our kitchen. There were tinctures, oils, salves, cough syrups, teas, spices, powders, and natural foods she sold in the local farmers' market, and she soon became famous in our little valley. Then she became famous in the state and later nationwide. Eventually, she would oversee a small corporation and do very well for herself.

I know now my mother rarely talked about her father with me because one of her greatest fears was I would not be able to control my free spirit, and I, too, would blow away from her life just like he did. She resolved to allow my free spirit to run through the forest that was close to home, and she rarely allowed me any other freedoms. That is until I got Blue. Just the mention of his name overwhelms me with emotion. He taught me unconditional love, never yelled at me, criticized me, or was disappointed in me. He listened and didn't judge. He was different; I know that now. I thought having a dog meant I would make the decisions. I would be in control. I thought a dog followed while I, the master, led. But Blue was no ordinary dog.

Chapter 2

Finding Each Other

I recognize her voice. It awakens a memory so deep inside of me. I cannot contain this antecedent yearning to be near her. I never forgot how her love felt, no matter how many lives I've lived. Hers was a love that walked through my open heart and then dragged the rest of my lives on this earth with it. I shut my heart from that moment onward—for an eternity. I heard her voice in every beautiful sound the earth gave me. I have seen her face—this face—in brilliant flares of memories, every moment of my soul's existence.

Everything I have ever sensed, felt, touched, and saw about her has lingered within my soul. This is true for all souls. The things you may only barely detect, like a bird that lands on a rail in front of you, or the sound of distant laughter have an infinitesimally small effect on you. Yet some things, like witnessing a hero's triumph or the look of gratefulness in desperate eyes, or the feeling you have as reciprocated love leaves its mark on your heart, these never leave you. They change your life and lives to come through a cellular resonance.

I peer over my unsophisticated littermates. Her voice and scent pull me like a magnet. I am frantic to have her notice me. I will do the best I can to get myself right inside her arms and have her gaze into my eyes. Maybe then she will see who I am. As I clamber on top of my canine companions, I wonder if I act as dumbfounded as they do. All of them apparently new souls while I, on the other hand, am a seasoned soul transmigrator now apparently locked in a canine-shaped safe with no combination to set me free. Once again I have been returned to this earth for further attempts at redemption. Such agony at not being able to feel the true joy of reconciliation as two humans. Am I never allowed to be human again? Apparently, this life I am to be persecuted in a prison of fur and four legs, keeping me painfully distant from showing the immense love I am meant to give that I felt only once before many lives ago. How can I, as merely this insignificant creature covered in fluff and slobber, make right the wrongs that are centuries old and overdue?

Sparkling bits of vivid memories and images flooded back like déjà vu as soon as I first detected her with my astute sense of smell. Yet through all my past lives I have never forgotten the feelings of love, remorse, and an overwhelming need to repair my past wrongs to her. Out of all the creatures I have been in my past lives, with deep regret, the weakest was of being a human. The weakness had allowed me to destroy lives with such purpose and not for food or protection, but only for ego.

Now this rebirth and seeing her has resurfaced my instincts for love. Can this girl allow me to love her in a capacity that exists only in some fashion of canine loyalty? I am the one you need to pick from these scoundrels, these weak new souls. Take me away from this hoard of drool and mayhem. Find me. Here I am. Pick me.

I never thought any kind of excitement could be topped, until the day I met Blue. I remember I couldn't decide which pup would be the right one. I had read somewhere if you sit down in the middle of them, one will choose you. Out of the litter of eight chubby, soft balls of fur, a distinctive white-brown-and-gray one climbed over his littermates, tripping on his stubby legs, rolling and somersaulting in his effort to get to me while wagging his sprig of a tail. He ambled his way right up onto my cross-legged lap, stood up on his short awkward hind legs, forelegs extended up onto my tummy, and peered up at me. I picked him up and stared into his cloudy gray eyes that were talking a language I could feel but couldn't understand. I sniffed his folded, sweet-smelling ears that seemed too small for his head. He wiggled and licked my nose. The rest of the pups were just as cute and in a variety of colors, but none of them were as strong and determined as this one. He didn't cry or whine like the others. He only stared at me. His soft paw landed on my lips as we inspected each other. The owner wasn't sure of the breed, as she rescued the mother off the street, and she was already pregnant. She guessed the litter was a mix of husky and border collie or Australian shepherd.

"They may turn blue in the future. Hard to tell when they are so young," the dog owner explained. His eyes did indeed turn a multitude of blues. We did not buy a pup that day. It was my heart that was sold to a dog I simply named Blue.

Chapter 3

Blue

She hasn't let on she knows who I am—who I really am—or even if she knows who she truly is. I am doing my best to show her as we spend every living moment together when she is not in school. I have so much to tell her, so much to say, but I can't. My voice is trapped in this canine cage with a futile tongue that gets in the way. I can't pierce my lips or form logical sounds in this oversized mouth. Every word I attempt starts and ends in my throat, with nothing to push it out. I will have to show her how smart I am. Maybe she will figure out the connection between the two of us, and I can tell her everything will be all right now. I will show her through my vassal love that we are soul mates, and I would go to the ends of the earth and to the end of time for her.

There are things I like about being a dog. I grow into my paws while my legs grow faster and stronger. My senses are incredibly acute. I can hear a fly sneaking up on my tail or discern whose car is turning up the lane two miles away. I can smell the weather changing in the wind, the gofer in his den, the squirrel at the top of the tree, and my tennis ball in a bush. I can smell cells of all living things—every organic chemical upwind or near my nose. I can smell emotions.

If all life began in the ocean a few hundred million earth years ago, and all mammals are connected by the history of our saltwater cells, I have truly discovered the connection of our common ocean of blood, sweat, and tears through the nose, heart, and tongue of a dog.

I immediately shared my love of nature and horses with Blue. I discovered he had no concept of size or difference in creatures. Anything or anyone had to be within his control or at least watched. It was like he was a commander of an army or something. Everything from bird to animal to human had to be in line, according to him. That didn't work well for almost everything. The horses barely tolerated him. He nipped and barked at their hooves, successfully dodging any hasty kicks. Once they were rounded up, he would lay down proudly as if to say, "The soldiers are under control, Captain."

I started to notice interesting things about Blue I didn't think were normal in dogs. If I so much as glanced his way and nodded my head to come, he would respond as if he had read my mind. He always listened attentively to me. He rarely disobeyed a command. As he began to recognize my signals and commands, I tried to unlock his language. His methods of communication came in the tilt of his head—ears up, back, or to the side—the narrowing of his eyes; his smile with his teeth showing or lips closed; his different panting, with tongue out or in; and all the various hums, huffs, growls, moans, sneezes, coughs, whines, whimpers, sighs, and various barks and howls. I learned to speak dog. But whatever I thought I understood about him, he appeared to know way more about me. He seemed smarter than me in many ways I cannot explain and may never understand.

I guess the counselor was right: Blue did bring me out of my shell, but not out of my solitary one. I was now solitary plus one. My shell just opened wider to more adventures. In his young months, we went for very short walks. But as he grew stronger, and after he was a full grown and got the go-ahead from the vet, we would run for hours. Blue and I became Lewis and Clark, going further away from the farm, mapping out new routes, and sometimes getting completely lost, but he always found the way back. Soon our adventures together went deeper into the mountains. When I got my driver's license, off we'd go to the higher mountain ranges and camp overnight. I never feared anything with him by my side, and Mom trusted him to watch over me. It was a battle at first, but she eventually relented. She didn't have a choice. I had great grades, won the state cross-country championships, and later the nationals. Her threats motivated me to be a good kid because I never forgot the words she said when I first got Blue: "If you get into any trouble, Giselle, or give your dad or I any back talk, we will take the dog away."

And I believed her.

Chapter 4

Running Together

OK, I pooped. There. Happy? Oh, Ellie, do you have to pick it up? Are you keeping it? Oh, it's going in the big can. This is a no-poop zone like in the house. Do I have to wear this shirt? Dogs don't wear clothes. What do you mean I look cute? Damn these people! Get in a line and stay together! Come on, people, run together! You, slowpoke, get moving. I am at your heels. Stop screaming! I hate when you humans scream! Ellie! Ellie! Hey, wait up! How did she get so far ahead? People, there are predators out there. We must stay together.

I don't understand the disorganization of these people. You are soldiers in training for battle, aren't you? If you scatter, that means the enemy has separated you, and when you are alone, you are weak. Together you are strong. Oh, that darn piercing sound hurts my ears. Damn it! We are to gather in front of the general. Thank you, strange human, for scratching my ears. The tall man with a board in his hand is yelling at us. He sounds the high-pitched sound again. I howl, they laugh, and we all stand at attention. It's quite routine. These humans respond well to annoying screeching sounds and not nipping at heels. I must remember this. I sit on Ellie's feet. Please scratch my butt with your toes. We wait. Now we run again. Ellie tells me to stay by her side and not to bother anyone, or I go back in the car. OK, no problem. After a long while, we arrive back, and the humans fall to the ground, whining, so I scratch my back on the grass and take a dog nap. Then we stand to say goodbye. Can we stop for ice cream now?

I like running with people, but my favorite times are when I'm alone with Ellie. No loud noises or talking is necessary. We have a conversation that doesn't need words. We both know the rules to stay close. If anything ever happened to her, I could never forgive myself. That would be the end of all my lives of trying to find her, and my soul-saving mission would be over.

In the trails, just the two of us, is when we have our true freedom, with lots of jumping on and off boulders, crossing water, running through trees and bushes, or a field of grass and wildflowers with views only I can imagine from distant dreams. I love the smell of the crisp air flowing off snowcapped mountains and the distinct sharp smell of pine trees.

I am set free in a bounty of scents and sounds from various creatures, each beckoning to tell their story through the hints their bodies left behind. The calling cards of other males must be rewritten with my scent, as I am the leader of our nomadic pack. She lets me do reconnaissance in the beginning, but I must stay close, or I will lose her. I never let her out of my sight. She sometimes picks deer trails where the scents are divine, providing tasty snacks left for me by the deer. I am embarrassed by my cravings, reduced to a deer-poop eater. Other times I find poops from other animals that are not always tasty. If it is bad food or if they are sick, I must pussyfoot away. There are particular poops we come across, and if fresh, they signal the end of the trail for us.

When we stop for water or a break, I check her out. There might be a scratch that needs cleaning. I can do that because I am a skilled soldier. Medic Blue. But I am not just a soldier; I am a general. At least I once was one.

Chapter 5

Mother

After my parents' divorce, my dad went off to live his life on the road, always ineffectually apologizing for not being there for me in person. He felt more at home being a nomad rather than being restless and unhappy after a few days of being stuck in one place. I pacified his guilt by telling him I understood the idea of being stuck. If I didn't get out to my forest or trails, I, too, felt caged.

He bought a bigger truck with a luxurious sleeper cab containing a bathroom, shower, kitchen, and storage for his motorcycle. He would call me from the road, entertaining me with his stories of who he had met at the truck stop or what he had seen on the highway. When he happened to be passing through, he'd stop by to resuscitate our relationship with praise and gifts. All I wanted was time with him and an opportunity to hide away from my mother, the matron of mystification and moodiness, so Blue and I would join him on some short-haul trips.

He never criticized me about what I was doing with my life like she did. He simply told me I had always had a choice in life. "In everything you do, you have a choice of attitude. I have seen hotel cleaning staff, waitresses, and gas pump jockeys singing and enjoying their work. Ellie, your life is an open book right now. Do what you love to do, and if you can make money doing it, you got it made in the shade. If you put your heart into it, you will be successful. But always have a backup plan."

He would talk about his life on the road, roaming, and seeing so many crazy things that he could fill a book. "Ellie, I have learned to be calm in the face of tragedy. I have seen way too many accidents and no longer take life for granted. One of the dearest and most touching moments in my life was holding you when you were born but also holding a man I pulled from a wreck as he shared his last words with me. To receive life and to watch it transcend to another plane is a gift. As you know, I don't believe death is our final destination. There is no finality to existence in time. I also learned the pursuit of peace of mind. Feeling content with life should be a priority while we are living, because one day it could all be taken away."

Ain't that the truth, my captain. We don't get a chance for a do-over in the same life. I am tucked in tight next to Ellie, watching the world zoom by and leaving wet nose tracks on the passenger window as we both listen to Dad's nonstop talking. I guess he spends a lot of time alone, so he makes up for it with us. I am triggered by his words to memories of my human life. I was calm leading an army to battle, in what I remember of my life when I first fell in love with Ellie's soul. I had nothing left to lose that mattered to me after she died. I let true connections to anyone go because the pain of loving and losing was unbearable. I resented happiness, wondering how anyone could be happy when I suffered, so why not pull everyone down with me. I became empty to avoid the pain. I would have killed myself to feel peace, yet I had a visceral awareness that ending my suffering that way would never allow me to redeem myself. I am grateful I made the decision to try to redeem myself for my sins because everything is on a time continuum, and everything in nature has a connection, even the smallest, most insignificant atom. Even yeast have lifetime relationships. I have been at the bottom of God's list of complex creations in my past lives, but the Creator always treats us as equals. Man's intelligence is the problem and his assumption of superiority, when in the universe everything is equal and continuous.

I started to live each new life with intention. I found a purpose, even if for many lives it was simply to become worthy enough to make it to the next life. I look Ellie in the eyes—the window to her soul. I want to tell her reality as you see it is nothing more than an illusion, because there is another reality beyond what you can see with your eyes—a reality you must feel with your heart. I hope she will figure it out. Eventually my thoughts fade and I am lolled into a dognap on Ellie's lap, coaxed by the movement of the truck as she runs her fingers up and down my back.

"What about déjà vu, Dad? Sometimes I feel like I have been in a place or have lived this moment before. It's like I am getting a glimpse of something in the past, and if I hang on to it long enough, I would be able to control it and thereby control my future." I remembered the countless times, especially with Blue, when I swore I lived that exact moment before.

"There are many theories on déjà vu, Ellie. I think of it as time warping around on itself. I believe there exists a time continuum like a flat piece of paper. For some reason, the paper folds like a Japanese fan. Future experiences on the tip of one fold transfers between the fold of the present time or a fold from the past touches the present. Time warps, pulling us forward or backward for a split second, giving us glimpses of our deep past and our future. Someday we may be able to control it, as you say. We will be able to travel through time by controlling our thoughts."

"I really wish that could happen." My father could go on philosophizing about life in general, but I wanted to ask about our life, so I took a turn into a topic, debating whether I wanted the truth or not. "How's it going with Mom?"

"Giselle," when he was serious, he didn't use my shortened name, "I will love your mother like I will no other woman on earth, still, even after our divorce. I long suspected what she was up to, but I felt guilty for being on the road, yet I didn't want to change my life for her. No amount of flowers, gifts, or phone calls from the road can replace a warm body next to you, a hug when you are sad, or a foot rub after a hard day. She is a very physical woman, and I am a ghost. I fly in, hover around, and fly out, leaving only a sense of my being and the smell of my aftershave in the house. She is brilliant, strong, and passionate. I am quiet, introspective, and stubborn. And so are you, I might add. Good qualities to have if you use them in pursuit of your goals, but not in a relationship. You must forgive your mother, because I have."

We discussed more and then changed the topic, leaving me with enough insight to understand my father's role in their divorce, and this forced me to reconsider my mother. I always blamed her. My judgment of her created a wall I couldn't see over. I peered at her through the cracks, seeing only parts of her moving and talking. I never acknowledged the whole picture of who she was until I was forced to chip away all the concrete that blocked my view. My mom was stubborn and self-centered, but I didn't realize she was also fragile until I was forced to confront it.

Blue and I had returned home very late from a long run. Whenever I was later than I expected to be, I called her out of courtesy, but my cell battery had gone dead. I was fully bracing for and afraid of her impending wrath when we returned, but we found her leaning against the kitchen counter, staring ahead at nothing, not responding to my explanation. I became emotional with her, when I was normally detached and indifferent. She was playing with me by being unreasonably vindictive.

"Say something," I demanded. "Don't you care where I have been?"

I courageously stood across from her, inviting her to scream at me. But when I finally caught her eye, for the first time I noticed the wrinkles around her eyes and mouth. She looked older and tired with no makeup, wearing her apron covered with splotches of various colors of plant stains. She looked like a mother and not the fashion model I was used to seeing. A stray hair was stuck to the sweat on her forehead, and I impulsively reached out to move it away out of my own irritation. As soon as I did that, I was afraid it was too personal, like seeing someone naked in a changing room, and I quickly turned away in embarrassment. She must have seen it as a show of compassion because she grabbed my hand, kissed it, and held it against her cheek as tears filled her eyes. I became too confused to console her, locked into position questioning how I was feeling. I didn't like her kissing my hand, wanting to pull it away, because I was being pulled into something I wasn't ready for. It was much too personal. We had become only roommates, existing together, but we weren't connecting. I had grown comfortable with the distance between us.

I let her hold my hand as she looked at me through her wet eyelashes. She was the strong one, the alpha female in this house, and here she stood, breaking down in front of me, and she wasn't embarrassed. At that moment, I realized she was not as stoic as I thought. She was alone, with no one to share her emotions or the events of her day. I was the only one, and I did a good job of ignoring her, pretending to listen, apathetic, never responding out of genuine curiosity. I realized how self-absorbed I had become, but I did it to protect myself from being hurt by her constant criticism—her envy or dislike of me. To see her like this was different. She seemed so vulnerable. Was it a trap? I remembered the words of my father. Was she human and not just my detached and critical mother? I wanted to console her, if only she would stop squeezing my hand.

We stayed that way too long for my comfort, like she was afraid to let me go. I gently pulled my hand away, sliding it out of her grasp. She dropped her head in response. I immediately scratched my head, showing a need and not a feeling of overwhelming emotion that I had to pull away. I quickly moved to pet Blue as the next distraction from connecting back with her. He had sensed the emotion between the two of us and took his place stuffed in between our feet. I glanced up to her, meeting her sad eyes, and broke the silence with the only explanation I had: the truth and an apology for not being able to contact her.

"You don't know how much I worry about you," she whispered. Then her attitude changed completely, and she raised her voice. "You don't seem to care. You care more about that stupid dog," she snapped as rolling tears hit her lips.

"Are you jealous of Blue?" I was shocked.

"How could I not be? You are with him twenty-four hours a day and don't have a minute for me, your own mother."

Her words stung me. How she could spark feelings so instantaneously in me by her overdramatics.

"You can't mean that. He just follows me around. He doesn't demand anything and doesn't force me to do anything I don't want to. He never yells at me." I had shot back, but I instantly regretted it when I saw the look on her face. I suddenly became overwhelmed with guilt and sympathy as my dad's words swirled in my memory and yanked at my heart. "Oh, Mom. I'm sorry. I am being selfish. You are right. I won't let you worry again, and we can plan some things to do together." I tried to rescue myself in her eyes.

"Don't worry, Giselle. I am not a child. I don't need to be pacified. Wait until you have children of your own. In fact, tell me how you would feel if Blue disappeared for hours, and you didn't know where he was." She locked her intense green eyes with mine and raised her eyebrows.

Her words hit my heart as my imagination took flight. I imagined if Blue was the closest I would come to having a child, and I loved him as I do—how much she must love me. I never thought of my mom as a human being. I always felt that I was an accident—that it was her role and a duty to raise me to the best of her ability. But she just didn't have the desire. She didn't have to take an oath of expertise when she had a child. My parents were unlicensed agents of creation. Some of my friends had far worse parents, but my mother's parenting boundaries were like an invisible force field that got turned off and on without warning. I grew panicky not knowing when I would get zapped with a rule or left free to roam freely for days. I compensated for the lack of consistency and family cohesiveness by making my own family with nature and then Blue, which left my mom completely out of the picture. We rarely saw eye to eye and had virtually nothing in common. Her revelation left me not knowing how to respond. She watched the expressions on my face as I worked through my thoughts.

"I know how much you love him, Giselle, but he is just a dog and one day will have to leave you. He won't live as long as you, and my greatest fear as a mother is that the same thing happens to me—that I will lose you too soon. Despite our differences, the bond we have is deeper than the one you have with Blue. It is in our blood."

I didn't want to tell her I felt blood had nothing to do with love, but I gave her that argument as if she scored a point and smiled back at her. She smiled in response and reached forward to hug me. It felt awkward angling forward over Blue, barricaded in between our feet. We hadn't hugged since the time I needed stitches in my knee a number of years ago. Now I was old enough to repair myself. I stepped way outside myself and found the courage to whisper in her ear, "I love you, Mom." I felt the vibrations of her shoulders as she started to cry again, then she pulled me in tighter.

"I love you so much, Giselle. You are my life," she whispered through my hair. My eyes burned as I tried to hold in the tears but couldn't. I sniffed, so she pushed us apart to look intensely into my eyes.

"I guess I just never hear you say it," I whispered through the tears that came from an unknown place.

Her smile lit up her eyes, removed the sorrow from her face, and replaced it with a look of compassion. I didn't know if I would ever experience this connection with her again. There are these very rare moments in life when you are vulnerable enough to hold a stare—maybe between lovers or during a shared toast or in a game with a friend of who blinks first—but nothing can come close to seeing through to a person's soul, showing it is full of love—honest, wounded, and forgiving. No words are necessary and saying too much at that moment would take away from its purity.

Sensing my discomfort at my vulnerability, she said, "Come on, let's get to know each other and celebrate your arriving home safely." She wiped her eyes and reached out to me to push back my unruly hair from my face and soak up my tears with her thumbs. She cupped my chin in her hand with the other resting on my cheek. "You are such a beautiful girl. More beautiful than I ever was at your age."

I wanted to contradict what she said, but she pleaded, "Please promise me you will stick to Blue for a relationship and not a boyfriend for a long, long time."

"Oh my God, Mom. I don't have time for a boyfriend! I barely have time for a dog." We both laughed. And the tension between us vanished, if only for that day or that moment, but I took what I could get.

"Good." She took a deep sigh. "I know I haven't been there for you as much as I should have been. I always thought I would have time to make amends for, for my past. You know. But…"

I cut her off, "There is no need to explain. Please, let's not go there now."

"Where does the time go, when it gets away on you? It seems we were just getting Blue and suddenly you are graduating from high school." She said this mostly to herself and then quickly spoke up. "I know I socked away a bottle of wine in this kitchen somewhere. Help me find it. We never did celebrate your scholarships. You are going to have to pick a college soon."

I remember that day when the mood in the house changed. When these two females cracked and broke down part of the barrier of concrete tension that felt so thick since the day I had arrived in this small family. It felt like the wall became a lattice, and light was streaming in. I tried sticking my nose in between them to be a part of this consolation. Ellie only gave me a half-hearted pet, so I kept circling and trying again. They were back at the hugging and laughing.

I moved to sit by my food bowl, waiting. Story of my life: waiting for humans. I licked my empty bowl, clanging my tag against the metal. Do you see me standing here, starving while you and Mom are having a good laugh? I tried the death stare. She was purposely ignoring me. I laid down because I knew this would be a while until she returned with an enticing treat, human food. The heavens have blessed me today for two reasons: cohesion among the pack and elk sausage. I had all I needed right now—the heaviness of confused emotions drifting away, and my food bowl full.

Chapter 6

Running to Hide

What are you doing in the small room, sitting on the big water bowl again? Peeing in my water bowl, again? I will put my head on your lap for a few minutes of good petting time. Sometimes she locks me out of the bathroom. Not this time. I pushed the door open with my nose. My nose has hardened to the door opening I have to do around here. Why are you yelling at me? Sorry. OK, I will leave. Humph. That is the third time you are in there. Let's go already.

The running shoes. Sniff. I will help you tie up the shoelaces. The backpack with water. Where is mine? Oh yes, there it is. Leash? I will get it. Get in Mom's car. Seat belt on. No, don't sing that song. Oh, there is that note. Ouch. There are lots of stops and starts that keep throwing me back and forth on the seat as usual. I am up on all fours to gain traction or I will bounce right off the seat. She is forever learning how to operate this machine.

We stop completely. I am let out and sniff around. I love this area. There are lots of smells of my kind everywhere. Ellie locks the car, but we leave our packs behind. This must be a short run. We take off slowly down the trail. I can see there is a lot on her mind, completely distracted because she left my leash in the car. I hate the leash anyways. It is completely demeaning for someone of my stature. I follow on her heels but get distracted by the fresh smells released by the crisp spring morning dew. I get a flash of a memory. I am a cat watching a dark-caped man standing before an easel with a paintbrush held contemplatively in midair. Inspired, I set my artful markings on my easel of grass. I have conquered this territory once before, but I see the enemy has infiltrated the land. I am reclaiming it as my own. Come, Princess, let's get conquering! We are on a mission until a small chubby ball of fur bounces up beside me. Oh no, a puppy. What on earth are you doing out here all alone? I try to ignore him, but he keeps pestering me, wanting to play. We trot along, all three of us, and everything seems fine.

Running at its best is not about running or breathing or taking a step. It is about what happens in between each step and in between each breath. It is about feeling the air in between the landing. That split-second when nothing happens. Like in music, sometimes it is not about the note, but about the pause in between the notes that carries more meaning. I have spent so much time reviewing each step: Where are my shoulders, my knees, my hips, my arms, my head? Where is my foot landing? After a while I can let go of these thoughts, relax, take my head out of the process, and just be. It is a magical feeling when everything is in sync, and I do not feel anything at all but the silence between my steps. I heard this is called being in "the zone" or "flow." It feels effortless, and my mind can wander. I am on autopilot. That is on a good day.

I was having an off day. There is no zone or flow. When I left I had a sneaking suspicion things were not going to go well. Call it intuition. I often play this game with myself. If things don't line up right as the day gets going, almost like little warnings to pay heed, I force myself to rethink what I have planned to do. Sometimes I go ahead anyway to test if my instincts were correct or not, and I surprise myself with my accuracy. Sometimes I feel foolish, and my rational mind overrules what my gut feels. It was one of those days. I decided to go out for twenty minutes, and if I still felt the same way, I would retreat. Maybe I was feeling off because I had a meeting later in the morning with a college scout. I thought it was a good idea to take a run around town to settle my nerves and shower at the pool before meeting him.

Meetings with coaches were happening a lot with college application deadlines looming closer. I needed to choose a college, and being national cross-country champion was a ticket to a free education. But a part of me wanted to run away from it all, no pun intended. I didn't want to go to college. I really wanted to try my legs in a marathon distance trail run taking place in a few months over joining a college team, but I couldn't admit that to my parents. My ultimate dream was of running one of those ultraendurance races. I knew being on a college team would not allow me the time to train for a longer race. In truth, I wanted open air and nature, not a classroom, books, exams, and deadlines.

My mind was caught up and preoccupied in these thoughts, when I heard thumping sounds so loud I felt the vibrations in my chest. Someone was playing their stereo annoyingly loud, perhaps carrying on from a late-night party, as it was only just past sunrise. I scrutinized the houses across the street from the trail I was on. The trail bordered a river and was lined on both sides with sizable poplar trees and wild rose bushes. The music was getting louder, so I assumed we must have been getting closer to the party house. I kept running, but the music stayed at the same volume, with a deep, resounding bass vibrating in my bones. Something in my peripheral vision forced me to turn around, and that was when I saw a pickup truck following slowly on the road beside me.

I immediately scouted around for Blue, but he was nowhere in sight. *Darn, I forgot his leash.* I stopped and yelled for him. The truck stopped directly across from me. I wondered who sat behind the closed, tinted, dark windows. I rationalized that he was slowing down to make a U-turn. I turned around to retrace my steps and search for Blue. The truck stopped and reversed, following my retreat. No Blue.

I ran back a little faster, and the truck kept up with me, driving backward with no regard for what might be behind him. My solitude accelerated a growing sense of fear. I wanted to ignore it, rationalize it, but it grew more intense inside of my gut, moving its way to my throat. It was too early in the morning for much traffic, and there was no one around on the trail either. And no Blue. I stopped, and so did the truck.

For some reason, I assumed the driver was a man. Did I know him? Was he having fun with me? Is there more than one person inside? The truck carried no wave of familiarity. The hair on my bare arms started to rise, and I shivered. *Where is Blue, damn it?* It was probably only a few seconds, but it felt like minutes since I saw him last. My growing discomfort expanded every nanosecond.

As soon as I started calling again for Blue, the music from the truck got louder, drowning out my voice. I swallowed hard on the fear building inside of me, questioning its irrationality. I needed a plan of what I would do if he got out and chased me down. No one would see us, because of the trees and bushes along the path. I must get off the path onto the street.

I ran as fast as I could back down the path while still shouting for Blue. I had given my fear away. He suspected I was on to him. The truck made a rubber-burning U-turn and was now following me from the other side of the street. My heart pounded in my throat in time to the thumping music, and my mouth had gone completely dry and sticky. I had nothing with me—no pack, no leash, no dog, no phone. I felt trapped, with the music drowning out my thoughts, and then I spotted Blue running toward me full force from up the trail in the direction I was headed. He jumped up at me, almost pushing me down.

Where have you been? What is that hideous noise? What is wrong with you? The fur goes up on the back of my neck without my control. I am disgusted with myself. I was right by her side until that puppy came up to me distract me from my command while the enemy appeared. I see an ominous dark truck with a strong smell of diesel. The noise and smell are overwhelming, but the vibration in the air feels much more toxic. When I sense the emotions coming from Ellie, I stand against her. She steps over me and calls me to come with such demand, I don't think twice, and I am by her side as we turn around, sprint up the path, cut a hard left to run across the street, down a side road, and then turn quickly up an alley full of overloaded garbage cans. The temptation of aromas

coming from the garbage are overwhelming, but an electrical field of fear coming off her body overrules all scents. We turn up another alley, when we hear the music mixed with shooting rocks hitting garbage cans and fences. He is around the corner, gaining on us.

Suddenly the music stops completely. We keep running to the end of the alley and turn up to another street. We stop and wait. She rarely breathes this heavy, so I sit and stare at her, waiting for a command. She squats to hug me, her heart pounding into my neck as my fur goes up, senses tingling. The noise comes on loud again, and she stands up, staring down the street as the sound of an engine revving grows louder. We run back in the direction we came.

The worst thoughts and scenarios were running through my head, and I can't make them stop. I envisioned being caught, Blue being hurt, and I am attacked or raped. I have nothing to protect myself. Everything is in the car. I never thought this could happen to me. I was in a neighborhood full of houses, yet I felt so vulnerable. No one was opening their doors, offering to help. Where was everyone?

We darted into someone's side yard and crouched low behind a dense bush. Blue was calmly standing beside me, reducing my anxiety a little. I listened for the truck or footsteps but couldn't hear anything because my heart was pounding in my ears. Blue was in close, pressing so hard against me I could barely stay balanced in my position. I peered through the branches of the bush that was still bare from its winter sleep and saw the truck rolling by slowly, then it stopped completely. I was sure he couldn't see me, but as I glanced down at Blue, I realized I was wearing fluorescent colors. Surely he would see me through this bush. I got down as flat as possible, smelling the snow mold around me. Blue shuffled in low, almost lying on top of me as if he knew to hide me with his earth-colored body. No more loud music. I heard the gravel crackle under its tires as the truck crept incrementally forward.

We waited through countless stifled, heavy breaths. I couldn't coordinate my legs to lift me up. They were stiff with adrenaline, but I managed to crawl through the wet, empty flower bed to peer around the corner of the house. The street was empty except for a few parked cars. I pushed against my legs to stand up and leaned against the side of the house. I was too nervous to move, but I knew I had to do something because doing nothing was a risk.

"Let's go to the car, Blue," I said in a harsh whisper. My attention to running away completely disorientated me to my surroundings. Giving the option to him on the direction to take was the best idea. He had his body pressed hard against my legs as if to help hold me up, but he was forcing me into the side of the house. His ears perked forward as he held his nose up and sniffed the air, then peered up at me.

"To the car," I commanded. He started to pant and eased off my legs. I took a few steps away from the house and glanced around, blinking the sweat out of my eyes to see clearly before moving. We were lost. Blue padded forward a few steps, with his head down, then checked behind if I was following him. When I noticed the direction he chose, I raced ahead, and he pulled up alongside me. I scrutinized the houses as we ran by trying to decipher the ones that looked inviting. I kept envisioning knocking at a door with no answer, with the stalker sitting in his truck, grinning, knowing I was trapped.

My dubious trust in Blue to lead us back was unfounded, as the surroundings eventually became welcomingly familiar. I sprinted to the car, struggled foolishly to unlock it, and aggressively pulled open the door, then signaled Blue to jump in. Without hesitation, I locked all the doors and hunched down low in the seat, peering over the dashboard in every direction. My heart refused to stop its pounding. Where was he? I couldn't think. I needed to calm down. Blue came over to me, but I pushed him back to the passenger seat floor to hide, telling him to stay down. I heard a car drive by and checked the side rearview mirror. It was a truck slowly moving down the street away from us. Was that the truck? Fear filled my chest, and my hands started shaking uncontrollably. I slipped right down to the floor as low as possible and reached over with my hand to keep Blue lying low. Thoughts of my parents, going to college, my future ran through my head as I realized none of that mattered right now. Was what was happening real or something I fabricated in my mind?

I stayed crouched low until I heard female voices talking together and laughing. I took a deep breath and peered over the edge of the car window. A couple of women had passed on their morning walk. I felt safe enough to sit up and allow Blue to come up out of hiding. He jumped up on the seat and stared at me. I eased into my seat and started up the car with my eyes looking everywhere. We pulled out on to the street a little too fast kicking up pebbles, throwing Blue against his seat. Poor guy. I slowed down and put my hand on his head to reassure him and headed back toward home. My hands were too sweaty to hold the steering wheel, slipping slightly forcing the car to sway slightly to the side of the road. Blue bumped into the side of the door, and I realized I was still too frazzled to drive. At the street corner, I pulled into a gas station and backed up into a parking stall to face outward to watch the traffic. I needed to get control. I rationalized that guy was only trying to scare me. Maybe I shouldn't be rationalizing anything but to see it for what it was, and that scared me even more.

The security of Blue's warm body pressed against me felt reassuring. All those times my mom had warned me about running alone were beginning to hit home. I didn't want to stop running, so I would have to look into arming myself with something. What could I do to defend myself? What would Blue have done if this guy decided to kidnap me or hurt me? I grabbed his head in my hands and looked into his eyes. He made me feel so safe, but a gun, a knife, or a swift kick could put him out of commission. The pain of this vision hit me hard, and I immediately started to cry. Blue put his head hard against my chest. He sensed the situation, as he always does. I hugged him tightly, squeezing his body a little too hard.

Realizing I was too frazzled to drive, I sat in the car and took the time to contemplate the purpose of my life. It took this scare to shake me up and make me think. I realized that if I did not pursue my dream, if I left it until after I graduated; I wouldn't be happy. I sat there strumming Blue's fur reflecting on my life and dreams, and after what seemed like hours. Then I buckled us up and drove back home with my eyes constantly shifting to the rearview mirror.

Chapter 7

Damned Dream Again

The heat is searing my skin. I am screaming to be saved. Red flames and smoke everywhere I turn. I am trapped. I try to yell, but I cannot. My chest hurts from pushing dead, dry air. My clothes are melting into my body. I reach to pull them away, but I no longer have hands. I look for my feet, but I cannot see through eyes that are burning and dry, with eyelids of sandpaper. I am moving. My feet are still attached to me, so I try to run. I am yelling a name. What is the name? I am sinking deeper into the ground as my body melts, yet my eyes can detect a shadow in the smoke. The shadow does not move. "Please help me," I plead.

I woke with a muffled scream stuck in my throat, startled at the reality of my location, a haze of images from my dream still moving around my bedroom. Flames sweeping up the walls. I hate this dream. I have had it for as long as I can remember. It always startles me awake, covered in sweat. I had it again the night of the stalker.

When I was younger, I would scream aloud, and Mom would rush in, petrified. I would be yelling a name she couldn't recognize. She would say I was manifesting guilt for my insolence toward her. I stopped telling her how often I had the dream. I was sure another counselor would have to be consulted. I would have to sit and explain the dream in detail, go through what is bothering me, how I feel. I don't know how I feel. Normal. What does normal feel like? This is normal for me. No, I don't have suicidal thoughts. No, I don't want to kill anyone. Yes, I have friends. Yes, I like being alone more than with people. Is that wrong? God knows what crazy idea they would come up with. Did I mention their fighting always happened the day before my dreams? But the dreams never left, even when my dad moved out or Blue moved in.

After Blue came into my life, I learned to control the yelling. Blue would jump up on my bed and lean his body on top of me, pressing into my chest, laying his head on my shoulder until I slowed my breathing. I wondered if he was in my life for this reason, like those dogs that sense seizures, smell cancer, or calm anxiety. Some people would think it odd of me not to let him sleep on the bed with me all the time. I tried that once, but he hogged the bed with such command I had to constantly fight for space and covers. If I pushed him away, it was only a matter of seconds before he would pick himself up and plunk himself against me with such force, I ended up on only a fraction of the available real estate the bed offered with a sleepless night ahead of me. I decided if I wanted to keep my sanity, he had to sleep in his own domain. But when my sanity was in question, he broke all the rules.

I was so shaken by that truck following me that I forgot to meet with the college scout. I called him to apologize, but he had already headed out of town. He understood how I could be shaken up and suggested I carry bear spray and never run alone. I was never alone. I had Blue.

While lying under the picnic table's shade on the first day that hints of the inevitable heat of summer, I drift in and out of sleep. A bird landing nearby to pick at the crumbs has forced me to open my eyes, but not enough to move my body. The grass is cool, and a blade tickles my nose. I rub it with my paw and roll over on my back to scratch it with the grass. Nothing to see under a table, so I roll over to my other side and watch the finches peck at seeds that have dropped from the tall grass of the uncut lawn. Ellie has stayed in her room for half the day. Mom is baking, and the yard is looking haggard. I have lots of time to think.

I have been contemplating the recent events of the humans in this house. If our eyes are the windows to our soul, our dreams are the windows to our subconscious. In our subconscious, locked in a perplexing timeless code, is our past, present, and future. If we suffer in our dreams, we awaken to the relief of peace, and the yin and yang of suffering and happiness make us aware of their differences. Come to think of it, if we do not suffer pain, then we how do we know the feeling of joy? If you don't know yourself, how can you truly be happy? I am getting too philosophical. Ellie's experience with fear always presented itself in her dreams as ghosts who should have been laid to rest in an ancient burial ground lifetimes ago—ghosts of things left unresolved. I can't see her dreams, but I know what they are. Her subconscious is forcing her to deal with her fears, which are caused by things out of her control. I have learned that either you have fear or you have faith. They are both the same thing. They are both a belief in something you cannot see. Both can manifest in your subconscious and direct how you make decisions. And Ellie has a big decision to make.

The finches have moved on. I stand up, stretch, and move over to the base of my favorite tree located on a small rise to guard over the herd. They, too, are lying down, with their strong legs jutting out from their sack of a belly, intermittently flicking their long, thick tails. Horses are not as smart as humans like to think. I was one. I was one of those horses who spooked easily, fearful of loud noises and peripheral movements. I detested being jittery, but I couldn't help it. It was ultimately my demise. No cavalry wants a jittery horse.

Both of these women are jittery. They are jittery with each other, imagining fears in their peripheral vision. They manifest their fears in their unresolved issues and inadequacies they don't want to face head-on. Fears hide in feelings of abandonment or lack of self-worth, confidence, or self-love. I entered this family with many observations of how living things interact. I figured out a common denominator: man's overthinking has always gotten in the way of the fundamentals of living—overthinking their fears, their purpose in life or their deficiencies while looking for someone to blame or looking for something more perfect than what they have, who they are, or who they are meant to become.

I watch the trees that border the other side of the pasture as a breeze strums through the branches like harp strings. I sniff the air for the scents it carries from its journey across the land, then lay my head back down between my front paws and sigh. I wonder what my purpose as a dog is in this part of my karmic cycle. Why am I just a dog? If I could speak, I would have so much to say.

Chapter 8

Something Bigger

Winning the nationals for cross country in my senior year provided lots of opportunities for scholarships to different universities. Even though I loved the idea of moving away from home, gaining independence, more than anything; I wasn't ready to commit to any one school. It was overwhelming, and I needed more time to decide, which I didn't have. My mom was insistent on my going, hounding me daily to make a decision. I assumed she also wanted her independence, too, but surprisingly, after my parents divorced, she never dated. She had all the freedom she wanted and never took it. She was annoyingly present all the time. And annoyingly persistent.

"What in Sam Hill do you mean you're not going to take the scholarship?" She stood with one hand on her hip, and the other pounded the kitchen counter to accentuate her words, causing the dishes in the cupboards to rattle. "What on earth is wrong with you? I never had such an opportunity. I would have jumped at it, and you are throwing it away."

"Mom, it's the running that got me a scholarship." I flinched every time her fist slammed down. We tended to increase a few decibels and octaves when we got into a disagreement, and we were headed for jet-engine levels. No one but the horses could possibly hear us, so we blasted our words back and forth at each other. I was adamant about this. I didn't find any reason to go to college, because there was nothing I wanted to study, and my heart wasn't in it. It would be a waste of time. Weren't those enough reasons?

Here we were, two soldiers with our bayonets at the ready. After we both scarred each other with our jabbing words, she had to relent to my decision. I felt proud for standing my ground and not letting the enemy gain any territory. I was going to enter some bigger races—the races I had been dreaming of for years, ever since I had heard about them, studied them, watched the videos on YouTube, and listened to the competitors' interviews. There was an incredible desire deep within me to push my physical limits that I couldn't find the words to explain. I wanted to experience all those feelings endurance runners talked about. Just how far could I go? How much pain and suffering could I endure? I couldn't explain this innate desire to experience that kind of fatigue to myself, let alone to my mother. If I tried to explain it, she would overreact, send me to a shrink, and I would come back with a hamster as a new coping device to keep me grounded. Or maybe a goldfish.

Training for a five- or ten-kilometer race was too elementary. I didn't want to be limited to collegiate or national races that didn't have the long-suffering distances. I wanted to run fifty miles, one hundred miles. My mom thought I was crazy. It felt rational to me. If I could run twenty miles on a trail, why not test myself in a longer distance race? I would work at night and run during the day. It sounded like heaven to me.

"One year, Giselle. I will give you one year to prove to your stubborn self, to the world, and to me, and then you are going to school, scholarship or no scholarship." She was fatigued from her fist pounding. I wore her out with my cannon fodder.

"Realize it will take me a year to train for one of these long races."

"It's your life, Giselle. You'll learn from your mistakes." She relented but, as always, tried to end with a final sting. "Maybe all those hours pounding your body will give you ideas on what you seriously want to do with the rest of your life. What will you do when you get injured and can't run? You won't be training with a team, Giselle. You will be out there all on your own, and you remember what happened that one morning when you were running." Touché. Nice jab.

The more negative she got, the more determined I was to succeed. I had to take on adversity in many forms: my fears, bad weather, mental fortitude, fatigue, fueling properly, recovery, but the one that concerned me most seemed to be overcoming my mother's constant negativity and proving her wrong. Even though we were a little more tolerant of each other since I turned eighteen, she still wanted to dictate what I did with my life. She wanted me to follow her rules. I know she was proud of my accomplishments so far. She framed some of my bib numbers, medals, and newspaper articles about me, and she bragged to her friends. But for some reason, I was still always looking for her approval.

Tension was rising in the house again. I pull my ears back and circle a few times to tuck deep into my bed. Why so loud? Don't you know I can hear that fly on the windowsill in the other room? I had seen this throughout lifetimes when the parent is losing a child to chase a dream completely different from what was expected since the day she or he was born. Mariella did not want to let go of control. She was so attached to one plan for Ellie. She needed to detach herself. The hardest part is letting children make their own way. Make mistakes or not. Birds falling out of the nest. They get eaten or they fly. Laws of nature.

I couldn't settle down to a nap, because they continued battling over who could yell the loudest and still be heard, so I grabbed a squeaky toy from my basket. Every time the fist pounded, I squeezed the toy with my teeth. Bam. Squeak. Bam. Squeak.

Chapter 9

Success and Failure

I took my training very seriously, no longer having a coach or teammates. I educated myself about running long distances, leaving no stone unturned. It was one thing to dream, but there was no way I was automatically and miraculously going to become a skilled long-distance runner. It involved a lot more education and training than I was used to. I had to learn to pace myself, fuel myself, and to feel comfortable with pain. Because I was cautious about running alone, Blue trained the distance right along with me. We became an inseparable team of two.

I never found nirvana, but this must be as close to it as I could have imagined. The freedom to run unencumbered by the pursuit of enemies or predators. It took me a while to realize not to chase the squirrels, rabbits, and birds, no matter how tempting. If Ellie put a pack on my back, it meant a long day ahead, so keep my nose in the air and my eyes on Ellie. She will not slow down to let me nibble a little on the deer poop. That is what life is all about, slow down and smell the stories of nature's creatures, but not when she is on a mission.

When we do stop for a rest, she talks about the views, which I can only imagine are as beautiful as the tone of her voice, as I cannot see as far as she. I try to dig deep into the caverns of my memories for some link to the colors associated with the intense scents floating through the air from the mountains and trees that surround us. When we finish our rest, I mark our location, and she does too. I re-mark the spot just to be sure that others know this is our kingdom. We have marked hundreds of miles together.

The weather changes colder as we run through fallen leaves and snow. My paws get caked in ice and snow, so Mom has made me booties. I try my hardest to shake them off, putting on a skilled dance to make Ellie laugh. If I can be by her side to chase the wind, the rain, the falling leaves, and the falling snowflakes until my eyes freeze shut, I am there, boots or not. When we go inside, she wraps a warm towel around me, hugs me, and tells me I am the best. I would go through mountains of snow for her.

I was ready to tackle my first race, the Great Divide Mountain Marathon in the spring of the next year. I camped out with Blue for ten days before the race to get used to the eight-thousand-foot elevation. We huddled together in one sleeping bag because it got so cold at night.

The race organizers would not allow Blue to run with me, even though I assured them he would not be in anyone's way. I pleaded the fact he has run the distance, but they wouldn't relent. It was hard for me to explain to him that I had to go alone, but mostly I wondered if I could. It would be like running without a part of my body, an empty space beside me. Reluctantly, I found a volunteer who would watch him for a few hours. It incensed Blue that he couldn't come, and he sulked the whole time I was running, which transformed into the perception by the sitters that he was the best-behaved dog on the planet. I knew better.

It was a well-known race for its spectators, as it finished at the bottom of a ski trail close to the main lodge of the major ski resort. I arrived at the start area in the dark. Everyone there looked the same as me, wide-eyed and anxious to start. My nerves forced me into myself, ignoring the others until we lined up at the start. I kissed my best friend goodbye and took off toward the rising sun, with a french braid tapping on my back as my one constant companion. I turned off my emotions, mechanically following at the heels of the leading group of men. A few of them threw backward glances with raised eyebrows, but the pace was comfortable for me, so I gave a nod back in salute. We ran in a unified rhythm of footsteps and breathing in the first ascent as well as a series of successive climbs. I strived to stay a few meters behind them, and no one passed me.

The tall, lanky, long-haired guy with a bandana around his head and tall white basketball socks that I had focused on the whole way, never letting the socks get too far ahead, turned to me so I could see his face for the first time and said, "You are quite the spitfire, aren't you? Sticking with us this whole way. You dropped Maggie a ways back. Sheet, she won this a few years in a row. You aim to stay ahead of 'er the whole way?"

"Who's Maggie?" I asked.

Laughter broke out among the line of six men snaking ahead of me. "It's better she doesn't know," someone yelled out from the line. I kept my eye on Mr. White Socks until the final aid station at kilometer thirty, where I got distracted by the tables laden with various fruits, bars, and cookies.

"Go on, darlin', you are doing fabulous. Go give these hoodlums a run for their money." A plump, bundled-up older man handed me a bar and continued shooing me on my way after filling my handheld water bottle for me. I felt a sudden burst of energy, knowing there were only twelve kilometers left on the part of the trail I studied the hardest. I took off before a couple of the men to the cheers of all the volunteers.

During my parents' heated and explosive arguments, when I took refuge in the forests behind the farm, I found my alter ego. She was an Indian warrior. I counted on her to bring me through the turbulence, to escape from the reality of the heartbreak of hurtful words. I could count on her strength. She had no relation to the couple who hurled objects and obscenities. Hers was a culture of respect and strength. In my darkest moments, she has been there for me, pushing me aside so she can bear the wounds she knew I couldn't handle. After kilometer thirty, she appeared again, her spear in one hand and my hand in the other. We ran softly together, becoming one and the same in the hunt for the end of the enduring pain.

I was getting desperate to find ways to keep up with the lead group. They were starting to pull away, and two men passed me with a pat on the back. I ran to an imaginary drum beating in my head. I sang a war cry deep in my throat. Since I had no energy left of my own, I used the energy of the men ahead of me and the ones chasing me down. I don't know what concerned me more: the pain that was crushing me or my ability to endure it.

Overruling the negative thoughts surging from the pain became an overwhelming task. There grew a mix between the sounds of my steps and my exhaled grunts that evolved into a religious chant: tap, tap, tap, huh, tap, tap, tap, huh. I began to connect spiritually to the earth. I prayed through my feet with each step, praying for the end.

I came out from the narrow trail onto a gravel path, unsure of which way to turn until I heard the rush of cheering and a muffled voice over a loudspeaker. I saw the finish line was about two hundred meters at the end of a steep downhill, so I let the encouragement of the crowd bring me in. My legs felt heavy, but the roar of the spectators dulled the pain as relief of seeing the finish line filled my muscles with an energy I didn't know I had left. I pulled the large ribbon strung across the finish line along with me as I heard Blue's distinctive bark with him running full speed toward me, dragging the leash once held by his dogsitters who were following close behind.

"Amazing finish, Ellie. You are incredible. Congratulations." Words were coming from every direction as I bent down to greet my teammate. He started sniffing and cleaning the sweat from my legs with his gritty, wet tongue. It felt divine.

I finished seventh overall and the first woman. I lapped up the admiration from the men who finished before and after me, enjoying their camaraderie and attention. I earned my place among them. I wanted to do it again.

I was congratulated by Maggie, a surprisingly small woman a few inches above five feet with short black hair and a pixie face and a welcoming smile that made me like her instantly.

"Wow, Ellie! Oh my God, I couldn't catch you. I got a glimpse of you in the straightaways—so far ahead. You turned on your afterburners and took off in the last half mile or so. There was no way I could catch you." She placed her hands on my shoulders and bowed her head down to catch her breath, her head reaching the height of my stomach. "Where did you find that finishing kick?"

"It was finally seeing that fabulous finish line and being chased by you of course!" I laughed, trying to pay her a compliment. We shared a deep hug despite the sweat and grime covering our bodies. I didn't find out until later she was one of the top-ranked runners in college before she quit competing, disillusioned by the college race environment. Knowing this solidified my reasoning for pursuing my dream. I wasn't the only one on this crazy path.

There was something special about the camaraderie of this group of athletes. Everyone was so easygoing and relaxed. I did not feel the tension, pressure, and stress that accompanied every one of my high school races. I flaunted my success over the phone to my mom, who sounded relieved I finished more than congratulatory. I told her about the check for $600 I had won along with a pair of trail shoes I so desperately needed. That's when she got excited.

I turned to Blue. "Next time I race, we will find a hotel that takes dogs rather than tenting before a race." My father was going to send money to help pay for a hotel room but forgot, and my mother kept reminding me if I wanted something badly enough, I would have to find a way without her blessing or financial help.

I picked up a brochure for another race called Finnegan's Fancy Fifty, a fifty-kilometer race in three weeks. Only eight more kilometers than this one.

"Just rest from now until then, Ellie, and you can do it," Maggie encouraged me. "And I'm glad I won't be there to compete against you."

The race was closer to home, so our local paper published an article featuring me entering the race. They had been following me since my regional and later national cross-country victories. The town was disappointed when I didn't go to college on a scholarship, but showing I could tackle these longer distances was justification for my decision. I felt more pressure to perform for this race since many people mentioned they would drive up to watch.

I succumbed to only three hours of restless sleep before getting up at 3:00 a.m. to make coffee for the road. Surprisingly, I found Mom up with the coffee made and some warm muffins on a plate with melting butter slathered on top.

"What is this all about? Why are you up too?" I shuffled into the kitchen, almost hitting a wall while rubbing the sleep out of my eyes.

"I could hear you rustling around last night, and I knew you weren't sleeping well, so I thought I could drive while you try to get a little more sleep in the back of the car," she said matter-of-factly.

I was puzzled, or was I dreaming? I didn't understand this gesture. She read my expression adeptly, and she quickly replied, "Don't overthink it. Get ready to go. Blue will keep me company while you run. We'll go have lunch or something. Doesn't seem like it will take you long, since the last race was around three and a half hours."

I didn't disagree. I wanted to play the stubborn you-said-you-weren't-going-to-help-me reaction, but I talked myself out of it. I was debating about going, but a few more hours of sleep would make a big difference.

This was the race that killed my ego, and my alter ego didn't even bother to show up. Maybe I needed a good thrashing. I stood at the start line, waved to Mom and Blue, and took off with the leaders. Where I got it in my dumb head I was superhuman is beyond me. I was OK for the first forty kilometers, and then I blew up. I completely lost control of my emotions, and I wanted to quit. My legs turned to lead, and my stomach felt like a taunt balloon. All my body parts took turns aching and cramping. As each runner passed me while I slowed, I felt more and more like a failure. I couldn't bat away the negative thoughts buzzing in my head like pesky flies. I had never experienced this before. I had always loved to run, but I hated this. I started to hate each runner as they padded past me. From the ones with a serious look on their face to the ones with smiles, saying, "Come on! You can do it!" I felt like a failure and I wasn't used to that.

Why was my body betraying me? Why was I taking it out on everyone who was trying to be nice? I grumbled through the aid stations without a thank-you. I kept my head to the ground so I couldn't see people as they passed me. I started to hate everything, and it complimented how I felt about myself. Dragging myself along the trail, I was in a deep funk. My body betrayed me with cramps I had never felt before. I had to run off the main trail to vomit my mother's muffins. I was a mess by the time I walked over the finish line over five hours after the start. I saw my mother's look of relief change to shock as she took off her jacket and wrapped it around me.

"This will be a great picture for the paper, won't it," I moaned.

My mother had never responded well to any whining. She would tell me to quit feeling sorry for myself—that there were people way worse off than me, who don't have food on the table or a roof over their head. I get that. But why am I not allowed to feel bad? But this time she was different.

"Count your blessings, Ellie. You have a gift of perseverance I have never seen in anyone." She wrapped her arm around my shoulder and pulled me into her as we walked to the aid station. "I don't know how or why you do this to yourself, but the important thing is you never gave up, even when I know you wanted to. You kept going. That is all that matters."

I managed a smile, but I wanted to be alone. Fifty kilometers of being alone was not long or far enough away from the unwanted attention of the locals who came to watch me finish. I had let them down. I found a quiet place in the shade to sit and stretch, and suddenly my emotions came boiling up from deep inside. Was I doing the right thing? Should I have taken a scholarship? Maybe I can't do this, and I am not good enough. Will this happen again?

I sat beside her as I watched her berate herself for something she had no control over. I couldn't make sense of it. Why do humans demand so much of themselves? I nuzzled up to her and put my head against her chest, and she gave me a big, deep hug, then sat back against the tree, letting me go. I pushed my nose under her hand again, stepping in between her crossed legs, sitting up against her. She could have freed herself, but instead she buried her head in my neck, held tight, and started to cry. She works too hard at keeping all her emotions inside. It builds up, and then it explodes. We sat that way until she could breathe normally.

With her head now resting against my back, her body restless with introspection, I realized that no matter what time in history, successful humans discover that making mistakes or overcoming problems are treasured lessons. Ellie, you deal with pain to train for endurance, and you will deal with pain when you grow in life. Each painful experience, just as with our painful training sessions, break you down so you can build yourself stronger, more resilient. When you try to overcome each new adversity, you look back on your past and say, "I have survived that trying time in my past. Now I will survive this." That, in essence, is the story of my many lives.

Chapter 10

Dirt Dive

The rest of the year came together with a string of successful wins in smaller races that paid a very small purse. It would be enough to allow me to fund the next competition and a tank of gas to get there. There were no lucrative prizes in these races. I had no sponsors, because companies thought I was a one-shot wonder. No one was knocking down my door to wear their running shoes or try their supplement.

I tested myself on another fifty-kilometer trail race called, Bunny Run. I wish I knew better than to trust a name. I didn't realize it was such an iconic race, because of its reputation for difficulty with its narrow, undulating technical climbs and steep pitches. But these were similar to the trails I was used to running at home. Good thing I was the new naive kid on the block because I would have been completely psyched out by the headliners who showed up for this competition. I started the race with the idea that I had nothing to lose. Give it all or go home.

I didn't want to be stuck behind slower runners trying to push past them, so I would have to get out fast, which wasn't always my best strategy. I am the one who can turn on the kick at the end, but I felt I needed to redeem myself from the last fifty-kilometer race. I was mentally prepared, muffin-free, and chomping at the bit.

There was nothing easy about this race, as it was all uphill and then all downhill to the finish. It was absurdly treacherous, with steep declines and hairpin turns that had your body wanting to go down the fall line while the path veered sharply across it. Running fast was nearly impossible for me, so when guys started to pass me, I was bewildered by their nimbleness and strength. I tried to follow in their footsteps, and it was a fine balance between falling forward too fast for my feet to keep up or falling sideways over a cliff while I turned. These runners seemed to defy the laws of physics, but I couldn't.

I remember studying about Newton's law of momentum in school. The total momentum of two objects before a collision is equal to the total momentum of the objects after a collision. In my case, the ground didn't have any momentum, but I did. There must be some sort of law about tripping, flying through the air, landing on your knees with uncontrolled momentum that can send a rippling effect through the hips, stomach, and chest so the final body part, the face, gets slammed into the dirt in a classic dual-action chin-first and nose-second reaction. Two men jumped over me, while the third stopped to help me up.

"Oof, that was a nasty face-plant, and you nearly caused a chain reaction. Don't mind those guys. They couldn't stop, but I could. Wow, what a spill. I give you twelve out of ten for style. Your feet kicking up almost touching your head from behind earned you bonus points." He laughed as he dusted me off. He pulled out a bandana and dabbed my chin. It stung, but I didn't dare say a word.

I inspected the blood as a few other men slowed to offer assistance. I pushed them all to keep going as I tied the bandana under my chin to the top of my head like a reverse babushka. I stuck my cap back on and continued to run without checking my hands and knees, which I eventually discovered were a bloody mess, but I didn't have time to pick the stones out of my palms. I ignored the cuts and stings to focus on my footsteps. After a while, everything went dumb.

Still, no women passed me, and I felt the warrior more than ever before as my alter ego, a newly wounded warrior, took over. I kept pushing. Not sure whether that was because I wanted to win or just get to the medic tent as fast as possible. I knew my crash victim appearance would add drama to the finish line, and sure enough, I did not disappoint the crowd with bloody shins, shoes, T-shirt, and hands. I had a wide ribbon to pull with me, signaling I finished as first woman to a round of applause and hoots before being escorted to the aid station.

As we gathered around after everyone had finished, I took in the moment by mixing with everyone, not shying away to be alone. Nothing like being in a group of like-minded people with the same obsession but different abilities all recognized for simply finishing something they started. We finished, not asking, "How did you place?" Rather, we asked, "How was it for you?" No one hogged the conversation with exhaustive descriptions. Just the mention of the mud or creek crossing was enough for people to nod in agreement with survival tales of their own as everyone took turns sharing.

We all had to laugh when one volunteer held up one muddy running shoe that got sucked off a foot, asking if anyone would like to confess ownership. "You know you are a seasoned distance runner if you continue running with only one shoe," she announced to the crowd, and we expected no one to lay claim. But we were wrong and whooped in unison when a pirate–like character limped up to collect his shoe while shrugging in response to the resounding applause.

To finish off my first year of racing, I completed and won a couple of fifty-mile races. Winning gained me instant entry into a famous and notoriously difficult race called the Bullwinkle 100 in early spring. The thought of going one hundred kilometers frightened me, yet the fear was also motivating. I would have to train hard and consistently. I was unsure of how. All I knew was to go out, run, rest, and do it over again until I needed to rest more. It would mean training through the winter as best I could. This race entry also meant I was getting noticed. Mom cut out a short magazine article and stuck it to the fridge as her way of telling me she was proud of me. With the race on the horizon, I wanted to be more than ready. I wanted to be superhuman.

"What else am I going to do with my money? I would rather it go to your dreams. Besides, you will pay me back when you hit it big time and are on the cover of *Runners Magazine*," Dad sang to me over the phone to the tune of "Cover of the Rolling Stones." With the winnings and the help of my father, I was able to buy a used SUV of my own so that Blue and I could travel to training routes and camp in the back with the seats folded down, snuggled together on a thick foamy covered with a heavy down-filled quilt. When I look back, those were the happiest days of my life, with an open moonroof, staring up at the night sky, trying to figure out my life's true purpose, with Blue's warm back nestled into my side and his low dog snore rumbling over his lips.

Chapter 11

Bullwinkle 100

"Giselle, this is too much, too far for your young body. How can you run one hundred kilometers? How will you keep up your energy?" my mom asked, but she began to realize there was more to me than how I looked.

I was thinning out but also beginning to look stronger, with defined muscles. I grew taller than her and taller than most of the women I competed against at five ten. During my training, she took it upon herself to fuel me properly every day. I had my own private and knowledgeable chef who knew the best natural foods I needed for me to train and recover. She changed her recipes to suit me based on trial and error. We learned her muffins were definitely off the list.

I dared not miss one ingredient of a recipe out of superstition and fear that if I did, I might sabotage my chances at performing well. It had evolved through experimentation between my mother and me, but the key ingredients never changed. My mother was pleased I was more accustomed to her natural ways of eating than to the Western world's processed junk food. I never tried the power or energy bars provided at races, instead I ate her thick honey cookies filled with nuts and dried berries and salted yam chips. If I fueled properly, I knew I could tackle any race because gastric distress was debilitating for any runner.

As a result of my success in my latest races, and unaware I was gaining a reputation, I was asked by the race organizers to be part of the prerace interview involving several reporters asking questions to the distinguished competitors who sat at a long table along with the race organizers. I felt compelled to appear because they covered my race fee after I won the fifty-kilometer race earlier, which saved me considerable money on my minimal budget, so I could splurge on a hotel room that allowed dogs.

There was a film crew shooting a documentary. They had asked me earlier if I wouldn't mind being filmed occasionally, but their central focus was Lindsay Miller, who was favored to win. Sitting at the long, formal table, I was nervous about what to say when it was my turn, but I could hear my mother's advice to always speak from the heart. They asked me to give a short analysis of my race strategy. "One foot in front of the other," my heart said to a few chuckles in the group.

"Right. Simple plan, I guess," said the reporter sarcastically. "What about fueling? What about pacing?" He worked to drag answers out of me. I fidgeted and said a lot of hums and ahs, tilted my head to the side, my eyes looked up and around like I was being pensive, but I was simply as scared as a fox surrounded by hound dogs. They wanted to understand what accounted for my success so far.

"The formula for me is consistent hard work with scheduled recovery days, eight to ten hours of sleep, naps if necessary, lots of stretching, self-massage, and a lot of nutritious food. I am sure it's the same for everyone here. Sometimes I can't seem to put one foot in front of the other with any rhythm on a training run, but I just go out and try again the next day, and I celebrate the daily accomplishments," I explained. I sat back in my seat, hoping if I sank out of sight they wouldn't call on me again. Looking around, everyone was so seasoned, with their running history weathered into their faces and bodies. I was fresh, unscathed, and easily the youngest. Who was I to know anything more than them?

Another question from the crowd: "Where do you find your motivation to train, Giselle?"

"I think that if you are lined up for a difficult race you must have a crazy passion for torturing yourself." There was a lot of laughter, which took me by surprise, so I continued. "Actually, it is these people sitting at this table. They are my motivation. They are the ones who stir me to action when I don't want to get up out of bed to train; that, and the fear I am going to die of unbearable pain if I don't train," I declared, then glanced around to see a unified look of respect from the other runners at the table.

"What brand of trail shoes will you be wearing?" someone shouted out.

I looked upward with a few fingers drumming over my lips as I tried to remember. "Just a sec. I'll check." I glanced down to look at my shoes and sat up to more laughter.

After the media session, the race organizers gave their final pitch about the race rules and hazards. The runners and organizers mulled around together, but I felt overwhelmed and awkward, so I sneaked my way to the exit as quickly and quietly as possible without being stopped for a one-on-one interview, which was happening to all the other competitors. I beelined it for my car and back to the hotel where I left Blue waiting.

On race morning I try to leave her alone. She walks around at a quicker pace, scratching her head, pausing, walking again, moves things around on the countertop, puts them in a bag, takes them out of the bag, puts them back in. She never sits except on the big water bowl, which she does a few times. We sit staring at each other. I think she is praying, so I pray with her through my deep sighs, my head resting on her bare legs.

Her mind is weighed down with what-ifs. I wish I could tell her not to think too much. She cannot predict but only plan and if the plan doesn't work—and it rarely ever goes as planned, hence my many lives—be flexible and make the best of it. Reminds me of the time I came back as a cat—and no, cats don't have nine lives. I was particularly irritable most of the time with damn fur balls in my throat and an obsessive-compulsive disorder about scratching things and cleaning myself. No one quite understood the sophistication of my spiritual intelligence, which conflicted with my ego, making me appear aloof. I even annoyed myself at times. And I had a nasty habit of falling asleep in odd places—boxes, bowls, flowerpots. Come to think of it, that was how I met my demise—sleeping around where I shouldn't have been. A cat with no plan.

Our morning drive in the dark is quiet, except for the same songs I have heard before. We park and grab her pack, but nothing for me. We walk silently to a group, then I am handed off to another woman whom I have met before. I don't mind, because she can speak dog. Ellie crouches to give me a long, tight hug and muzzles me in closely, whispering in my ear that she will think of me every second. She thanks me for being her training partner, and she tells me she loves me. If I could cry, I would. My tail and head drop as she fills my face with kisses. We stare into each other's eyes as she scratches behind my ears in a way she knows I love. Normally I would feel better, but I don't. I cry out a short pathetic bark when she walks away. She turns briefly and waves. I will wait until she returns, exactly at this spot. She does not have to worry about me. The woman holding my leash should let it go. I won't follow. I promise.

How I feel on a race day is remarkably different. I always have electricity in my stomach. It makes my body feel like it is glowing with light. If something hurt earlier in the week, it no longer hurts on race day, because my adrenaline has erased all the pain.

We arrived at least thirty minutes early for me to warm up and pee behind a bush about five times. My nerves are always directly linked to my bladder. The more nerves, the more urine, and chilly air carried on a damp breeze didn't help. I remained in the shadows out of the temporary lights illuminating the start area and double tied my shoelaces while I observed the unfolding scene. Runners were wandering around with blank stares, deep in thought. Groups of runners with their support crew were gathered chatting quietly together. I saw some veterans talking and laughing like they were going for a short morning jog.

The older guys with weathered skin were the most jovial, raising their eyebrows with amusement at the nervousness of the newbies. Some runners were shuffling and shaking their arms to keep warm or to keep the nerves at bay as they checked out the others through wide-open, squirrelly eyes. Others were doing some form of warm-up. Others were sitting or lying on the ground while staring blankly into the night, occasionally watching others walk by but not focusing on them. Then there are the young guns bouncing up and down to loosen their legs. I was not sure where I fit.

The running gear I saw ranged from high tech to primitive—from old bandanas that have seen hundreds of miles and gallons of sweat to the latest high-tech outfits. Everyone invested in the best water-carrier backpack with pockets stuffed with everything from food to batteries and socks to Band-Aids. On display is an eclectic array of practical running fashion: long tights, short shorts, and ankle or knee-high socks that are color coordinated or stained and threadbare. I am sure, in a quirky way, superstition drives most of the clothing choices. If you had a successful race in one pair of shorts, they kept running with you until you had a bad race, kind of like a hockey player in the playoffs who doesn't shave or change his underwear, or so I've heard. I read about a guy who ran a marathon in every country in the world wearing the same black shorts until they faded to a light gray by the end.

I stalked my competitors from the shadows. I had researched the women in my category and the women in general. I knew what they were capable of doing. Now I studied their demeanor at the race start. I don't want to admit I felt great, because the running gods would put me in my place somewhere out there on the course. I learned to enter a race with great humility.

They played the national anthem, and a few people sang along off-key. Most stared at the ground and shuffled their feet in anticipation of the start. The race director gave a small speech followed by a loud cheer and clapping from the group. I quieted myself by saying a short prayer, a prerace ritual to calm myself. The gun went off, and we all slowly trotted off into the last hours of the night, bouncing along with the beams of hundreds of headlamps reflecting off backsides of the runners in front. From a distance, we were a bobbing sea of human fireflies.

The sun comes up, and I have slept restlessly from where Ellie left. I am given lots of treats from various people, but I refuse some things. Don't they know I am a canine? Canine means meat-eater. I still eat most of it, though. We walk a lot. We spend time in a coffee shop where I get lots of attention and cookies. I sleep under the table, in the shade at the feet of strangers. Finally, we drive back to the spot where we said goodbye to Ellie and wait.

I feel the excitement of the humans around me. I am getting more rubs and scratches than normal from a lot more people. They are smiling, so I smile too. I search in vain for a breeze to carry Ellie's scent to me. I hear some yelling. The woman who has my leash yells, "It's Ellie! Come on, Blue!" I run beside her with my nose on high alert. I smell her first, then I recognize her form, her gait, her bounce. She is illuminated by lights in the sky. The crowd is cheering, and I start barking loudly so Ellie can hear me. I am here, Ellie. Look up.

Her body is moving awkwardly, stumbling forward with uneven steps as she passes by us. People rush toward her to hold her steady and put a blanket over her. She is bent over with her hands on her knees, breathing heavily. People are patting her back, but giving her space. She stands up and looks over to us. I jerk the leash free and run full tilt toward her. Ellie squats slowly, in stages, then falls to the ground as I clamber on top. "No, it's OK," I hear her say, and she hugs me tightly. Her body is a pot of stewing scents—sweet, woody, salty. She has seen the world.

She hugs me tightly before being helped up and ushered to a nearby chair beside a fire pit and is given food and a blanket. She starts talking in a lively tone. Wow, she is happy. I start my reconnaissance. I sniff out the journey she took. There is pine, grass, moss, dirt of various elements, and river water. You are very salty, almost metallic, and very bitter. There are bits of dried blood. The Salt Lick News. I sense quite a bit of elevation gain from the lingering perfume of winds from distant mountaintops unfamiliar to me.

Below the foreign bouquet, is the warm earthy essence of my Ellie. Her scent takes me back in time and reminds me of something as I am pulled into an impromptu dog nap warmed by the hypnagogic fire. There are slight shadowy images coming forward in my dream. I feel emotions build up inside of me I cannot explain. I am in another land, with different scents. People are running in different directions. Scents are becoming stronger and more pungent, smoky, and spicy. I smell a horrible scent of burning flesh that tears at my heart and makes me choke. I am being pulled backward, forced against my will. I cough out, "Let me go!" as I struggle against the restraints. I am terrified as I watch. I wake up to the gentle tug on my collar. She tells me I was running in my sleep again. I was running to save you, my love.

Chapter 12

Race Fame

"You did it. I got your text. How do you feel? What's going on? I thought you would be exhausted and sleeping by now. It's late," my dad went on breathlessly.

I waited for him to slow down. "Blue woke me up to go pee, and I couldn't go back to sleep. I hope you don't mind me calling late. I thought you might want to hear from me, but I was too exhausted after talking to everyone at the finish. I came back to our room, showered, and fell asleep on top of the covers until Blue woke me up."

"No. No, of course not, darlin'. I am here anytime day or night. How do you feel, Ellie? Are you OK?" I could hear his concern in his tone.

"My body feels like it is still running. It is tingling all over and numb at the same time. I feel a fatigue deep inside." I laid back, attempting to stretch legs that felt like wooden planks while I described the feeling of winning and how it felt to take the lead from Lindsay Miller when I hit the last aid station, learning later that she had to drop out. I ran on a cloud, wiping away tears all the way to the finish. The whole event was surreal to me. After we went back and forth, me sharing details and Dad asking questions, I closed off and lay awake staring at the stippled ceiling with water stain spots near the light.

Blue had his head on my stomach staring up at me, his eyes large and full of an eerie adoration. He sneaked his way on the top of the bed, and I had no energy nor desire to command him off. I grabbed the big bag of chips from the side table and struggled to pull it open, but the smell of salt and vinegar was well worth the effort. I awoke later in the morning to find the bag still in my hands, licked clean.

There were a lot of calls and messages on my phone with quite a few from magazines and newspapers. The first order of business was to call, for a fourth time, The Worrier. When she answered, I dove into my thoughts, "I need to have someone to lean on. To help me sort through all this."

I told her about meeting Jake Wellington, the top male finisher, and how he put me under his wing. Jake was a calm, down to earth kind of guy. He had short dark hair that never needed combing. He spoke volumes through his large saucer-sized, deep brown eyes framed with arched brows making him appear hopeful like he is searching for a friend in a crowd. He was the first one to greet me at the finish line and later helped me move my wary body through the crowds of well-wishers.

"The film crew who were doing a documentary wanted me to give an interview right after the race. I bet I sounded stupid. I didn't know I would win at such a famous race. It is going to take me another couple of days to get my head out of the clouds. The film company is paying my expenses to stay another day after the banquet to discuss some footage and narrate what was going on. I don't think I could drive back eight hours, anyway. I need to keep my legs moving. A doping organization did a drug test on me!" I rambled on without taking a breath. "People are asking for my autograph. Can you believe it?"

"Of course, Ellie." I heard her take a deep breath. "Your dad and I have been talking. You are moving into new territory, and you need guidance. We don't want you to be taken advantage of. It's all good that you won, but now all this. I thought you'd win a few little races and then go to school, where you should be. I didn't realize you were this good. But it could be beginner's luck. Prepare for future disappointments. It won't always be like this."

Way to rain on someone's parade. It was no use getting the advice I wanted from her. "Mom, thanks for your advice, but I have got to go now. I wanted to let you know I won't be home for a few days. I'll call you soon. Bye." I closed off before she could say anything further. I felt this burning need to fire my hands through the phone and grab her by the shoulders and shake her. Didn't she understand what I did? I called Dad.

"My Lord, sweetheart, you are a superstar! Not only a superstar, an ultrastar," he teased. "That is bigger than a superstar. You are a supernova ultrastar!"

"Oh, Dad, I am just me," I replied. I told him about mom knowing I was unfairly tattling on her.

"Ellie, I can't venture into that territory with you. I am sure she is proud of you but doesn't know how to show it, so it comes out as being protective. She is probably more worried fame will take you further away from her. But for me? Heck, go be famous and buy me a new truck. But honey, you do need to take your time before jumping into an interview or publication. We want you to be sure you are painted in the right light. Don't let the excitement overrule the logic. Just one step at a time, OK?"

I understood that they were both being protective. Over the next few days, I latched onto Jake like a little sister, watching how he addressed people, quietly, humbly. He knew I was new to winning a big event from my deer-in-headlights approach to the media questions and attention. While others were talking, I could see him listening intently, not thinking ahead about what he was going to say. When someone asked him a question, he would pause and think before he spoke. He controlled the pace of the conversations. I was beginning to realize he had the knack on how to control the pace of a race as well. He had a long notorious history of running successful ultras and everyone clambered over each other to meet him. He took it all in stride, with a calm professional demeanor. I was learning a lot by watching how he dealt with people.

At the awards banquet, I watched the other top finishers admiring their athleticism and grace as they accepted their awards. We sat together and relived our own accounts of the race, laughed, and found the energy to dance, bonded by a common battle we fought. Even Lindsay, who had to drop out so close to the finish graciously congratulated me, making me admire her for her sportsmanship. She could have gone home with her tail between her legs, but she was there to the end.

Winning this big event felt surreal as if I was watching a video of myself. I stopped and took it all in, putting the video on hold. I wanted to capture and store the memory away, so I could draw on the special moment and the connection between all of us, when I felt alone. I met the eyes of others, without looking away, holding a silent acknowledgment of the massive feat we had accomplished. I came to acknowledge a new reality I saw hiding in everyone's demeanor, the pressing question tapping at the edge of our minds: What next? I was relieved yet depressed that all the daily training was over. What would I do tomorrow?

We got up before the sun, and she bundled into a lot of clothes to take me for a walk. She seems depressed about leaving. Ellie spent a lot of time hugging people. We both said our goodbyes to Jake. He has no pheromone scent on him. He smells like Ellie—fresh, woody, and with the same lingering hint of mountain adventures. The air around them when they are together is light, without turbulence, which doesn't happen much with Ellie. She is usually guarded and tense around new people. I liked that he felt familiar. It was the first time I didn't feel a little threatened by a male, except for Dad. Humans are the same as dogs—not all are made the same. I have gotten faster and more accurate at judging the vibration, like an electrical shock to me, demonstrated in their body posture, eyes, and their aroma. Ellie might be a hugger, but I am a sensor and a guard.

Ellie loads up our gear, and then we head home, stopping more than normal so Ellie can stretch her legs. Her finisher's medal swings back and forth off the rearview mirror keeping time to the thumping coming from the car. Ellie sings and talks. She tells me all about her what race she wants to do next, rationalizing her ability to run further. Next is 150 kilometers. I am not sure I know what that means. I am not sure she knows what that means either.

The relief I felt to take the turn into our driveway, knowing I was finally home and could throw myself into my own bed was quickly overtaken by butterflies of excitement when I saw Dad leaning up against his truck with his legs crossed and arms folded. He looked thinner, like an old ranch hand with his cowboy boots and ball cap. I told him I would be arriving home today, but he never mentioned being here to greet me. I couldn't stop the car and open the car door fast enough. It had been almost two months since I had seen him. I landed on stiff legs but managed a few awkward strides toward him as he moved away from his truck to me with his arms wide and beckoning.

"Congratulations, my dear Ellie. I am so proud of you," he sang as he swept me into his arms and swung me around, releasing the stiffness in my back a little as it cracked under his squeeze.

"You are amazing. I bought fifty copies of the newspaper to hand out to everyone I meet on the street. This is my daughter, I tell 'em, the youngest woman and new female course record on the Bullwinkle 100. 'Can you believe she can run one hundred kilometers?' I ask them. I have been getting calls from distant relatives and friends I never knew I had. We are all so proud of you, Ellie."

"Oh, Dad, I can't believe you are here. You never told me you were coming home. I mean my home. No, your home too," I stuttered out the words. Blue was there to greet Dad with his body wagging out of control. Blue had variations of wags from a slight twitch of his tail to a full body wag for family and certain people, most of whom I had no idea how he judged. His tail was like a barometer on how much he loved and trusted someone, and he was having a dog-wagging seizure seeing Dad.

"Does Mom know you are here?" I asked as he stepped aside with a wink in his eye to let me go first into the house. I opened the door to find a chorus of friends, led by Mom, yelling, "Surprise!" Half the town showed up and hid their cars behind our barn. I thanked everyone with a hug and received handshakes, high fives, pats on the back, and a pleasant teasing about not letting the win go to my head. My parents looked at each other, and I thought I saw a wink and smile exchanged that instantly heated my heart.

I didn't want to have all the attention, as people quieted down to listen to me, so I gave a very condensed version of the race. I told them about Jake and the offers for sponsorships from various companies who had reps at the race.

"I think I will have to go with this company," I announced as I presented a little high-tech blue T-shirt emblazoned with the company logo on its back. Everyone laughed as Dad gave a running commentary as I struggled to put the shirt on Blue, who was having no part of it.

I enjoyed mingling, seeing old friends, while I couldn't stop getting my fill of the delicious array of food people brought but was grateful when people noticed my yawning and started to say their goodbyes. My heart was warmed by their presence, but I was looking forward to a quiet night alone with my parents. It had been years since I had the two of them in the same room together when it wasn't stuffed full of tension.

"Dad, are you staying over?" I was so hopeful that my voice squeezed higher at the end.

"He is sleeping in the guest room," my mom yelled out from the clanking dishes she was piling up next to the sink.

"Damn, Mariella, you promised I could sleep with you," my dad yelled back, winking at me as I dropped my jaw. Dad got up to help clear the dishes and joined my mom in the kitchen.

Without my knowing, my parents had evolved their broken marriage into a quasi-friendship. I detected a little flirting, but maybe it was wishful thinking on my part. Home felt more like home than it had in as long as I could remember. I was not sure if it was the air of happiness and celebration, but it was a long time since I had seen my parents being so cordial to each other. Whether they were putting on a show for me, or they were getting along, I didn't want to disturb this feeling with false hope. We moved delicately around each other, dancing between the past and the present, trying to forget old tensions through laughter. The conversation felt easier than it ever had been in the past, and I wondered if it was because we had settled into our comfortable separate lives and came together as three separate individuals and not one bound together through obligation.

We each were drawn to find our way to a new path we may not have found if we were forced to stay together. My mom seemed very content in her growing business brewing and selling herb mixtures from her garden and the surrounding forest, for food and natural medicines. My dad started writing a book on what he experienced while trucking across the country. He found software to convert audio to word, so he recorded his thoughts as he drove along. We were all moving in the right direction. Our own direction.

Chapter 13

The Letter

She is opening her eyes. It's about time. I have been jumping up and down beside the bed for a while now. I managed to stick my wet nose under the covers and poke her in the back. She turned over to look at me, one eye opening at a time, half in dreamland. She has had a restful sleep. She reaches out to give me a pet. Her hand is warm, and her claws give my head a nice massage. I relax a little, but when she pulls her hand back under the covers, I jump up and down again. "But Ellie, I have to check the yard! Are you getting up?" I circle around a couple of times to show her she needs to get moving. Things always happen out there at night, and I need to inspect the area.

"OK, Blue." Ellie sighs as she pulls back the covers and swings her legs around to get out of bed. I sit, pant, and wait. It has been the same routine ever since I could reach my nose up to poke her awake. Sometimes she is up earlier than I am, but mostly we wake up to the same alarm nature has given us, although I keep one eye open all night. I am a light sleeper. I was trained to be this way. No animal life involves a deep sleep unless watched over by a comrade. It is only when she is awake and busy that I can get in a deep sleep full of dreams. I feel responsible for her safety. It's an important job.

First, we go to the big watering bowl petting zone. She sits, and I sit facing her. I don't know why she keeps yelling at me when I want to drink cool water that is freshened up all day long. I know it is not allowed, but I sneak in a drink all the time when she is not looking. I am let outside to investigate all the night critters that have their scents. Time to do my markings. This is my territory.

When I am allowed back in, I am always greeted with the smell of coffee and a bowl of my food and freshwater. I don't drink coffee. If Mom lets me in, I can always find Ellie in her room sitting quietly with a smile on her face. I put my head in her lap, and we meditate together. She is saying her gratitudes. I am always grateful for the same things, that I am able to be with her again, and I will be able to redeem myself in the eyes of my creator for her soul and for my soul. Nothing else matters. After our gratitudes, she sits still and deep breaths. Each of her breaths create an aura of calm, and I am soothed into dreamland.

Today we are going for a run. I know this because my gear is out. This is quite the show with Ellie pulling all kinds of shenanigans to delay heading out the door. It happens every time. She goes to the bathroom, again and closes the door. I don't like closed doors. I try to scratch it open. I throw myself against it. I get yelled at, so I lean against the door and slide to the floor. This could be a long time.

"Good morning, Blue," sings Mom. "Ellie in the bathroom I see." She laughs as she steps over me. I keep my head down between my paws and look up. Yep. I'm on guard duty.

Let me help you with your shoes, Ellie. Here they are. Put them on. Noise comes from the little box in her hand, and she sits to stare and move her fingers back and forth on it. I wait, patiently, panting. OK, she is up! Good, another thing done. My leash. Get my leash. No. She passes it by talking into the lighted box that is talking back.

It is a box where some humans are kept. Sometimes you can see them and other times it is only their voices. Humans exist in many boxes like in her room, on the big box that always stays in the living room, or on a box that can go with you. A transportable human box. Sometimes there are many humans in the box, and they come out at different times. I am jealous of this box because it demands attention. It is rarely ignored like I can be. The box is frustrating me, so I step on Ellie's toes. She yells at me to get off because she is losing a toenail, whatever that means. I walk to the door and back like I must go pee. I circle around, sit, and shoot out a few quick short cries at her.

"One minute Blue. Please wait." I hate that word, wait. I go walk around in a circle on a blanket and lie down with a thud and a huff of air from my mouth. Here, see? You have hurt my feelings.

"Ellie, you have got to give a guy called, Jake, a call. Here is the phone number where he can be reached. He said it was important," Mom yelled from in front a steaming pot of bones brewing. We were not the only family in the area with a landline. The cell coverage in our part of the country was hit or miss most of the time. I hoped she didn't interrogate him with a million questions.

Empty jars were lined up on the countertops and kitchen table waiting to be filled. Her latest product was bone broth. She sold out in every farmers' market and health food stores in our area. She couldn't keep up with the demand, and I helped as much as I could. It was a recipe passed down from her great grandmother. Every bit of the animal was used back in those days. Not like now when only 60 percent of a cow is used. My ancestors took the bones and cooked them for a day, mixed with various vegetables and herbs, salt, and apple cider vinegar. My mom would make me drink a cup every day growing up. I don't remember ever being sick.

I was excited about calling Jake, he didn't answer, so I left a message. We hadn't talked since the race, so he must have something interesting to tell me. I was halfway out the door when I could hear my mother's muffled voice, "Could you get the mail on your way back," yelling into a steaming pot.

I felt the stiffness in my legs even though it had been a couple of weeks since the race, so Blue and I walk, taking our time to enjoy our exclusive route I named Deer Run off from a public trail. I discovered a deer track a few years ago and so far, no one else has because there is always deer poop and no sign of humans. It is Blue's favorite run because he has a stupid obsession with deer poop. I guess it was his way of getting vegetables - his version of bone broth.

My head was full of ideas of what was next for me, but it was unsettling because I had no plan. I was in a void space and a little lost waiting for my body to heal and wanting to train. I was hoping the trail would clear my head, but it only confused me more. All my purpose for the last year ended at the finish line and now I felt like the trail, meandering all over with no end in sight. I needed a bigger goal.

Arriving home I saw his truck parked outside and thought something must have happened for Dad to come to visit again so soon. I was excited and nervous at the same time and pulled up quickly beside his truck forcing Blue to strain against his seat belt.

"Sorry, little buddy. Let's go see what Dad is doing here." I rushed into the house almost expecting to find my parents in a heated argument. Old presumptions die hard. The house was strangely quiet, and I turned into the kitchen to find them both standing relaxed.

"What brings this surprise visit so soon? I thought you were headed south of the border for a long haul," I asked as I nuzzled into my dad's neck for a deep hug, inhaling the familiar hint of his aftershave, Old Spice. It never changed, and it defined him as my father. I would be able to pick him out of a lineup with my eyes closed. I released him, but he still held on to my arms as he tipped his head nodding toward a stack of magazines on the countertop with a curious-looking package and a couple of letters sitting next to it.

"What is this? Did you get the mail, Dad?" I drew out the words, slowing in anticipation. I noticed the package was addressed to me.

"Cover of the Ultra World," Dad sang to the tune of "Cover of the Rolling Stones." I grabbed a magazine from the top of the stack. "I bought out every store from the border to here. Don't you people get your mail? I still have my key, thank God."

Mom rolled her eyes. She held her arms folded, leaning against the cupboard. I could see she had hastily brushed her hair back with her hand because there was a streak of flour across the top of it. "And here I thought the smell of my pies brought you here," she snorted.

"You drove all the way here after buying all these magazines," I clarified, examining the glossy stack. I knew they were releasing it this week. Jake had called to tell me he had received his copy and called to ask if I had seen mine yet, but of course, I forgot to drive into town to collect the mail, with my mind wrapped up in my unplanned future.

Mom and I only collected the mail once a week for months now. Nothing but bills, so we avoided the effort of the task. It was the one thing she did not hassle me about doing. The postal service stopped putting a mailbox on our country road because it always got destroyed by either someone with a shotgun or with a bat hanging out of a passing truck, or it was knocked over by a snowplow.

I picked up a magazine and examined its cover. It was the first time I had seen this photo. I had to admire the strain of each contracted striation of muscle fiber in my thigh as I touched down on the trail. I had a focused expression on my face, not to be mistaken as a grimace. It looked more like a little grin of annoyance. I had seen the photographer down the trail hiding in the bush yelling at me to smile, but I was too focused on picking my way through the precarious rock garden of a trail. The grin was all I could manage. One misstep and down I would go. The photographer was down slope from me and used a flash. I kept seeing the flash in spots in my peripheral vision for a few minutes as a result. I remember feeling annoyed with him but kept my usual impatient tongue silent. Now I was thankful because the photo captured me perfectly illuminated against ominous dark gray angry-looking storm clouds over a slate blue sky peeking through in slivers. Leafless branches at the edges of the photo, reached out toward me like witch's arms. I was making my way through a scattering of rocks and roots over a narrow dirt path.

For some reason, the stormy weather during the race made me feel calm as if the wilder the wind blew, the more control I had. It reminded me of my childhood days caught out in a storm in the forest. I had a strange kind of strength knowing the wind could not blow through me, but I could run through it. The weather wasn't cold, but it was angry. And the angrier it got, the more I felt in control. The harder it blew, the faster I ran to defy it.

Both my parents were silent, watching me with raised eyebrows in anticipation as I carefully opened the box and unwrapped a beautifully framed photo. It was the magazine cover photo of me, but it was much larger than the actual magazine cover. There was a handwritten note attached, congratulating me for my success, and signed, Chilton Murray.

Mom spoke first. "Who is Chilton Murray, Ellie?" She took the edge of the photo gingerly in her floured hands.

"I have no idea," I replied, searching through the stack of letters finding another one addressed to me. "I wonder why he did this for me. Who is he?"

"A huge fan, that's for sure." My dad was sniffing the card while my mom watched him and rolled her eyes.

I opened the next letter and found a check for $500 from the documentary film company from the Bullwinkle 100.

"Oh, look what you have there. Perhaps you could be chipping in with the expenses around here." My mom grabbed the check to take a closer inspection.

"I cover her expenses, Mariella. Start a savings account, Ellie." My father turned his glare from her to a softer look toward me. I quickly worked to smooth the tension by saying I would gladly share my income.

"It is fair, Dad. I am OK with it." I responded as Mom held a smirk on her lips as she set the check aside and finally noticed the flour on her hands.

"I'll give you a pie, Frank. They are at least worth a few hundred each."

"In your dreams, Mariella."

I quickly opened the next envelope. It was a registered letter with the stamp of Evotech on the envelope. I tried to think of all I knew about this company.

"That company is run by Asgood Murray," my dad explained. "Hey, wait a minute. Chilton Murray. Yeah, Asgood Chilton Murray. He created a device to help Alzheimer sufferers repair their brain function to almost normal. It was revolutionary and earned him Time magazine, Man of the Year, a few years back."

"How do you know all that? And who calls their child, Asgood? As good as what?" My mother piped in. "I bet he got teased in school."

I grabbed my phone and googled the company before I opened the letter.

"It is probably advertising disguised as registered mail," she continued with her typical sarcasm.

The logo for the company slowly appeared on my screen with a photo of a middle-aged man with curly dark brown hair. His head slightly tilted upward as he was looking down at the photographer. He was wearing a white lab coat, but it was open showing his open-collared plaid shirt, pair of jeans, and Converse sneakers. I paraphrased as I read, "He created a device patients wear on their heads, and if caught early enough, they could use it in combination with a program on a computer to rewire their brain and build it up to compensate for parts of the brain that are not functioning properly. Apparently it was a huge success and has helped rewire the brain of those with brain injuries, or damage due to brain tumors. There is a link to a TED Talk he gave. He has other various projects on the go, mostly medical or human performance related. It says he is seventy years old. No, that's not possible," I said in complete disbelief as I thought that by seventy you'd be retired, playing cards in a seniors' home.

Wikipedia had a long list of his credentials including doctorates in medical technology, biological engineering, and biochemistry, and plus were a slew of credentials in other sciences. He has been dubbed the modern-day Leonardo da Vinci—an inventor and innovator.

I sat in a chair to open the next envelope as Blue rested his head on my leg, staring up at me as if the letter were for him. I glanced up at the anticipated looks of my parents. My dad pressed one hip against the counter, leaning his weight all on one elbow to brace himself as he stretched his legs out to the middle of the kitchen and crossed his cowboy boots at his ankles. He drummed his fingers of one hand over the wrist of the other. I wondered when he was going to slip on the flour that covered the linoleum floor. I'm sure mom thought the same as we watched him balance precariously, and she nodded for me to open the envelope. I read it aloud.

Dear Giselle,

I would like to take this opportunity to congratulate you on all your running successes. I have been following your running career with great interest because I am a tremendous admirer of the capabilities of endurance athletes especially those who not only excel in their accomplishments, but also far exceed normal human capabilities.

I am not sure you are aware, but at Evotech we have been studying the science of human achievement and performance in all capacities for many decades. We are greatly interested in what makes some humans exceptional. Our business is to study how good organic and ethical science can make humans perform to their ultimate capabilities. We understand it is much more than science, but also the mental abilities of those athletes, such as yourself, who must overcome not only great physical adversities, but psychological as well, in order to achieve amazing goals the average person would not even dream about, even with all the proper genetic makeup. We have worked many years taking what might seem a whimsical idea, researching and expanding on it further to see if there could be substantiated and efficacious results. I think we have succeeded on many fronts.

Now I am sure you are wondering why I am contacting you. Of all the successful and outstanding accomplishments many athletes achieve, I take a special interest in running athletes, and for me personally the ultraendurance athlete. We do, in fact, have many significant individuals and athletes working with our laboratories currently, astronauts, race car drivers, mountain climbers, marathon runners and sprinters, but now we are looking for an extraordinary team of superendurance athletes, those whom we hope, not only have the time to help us, but also have the mental and physical health as well as other specific qualities, we feel could significantly help further our research.

I am extending an invitation for you to visit our laboratories and meet with me personally as well as with the specialized team of scientists to learn more about what we think will be the greatest opportunity afforded to any athlete worldwide. I assure you none of this involves performance-enhancing chemicals or procedures that could damage the body or be misinterpreted as cheating. On the contrary, our goal is to use only healthy organic processes and optimal living conditions to improve the performance of all our athletes. Nothing we do breaks IAAP or WADA rules for doping. We are strictly manipulating the natural day-to-day routines of our athletes.

I would like you to see for yourself. I look forward to meeting you personally. Please accept my invitation in order that you make an informed and educated decision on what could be the greatest opportunity of your entire life. I hope my reputation precedes me.

Sincerely, Dr. Asgood Chilton Murray

"Sweet," I gushed. "Blue, what do you think?" I swear I could see his eyebrows go up. He opened his mouth and started panting, his tongue hanging out loosely. I wanted to pack my bags and leave immediately, but the logic in the form of two parents woke me up.

"What the Sam Hill kind of prank is this?" Mom spoke first with her typical distrust of everything.

"What are those papers, Ellie?" Dad stood up and pointed to the additional papers that filled the manila envelope laying on my lap next to Blue's nose.

"OK, uh, there is a plane ticket for, let's see, it's this Monday and one for a return flight for late Wednesday. And here is a reservation confirmation for a hotel and phone number with names and details. Here look - a travel pass for Blue and a confirmation slip for delivery of a travel kennel arriving tomorrow. There is a credit card for five hundred dollars and a note saying it is for travel incidentals and should I need more to please contact them."

I sat stunned with my mouth agape, passing the papers to my parents, who examined them with an uncharacteristic quiet. Blue broke the silence with a loud bark. I slipped off my chair to the floor and invited him to sit in my lap, squeezing him hard to try to calm the excitement building inside. My life was about to change and anyone who thought enough to include my dog, must have the best intentions, but also knew a lot about me.

My parents exchanged the letter and tickets, reading and checking things over a few times with an obvious air of disbelief on behalf of my dad, while distrust was seeping from my mother's every pore.

I waited until they set the letters down with no further comments. I stood up and did a little dance with Blue in the middle of the kitchen. My dad joined in twisting and jiving to imaginary music sliding our shoes over the floured-up linoleum. We danced into a hug, while my mom leaned back against the sink with her arms crossed.

"Come on, Mariella, it is time to celebrate our little baby girl's opportunity here." He grabbed her arm from its folded position and pulled her into our dance troop with a swirl, and twisted back and forth, teasing her until she relented with a half-jig move. We danced around Blue, laughing and when we finally stood apart, I thought I saw happiness and pride glowing on their faces. At that moment, I felt happier for them than I did for myself. I was making them proud and that was the greatest feeling in the world.

Chapter 14

Evotech

I haven't been in such a big place with so many people rushing in all directions, pushing, pulling, and carrying things. They are looking at their little human boxes, stopping, talking, crying, spinning around. What a mix of lost and found humans. There is an annoyingly loud voice booming from nowhere every few minutes. Groups of people sitting together and getting up together and heading out a door in a straight orderly line. Well-trained humans. I am trying my best to act like one of the humans. I sit when I am told and wait when I am supposed to wait. This is peanuts to me. Simple stuff. I could be a human. And then I am put in a box.

Ellie gives me too many kisses, so I start to wonder if I am going to my death. The box and I move along, with Ellie disappearing while waving, and I think she is crying. Certain death is impending. There is not a human in sight until I make it to the bottom of a giant bird with huge wings singing a horrible hum that hurts my ears. In all my lives, I had never seen a bird so big. Some males lift me onto a moving floor to another human who talks nice to me and sets me down securing my box to the floor. The dog in the box next to me looks petrified. He reminds me of distant memories of soldiers about to die. Why would Ellie do this to me?

I lay down my head between my legs and let out a few nervous whines. What method of life-ending torture awaits me? After the rush in my ears and a push of my body into the ground, nothing happens. I am still breathing. I eventually fall asleep to the vibrations underneath me and the cries of my buddy next to me. I wake up as

I feel incredible pressure coming down on me and then a horrible cranking sound—a big bounce that sends me to the top of my crate and pushes me forward. The sharp whirring sounds softens and stops, but the tremor in my body continues. After a while, the side door opens with a swish, and I am pushed out into the bright sun and can't see.

It was only my second trip flying in my life. The other time was for the Cross-Country Nationals when I was in my final year in high school. Our family vacations were always by car, so everything about flying excited me from the check-in, security, boarding the plane, and buckling in. Letting Blue go was devastating, but I tried not to let him see my feelings.

My first time at a window seat, I leaned in against the cold plastic window with my headphones on, tuning out the hum from inside the jet and watched as the geography changed below me. It brought a realization of how I was so focused on my own piece of the earth without the slightest awareness of how vast and magnificent this world is, and how insignificant I was compared to it. I followed the roads surprisingly straight suddenly snake through towns, farmland, and around mountains and lakes. There were crop circles mixed into the flat checkerboard farm sections. The topography rose and fell only detected by the early morning shadows cast from the hills and mountains. I imagined myself running through the mountain ranges and valleys wondering if someone had run there before me. So much of the land looked as if no one had set foot on it. It appeared empty of human existence, and then there would be a little town or a section stripped of its vegetation. I couldn't help but wonder why there were so many people living homeless when there was so much empty land? Well, of course, I realized it wasn't that easy, but if a huge worldwide catastrophe were to happen, there appeared to be lots of unoccupied land to hide in.

After worrying about Blue's first-ever flight, I collected him from cargo. I let him out of the state-of-the-art, climate-controlled kennel as soon as I found it in the baggage area. He had stepped into it with no hesitation trusting me. The flight was only two hours, but I was concerned for him. He was none the worse for wear when I let him out to freedom, and he immediately drew attention to himself, by acting as if he hadn't seen me for months. He wagged his whole body while singing his reunion song of squeaks, whines, and yips, followed by a lot of sloppy kisses. From the corner of my eye, I realized someone was filming his performance with their phone. I was afraid he was going to pee from his excitement, so we quickly rushed over to the dog area. Who knew a dog could hold that much urine? We finally made our way to the curb and searched for our transportation.

In the midst of an anxious and tired looking group of travelers searching for their rides, shuffled a short little man dressed in a suit and matching cap. He was amusing to watch as he sure-footed a quickstep dance move through the disordered crowd without so much as touching them or their bags. He was on a mission. I noticed he was carrying a placard with 'Giselle and Blue' written on it. He moved it from in front of his chest like a shield, to above his head like a newspaper hawker. We locked eyes through the crowd.

"Miss Giselle, Miss Giselle! Blue!" he yelled out with a French accent like Inspector Clouseau in the *Pink Panther* movies my dad loved so much. He shuffled toward us using his sign as a paddle to push passersby aside.

"'Ere I am. Let me get your bag and ken nel. Monsieur Blue, mon cherie. Comment allez-vous? Ahh. How are you?" he asked as he reached down to ruffle Blue's ears.

"I trust you 'ad a good flight, mademoiselle, Je-zelle. Come, we will go zis way. The car is over 'ere. Come. Follow."

He grabbed the kennel and jut it out in front of himself to clear the path, poking unsuspecting travelers in the butts if they didn't hear him coming. I hoisted my backpack and quickly slipped in behind him with Blue in tow.

He stopped in front of a long black limousine pausing, looking one way and the next as if he was not sure this was our ride. The trunk opened automatically, and he inspected it with the kennel clutched in both of his hands. "I think, ahh we must poot zee ken nel in the salon because, ahh, it will not fit in the boot."

He shuffled with the kennel to the last door on the limo as we followed behind, and it opened automatically. He shoved the kennel in first, then disappeared inside the limo as Blue and I waited. I looked down at Blue, and he tilted his head to the side as the little man popped his head out of the car.

"Oh, mon Dieu. Forgive me. My name is Oliver. I am your driver. Nice to meet you and aahh, Blue too, of course," he said excitedly bumping his head on the door frame as he moved back outside the vehicle while still talking.

"How was your trip? Good I hope," he asked without waiting for an answer. He scuttled to the side, ushering us to go in with an outstretched hand. "The drive will be for two hours, mademoiselle. So please enjoy the refreshments I have prepared for both of you." He waited as we slid inside. I didn't know where to sit because the limo was lined with seats at the back and along the side, so I took a seat at the very back next to where he was standing. Blue hopped in and made his way up to the front where his kennel sat and started his sniffing expedition.

"Look, 'ere is the fridge with delicious snacks and the drinks are 'ere. This screen you will play a short video Doctor Chilton would like you to watch to become familiar with ummm, the facility, and itinerary for your vee sit. But first we will stop at the 'otel, and I will wait while you freshen up and you can change into something comfor table for your meeting this afternoon," he said all in one breath.

I sat wide-eyed as Blue barked a quick hello.

"So, if you want to go anywhere or need anything, pleeze, here is my card, and I will be at your service, but I am po seetive once you enter Evotech you will not want to leave, and you will want for no ting," Oliver stood up to his full length, took off his cap, rubbed his head, reached into the breast pocket of his suit jacket to pull out his business card.

Blue and I examined the card. I thought I could see him raise his eyebrows and smile as he opened his mouth to pant, releasing a few drops of saliva from his long red, wet tongue. He circled a couple of times and sat on the seat near the far window as if he had been there before and this was his regular ride.

"Regardez, we could all learn from the carefree nature of a dog," Oliver pointed out. I kept thanking him. "No need. My pleasure." Oliver held up his hand in protest. I noticed he had a soft round face, with kind yet black, marble eyes peering out from under a black bushy overhang of eyebrows. Little tufts of black hair stuck indiscriminately out from under his chauffeur's cap. I was mesmerized by how he wiggled his mustache as he talked while leaning in over me to show us the command console for climate, seats, windows, roof, and a myriad of different things I lost track of. He invited me to sit back.

"If you are tired, you can push this boo ton to recline your seat." And with a quick demonstration my seat folded out into a position that reminded me of my dad's lazy boy recliner except with a built-in headrest that inflated lightly into a softer leather cushion.

"Oof. I lose track of all the mechanisms of dis car. We have a company jet, but it is used only if necessary. The doctor does not like to leave a carbon footprint, as he says. He prefers to leave a fingerprint." He laughed by inhaling with a snort, then laughed harder, which became contagious to me. I held my hand over my mouth so as not to giggle at him, while watching Oliver set the chair back to its normal position in a smooth motion. It was not a jerky movement like my dad's old recliner that practically sent you flying across the room if you weren't holding on tightly. Oliver showed me the intercom to talk to him, gently closed the door with the push of a button, and ran around to get in the driver's seat on the other side of the world to me.

A gathering crowd appeared to be as intrigued with Oliver's demonstration as I was. This must be how the mega-wealthy live. I could get used to this. I settled in and texted a few pictures and a short video of the limo to my parents. The time went by too quickly. I had explored the snack cabinet that was within my reach, and sampled a variety of foods I had never seen before, let alone tasted. While Blue snored, I watched a company initiation video that gave a tour of the Evotech facility, briefly explained all the research done in the past and currently at Evotech including a short commercial-like video of the program I was there to be a part of, I assumed, as it focused strictly on athletes. It explained their research into nutrition, supplementation, technology and various devices that improved health, sleep, mental state of mind and performance in athletes, using the latest technology to heighten the athlete's natural capabilities, basically providing all that is possible to create a perfect world to which an athlete could excel without doping of any sort. If they are successful, Evotech would have access to a huge market of weekend warriors looking for an advantage for their next marathon, tennis match, or golf game.

After leaving the airport, most of our drive was in the country. So I was surprised when we arrived at a magnificent building on the outskirts a different city. Later I would find out this town was made up of Evotech employees and the economy they generated. We unpacked the limousine and Oliver led us into the hotel and through the magnificent lobby the size of half a skating rink. We were greeted upon entering the foyer with the largest table, vase and flower arrangement I had ever seen. Off to each side were dark red-and-purple baroque sofas a mile long against the walls as well as there were impressive dark leather fanback chairs put in groups of four with marble-and-iron tables in the middle. I wanted to take photos, but it would become extremely apparent I was a hick from the country. I tried to keep my mouth closed and act like this was an everyday thing for me.

The staff greeted Blue and I by name. I felt significantly underdressed for the environment and the crowd of people standing around. They had a stately appearance while I was in jeans and a T-shirt. Oliver could sense I felt out of my element, like Julia Roberts in *Pretty Woman* when she went shopping for expensive clothes, and no one paid attention to her.

"I feel the wealthiest people in the world are the ones who don't feel like they need to impress anyone in any way," he said while we rode up the elevator. I shuffled my feet and glanced up to see him wink at me in the mirrors encasing the elevator car. I grinned back at him.

Oliver slid a card into a slot and the light went green, and he opened the door and handed me the card. I stared at it and then turned my head to see a room beyond my wildest expectations. I compared memories of the dingy, old hotel rooms I treated myself to so I could have a real bed on the night before a race. The room was enormous, with oversized windows, and the curtains opened fully to show a magnificent view of the mountains in the distance, with the town's small skyline in the forefront. The room had dark brown leather furniture in contrast to the plush light blue carpet. On one desk was a wicker basket full of fruit, chocolates and bottles of mineral water and juices with Evotech label on each one. There was a hip-height king-size bed with a headboard of intricately carved wood that reached halfway up the wall. Blue started his sniffing recognizance. How was a dog able to stay here when I had to promise my firstborn child to managers of dingy hotels to let Blue stay in a stinky, stained room with me?

Oliver said he would give me an hour to freshen up, as he had to deliver me to Doctor Chilton on time. He saw the panic as it crossed my face.

"Don't worry about what you wear, my dear. The doctor is the least pretentious man you'll ever meet. Be yourself. You 'ave no one to impress. Besides, with your beauty, if you wear a potato sack, you would still be the most beautiful woman in the room."

I didn't know how to take the compliment, and felt my cheeks heat up as I mouthed a thank you. He winked back at me with a clear sparkle in his black eyes.

When he closed the door behind him, I took a running dive onto the bed and Blue immediately followed. "Oh no, Blue," I started to say but changed my mind. I grabbed him in a deep embrace and wrestled with him until we settled, sinking into the feather quilt with his head tucked into my armpit and all four legs up in the air. I rubbed his belly, thinking how I might not have a boyfriend, but if I did, I would hope he was as easy to be around as Blue. I love Blue but it would be wonderful to have a two-way conversation with my best friend.

After playing with his paws staring up at the beautiful designs on the ceiling, I bounced off the bed to I take a few selfies and admired the cityscape reaching out to the mountains silhouetted against the midmorning sky. I imagined I was wealthy enough to own all this. I planted that thought in the dream part of my brain to become my happy place—a memory to escape to when the real world was too much to take.

I walked over to check out the bathroom. It was a place I could spend the rest of my life in. There was an enormous white tub positioned under an immense window overlooking the views of the town. It was surrounded by a ledge holding strategically placed vases of fresh flowers and candles in tall holders. It was big enough for three people. On the adjacent wall was a long marble vanity with two raised marble sinks. I had to turn the water on to watch it flow like a waterfall from a ledge protruding a few inches above the sink from the beautifully tiled wall. The countertop was full of all the amenities. One bottle was labeled bubble bath, so I checked my watch, forty minutes until pick up.

With the taps running full blast and half the bottle emptied, I soaked in the tub of fragrant bubbles while Blue chased the foam I blew at him. After my fingers were pruned like raisins, I glanced at my old Timex, realizing I was going to be late. I rushed to get dressed without a care for any makeup, as my mom would have insisted, threw my hair in a ponytail, hooked Blue to his leash, and we dashed excitedly to catch an elevator heading down.

"I hope Blue is welcome to come?" I asked Oliver who was standing in the lobby patiently waiting. "What would I do with him, if he wasn't?"

"Evotech is a family friendly environment and pets are family. We have a pet daycare facility I am sure many humans would love, I assure you. He will be treated like a king, so have no worries."

We drove about twenty minutes and turned up a winding road heading uphill. Oliver stopped the car and came around to open the door for me. "Miss Giselle, before we arrive, I took the liberty of taking you to a viewpoint so you get a bird's eye view of Evotech or EVT as we like to call it. From this vantage point you can almost fully appreciate the architecture and surrounding area," said Oliver as he led us to the edge of a viewing point about one mile away and several hundred feet above a barely detectable, flowing structure covered by vegetation and surrounded by trees and grassy areas. I was sure I saw a few animals grazing. There was a bench to sit nearby and Oliver invited me to sit while he described the area to me.

"The building is completely self-sufficient because it is cooled by water from the ground and 'eated by solar panels located on the 'ills just beyond and powered by wind as well," he pointed out. "In the surrounding 'ills we 'ave what we like to call, an efical farm. Let me try zat again—ethical," he pronounced to erase my confused expression.

"EVT grows its own organic food as well as experimental plants. We do not do any genetic modification. We 'ave our own 'erd of grass-fed cows as well as pigs, chickens, sheep and goats. All are raised and treated in the most humane manner and when we need to end their lives, we do not slaughter them. We use a pain-free met'tod. I know some people are against the consumption of meat, but at EVT, we believe the choice should be yours. We also manufacture essential amino acids to supplement the diet; therefore, we do not eat so many animals. We also use every part of the animal. We create a lot of bone brot."

"Oh, my mom makes bone broth, so I know exactly what you mean," I replied, covering up his embarrassment over his thick French accent. "I like your accent. I have never heard a French accent in person, only in movies."

"Oh, mon petit chou. You are so sweet." Oliver patted my hand, then continued. "Dr. Chilton wanted the building to be unobtrusive to blend in with its surroundings—to flow with nature, so to speak," he continued.

The building flowed with the rolling hills that surrounded it and appeared to be built right through the hills and valleys as if someone had dropped a liquid building from the sky, and it molded to the earth in whatever way it could, and then the earth grew over top of it.

"All zee parking is underground so we don't waste zee land space," Oliver stated. "Our water comes from underground springs as well. We collect water through a condensation process and reuse it. We use recycled water for zee vegetation and animals. As you might know, animals are a huge consumer of water. One cow can consume one gallon of water per one hundred pounds of its weight per day. It is zee same for humans when it is hot. It can be more for a lactating cow or an ultrarunner who can consume four times that amount," he said with more excitement than I thought warranted, then he gave me a side-glance with a slight grin on his face.

"That is fascinating," I replied, wondering how a chauffeur took an interest in knowing all this. It truly was a wonder, and it all made sense to me. Why don't we do this in our cities? What a different world we would have.

"We have trails that go for hundreds of miles into the hills. We run a trail running competition every year. You will have to participate. It is only for fun, and to make it fair, we will have to make you walk." He huffed out a chuckle from under his moustache.

"Oliver, you always use the word, we, when talking about EVT." I hinted for an answer.

"That is part of the EVT philosophy that if employees feel they have an ownership in zee product they are creating, we vill take a more active role in the success of zee business. Everyone who works at EVT is a shareholder who gets paid in salary but also dividends, organic food, vacations, and technology. Must seem weird to say we are paid with technology, but when you see zee technology you will completely understand." Oliver slapped his palms to his thighs, stood up, and motioned we should head back to the limo.

There was only one unpretentious sign carved in wood with copper inlay letters announcing Evotech. Oliver pulled up to an entrance way with a man standing waiting for us. I thought it might be a doorman, as he reached down to open my door and offered his hand to help me out.

"I know the limo seems too luxurious, but it's actually powered by bio-fuels," he said offering his hand. My brain tried connecting the image from the *Time* magazine cover, but it didn't compute immediately— this was Dr. Chilton. I stood up puzzled.

"I am Dr. Chilton. Please call me Doctor." He laughed and extended his hand to shake mine. He was not as tall as I imagined him to be. He was slender, athletic and muscular, stretching the fibers of his bike shorts and jersey. His hair was dark brown, thick and messy. He had recently taken off his bicycle helmet and was trying to smooth it back with his hand. I couldn't help notice his surprisingly well-groomed eyebrows that dipped down to meet the smile lines making his soft blue eyes kind and friendly. He had a strong jaw and narrow nose, with thin lips that spread open slightly when he smiled, bracketed on each side with smile lines. I shook his hand heartily as my father taught me.

"Strong handshake, D'Angelo." I immediately felt like I could pass as one of the boys on the team. "Very nice to meet you finally and thank you for taking your time away from training to visit us. I am sure you will be quite impressed. I don't normally come out to formally greet visitors, but I happened to be arriving at the same time." He pointed to his bicycle. "Thirty miles one way. I am quite proud of myself for my age. Must be the supplements." He laughed as he puffed out his chest. "Come on. Thanks, Oliver, for your services. You are always my main man." He threw a pointed finger in Oliver's direction and received a tip of the hat in return.

"Let's drop off your little buddy, Blue, on his vacation first. What do you say?" He bent down and gave him scrub behind the ears. "How are you, Blue? Beautiful dog, Giselle. No wonder you take him everywhere."

We took an elevator up while we chatted about my trip and the hotel while Blue took the opportunity to sniff Dr. Chilton's ankles. The doors opened to the outside. We were on the top of the roof. Off in the distance was a fenced-in area with a small building where we were heading to leave Blue. The attendant dressed in an overcoat covered with cats and dogs, asked me all kinds of questions and assured me he would love his stay. Blue immediately spotted a dog pool across the way. She picked up a ball and threw it in the water and Blue took off after it, landing with a flying splash. He didn't even say goodbye.

"Don't worry we will bathe and style his fur at the end of the day," she quipped. "He is going to have fun at the dog spa."

"Oh, can I stay too?" I responded, and we all laughed.

"Oh, you are going to have a spa kind of day too, Giselle. Come on. Lots to show you. Blue is in terrific hands, and you can check on him later if you want or watch from one of the monitors anywhere we are. You can see what he is up to and even talk to him, if necessary, via a video screen," Dr. Chilton said as I took one last look at Blue swimming and splashing in the pool, oblivious to the other dogs around him.

I turned around as my eyes explored the rooftop. On the far side was a regular park area with trees, benches and pathways except for the odd glass bubble popping up from the ground. Dr. Chilton waited while I took in the views, but said nothing.

We took the elevator to another floor and walked along a white-walled hallway covered with various photographs showcasing Dr. Chilton's achievements. He was either giving a lecture, receiving an award, or holding a device. On two occasions we passed by sections with a small waterfall trickling down through vegetation of vines, small plants and flowers growing on a rock wall. Above was the skylight I saw from the rooftop. Dr. Chilton explained the history of the building and a bit about their ongoing projects. We passed by labs that were open to view from windows lining the hallway. The people inside always smiled and waved. Dr. Chilton greeted each person by name as we passed them in the hallway.

"How many people work here?" I asked, wondering if he knew all of them by name.

"About three thousand. We are one big happy family. The town you are staying in is home to the employees and their families. We have a school system, restaurants, businesses. And if someone has a family issue, we can help with that too. I try to set a tone here that we should all know each other, help each other and learn from each other, but we all don't have to be best friends. We should be kind to one another with a simple rule of respect. If one person is successful at his job, we all should celebrate and be rewarded. We do have rules and order. We have methods to deal with all kinds of issues from discrepancies, arguments, marriages, births, divorces—all the things that make us human. To me, it is like a human study as well as a biological technology facility. We try to make the best human possible and that means dealing with the emotional and mental aspect of being a human, not only the physical. Everyone here is a 'test subject' whether they realize it or not. No one has complained so far, as far as I am aware of. They sign a disclosure agreement keeping all that happens here stays private until made public. We've never had to sue anyone yet." He glanced toward me as we walked down the hallway.

As if reading my mind, Dr. Chilton said, "Yes, Giselle, you will have to sign a nondisclosure agreement. Sorry, but it is the way of the world. It is a business, after all. We have arrived." He stopped at a doorway and let me proceed before him.

Inside was a bright open conference room with a massive oval dark polished wood table in the center. There was a wall of ground to ceiling windows but darkened so your eyes were not drawn toward it and distracted. Off to the side was a table of fresh fruit, nuts, sliced meat, cheeses and pitchers of smoothies of various colors. There were not the usual doughnuts and cookies. Jake was already sitting at the table but had jumped up and skipped over to greet me with a hug.

"It's amazing, Ellie. Simply amazing. Just wait," he whispered in my ear.

"We are going to wait a few minutes more until all the superstars have arrived. Meanwhile, I am going to take a quick shower and change, so I don't stink you guys out of here. I'll be right back." He turned and left with an assistant following close behind taking his bike helmet from him.

Jake and I quickly updated each other on our trips. Well, mostly it was me talking about the hotel room, my bath, and the view. He couldn't get a word in as more people started to arrive. They each came over to shake hands and make introductions. All of us were endurance athletes and some—their reputation preceded them—were easy to recognize.

I was immediately intrigued with Jack Wilde or Wild Jack, as he was known. He would be difficult not to remember because not only was he intimidating looking, but he had a reputation as a wild mountain man with the entire persona of one as well. He looked weathered and was bearded with long hair pulled back into a ponytail. He didn't say much during the introductions, and I didn't dare ask him any for fear he would growl back. He observed, keeping his mouth closed while his eyes darted back and forth watching everything like he was about to be attacked by a mob. He occasionally pulled at his beard like a habit he couldn't control. Not only was he a master ultrarunner but he also did well in extreme multisport races and has run up a few mountains, like Kilimanjaro, for fun. He didn't like to do the same race twice, so he held the most ultradistance titles from around the world of any man. I wondered how science could improve on his genetics and his mental strength?

I was soon surrounded by a table of athletes who had done something extraordinary, such as win an Ultra Ironman, run at the highest altitude, the fastest one hundred miles, the farthest in twenty-four hours, or ran through all the deserts of the world. These were individuals who had overcome the most difficult obstacles to achieve greatness, and I had no idea what I was doing in their company.

Most of them have never heard of me. I could tell by the puzzled look on their faces, leaving me feeling like an impostor. My running experiences were so few. As the introductions continued, it became apparent most might know of the other person's reputation but never met officially. I was in a room of people who spent a lot of time alone. If they were anything like me, they felt more at home in nature than at a boardroom table.

The afternoon was spent with Dr. Chilton explaining his mission and how we could contribute to science. A lineup of scientists came to discuss their expertise, sometimes bringing in food to sample along with graphs and charts to explain its effects. There were various devices I had never heard of before or even imagined in my wildest dreams, since the most technology I had ever worn was my cheap Timex watch. I could never afford anything this high tech. Some of us openly expressed skepticism and no one seemed overly excited in letting technology or science interfere with the purity of what we did. Dr. Chilton would have a hard sell with all of us. We sat around the table most of the day with our arms crossed, as if protecting our immaculacy.

Jeep Jenkins who was famous for skiing unaided to both the North and South poles, was sitting on the other side of me, watching me take furious notes on the recycled paper they provided each of us. I noticed his was full of doodles. At one point he bent over and whispered in my ear during a demonstration of the clothing we would be given with the ability to read all our vital signs through the cloth fibers. "They sound like politicians, promising a bridge when there is no water."

I nodded in agreement and stopped taking notes. He reminded me of a picture I saw in a textbook of Vladimir Lenin. He sported the same goatee and round balding head with piercing eyes and dark full eyebrows that were always slightly creased in the center, as if he held in those creases, his apprehension and disbelief.

There were a couple of people at the table who were curious enough to try out a demonstration of the items, but I thought it better to stay seated, not to stand out, and try to remember every detail of what was happening. It felt like we were characters in a science-fiction novel, and I had trouble keeping up with the plot.

Hans Wagner, undeniably the most famous ultradistance runner in Europe was one of the first to try a contraption that provided instant pain relief. He laid his tall lanky body on a table and pointed to his psoas muscle as a point of annoying pain. He brushed back his long straight brown bangs out of his eyes and left his hand on his forehead, bracing himself for the type of reflex that occurs when someone pushes on a pain point. "Oof take it easy, ya. I am bracing for zee vorst," he cautioned through gritted teeth. We all stood up to watch the technician place a device over the area and left it quietly humming while admitting flashing lights of various colors.

"Ya, ziss feels good ya. Zee pain is gone, unt it feels almost orgasmic," Hans moaned." I vill sign up if I can take dis contraption vit me." We all laughed.

At first, I found Hans intimidating, towering over me at six foot four inches, looking down over his strong straight nose, square jaw and cleft chin, but his broad smile lit up his deep-set eyes, and his overwhelming presence defied his gentle fun-loving nature. He would quickly become the jokester of our group.

I watched in amazement at the amount of food some of these guys could pack away. Tim Donaldson, who I learned was only a few years older than me, ate nonstop. He had recently finished biking from Alaska to the tip of Chile. I had listened to a podcast interview he gave a few weeks earlier. I couldn't fathom the effort and logistics. He had talked about getting his bikes stolen, being woken up in the middle of the night in a central American country with guns to their heads and told they shouldn't stay where they parked because it was too dangerous. He was gorgeous in a rugged, bad-boy way and ate unabashedly and with enthusiasm, like every morsel was his last. I was fascinated with the collection of leather bracelets and strings around each wrist and the necklace collection around his neck. He tucked the layers of blonde waves behind his ears, while his earrings reflected the light as his jaw muscles strained with each chew. He had such amazing muscles in his jaw I could only imagine what the rest of him was like. I had to stop myself from staring so much before he noticed, but it was too late. He glanced up at me and winked. Embarrassed, I stared at my notepad as if contemplating a math equation. I tried not to look at him for the rest of the afternoon.

There were other fascinating people in the room to watch. Every time a new person spoke, it gave me the opportunity to focus on every detail about them without being obvious. Each person at the table was a unique character, and I wanted to steal away a piece of each of them to make myself more interesting.

Finally, after four hours of sitting, we were invited to take a run or walk in the hills surrounding the building and then come back for dinner. None of us had brought any change of clothes, but it didn't matter because all of it was supplied in the correct sizes. We all chose to go for an easy fun run in the hills, and I was happy to retrieve Blue and take him with us. It gave us a chance to run beside each other and share thoughts about the day so far. The consensus was we were going to be asked to be guinea pigs.

"He sent us out here to compare notes," Anabel Creston offered up her opinion to the group. Like me, she had sat quietly during the presentation, simply observing with a slight air of rebellion surrounding her as if she would blow a chewing gum bubble and pop it just to disturb the solemnity of the presentation. I was most familiar with her through a documentary on YouTube showcasing her competing in the Big Grizzly two-hundred-mile ultradistance event, in which she placed first overall. She had also won countless races around the world, but was most famous for her flamboyant race kits of bright colors, tall socks, short skirts combined with a myriad of hair colors to clash.

She was rumored to be one of two women to finish the notorious one-hundred-mile Bentley Marathon but would never admit to it. I felt like I was in the presence of royalty, and I told her so earlier during the break. She said she felt the same about me, but I think she was just being nice.

"Let's wait to see what happens next and not jump to conclusions," Jake dropped into the conversation. He seemed the most enthusiastic out of all of us during the day, asking a lot of questions. He knew a lot more about the biohacking devices than any of us.

"I got nothing to lose," Wild Jack said with a sarcastic tone, pulling at his beard as we ran along, "only my sponsors. They might freak. They have been good to me. I gotta really think about this."

"We all have sponsors. Sorry, Giselle, you are just starting, but we all have been at the game for a while," said Joe Bosko, or Boz, as he was known in the Ironman world. He was world champion for a few years then transitioned to extreme triathlon, completing each one with his worst finish being third place. Extreme triathlons were Ironman distance of 140 miles of swimming, biking and running but in harsher conditions, higher elevation gains, and colder water. I was intrigued with his grace and good humor. He wasn't much taller than me with a rough Australian accent that made him a little hard to understand when he spoke fast. He had a wonderful mess of curly brown hair looking like it would fuzz up if he combed it. I wondered how he got the curls to be so perfect. His face was framed with high cheekbones, wide forehead and pointy chin that hid behind a short bristly beard. His deep-set hooded eyes were kind but studied a person intently when speaking to them, making unnerving eye contact.

"Why us? Where are our competitors? There are hundreds he could have invited. Are we the only ones?" piped up Richard Wilson, who earned his nickname, Rocky, by being the five-time winner of one of oldest and most famous races in America, The Rocky 100. All these guys, except for Richard, were sinewy and a little disheveled. Rocky did not appear to match his nickname, looking neat, and conservative like an accountant. Hans would always refer to him as Richard, saying he was no Rocky.

Jake piped up, "Well, look at it this way. We all kind of do this for a living. We don't have real careers, except for Rocky who does his freelance computer stuff. Do we? I write a blog and articles for magazines. Some of you earn enough from races and sponsors. But for each of us, correct me if I'm wrong, we aren't leaving much behind. That is what we all have in common. None of us have serious obligations we can't leave behind for a couple of years becoming the common denominator. We all rent our apartments too. Right?"

We all nodded our heads while glancing around looking for someone to disagree.

"So, out of all the athletes out there, who are successful, we fit their needs. We are available. They have done their research. They know everything about us," Boz added. We remained quiet to ponder his words.

Olivia Nobel spoke first. "I have a very supportive community where I live. I love going to med school and doing a few races a year. This is a big move for me. I am not sure what I am going to do if they ask me to take part in this crazy experiment, although the medical research aspect of it intrigues me."

I had been observing and admiring her all day. People would call her a cute tomboy over beautiful because of her boyish mannerisms with her thick blonde hair cut short. If she wore a dress and heels, she would look quite striking, but somehow I got the feeling she has rarely worn a dress, just like me. I don't take the risk of stumbling around like Bambi in heels when I felt way more at home in running shoes. She could pass as one of those clean and healthy beach volleyball California girls who model for a wholesome food or face cream. I was amazed she had time to train and study, but she told me during a break, that Roger Bannister was in med school when he trained and broke the four-minute mile. She found running was a great way for her to review her oral notes, listen to taped lectures and help her to remember. She could recall certain things on a topic if she happened to go back to the same area where she was running when she had been listening to that topic. This amazed me.

When we finished our run, I took Blue back to the pet care and we headed to the spa to shower. The change room was spectacular. The walls and floor were an opal white providing a blank canvas highlighting the colorful watercolors on the walls, vases with tropical flowers and colorful furniture. There were soft pink benches, mauve comfy chairs and orange marble countertops. The room smelled of jasmine, grapefruit and sweet peas. There were three types of saunas, infrared, steam and dry, but we all eyed the massive whirlpool.

We were offered bathing suits and once changed I couldn't help admiring our lean and muscular bodies. The two women had visible abdominal muscles, and I envied their bodies, as I still had a little baby fat. Together we raced through the side, leg, and back jets and walked over the foot massage jets. We tried the underwater massage chairs and stood under the waterfall. To the side was a deep cold pool. It was painfully cold, but I managed to stay for thirty seconds before rushing back into the hot water. It was so invigorating that the others followed suit and soon we had a routine of follow-the-leader from jets, to waterfalls, to cold pool and back. After about twenty minutes, we were signaled to come out and told we had twenty minutes to change for dinner. There were fresh tracksuits, T-shirts, sports bras, and sneakers laid out in our individual shower stalls.

I fiddled with a few knobs with no luck until I heard Anabel yell out for instructions. Attendants came into each of our rooms to turn things on, and soon scents of ginger, watermelon, hibiscus and lavender diffused into the air from body wash and shampoo. My body was still tingling and alive from the cold pool. I buffed, scrubbed, and patted dry, then changed into the fresh clothing feeling as if I had recreated a newer better version of myself. I hoped this was a hint of things to come.

We were dining in a charming courtyard under the open sky, which was glowing with the last amber rays from the sinking sun. The circumference of the area was glowing from hidden floor lights while strands of small white lights hung above our heads. Tall torches burned bright in the far corners of the courtyard creating an exotic, tropical feeling. It was surrounded by glass partitions on a track that slide to create bigger or smaller spaces. On the other side of the windows, in a larger area, were fruit trees lit up with tiny white lights and various plants spaced around a small canal of water illuminated from dim underwater light that highlighted the various colored koi fish. I could have gotten up and plucked an apple from a tree on the other side of the glass.

After we took our seats, Dr. Chilton stood at the head of the table and began to speak. "I know you have all come to realize we are going to ask something from all of you. The food and experiences you have had so far are not offered as bribes. This is part of the deal. In front of each of you is a very individualized contract. The very first page is a Confidentiality Agreement stating you will not share information about this company, your experiences and your individual contract with all its details with anyone, including each other. Please read through it now and sign it. I know we did have you sign a similar document when you arrived, but this includes the future, whether you are with us or not. I am sorry we ask you to do this, but I'm afraid many companies have tried to infiltrate our organization to steal our ideas and research. There is no way around this."

We are given time to read through it, and I noticed many signing right away. As soon as I saw Jake sign, he looked at me and winked, so I signed as well.

"I don't ask you to sign your contracts tonight but take it home, discuss it with your lawyer and think deeply about it. It is a commitment for two years. We are asking you all to be part of an endurance team, with everything provided for you: a coach, place to live, all food and supplements, proprietary technology, and a training and race schedule that is mutually agreed upon. Everything you could possibly think of will be provided. All your living accommodations have been set up with the latest in technological advancements for ecological and healthy living. Ninety percent of which most of you will never have heard a hint of before. All you have to do is what you love. You will be paid a salary. A handsome one, I might add." Dr. Chilton paused with a sincere expression on his face that made me desperately want to believe whatever he said, but it sounded too good to be true.

"I have thought a great deal about the team I wanted to create. I needed an extraordinary and eclectic mix of individuals. Those with an unusual drive to push themselves to their limits and yet still want to discover what more they can endure. I assure you nothing we do will harm you in any way. We are providing optimal living conditions to discover how far humans can go, organically. You will be living as close to a perfect life as possible in regard to quality. Let's do this together and see what can happen if we optimize ourselves on every level, every cell, every body function, every thought possible. Join me," and with that he sat down and gave us a silent toast. "Go ahead, take a look," he nodded toward our contracts. We all lifted our glasses to return the toast and quickly opened the folder containing our contracts with excited curiosity. The lights above the table grew brighter.

We all took a few minutes to glance over our contracts, which I found was full of words I couldn't pronounce, let alone know the meaning. I searched for my salary, but Dr. Chilton started talking before I found the number.

"The farewell dinner prepared tonight as well as all the food you have eaten are samples of the food we will be providing for you. The important thing—and I will stress this repeatedly in the future, should you come on board—you are not to stray from any of the protocol. You cannot use any other products for anything other than what we provide," Dr. Chilton continued. "In fact, even feminine products and condoms are ours." We all glance at each other wide-eyed.

"We have shown you our methods of raising animals as well as the methods for growing crops is strictly regulated here. There are no chemicals involved whatsoever. In fact, the earth, which supplies the nutrients for our fruits and vegetables, is heavily enriched with all the minerals you need. In the real world, it is doubtful the vegetables you are eating have the minerals they are intended to have when crops are not rotated and the soil is stripped of its nutritional value. How well does our government control even the organic markets? These things we do not know completely but what we know is the quality of food is minimal compared to a hundred years ago. We have found ways to use enriched soil to provide the optimal levels of nutrients we need."

Dr. Chilton continued as the food was in front of us, "All living beings need to help their bodies repair at a cellular level from daily damage caused by the environment, stress, chemicals, air quality, food quality and even stressful forms of exercise. This is especially important for unhealthy people, developing children, and super active athletes when the body is under constant and heightened demands. The best way is through nutrition. So bon appétit!"

"But Doctor, I luff my shnickers bars and shkittles. I am not going to give them up," teased Hans.

Dr. Chilton laughed. "Oh, Hans, we know, but I assure you our version of chocolate will taste as good, and you might be able to eat Skittles on a long run with no problem, but not every day like an addiction. You can run so very well now, just think of giving your body the best fuel, the best of everything possible...think of the possibilities. And if there is nothing, no results, then you can go back to eating your snickers bars. But I think you will find out our organic chocolate is delightful. Nothing here is cooked in using any method that would adversely affect the complex cellular function in your magnificent human body, Hans." Hans stood up to show his biceps and took a bow. A few of the guys collectively threw out some jibes and told him to sit down.

Doctor Chilton turned more serious in tone and reminded us of what we have been learning, "The greatest thing we can do here is to show the world, or at least governing bodies and policy-makers what will happen if we continue on this path of malnourishment of the human population. We are fed up and angry with the misdirection of what is proper nutrition, and we are fed up with big corporations dictating what we eat and false advertising it as healthy. Who can take on these corporations? The government? No. It takes another big corporation to show the way."

Dr. Chilton took a breath, then continued. "In your contract, you must consent to genetic testing, and when we show you your DNA results as well as ancestry and discuss some areas of possible concern for you, we do not want to create fear. We want you to be aware of your possible, and I stress possible future, if you continued or started to indulge in a daily unhealthy diet and lifestyle. Of course, we know you are far ahead of the population in fitness, but how are your cells? Personally, as a scientist, I would want to know everything about my genetic makeup to ensure I am doing all I can to prevent disease. Whether you believe this or not, the nutrition we provide for you will be designed especially for your specific genetic makeup. This type of nutrition protocol will be how humans will eat in the future. We know it is expensive right now, but we want to be able to influence farming technology and regulation to make it mainstream. We will know more about you than God. Sorry for that. Maybe not God. But we are God's laboratory."

Dr. Chilton concluded, "OK, enough of that. Enjoy and celebrate our new journey of discovery. Enjoy the facilities tomorrow. I will be away. So, as I say my goodbyes, for those of you still debating on whether you will join the team," he paused and looked around at each of us until his eyes landed on me, "don't miss this opportunity of a lifetime."

The next day we enjoyed getting to know each other while enjoying the facility. Surprisingly most of us did not talk about the contract. The topic was purposely avoided. It wasn't until I was picked up by Oliver that I decided, without a doubt, this was my golden opportunity.

"Miss Gee zell, I must tell you some ting," Oliver said to me as we stood beside the limo at the airport, saying our goodbyes. "I was a crippled old man when I came to work for the doctor. I was a taxi driver who drove him to the airport in Paris when we first met but because zee Doctor's French is excellent, we talked the whole way like old friends. Mademoiselle, he cured my art'ritis. I know people do not believe me. It's crazy, they say. But no. It is true. I could not fully open my fingers. Now regarde. Look!" Oliver held his hands open flat with his fingers splayed straight and wide. "I no longer 'ave pain. I can hold scissors! Mon do. Gee zell, this is the most incredible opportunity to give this science a chance to change your life."

He gave me a tight hug and squeezed my shoulders, then bent down to hug Blue who responded with a lick across his face. I believed him. This was going to change my life forever. But not in the way I expected.

Chapter 15

The Contract

"Well, Mom and Dad, it's quite simple."

We were all sitting around the kitchen table. Blue hopped up on a chair and sat up tall as if he was about to contribute with his experiences as well. We all looked over at him, but no one told him to get off the chair. It was like he needed to be part of the decision-making.

"Dr. Chilton wants us each to move into our own condo, all paid for, and Blue can come, of course, and they would supply state-of-the-art everything, from ..." I started to ramble, until Dad put up a hand for me to stop, which I ignored. My excitement was still balled up in my stomach, and I had to get it out. "They provide all the food, supply our clothes—I mean, they supplied specialized clothes to wear running, and when we came back, they provided a computer analysis of all our body functions from oxygen intake, heart rate, heart rate variability, muscle usage, stuff I don't understand nor care about. All the information came from the fibers in our clothes! Our clothes and even our socks gathered information about our running dynamics."

"Wait, wait, wait, Ellie." My dad took advantage of my taking a breath. "They are going to supply living accommodation, all food, and clothes. What do you have to do?" He squinted his eyes and titled his head toward me.

"Dad, what happens is we train and compete as usual. I, I mean, we test their theories and technology and food and supplements and, and," I was cut off by my mother.

"Something smells fishy. They pay you, support you, and you would be giving them all the control to test you? Correct, Ellie?" She was playing devil's advocate. "There must be a substantial price to pay from your end. What do you have to do, Ellie? Sacrifice your body to science?" She scrunched up her nose and eyes together as if she smelled something terrible while my dad rolled his eyes, then looked at me.

"No, Mom. I mean, they are testing technology on actual people and then in hopes people would buy it when it goes on the market. If we use it, and it works for us, improves our performance, I mean, we are already top of our game. Well, some of us are. Not me, but some of these guys have been winning or doing incredible feats for years. If we notice a difference, think of how the average guy would want to use it. Anyway, their idea is to support us and provide this advanced technology to create a perfect environment in every aspect of our lives."

"You said that, Ellie, but what's the catch?" my dad asked. "They pay for everything, and all you do is train and compete? Sounds too good to be true. Where do I sign up?"

I laughed but felt a lot of relief when I got him on my side, but I hoped Mom wouldn't purposely put her foot down to disagree. I needed their support because I wasn't old enough to be considered a legal adult to sign this contract. "Oh yes! And I get an allowance of four thousand dollars per month!" I pumped my fists up and down in front of me and wiggled in my chair. I tried to contain my excitement but couldn't wipe the grin off my face.

"Blue! Get your paw off the table," scolded my mom. "OK, that seems a little ridiculous. What is the catch, Ellie? Come on, that is a lot of money," my ever-skeptical mother replied. She had her hair pulled back into a tight bun making this look more like an interrogation by a prison guard.

"Well, we have to sign a contract for two years, but it can continue, and they hope it will. We must stop what we are doing now and move to a new location, start a new life and give up control, I guess. I mean, no. I am in control, but I can't eat other food or buy stuff on my own.

It is a controlled study. That means they want to make sure there is no way another organization could criticize the results. So there are rules. I can leave to visit you and you can come anytime to visit me anytime. It's not like a prison or anything. We must eat only their food grown right there. If I go somewhere, they pack us food to take."

"Hey, I take offence to that. You do not eat junk food here." My mom was quick to defend her cooking. "They can't provide better food than my garden and that forest out there."

"I know Mom, but we are not allowed to eat out anywhere and if we happen to, we must tell them. Like if we go to a wedding or party, they will supply snacks and meals for us, but not make it obvious to others. None of us want to be seen by others as being different, if you know what I mean. I'm sorry about those rules, Mom, but not everyone has a master chef cooking for them like you." I was hoping my compliment would soften her attitude enough to sign the contract, but she put down the pen she had picked up.

I changed the topic, "It is all set up to be like a team with a coach, and Evotech is sponsoring us. Some of these guys are mega-famous and I've admired them for years. I am in the same room with these people! But for them, they must drop their sponsors and announce Evotech is their new sponsor, or EVT. That is the label for all our clothes and running shoes. The logo is on everything." I am exhausted and slowed down to rest and let it all sink in. I had so much to say, but nothing came to mind.

"What an opportunity." My dad sat forward with his hands on the table as if he was going to lift himself up. "And if you don't like it, can you leave?" he shifted back in his chair to await my answer.

"Well," I held the word a bit long and got their attention. "There is a non-disclosure clause in the contract. We can't divulge industry secrets, although I don't know how to explain to others how half of the stuff works, like how and why earth-grounding tiles in our floors are going to make us run better, but also." I paused. "There is a penalty for quitting. We must pay back fifty percent of our income for the time we were with them. They stressed they would sue our asses off if we gave away any trade secrets, started our own company using their technology, or gave away anything they gave exclusively for us to use. We must guard our stuff from theft. We also get a bonus at the end of each year, and we get bonuses if we win or place on the podium."

"That makes sense," my dad added. "But what if you get injured? Is it game over?" My mom sat back in her chair with her arms crossed, nodding her head to this.

"No Dad. They said it would give them another opportunity to try new things. They have doctors on staff. A lot of doctors, actually. We met some of them. I would have the best care. It's just unbelievable. It doesn't seem real. I really want to do this. I want to take advantage of this opportunity, but I need your support. I need your signatures."

I studied their faces. My dad was tapping the pen to his forehead, looking to the side as if thinking of all the negative possibilities to this, but not coming up with anything at this point. My mom has her arms folded and stared at me first, then my dad, and then at Blue. I tried her first. "Mom, what do you think?"

"Let's see what your dad has to say." She tilted her head toward him first before shifting her eyes. "He looks like he has all the answers," she said with a hint of sarcasm.

"OK. Let me have the contract, and I will get Pete to look at it," he stopped tapping his pen and pointed it at the contract.

My mom interrupted, "Like that two-bit lawyer is going to decipher an EVT contract written by Ivy League lawyers."

"Why do you always have to be so negative, Mariella?" he spread out his hands.

"Wait. Don't fight. Please." I was not in the mood to have them ruin my excitement. "They are giving us a week to decide and some said yes, right away, like Jake, and some said they were going to talk to their lawyers. But to be honest, I really, really want to do this. I think it is an opportunity of a lifetime and would kick myself for not doing this. I trust them. Besides, what else am I going to do with my life? I don't know what to study. Maybe this will give me ideas. Maybe I will become a doctor after all this." I knew this would peak my mom's interest, hoping to sway her approval. As I suspected, she replied.

"I know where you are headed with this, Ellie." She caught me. "But I do agree with you. There is a lot to gain, a lot of upsides and not much downside I can see right now. So what if you have to give back half of the money? Two thousand dollars a month is a lot more than you are making now waiting tables." I could see my dad nodding his head in swoops of agreement.

"You have my full support, Ellie," said Dad, ignoring Mom's hands up in the air and rolling eyes. "And I couldn't be prouder of you, baby girl. It was you who landed this." My dad's lower lip was starting to jut out like it always does when he shows emotion. My mom used to tease him about it during an argument, but I tried quickly to erase the memory from my mind. My father had always been more emotional one. It was like a role reversal. He had a soft spot in his heart for everyone, while my mom was the stoic one. She was the one who doubted and questioned even the door-to-door salesman until they gave up and forwent a possible sale rather than go through her interrogation. Now I know exactly how they felt. She was a hard sell.

I was exhausted but memories of the trip kept running through my head. If they agreed to the contract, Blue and I could move as soon as possible to our new condo. I started to imagine what it would be like to have my very own space. No sharing with Mom. No more fighting over bathroom time, tension in the air for hours after we argued and the need to feel I had to run to get as far away from her negativity, but yet feeling trapped and compelled to stay because I had nowhere to go. I realized this opportunity was freedom beyond my wildest dreams. Focusing on the positive reduced my guilt of leading this new life away from her, leaving her behind alone, with the image of her waiting for me to come home. I didn't want to wait for lawyers to approve of a contract. I was ready to go. I didn't have anything to pack, just my dog.

Chapter 16

Biggest Fan

My new electric hybrid all-wheel drive SUV was delivered to the house on a flatbed truck. My mother forced me to call Dr. Chilton on his private line. "Doctor, ah, there must be some mistake. I am looking at a brand-new SUV sitting in my driveway. I am very confused. This is too much. I can't accept this." I was trying to talk and shoo my mother away from me as she was mouthing the words she wanted me to say.

"Ellie, think of it as your parents' car. Fill it up with gas, pack it with your things and Blue, and drive it out here. It is a hybrid, so you will be plugging it in at night, but it will get you around. We are happy you agreed to join the group. That makes one hundred percent participation. Inside of the vehicle are a few surprises and some snacks for the drive. I won't be there to greet you, but someone will let you in and show you around your new home. Safe travels, Ellie, and welcome aboard." Dr. Chilton closed off, and I turned to my mom.

I felt guilty and foolish for disturbing such a busy man, but he was completely accommodating. How many people can say they have his private cell number? My mom stood up straight, crossing her arms and let out a mix between a growl and a sigh.

"Why can't you be excited for me?" I asked.

"Ellie, I am nervous for you. There is always a catch to these things that look too good to be true," she warned me, then turned on her heels to go back to her steaming pots in the kitchen.

"Want to go for a test drive?" I yelled out to her, trying to get her excited for me.

"No, Ellie, I have work to do," she said without turning to me and walked briskly back into the house, letting the screen door slam shut—something I always got yelled at for doing. I shrugged and turned back to inspect my new toy.

"She is not going to make me feel guilty," I said to Blue, who was at my side, equally excited about the new item for him to sniff. I wasn't going to make an issue. I foresaw an argument. I didn't want her to dictate how I would feel the rest of the day or let her get under my skin, so Blue and I hopped into the car to inspect it. After reading most of the manual, especially how to operate the music and Bluetooth, I synced my phone and sat there taking in the scent of the new vehicle, while Blue sat patiently waiting. I'm sure he was confused and after a while he lay down and fell asleep. OK, time to start it up and drive. I buckled him in with his special seat belt I transferred from mom's car, and we set off for a test drive with the satellite radio blasting out electronic beats. The excitement and novelty of the experience erased my thoughts about leaving, as we headed up to our favorite trail for one last run.

It was a popular trail for walking, hiking and running. I usually came across people from time to time, but if I wanted to go further out to Deer Run there were less and less who ventured out that far unless they were camping overnight. I figured out the vehicle fairly handily. It was so clean. I needed to get seat covers because Blue and I got pretty dusty and sweaty out on the trails. Today we would simply walk. I entered the parking area, found a spot away from all the other cars, and locked up.

"Dope ride," I heard a male voice echoing. I turned and looked around shielding the sun that was directly in my eyes when I noticed a shadow of a guy walking toward me. "Hi, Blue." He bent over and slapped his legs to call Blue over, but Blue wouldn't respond. When I stopped walking to see who he was, Blue circled my legs and sat on my feet.

"Ah, he's not good with strangers. I mean, sorry, do I know you?" I tried to balance under Blue's butt while shading my eyes.

"Ah, come on, Ellie. We went to school together." He stopped a few feet away, eyeing the position Blue took at my feet.

"Ummm, sorry, I don't remember you. It must be your cap and sunglasses." He removed them both, put on a large grin with one hand directed to his face, and put them right back on again as if embarrassed. I couldn't help noticing his hair was thinning when the sun reflected off it, making him appear much older than me.

"What? You don't remember me? I am heartbroken, Ellie. Come on, I sat next to you in science class. But hey, that's OK. I understand because you seemed all caught up in your running. You were running in and out of class too." He huffed a laugh at his own joke. There was a slight smell of something sweet lofting downwind from him toward us.

"I'm so sorry. I guess I was too preoccupied." I struggled to find some memory of this guy. Maybe it was because he wouldn't be the type I would give any attention to. He was unkempt as if he had slept in his clothes for a few days. He had a five o'clock shadow of a beard that ran down his neck. It was supposed to be hip if you could pull it off, but he simply looked like a hobo—pale and weak.

"Oh yeah, well, you know. I didn't talk much in class. I kinda hated school." He scratched at his chin. His cap was from our old high school baseball team. He shoved a hand deep in his pocket, forcing him to lean crooked to one side, and continued, "Yeah, you were running, and I was playing ball. So we were hanging in different circles."

I faked a smile and pulled my feet out from under Blue. "Yeah, that's cool," I replied. "What do you do now?" I felt I needed more information.

"Ah, nothing much now. Kind of work here and there. I was going to try out for the Cannons, but I kind of got injured, so I'm hanging out trying to figure out what to do, you know." He shuffled his feet and kicked a stone that stopped just to the side of us. "Now I ride my dirt bike on the same trails you run. Man, they are tough, and you run those? Yeah, I try to make sure I don't run over any runners." He laughed to himself again. "Hey, I don't go out there to run over you guys, don't get me wrong."

When I didn't say anything in response, he continued, "I follow you on Instagram! Yeah, I'm your biggest fan. I mean I can tell people we went to the same high school. I like following you. Like maybe, I can go for a run with you some day. I need to get back in shape for the try-outs."

He didn't seem the type to be able to try out for The Cannons, the minor league team in our area. His shoes were old worn-out high tops with the laces undone. I didn't think he could run across the parking lot.

"Oh yeah, I mean, I can't go as far as you, but I could follow, you know, maybe on my dirt bike. A girl like you shouldn't be running alone up here anyways." He tilted over even more, and I could feel his eyes glancing up and down at me. It was a feeling I had felt a few times from men. They think you don't notice, but when they have that glare in their eyes and smirk on their faces while it feels like they are stripping you naked with their eyes, I feel it instantly. It is an invasion of my privacy, and I feel as if he has touched me. I feel dirty when I know I shouldn't. It's not my fault. I was so glad Blue was standing up against me, pressing his weight against my legs as if to say, "Don't worry. One step and this guy is toast."

"I have my trusty companion and have run here hundreds of times without anything happening. So we are OK, but thanks anyways." I wanted to end the conversation quickly. I had a strong intuition to leave. "Ah, we are going to get going, have a great day and nice to meet you. Again, I guess. Sorry about that. Good luck with the baseball." I moved back away from Blue and took a few steps backward toward the trailhead and called for Blue to follow, but he stubbornly sat and stared at the guy.

"Oh yeah, no problem. Looks like Blue wants to stay with me, don't ya, guy?" He took a few steps toward Blue putting his hand out to pet him and Blue growled a warning.

He yanked his hand back quickly and laughed nervously. "Whoa, buddy, just wanted to pet ya."

"Oh, I'm sorry. Gee, he never does that. What did you say your name was?" I felt a name would trigger a memory for sure and in case I needed a name for the future for whatever reason. I got a feeling in my stomach that was a bit unsettling, but it was mixed up with a bunch of other feelings of the day and the future, so I couldn't tell what I was feeling.

"I didn't say," he replied, staring at me, standing at half kilter. If he leaned over too far, he would fall over. "It's Joe, ma'am."

"Joe Mam?" I asked.

"Ha! No, I was like saying, 'Madam.' It's Joe. My name's Joe Wilson."

It didn't ring a bell in my memory. "Sorry, I am running late. Have a great day." I waved as I turned to move this goodbye along quicker. "Blue, come," I demanded.

"Yeah, of course," he yelled out. "I'll be tracking you, Ellie. Biggest fan, remember. Wicked seeing you again."

I heard him yell out without turning to look back as I skipped into a slow jog with Blue following behind me a few feet. I could feel his eyes on me watching me go, but I wasn't going to turn around. I knew Blue would be, however. He was guarding me, stopping and checking if this guy was going to follow us. I guess he thought better, because when I stopped next to some other people who were looking at the trail map and glanced back, he was still standing in that same crooked stance. I began to wonder if he was disabled, then I worried he would key my car or something ridiculous and had to wipe the thoughts out of my head.

On second thought, I pretended to look at the map while taking sideways glances as to what he was going to do next. He got in a diesel truck caked in mud, started it up with a puff of dark smoke and pulled out kicking up some loose gravel. He gave me such a creepy feeling; I wanted to leave. Mom always said it was my woman's intuition talking to me. I have felt it many times and every time I predicted something would not go so right and there was a good chance something wouldn't, like a flat tire on my bike ride or I would fall on a trail run. My intuition had a mind of its own, and it was in sync with Blue's because he was walking back to my new SUV without me.

"OK, Blue, let's go pack the car for our drive in two days. We need your blanket and leash, and that's about it." I laughed, realizing everything we both needed, including my training clothes, would be supplied, and that was about 90 percent of my wardrobe. I guess I could pack a dress and shoes. The weird intuition left my stomach and was replaced with excitement as we got back into my fresh new-car-smelling SUV and started her up to a soft purr.

The next day there was a small going away party at our local diner with some of my old track mates from high school. I wanted to slip away and tell people later, but thought I should share the news with someone, then word got out pretty quick, and an impromptu lunch was arranged on my last day in town with my old teammates, who were considerably more excited for me than my mother. Our track coach, Mr. Larsen, showed up and surprised me one of our high school track T-shirts we were not allowed to take home and only wore at meets.

"No, we are so proud of you, Ellie." He had a habit of starting his sentences with the word *no*, which confused us in the beginning. We always joked it was because he had seven kids at home, and was constantly telling them no, so it had become a habit.

"No, I know you won't wear it on a big race, but maybe frame it on your wall." He held it up as if it were hanging up against a wall, and we all laughed. Mr. Larsen was a great mentor to me. He never looked the part of a track coach, being slightly overweight and unable to run, but he knew his stuff and taught me how to relax when running—how to let go and find my chi, as he would say. We reminisced about all the run meets and the nationals, which put him, our school, and our little town on the map when I won. He beamed with pride for weeks afterward. He told me it was the highlight of his career. I wanted him to know how vital he was to my success and when I finished telling him how I felt, he pulled me into a big hug. When we separated, I could see tears glistening his eyes before he quickly rubbed them away.

"No, too bad we couldn't have a big going away party for you, Ellie. You are picking up and leaving so quickly. One day's notice is not enough time," he said with emotion as he held me with outstretched arms, his hands heavy on my shoulders. He was watching one of his kids leave into the big world. I clutched the T-shirt to my chest with a pang of compassion hitting my heart as I watched him walk away.

When he left, I observed each of my friends giggling away with each other and a disconnection started within me. I sat back watching them talk, knowing I was ready to go on this new adventure with a quick exit from this town. These teammates were the only true friends I had in high school because they were the people I saw the most. I never had a sleepover with a friend or went to a high school party with them. I was never into that scene where everyone gets drunk and someone falls into the fire pit at the end of the night. I felt different, but we did connect on the track because that was my territory, my home, where I felt comfortable. They befriended me, but I was never one of them.

The conversation turned awkward for me when they admitted their jealousy of my new adventure. What do you say when your life is changing rapidly while theirs was staying the same? Their interests were about who was seeing who, who looked the skankiest on their Instagram, or who was the latest to get pregnant? Even though we ran together, we didn't have much in common anymore. Only a few of them kept up with their running. The girls who put on some extra pounds since high school commented I was too thin. They told me everyone in town saw me as a celebrity because I was bigger news than the local baseball team and the cat stuck in tree stories printed in our local paper.

Most people in our town did know who I was and would often stop me on the street to wish me well or congratulate me, but I didn't think they or my friends sitting around the table, had any concept of what I did. Most of them couldn't imagine driving a hundred kilometers, let alone run it. They thought driving ten miles to the next town was too far to go. The only thing they could relate to was I was one of their own. But now, I felt little connection to them, and I hoped it wasn't obvious. I felt like I was years older and had already seen more of the country than they ever would. I felt guilty for judging them, so I smiled and laughed too eagerly as I watched their TikTok videos. I had no idea what TikTok was, and I never had time to watch Netflix or engage a lot with social media. We had a lousy internet connection on the farm. I had a lousy connection to their world. It was time to move on.

I was embarrassed when I showed them my new SUV as we walked to the parking lot at the end of lunch. I didn't want them to feel bad or inadequate, so I tried to point out the downside of the whole deal. I struggled to think of anything, so focused on how I was totally owned by EVT, and I was a laboratory rat, taking the words straight from my mother's mouth. I wondered when her negativity would pay off. It finally did. They shook their heads in disagreement and said they would be following me every step of the way, just like everyone else in town, which made me think of something as I was about to leave.

"Do you guys remember a Joe guy from our school? Kind of scrawny looking, like a gamer, but says he played on the baseball team. He is kind of losing his hair already. Do you guys know him? He seems to know me, and he knew Blue too, but Blue definitely did not like him."

"No. Nope. Doesn't ring a bell. Not sure. Don't think so. Why, was he creeping you? Stalking you? Watch out for creepers, Ellie, God knows there are enough of them around here," were their collective answers.

"Oh well, OK, thanks. Love you, guys." I blew kisses and closed the door. I could feel the excitement tickle up inside of me as soon as I started the car. Saying goodbye to my friends was one of the last ties to this town. I might not ever come back and that would suit me just fine. Maybe I could put our little town on the map. Maybe they would name a street after me and tourists would come to see it and dine at this exact diner, where I waited on tables before my life changed forever. I had a strange feeling my destiny was reaching out to me, and I had to take its hand, which meant leaving things behind. I was excited, scared and melancholy all at the same time but so thankful I was not going to be alone, as I looked over at Blue's dusty paw marks on the leather passenger seat.

Chapter 17

Goodbye, Mom

On the long drive to my new home, I reflected a lot on what transpired between Mom and me. We had a few arguments about packing, as expected. But the bickering stopped with the realization I was soon leaving home, separated by a lot of distance. I was in a tangled mess of emotions. Every time I looked toward the car, I saw it as a symbol of adventure and the future, while turning to look back to my home, with Mom being overly helpful as the hour drew nearer to leave, I felt melancholy and my heart weighed down with sadness pulling my face with it. We were both on the verge of tears. I would glance sideways to catch the sorrow on her face, and I wanted to grab her and hug her, but thought if one of us started to release these emotions without preparing a stiff indomitable defense, it could wreck us both and recovering in an empty house or a long road was not a good idea. At least I had Blue to share my heavy heart, but she would be alone. We navigated our final goodbyes by reducing eye contact and finding distractions.

I wished she could be just a bit crankier rather than overly helpful and gentle. I knew she would miss Blue and me terribly. She felt it was her job to prevent me from moving too quickly. She made me think and analyze things before doing anything, and now I was left to my own devices and started to doubt my skills. As I drove away, watching her standing alone in the dust of the lonely farmyard, she would have to convince herself I was ready, and I imagine it would take a few sleepless nights. I thought of how she reminded me being a mother was a thousand times more complicated than being a dog owner and I tried to empathize with her words.

"Multiply the feelings you have for your dog a thousand times, Ellie. When he goes missing for a few hours, multiply your worries a thousand times for your own flesh and blood. When you come home late or go running, God knows where out in the wilderness, you kill me with worry," she would say. I killed her with worry, and she killed me with guilt. We were the walking dead attached through her apron strings, which I was slowly untying.

The horses had a sense we were leaving. Mom was sullen. She was not singing nor cooking. She did not want her tears to end up in her herbs, she told me, as I sat with my head on her lap. It would affect the people who used them. She always talks to me. I know all about her life story. When Ellie is away for the day, we have it to ourselves. I know she fears growing old alone. She talks about the mistakes she made trying to find love, being needed and wanted. Ellie didn't need her when she was growing up. She was so independent, always outside on an adventure, like her father and grandfather. All of them never wanted to be within four walls. She wondered why she married a man and raised a daughter exactly like her father? Maybe because that was all she knew. Her whole life felt like she was waiting for someone to come home.

Chapter 18

Hello Home

I texted Mom every time I stopped for a break for Blue and to stretch my legs. I let her know everything was OK. It made both of us feel better. When I needed her as a safety net, she always answered back. The melancholy music on satellite radio was making me homesick already. To stop the tears from blurring my vision, I switched to a comedy station providing much needed solace. I would laugh out loud and Blue would sneeze, something he did whenever he was startled. We laughed and sneezed our way to our new home.

We arrived, exhausted, to the exact spot by using the navigation system—a few miles northeast of the EVT facility. The nav system said we were at a five-thousand-foot elevation. Certainly a plus for training. There was a tall, thin sharply dressed man waiting at the community office for us. He introduced himself as Alex. He was exotic and beautiful. I had never seen a more stunning man. His eyes were an embroidery of gold fibers converging on a chocolate brown iris. His skin was flawless and reminded me of peanut butter truffle. His jaw was square and strong with a perfectly centered and symmetrical nose that flared slightly when he smiled. He had very short dark curly hair that looked painted on. I became so mesmerized by him that I didn't hear him ask how our trip was. He stared at me waiting for a response until I came to. After introductions, he led us both to the ground floor door to our new condo. The campus where the team would be living was spread out in a park setting. Most of the buildings were only one story.

"Ok there is a lot to explain here, so here is the manual and the keys. Let's get started," he said with gentle authority while opening the door. "Open to page one."

I walked inside and stopped to swallow my excitement. We entered into an open and bright living space with both kitchen and living room combined, all furnished like a show home.

"Is this all mine?" I whispered.

"Yes of course. Yours and Blue's," he acknowledged as he bent down to give Blue a pet. "Your responsibility. Page one."

I didn't open the book. "Just give me a minute," I urged. He smiled and leaned back against the front door with his arms crossed as I walked around running my hand over the sofa, touching the counter tops, opening the fridge and cupboards while Blue took off to inspect with his nose.

It was almost as beautiful as the EVT hotel. I was used to living in an old farmhouse circa 1970 with chipped linoleum floors, threadbare carpets, white travertine countertops with gold specs, and painted plywood cupboards. This kitchen had white cupboards filling one wall, with a marble countertop that swirled with colors of a tropical beach. The backsplash tiles were a mix of shades of robin egg blue, and sand that matched the walls. The whole color scheme was natural and calming. There was a stone fireplace in the corner next to sliders that opened onto a deck surrounded by greenery. The sand-colored walls were decorated with photos. I stopped to read the caption on a photo of a mountain trail that hung one of the walls: *"Do not go where the path may lead; go instead where there is no path and leave a trail."*

I turned to see the amusement on Alex's face as he watched me. I had to read each caption under each of the beautiful landscape photos of runners going up mountains, down valleys, or standing on the edge of a cliff. In small print on the bottom of each was a motivational quote such as: *"Don't stop when you are tired, stop when you are done." "When you feel like quitting, think about why you started." "Your only limit is you." " If it doesn't challenge you, it won't change you."*

"Giselle, get back here," Alex hollered, so both Blue and I came running and stood at attention. I was so full of excitement I got the shivers. "Are you cold? You shouldn't be. We have temperature control." I shook my head no. He turned his head toward the kitchen, but his eyes were still looking at me as if he thought I'd take off again. I opened the book to page one as instructed.

"To the right of the front door, you see a small closet for your running shoes and pegs for jackets and a shelf for caps and things. You must keep this condo spotless. No throwing your stuff around. I will be worse than your mother." He didn't realize that I was the neat one in that relationship.

He proceeded, "Behind this all along the wall is your pantry." He opened the sliding door and started pointing out items. "All your dried goods are stored in here and other devices as well, all of which are explained in the manual, but I will be able to show you, if you need help. For example, here is the portable muscle stimulator, an ultra red-light laser device for muscle recovery and healing. We have a full bed in physiotherapy room next to the gym I will show you later. Anyways, here is a pulse electromagnetic device for performance optimization you will use every day. We tune in that program specialized for you to enhance your capabilities." He picked up random items, and held them up for me to see, then placed them back in their spot and stood back, allowing me to peek inside.

One gadget reminded me of a magic wand, another one a large white egg and another scary contraption was full of straps, pads and wires. There were oversized headphones with spikes pointing down from the part that would sit over my head. There was a small device with light tubes sticking out labeled Theraluminator. It looked like it could be used to torture someone with electricity. At the back was a metal case I was afraid to open.

Alex noticed the apprehension on my face. "We will tune it all in for you, so don't worry. You will be going through a tutorial about all these devices for one whole day," he reassured me, then snickered as if withholding a secret.

"What are all these jars filled with powder?" I held up one marked Recovery.

"Oh yes." He grabbed another jar from off the shelf. "These are your athlete supplements specially formulated just for you, so you cannot share with anyone else. See the label on the back? It lists the ingredients so you don't think we are poisoning you." He chuckled and pointed.

I picked up a jar and read the label: Hydrogen Negative ions, B vitamin complex + B12, D Ribose, DHA, Essential Amino Acids, among other ingredients I had never heard of before. Alex saw me looking with a confused expression on my face once again.

"Giselle, they did blood work and came up with things that would be beneficial to you. Nothing would ever be harmful."

"Oh, OK," I responded, but I heard my mother's words come to mind once again: "You are just a guinea pig, Ellie."

"Here we have your fridge fully stocked with what you are to eat each day. Each container is measured for calories and nutrients and will be labeled on how to prepare it. You must stick to the eating plan that will be set out specifically for you." Alex was talking without taking a breath while opening doors and waving his hand like a game show host.

"The water from the tap is drinkable because it is already set up running through an infrared light and a little extra oxygen or hydrogen, depending on what you need, pumped into it. Next to the fridge you have counter space, a lovely window over the sink, next to a corner space for the coffee maker and handy jars of nuts and whatever else Dr. Chilton wants you to eat. Oh, and this one has organic dark cacao nibs, no sugar. You will grow to like them. There is no dishwasher. You will hand wash and leave to dry."

"Alex, we don't have one at home either. I wouldn't know how to use it."

"Good girl. Good old-fashioned living. Makes you strong. Dr. Chilton would probably have you ride a bike to power a dishwasher if we gave you one, anyways," he huffed, then chuckled. "All appliances are energy efficient and solar powered. The whole place is solar powered, of course. All organic soaps are under the sink. Use nothing other than the products supplied. There is no microwave oven. Dr. Chilton believes they are evil," he sneered.

He turned on his heel and swung out his arm as if displaying what was behind game show curtain number one, a breakfast nook, dividing the kitchen from the living area. "And this is your island with four tall chairs. Sorry, Giselle, no table. You can stand to eat or sit with this arrangement and have room for three other guests, should you choose." He made one of the chairs spin around as he spoke.

"The flooring is bamboo and the countertops are marble, of course. You can cut on them with no problem but use the cleaning spray and do not mix meat and vegetables in the same space. In fact, we have a special board for cutting meat in this cupboard. Here it is." He whipped out the board like a sword and placed it on the counter with his other hand held high in the air.

"Look how the island lights up when you flip this switch." He pointed to the sides of the island, which glowed from behind to illuminate the snow-white color of the marble stone exposing various cracks and smudges of blue and rivers of gray, yellow and even mint green flowing throughout. I was fascinated, never having seen anything like it before. I stood back to notice how everything blended together, feeling clean and modern, making me feel warm and happy inside.

Turning completely around he used his game show arm to indicate the other half of the open kitchen-living area. "Next section, page ten, turn to the next tab, Giselle," he ordered, peering over my shoulder. "The relaxation section has four chairs. They are meant to be movable for conversation and fit together. One is a massage chair. This one I believe. You can try it out later. See the instructions in your book. Right there," he indicated, and I nodded my head. "Good. The TV has no cable. Well, it's not really a TV. It is only a monitor, but no gaming device, so if you are a gamer, you will be in withdrawal, but you don't strike me as a gamer." He turned to finally notice me and stood back to give me a once over head to toe inspection. "I think you can link to Netflix, Apple TV, Pandora, Spotify, or something like that, but believe me, you will have enough educational videos sent to you to watch that you will have no time for frivolous stuff. Besides, who needs to listen to the dreadful news?" he asked rhetorically.

He passed by the sliding doors that led to an outside deck, to a desk situated against the corner of the room. It was a desk as far as I could tell but there was something different about it and the saddle-shaped chair next to it.

"OK, Giselle, this desk can raise up to match your position standing or move down to floor height should you want to sit, lie or do yoga and work at the same time." He demonstrated the levels of the desk. When he dropped it to its lowest height, Blue came over to inspect it as if it were set up for him. Blue and I both stepped back out of the way as Alex suddenly squatted down on the floor and swung one of his pant-suited legs around behind his head with his shiny leather oxford loafer positioned next to his ear like a picture of a yogi I saw once. I was afraid for him. He reached out to pretend to type on the desktop with his other leg jutting out to the side. "See!" he said. Blue, as if on cue, walked over with his head down, ears back, and aimed his nose at the open opportunity to sniff. Alex jumped a few inches back across the floor while still in his locked yoga position. I didn't realize a person could move that fast with his leg wrapped around his head. I started choking from trying to hold back my laughter, bent over and couldn't breathe. He unlatched himself and jumped up to slap my back.

"Oh dear, I haven't had that reaction yet. I have had some interesting responses to my yoga positions, but I've never had to revive someone from choking after my being sexually assaulted by a dog," he laughed teasingly.

"Oh my God, I am so sorry for Blue, but," I trailed off, still laughing. I had to sit down for fear of peeing in my pants. "Where is the bathroom? I have to pee!" I squealed.

"This way. This way." He led me a few steps around a corner to a door and held it open for me to pass. I closed the door only to hear, "Well, aren't you the friendly dog. And we don't even know each other that well. Come here. I have a treat for you."

I quickly got on the toilet for some grateful relief still laughing a few more minutes before I took in the room. The skylight above my head brightened the light green bamboo flooring under my feet. The corner shower had beautifully sand colored tiled walls with all the similar display of knobs as the EVT spa. The shower floor caught my eye as it was made with hundreds of small smooth river stones.

I turned on the water over the sink to wash my hands and watched as it flowed over the lip of a pouring vase attached to the wall, into the oval granite bowl serving as the sink. The back splash was the same river stones as the shower. I opened the mirrored cabinet that held four separate sections of shelves filled with jars, toothpaste, brushes, cotton, and various other items all in glass containers labeled EVT. Everything struck me as so clean. Nothing was manufactured except for the toilet, which had three separate buttons. I guess I would have to read the manual to figure those out.

I walked out to apologize to Alex and found him playing with Blue, getting him to sit and rollover to receive some treats. "I'm so sorry for his behavior. I can't control him all the time," I said as I glared down at Blue.

"No problem. I have a dog as well, but my Sasha is only a tiny puffball. They have no inhibitions when it comes to sniffing," he agreed and continued to play as Blue had his nose down and butt up in the air waiting to jump up in the air for another treat. Alex teased Blue a little, then threw it four to five feet above Blue's head, which he responded with a perfect jump upward to catch the tidbit in midflight, then land softly on the floor, and trotted over to Alex's tapping next to him and sat down.

Alex hopped up and we continued the tour in the bedroom. The bedroom walls were a warmer deeper sand color with a ceiling painted light blue with billowy clouds. I was mesmerized. The bed was double the size of mine at home and twice as tall with an ocean blue duvet and matching pillows. There was no dresser, only a small walk-in closet that was already stocked with my specially designed tech clothing and more tops and bottoms folded on the shelves as well as three new pairs of running shoes and two casual street shoes. In the corner in my bedroom was a dog bed that matched the decor. Blue went up, sniffed it, and walked away.

"Well, Blue, what do you think of our new home?" I had to ask him. He left the room without looking at me to investigate further. I was not certain he was convinced this was home for him.

"Giselle, this bed is made in heaven. I am not kidding. Dr. Chilton has a direct line to God. The mattress molds to your body, changes temperature to go cooler at night if your body is overheated from a hard training session. It also has a grounding or earthing mat connected deep into the earth below, so you benefit from the earth's free electrons to help restore the electrons lost during training. When you are in a higher metabolic state and experiencing higher inflammation as a response to your training, this mattress will settle your body right down. It is combined with acupressure massage that relaxes muscles while you sleep. Remember when they talked about this at the EVT center?" I nodded yes.

"Of course you must realize everything in this apartment is as organic and natural as humanly possible and this bed is the epitome of combining science and nature. We even provide you with a travel version of the acupressure earthing bed mat. Crazy huh? Go take a little lay down." He pointed to the bed, and I gingerly sat down on the edge, not wanting to disturb the beautiful bedding. "Oh, Giselle, dive right in, girl." He pulled back the covers, lifted my feet, took my shoes off, and pushed me to the center of the bed. He grabbed a small box from the nightstand and hit a few buttons. I melted into the pillows and felt a surge of coolness envelop my body in waves. I felt little pulsations under my butt and back and a rolling sensation under my legs. My body tingled in the refreshing and invigorating coolness.

"You can adjust the temperature for cooler nights. Dr. Chilton believes in cooler room temperature in the bedroom. The whole apartment is climate controlled in different areas for different needs. The flooring is heated because Dr. C does not like forced air heating. This room will completely black out at night. Not one light anywhere will disturb your sleep, which is why you are not allowed to bring in your cell phone or any other device into this room. It is used strictly for rest and relaxation. You can only read a paper book. Wi-Fi is forbidden in this apartment, Giselle. Dr. Chilton does not like Bluetooth or Wi-Fi, because studies show the radiation emitted can cause cellular damage. There is no Wi-Fi at the EVT center either. In case you didn't notice, all computers were on Ethernet cables."

"Oh yes, they were connected to the wall, which I thought that was weird because for such an innovative company, the fact you had to plug in your computer seemed crazy," I recalled.

"Well, Giselle, Dr. Chilton is way ahead of his time. The radiation from cell phones and Wi-Fi is the next unknown carcinogen, like cigarettes were forty years ago. In a few years to come, there will be warning labels on cell phones to keep them away from your body, especially when they are transmitting. You must use speakerphone and hold your cell phone two feet away from your body when talking. There is a measurable increase in body temperature produced by the cell phone and the radiofrequency exposure from your phone can cause biological issues such as cell damage, and not like the kind you experience after exercising. Many studies show changes to brain activity, reaction times and sleep activity from cell phones. If you can't use a phone on an airplane because it interferes with signals, what do you think it does to your body if you are on it for hours a day, like some kids your age are? You will connect with cables and there are no devices allowed in the bedroom, whatsoever. There is a tower located on the property to provide a cell phone signal but you can only pick it up outside, on the balcony. Inside for phone calls, you will use a landline. Also, your cell phone will be in a radiation-blocking case to block out the low-level radiation waves from transferring to your body."

"I have a question. You talk about radiation but EVT has us wear all this technology in our clothes and watches that transmits data. How does it transmit in a way that isn't dangerous?"

"Awesome question. It uses Bluetooth, but it does not transmit constantly, and the radiation is less because the signal only transmits so far and is collected in your watch or phone, which are both in protective cases. We download the information from it in less than a second, and then it stops transmitting. The information we pick up from all over your body is gathered in one place, in a protected case, transmitted quickly and sporadically to us," Alex explained.

He continued, "Giselle, there are rules about these things because we want to test the strategies we use and do not want to play interference from things we know have negative effects on our bodies. This information is scientifically proven. Even the way this place is built, and the air and water quality are set up to reduce the known negative effects that could affect this study. The rules of engagement, so to speak, are on page twenty-one."

I was not going to bother to look right now. I knew there were rules because they were discussed extensively in our contract. Did all this biohacking seriously make a difference to our performance? Only time will tell, I guess.

"You are to sleep and rest in this room, or whatever else, of course." Alex winked at me. "Which leads me to another topic. Although it is none of my business, unless you want to share, Dr. Chilton has made it my business. Being young and beautiful as you are, I have been assigned to act as a chaperone as well as your advisor. Yes, I know. Don't say a word. Dr. Chilton is afraid you will be inundated with admirers, and he believes you are sweet and innocent and need someone to run interference, and, well, I am a black belt. Even though I appear skinny and weak, I can divert them with my scrawniness and kick the living daylights out of anyone who gets near you." With that, he struck a fighting pose, and I started to laugh while Blue gave a sharp warning bark.

"What? You both don't believe me? Don't make me demonstrate," and as if on cue, Blue jumped up to place his front paws on one of Alex's legs as if to challenge him and Alex effortlessly picked him up high above his head, cradled him gently to the floor, and pretended to wrestle. Blue was in a state of shock at first, then soon realized it was a game. He grunted and squirmed his way out, running around the room, pausing with his butt up in the air ready to play.

"Yes, sufficient to say, I am your shadow," Alex continued after a quick chase session with Blue. He sat on the edge of the bed and turned to me still cuddled in the covers of the bed. "And I'm gay. Just thought I'd throw that in there, in case you didn't figure it out. So, I will not be getting in bed with you. Well, actually I can get in bed with you." He kicked off his shoes and got under the covers. "Look, I know this is all a bit of an overload for you right now, but Dr. C. has high expectations and has made a huge investment in all this high-tech living and in the team. You will be shocked at what is in store for you. Oh, this is nice." Alex paused to squirm as the coolness rolled up his body.

I smiled as we both lay side by side staring at the ceiling painted with a façade of clouds over a blue sky, taking in the sensations of the bed, a far cry from my dull stippled ceiling and hard bed at home. I never thought about having a problem with admirers, but the memory of that strange dude in the parking lot of the trail head came to mind as well as the truck that followed me, and I felt a sensation of relief knowing someone would have my back besides Blue.

"I don't think I will be able to get out of this bed to meet anyone," I joked.

"I agree. They will find us here, starved to death with smiles on our faces with my reputation gone to the dogs. Excuse me Blue." He glanced over to where Blue was sitting at the side of the bed, staring at us. "Don't worry little buddy, I am not going to make a move on your lady here. I am the least of your worries." Alex sat up and grabbed my hand to pull me off the bed. "Come on, we have more to see."

He pointed to a lounge chair and ottoman tucked in the corner. "This chair is not a clothes hanger. It is an energy chair. Dr. C. loves these chairs, see page 28. It does not go at your desk. You have an ergonomically designed chair at your desk, in case you didn't notice."

He opened a door from the bedroom to the outside and an enclosed patio deck that ran the length of the condo. There was a small private section cordoned off outside the bedroom surrounded by a lattice wall covered in blooming vines and curtains pulled back to the corners, which could be drawn closed to provide complete privacy on all sides. Beyond the lattice was a quiet forest peppered with trees towering over a forest lawn. In the corner was a small waist high tub and across from the tub on the other side of the door was a small one-man infrared sauna. I recognized it from the spa at EVT.

"Every day Dr. C. will want you to take a sauna. It is in your protocol in the book for daily routines. This here is a cold water plunge tub. About fifty-two degrees Fahrenheit. You will go from sauna to cold water and back again. It is the most fabulous feeling. If you didn't feel alive before, you will definitely feel alive after this. Don't worry, you will build up a tolerance to the cold water," he said while noticing the expression of fear on my face. "The water is recycled to water the plants and trees every few days. All the water here is recycled. Anyways, in the winter months, the temperature will seem warm," he winked at me.

We walked back inside, through the condo and out the sliding doors in the living room. A beautiful dark brown plastic wicker lounge with green cushions was in the corner against the wall that separated this apartment from the next along with a small table and one other chair. Hanging plants, a small water fountain and potted plants created a fresh, earthy and cozy feel. The patio was completely open to the park and beyond lay a majestic scene of dark green rolling hills before the rugged gray-blue Rocky Mountains. I wanted to cry with joy.

"And that, Giselle, is where you will do a lot of your training. Those hills lead to mountains that reach up to ten thousand feet." Alex stood beside me with his hands on his hips. And we both let out a collaborative sigh.

"Those hills, they are your real home, aren't they? Isn't that what you do? Run up mountains? They are only about thirty miles of rolling hills away. A nice warm up for you," Alex threw his head back and laughed.

"Not funny," I protested, but secretly I couldn't wait to set off to explore new trails.

"OK, we are done here, but wait until I show you the gym and pool." Alex grabbed the binder from me ready to lead me back inside.

"Alex, do we have to do that now? I mean, I can see it all later, when I am getting evaluated. I kind of want to settle in and not leave Blue here by himself. He should be taken for a bit of a walk, anyways. Is that OK with you?" I pleaded.

"Absolutely, my dear." He tilted his head to the side sympathetically. "Yes, that is a great idea. Go enjoy. The trails are all marked for one hundred miles, so you shouldn't get lost if you stay on track. Poor soul who had to mark those trails. Oh, wait, he would be someone like you." He winked and opened his arms for a hug. I dove in, feeling he was already an old friend, and it felt surprisingly good to have strong arms around me as I felt the pangs of homesickness.

No smells, no scents whatsoever, only Ellie. It reminds me of the big place we visited a month ago. It has the same smells, earthy but too clean and very confusing. The male had a different smell, heavy with soap but also very relaxed. I like him. He moves with grace and strength that I can respect. I can trust this one. Everything and everyone is new—the land, the house, the car. I am suspicious of so much change, but I can feel Ellie's excitement. I can also feel her nervousness, and she is a little sad. We both miss Mom. We miss the warmth of her kitchen and the familiar smells and routines. I miss my horses. They are probably wandering around aimlessly, no one to round them up. Soldiers without their General. I miss the farm smells. This smells too clean. It does not feel like a den.

We head off for a walk. This is where we will find our home. These trails are different. They are open with tall grass for a long time before eventually climbing higher into thicker trees. I smell deer, fox, rabbits, birds, and pesky squirrels. They must have followed us here. Stupid squirrels. We found berries and some plants Ellie recognized. We crossed little creeks with sweet tasting water. We sat leaning into one another on a big rock, her feet dangling over the edge. She described things she could see things way in the distance that I could only imagine. I know she is going to conquer those trails I cannot see, that may be too far for me to run, although I know I will try.

Chapter 19

The Coach

The next morning, Alex and I toured the gym facility, and I started over the next few weeks of a series of baseline tests, which nearly killed me. If I thought running one hundred kilometers was difficult, none of it came close to the do-or-die effort I was forced to give. They tested my body composition in a high-tech imaging machine showing in detail where and how much fat and muscle I had, my bone density, inflammation, and all my organs were checked for abnormalities. They had me wear various contraptions while I ran, to study my body mechanics. I did a maximum oxygen consumption test, while they took my blood intermittently as I ran as hard as I could on a treadmill. I did a variety of strength tests, lung tests, heart rate tests, agility, flexibility, and reaction time tests. They also had me try different foods, took blood, urine and feces to test. They measured my water intake, urine output and scraped the sweat from my body.

I had a brain scan while watching various images. They varied from difficult terrain with people running looking exhausted to high mountain ledges and pictures that were supposed to frighten me as well as loving and happy photos. They also monitored my sleep and told me they would be doing it every night from now on.

There were so many tests. My anxiety reached an all time high, and I was wondering if they had a test for that too. Later I found out they did. They kept assuring me I was doing well but wouldn't tell me the results. "It's only for us," they kept telling me. "You don't need to worry. Do what you normally do."

The problem was none of this was normal. No one wants to be poked with needles, hooked up to wires and cables, wear a mask and run to exhaustion on a treadmill. I was afraid to fail. It was all so matter-of-fact—do this, run here, lift this as many times and as fast as you can. I was completely exhausted. They would wait until I recovered and tested some more. I would go to the lab and test for hours, go back home to Blue and try to recover. I managed to walk him, and even then I was not allowed to walk him in the mornings before the tests. I knew he was feeling out of sorts. He was left alone even though Alex came by twice a day to walk and play with him, but I still felt so bad for him not being anywhere familiar. He was homesick.

I took my parents on a virtual tour of my condo, and they both promised to schedule times to visit. I was looking forward to seeing someone I knew. I ran into most of the team, whom I met at the first meeting back at the EVT facility, but it was only in passing from one lab to the next. We commiserated briefly before being shuttled to the next appointment. Everything was so mechanical.

After a couple of weeks of tests, I was allowed in the gym to go over a training program. There was more equipment than I could use in a lifetime. I didn't know what most of it was used for, but they assured me I would have a personal trainer who would walk me through a routine each day. I couldn't help but wonder if this was how professional athletes got treated. It still hadn't sunk in that I was getting paid to do all this. The reality of being twenty years old and making a living doing what I love, living in an amazing condo with everything supplied, and my best friend by my side reminded me to keep saying my morning gratitudes. I had so much to be thankful for. They encouraged me to continue with my daily gratitudes and meditation because they could see the results in my electromagnetic readings through the fibers in my clothes. Should I be happy or scared they knew that much about me?

The day came to meet our coach out on the track. We were told Lane Rogers was the best there was. I was excited to meet him and to see the team all together again, so I was surprised to see how many runners there were standing around in groups, as I got out of my SUV. There were others I did not recognize at all.

I stood back to observe everyone before I entered through the gate. Anyone could spot the difference between the groups gathered separately. My group were a motley crew in various outfits in contrast to the others all dressed in matching tracksuits. Some of them looked emaciated, while others were muscular and fierce-looking. They all had the confidence and appearance of Olympic athletes while we looked out of place and vexatious.

From a distance, I could make out Wild Jack, who was tall and scruffy looking with his caveman beard and unruly hair jutting out in all directions like he just woke up, which I'm sure he did. Jake was like a little brother being teased by Hans. I could hear his thick German accent from a distance. Olivia and Annabel were huddled quietly together. Anabel was in a bright orange running skirt and flowery shirt, while Olivia was the only one besides Jake to wear the EVT gear. Jeep Jenkins was wearing his trademark colorful chullo, an Andean style cap with ear flaps. Joe "Boz" Bosco was wearing lycra shorts showing off his incredible legs. He was a strong cyclist and kept his affinity toward lycra, which I aimed to relentlessly tease him about. Then there was Rocky talking to one of the other athletes. He was so famous for his feats that I was sure someone recognized him. Not sure how Tim Donaldson ended up here, because he seemed quite a rebel at heart with his tattoos, leather necklaces, and bracelets that he had collected from his adventures around the world. Maybe he needed the money and a free place to stay, like me.

The track felt welcoming and familiar. I had been to it a couple of times since I moved in. I was out driving around exploring with Blue when we happened upon it. We went back early the next morning because I was anxious to check out where I would be spending some of my time. Blue never comes along with me to the track, but because this was a new town I wanted his company. If we got kicked out, so be it.

We had arrived before sunrise and the track was empty except for in the middle of the infield where I could see a couple of people silhouetted against the horizon as the sun's rays were beginning to hint of the brightness to come. It appeared to me they were performing the graceful movements of tai chi. The air was fresh and made me feel alive. I love this hour of the morning. Blue and I are usually into our run day by the time the sun rises.

I had brought my doggie do-do bags for pick-up, so I ignored the sign that read "No Dogs" and closed the gate behind us, trapping Blue inside. I didn't intend to stay long, only until more people showed up and complained about the four-legged lawbreaker. I wanted to test the track. I love the discipline of track work because it measures success or failure immediately. The track is flat, fast and honest compared to a trail, and when you finish a session, you know exactly where you measure as a runner, and how much more work you have to do, which I hate to come to terms with. It is a definite love-hate relationship.

I stood and watched the couple of shadow figures for a little while, mesmerized by the elegance and grace of their movements. They looked like marionettes, their movements grandiose, disciplined, sharp, and fluid. A moving meditation not unlike running.

Blue stayed near waiting for me to give a command to run loose. A simple "Go" was all he needed to be able to run where he liked. I didn't think he could get into much trouble in this enclosed track, yet he immediately went to check out the moving figures. I am not sure how much dogs can see in the dark, but he was always my protector and no person anywhere goes without inspection. He never lingered for a pet. He was not that kind of dog. They kept up their elegant movements as Blue came close, then sat down to watch them like he wanted to join but was waiting for permission. They continued with their dance as if he wasn't there.

The rubberized orange track was perfect, the grass on the pitch was pungent, fresh, wet and the sun was now beginning to give a hint of the grass's green color. The smell of morning dew on any kind of vegetation was like a drug to me, always reminding me of mornings on the farm. I started to feel homesick, again.

I tested the track, and it felt spongy, beckoning me to run between its lines. I took one of the outside lanes. Blue broke free from his trance of watching the couple and came over to check my status. "Yes, buddy. You can go run." I knew his nose was excited with the reawakening of scents the morning dew provided from the night before, so I let him follow his nose as he ran with it glued to the ground.

After about eight laps, I picked up the pace and checked my watch to determine I could get away with some eight-hundred-meter repeats before anyone else appeared on the track. I hated them, but they kept me honest. I turned on my tunes loud, songs like "Running on Empty" by Jackson Browne and James McMurtry's "Off and Running," Tom Petty, and some Pearl Jam. It was the music I trained with and always motivated me to push harder.

After about six of the eight hundred meters with recovery of four hundred meters in between, I was finished. Blue was bored and had found something to roll around in. At least the tai chi couple found it amusing, laughing as they waved goodbye. Blue's attention span was spent. Like me, he would rather explore a bigger world, and he purposely got himself into trouble, so I would have to pay attention to him. I knew his game. The sun had shut down the dawn sky showing the true colors of the bleachers. Our time was up. When I turned to walk out, I realized there was a man sitting in the stands watching us.

"Oh, geez, Blue. Come on, let's go!" I commanded, worried it was the caretaker, and we're about to get chastised for breaking the "no dogs allowed" rule. As we had passed near the stands to get to the exit gate, the man stood up, stretched and walked toward us. I was in trouble. This feeling must come from my fear of getting yelled at as a child for always trying to get away with things, like I did here. Time to face the music. I was at the ready with a variety of excuses running through my mind.

He was tall, over six feet with broad shoulders and narrow hips immediately gave the impression that he was an athlete. He was wearing a loose-fitting track jacket but his muscled shoulders pushed back against the seams. It was zipped up to his chin, and he had his hands tucked deep in the pockets. His short straight blonde hair was close to his neck barely peeking out from underneath his ball cap. He didn't look like a caretaker. My heart started pounding. Not sure whether it was his presence or the cool breeze that sent a shiver, chilling the sweat on my arms and legs. He smiled slightly in such a way you could mistake it as smug and said good morning in a calm, relaxed tone. I smiled back more relieved than anything. Not the confrontation I expected.

"Nice yahoo eight hundreds. Two fifty. Impressive," he said, using a familiar track term only another runner would understand.

I stopped and turned to read his reaction. "You were timing me?" I was shocked.

"I don't need a watch to know your pace," he corrected while giving a slight nod side to side. I sensed he was waiting for me to take the bait and ask how he knew, but he was wearing it all over his clothes becoming obvious the more I studied him. If I was a track athlete, I would want to know about him, but I was proudly a trail runner and didn't follow track news. I still admired track athletes and enjoyed watching them on TV, but I couldn't relate to them. They were caged, while I was running free.

"Impressive," I replied. I didn't know what else to say.

He huffed out a breathy laugh. I tried to be nonchalant but as he stepped down toward me, I saw him clearly and the same shiver ran through my body again. He had a handsome face with a straight nose, thin lips and a cleft chin. His light eyes were friendly but small. What struck me most was the way he stood, tall and strong, feet squarely placed and balanced. Again, I shivered, but this time visibly. Previously, I was catching a chill from my sweat, but strangely, now I had started to feel hot inside. Geez, I hated when my body did that. I had no control when I was nervous; I started sweating. He was staring at me, and I began to feel awkward and self-conscious, like a nerdy teenage girl at a school dance being stared at by the captain of the football team. I nervously adjusted my knit cap lower over my ears, close to my eyes and peeked up from under it, hoping it would hide how I felt. Blue sat on my feet, and I welcomed his warmth against my legs as a barrier between us.

"You have a beautiful gait," he offered as he jutted his head forward and down, squinting his blue-gray eyes in order to see my face.

He stepped in closer, staring from one of my eyes to the next like my parents do when they asked if I was telling the truth. My cheeks flushed with color as they heated up.

I held his gaze for a few seconds to try to show I was not affected by his comment. I had no reason to be, but inside I felt he was challenging me in some way. With an amused look on his face, he continued, "Take the compliment." He tilted his head upward, still staring down at me through the end of his nose.

"Th ... thank you," I stuttered as I squinted up at him. People had told me I look like a gazelle when I run, hence the nickname Giselle the Gazelle. I have never been good at taking compliments. Mom always told me to simply say thank you and not make excuses or start apologizing. I fidgeted with my shirt, pulling it lower over my shorts, almost losing my balance with Blue sitting on my feet. I tugged one out from under his butt before I fell over, widened my stance and folded my fists into the bottom of my sweatshirt. I felt diminutive against his size, towering over us. Blue was beginning to push back harder against me as if to say, "Move back, Ellie."

"I was making an observation. You are just like your running, an elegant natural beauty," he paused, almost baiting me to see how much more he could make me squirm and when I didn't, he added, "You didn't stretch."

"I am not a big fan of stretching." I challenged a little too defiantly, not knowing why I lied.

"It would be a good idea to learn." This sounded more like a command than a comment.

"I'll work on it." I nodded, wondering why he felt superior enough to give me unsolicited advice. I felt a sudden urge to get away from his eyes, which he hadn't taken off me. He made me feel trapped and slightly defenseless, but not in a threatening way. I rubbed my arms, signaling to him I should get somewhere warm. My shivering got stronger.

"You better go before you shake yourself loose," he teased with a slight chuckle.

I managed a smile and a nod while I pulled my other foot out from under Blue and took a couple steps back. Blue stood his ground. I quickly commanded him to come and turned toward the gate, realizing he didn't even acknowledge Blue, nor did he bend down to pet him, which most people do. I also realized he never introduced himself. When I turned to call Blue again, he still hadn't moved from his position, while the man was already walking across the infield. I watched him walk away and thought I could see the letters *EVT* on the back of his jacket. Then the butterflies took flight in my stomach.

Here I was back at the same track, and I walked quickly toward the group, giving a slight wave and mouthing a hello when they turned to notice me. I was late. Their heads turned back to the voice of a person I had not yet noticed. I was walking up as he was beginning to address everyone gathered.

"Good morning, everyone. For the newbies, I am Coach Lane Rogers. I am your commander and chief." Everyone laughed at this. "And I am not kidding. Your job is to come here and punch your card with me. Get your work assignment, execute it, get evaluated, and leave. Come early and warm up if you want, but I will make you do it again so I know you are doing the drills correctly even if you have done them a thousand times before. I am the boss here. Please the boss, and you will have a great day at the office."

We eyeballed each other. Was he was joking or serious? He started back up again with the same determined, firm tone. "As you can see, there are two groups here. There are the ultradistance people and the speed group—marathons on down."

The voice sounded eerily familiar. I reached Jake in the group and quickly set in beside him. After studying for a few seconds, I recognized first the coach's size and then his ball cap.

"Welcome, D'Angelo. A little late but never late in a race." He was staring at me. As he acknowledged my reaction, a smile slowly formed on his face. "Everyone welcome the lovely and talented Giselle D'Angelo. New young superstar of the ultramarathon. The final member to arrive for Team Ultra. Next time you're late, it'll be fifty push-ups. Understand?" He nodded at me, then said, "This goes for everyone."

My cheeks flushed hot and red as I looked down embarrassed for being singled out. I thought I was on time. Jake squeezed my wrist. I turned toward him to see him smile and roll his eyes, setting me at ease. Running had never been a job to me. I guess I was a company girl now and had to punch the clock on time.

The team was friendly and everyone eventually introduced themselves as we warmed up. I recognized some of the names as some of the most talented runners in the world. I assumed many of them were already making incredible money from sponsorships and race appearance fees, so they weren't here for the income or condo. The ultra group, on the other hand, didn't make much money, if any at all, from our races. Our group counted on sponsorships to make an income, not prize money. I also knew the other group was used to structured workouts and events, while most of us ultrarunners were a ragtag team of nomads used to running alone for hours and sleeping on the ground during multiday events.

"OK, team, I brought all of you together because you have a lot you can learn from each other, even though you run different distances. I am going to dive right into it. The common denominator is controlling your brain. You all know this already or you wouldn't be where you are at in your careers. They can pump you full of organic crap and give you the best beds in the world, but what happens between your two ears is something we can only guide you with. You alone, are in control of what someone like Dr. North would call the Pivotal Governor or in better terms, your Pivotal Governor is in control of you, and if you don't flip the tables on it, you will not be able to push past the pain barrier into unchartered territory. The territory you need to get used to in order to reach your ultimate goal. Your brain is all that gets in the way for those of you striving to run the two-hour marathon or the sub three forty-three mile, run five hundred miles, or run up Everest. Physically, you have the genetics, plus you had a pretty decent history before joining us, but now you are really going to rock and roll and power-up your brain through nootropics, Dr. Chilton's unique brain supplements along with his high-tech gadgets. And by teaching you how to conquer the demons that lurk around in your monkey brain, you just might be successful."

I was confused not knowing whether he was complimenting us or putting us down. I felt the anticipation to understand more, grow in all of us. Coach continued. "Whatever your goal, if you don't cage that monkey in your brain that tells you to stop, makes excuses, or secretly says it's impossible, then you might as well walk away from ever doing the training. At this point in your careers, your biggest enemy to your dreams is you. It is not that you are not capable physically; it is that you must control your thoughts. So, from now on, the training on this track and other assignments is to conquer that monkey, control your pivotal governor, or whatever you want to call it. We will hone in on your dreams and aspirations, and make them reality. We start by believing your dream has already happened and you are already capable. You have to act as if you already are the person you want to become." He paused to let this sink in. Some people were shaking their heads in agreement.

"Your other job is to not only visit the pain cave but to move in. Get comfortable and make it your home. If you can't, then reassess your dream. Remember, each of you were interviewed. Each of you were asked about one particular dream you were passionate about. EVT saw the desire and passion, or else you wouldn't be here. The first step was to have a dream, an outlandish dream, something that scares you. One no ordinary human would ever think up, let alone attempt to achieve. You must have the physical capability to reach your dream and were willing to sacrifice everything to reach it because life would not be complete until you did." He stopped and studied our reactions. The group collectively grew a few inches taller right then and there.

There was a serious mood in the group, until Wild Jack piped up, saying only something he could get away with: "I think I'm scared, Coach." Coming from a big, burly man, we all started laughing.

"Don't worry, Jack. You should be. I might even make *you* cry," replied Coach Lane.

And he does make me cry. Over the next months, he found all my weak spots—in my running, my fitness, my spirit, and in my soul. As each training session got harder, I stepped up to the challenges, which often left me questioning why I allowed myself to go through the torture. He had a split personality. He was supportive at the beginning, convincing me I had all it took to make it through a training session and to embrace the suffering; then he turned evil. He would make me run until I was close to dropping, then pull up beside me in a car or on a bike, commanding me to sprint until I had to drop to the ground before I fell from exhaustion. I always managed to survive, and that's when his sweet personality would come out with just enough praise. I worked so hard for just a "Good job, girl."

Coach preached that anyone who was successful, first had a deep unrelenting desire that drove them to that success. They consistently accomplished something every day to toward their goal. Even rest days were important to move us forward. We were also instructed to act and feel like we had already achieved our dream. We had to get used to how it would feel to be successful, so that we wouldn't sabotage ourselves.

"Fake it till you make it, D'Angelo," he would yell at me if I had any doubts in myself. "If you believe you can and will be successful, then it is only one more step to believe you already *are* successful. Your mind doesn't know any different. Act like you are everything you want to be. You think this is tough, but it is what you would have done to reach that dream. You have no other choice. No whining allowed, or you can just go home and give up."

If my dream was to run two hundred miles, then how would I act as that athlete if I had already achieved it? I would have had to put in the work and be mentally prepared, full of self-belief, with no doubts. I had lots of doubts, even fear, but I had to brush the thoughts away— just roll right over top of them with positive affirmations. I read my affirmations, visualized them, and acted them out. I had to overrule my fears of not being good enough. My ego had to become separate from myself. Because my everyday Ellie had doubts and fears. My ego was already successful. She was who I wanted to be: a warrior.

I did already come equipped with a strong work ethic. When things got nasty with my parents, if I wasn't running, I would go hang with the horses, brush them, and clean their stalls to work away my frustrations and anger. No one loves to shovel horseshit, but the effort made me feel better afterward, released my frustrations, even if I didn't get thanked or recognized. I recognized my efforts within myself. This was the same work ethic I brought to training. And some of Coach's training principles were as repugnant as cleaning horse stalls.

I detested his arrogance. He was constantly berating us, demanding from us and rarely did we get any praise for our efforts, which brought us closer together, like it was us against him. Was this his plan? Our long runs were full of conversation in the beginning, but we always spaced ourselves out and went into our own heads to finish the run. Sometimes after training, we met at a local coffee place to discuss life at Evotech. I would grab a quick shower and Blue, arrive to a coffee waiting for me, and a bowl of water and cookie for Blue.

"Hey, Wild." We now shortened Wild Jack's nickname. "You got along for many years without a coach, and one of the reasons I joined this team is because you did. We all know Coach Rogers annoys the hell out of you. You could do this all yourself. So why are you here?" asked Boz.

"I love the torture," Jack replied with his typical one sentence answer, while characteristically pulling on his beard. He slouched down on the uncomfortable wooden chairs, pulling another over with his toe of his dirty trail shoe to rest his feet up on the seat. He dropped his hand and Blue walked into it knowing he would receive a scratch behind his ears. "I swear they put out the most uncomfortable chairs here, so we don't hang out all afternoon drinking one cup of coffee."

"I like Coach Lane and all the perks, you guys," confessed Annabel.

"Vell, it vas a dream come true for me. Zis latest project to design our own shoes according to vat ve like. Man, zat is very cool," Hans added. I could listen to him talk all day enjoying his strong German accent.

"The latest device I am not too happy about is the blue light nasal clip we have to wear for a few hours every night that is supposed to ensure we de-stress and get a deep sleep. That's a load of BS. That thing stresses me out, having to stick it up my nose," Tim pitched in a comment to which we all nodded in agreement.

"And screw the curfews and rules. I am the oldest here. It is frickin' demeaning to make me go to sleep and wake up at a certain time according to my *circadian rhythms*. And no Wi-Fi. Sheet, I can't work. Nor game," Rocky complained. He sat forward on the table. We all knew he had to detox from his gaming habits, and he was used to programming late into early morning hours. They analyzed his sleep patterns like all of us and gave us our own recipe for sleep. Most of us were not used to the stringent protocol set out by EVT. I couldn't help but think Rocky wasn't going to last. He was living up to a new reason for his nickname of being a rocky character, despite his conservative, dad-like appearance. He might be the first one to go.

"I think it's a sweet gig, but Coach Lane is pure madness. He draws a very close line between psycho and psychic," said Olivia. She and I weren't the only ones feeling that way. I looked over at Boz, and he nodded, eyes staring out to nowhere as he ran his hand through his brown curly hair as if in some faraway world of his own.

"For me, it is de discipline, ya. To haf a mission to accomplish, ya. Ve need to be pushed to go furder, test our limits. Zees all are de cutting edge of shtrategies fer training. Vel und of course, de supplements und food. All of dat is super, ya," said Hans. To hear undeniably the greatest European ultradistance runner voice such positive comments solidified the value of everything to me. The opportunity I had been given to dig inside the minds of these great athletes who were masters at their game was one of the greatest perks of being here.

"Vat about you, Giselle? You are so young and so much you have done vell. You now haf more pressure to perform. Can you handle dis? I see you being strong. Ya, you can do zee drills, zee distance, but can you handle dis pressure? Dis fame? How many followers do you haf now on de Instagram?" he asked because my account had grown the fastest since Evotech started their promotional social media accounts for each of us.

It was part of our contract to engage on social media and the EVT YouTube channel. Each of us shared personal marketers. Almost every training session, race or event had a few shots or videos posted. We had a media guy, Stanley, or Shtanly, as we had come to refer to him because of Hans. He was responsible for pictures and videos. We also had Agatha as a PR person in case we needed to make public appearances. We were supposed to approve everything before it got posted to sound as if we were posting, but that didn't always happen, to my dismay.

"Well, we all love the cleavage and leg shots of Giselle's. Man, girl, the last one was outstanding. I printed it and posted it on my wall," teased Tim.

"Ha! Zat is as close as you vill ever get, loser," quipped Hans as he flicked his hand against Tim's chest, which caused him to spill some of his coffee. The cafe was owned by EVT, so all the coffee was organic and tasted pretty good, but still stained clothing.

"I hate it all," I replied, completely embarrassed to be seen this way—for my body and not for my accomplishments.

"Hey, we know, and they are tasteful photos, Ellie. They aren't sexual," Olivia spoke up to support me and help me feel better. "I wish my shots were as hot as yours."

"See this is what I don't like. I don't like the comparisons. Women are the worst. We look at another woman and either want to be like her or we try to find fault, so we can feel better about ourselves," I surmised.

"No worries, Ellie. I feel good about myself and my age. I love being thirty-two because I struggled in my twenties, feeling uncomfortable in my own skin. Not saying that is you right now. I mean, look at what you have already accomplished. It's just that I truly feel content and wiser. I was still maturing in my twenties. Can you understand that?" Olivia wondered.

I smiled and nodded, wanting to be like her but knowing that maturity was earned. I still had a way to go.

"I am shtill growing up, ya, and so is Jake. He is forever thirteen," quipped Hans. He was on his usual mission to tease each of us.

"I get what you mean, Ellie," responded Annabel, who was sitting back and listening, sipping on her EVT latte, never setting it down on the table for fear Hans would bang down on it to accentuate certain words. "I am only a couple years older than Ellie. But, Ellie, darling, you are tall, beautiful, and a perfect poster girl for EVT and multiculturalism with your Aboriginal background, and that is cool. You have to accept it. I am more butch. I scare the guys completely!"

We all laughed because Annabel was one tough and intimidating girl. We didn't feel her name suited her, so we started to call her Steamboat Annie, thanks again to Hans, and she loved it. She only came up to my shoulders and looked more like an MMA fighter than an ultrarunner, but she sprinted the hills like a mountain lion, and if one saw her coming, I'm sure it would run out of her way.

"Come on, Giselle, I hear you get a marriage proposal every day," teased Jeep as he peered over his John Lennon–type glasses at me.

"And Tim's marriage proposals are all from ze gay community," quipped Hans, never one to miss an opportunity. "You know vit his long lovely locks, earrings, and jewelry. Geez even I vould date you, dude."

"Bro, you're creeping me out," snipped Boz.

"At least I get marriage proposals," quipped Tim.

"That is not very politically correct. What's wrong with a marriage proposal from the same sex? Ironman too macho to have gay competitors or followers?" Olivia teasingly nudged Boz.

"Crap. You know I'm teasing, but sorry guys, I would rather be on a poster in a girl's room over a guy's room. It might be politically incorrect, but I am sure a gay guy would rather have his poster up in a gay guy's room, right Jake?" Boz pointed his thumb in Jake's direction.

"Hey, you keep me out of this conversation. I am happily married to a beautiful woman. I am just sitting here minding my own business. And who has posters in their rooms anymore," Jake wondered while stretching his arms as he leaned back in his chair.

"I'd put a poster of Alex in my room," I pitched in. Everyone nodded in agreement, including the guys.

No matter what they thought, losing my privacy bothered me. I offered my thoughts again. "I think for the most part, we all love the sport of distance running because we love to be alone. And now amassing thousands of followers watching your every move, asking questions, making comments, good and bad, I don't know how celebrities do it. It bothers me and some comments more than others, especially if they come from one or two people constantly like they are stalking me. But Shtanley and Agatha say not to worry, and Alex is chomping at the bit to practice his martial arts on someone real."

"They are not shtalkers, Ellie. Zey are fanatics, hence the origin of the vord 'fan,'" Hans informed me.

"Well, I think I have some 'shtalkers' in my fan base." I nodded and slapped my thighs to accentuate my frustration.

"Just turn it off Ellie. Don't look at that BS," piped up Rocky.

I sat there and pondered, if I did that, how would I know what was going on in the world? How would I defend myself? Maybe he was right. I had to let it go and focus on the things that mattered.

We kept jawing back and forth about training and life at Evotech. I loved these get-togethers because this was when we could truly bond. We didn't often get the opportunity to share our stories during training. We had to concentrate on output, not input as Coach Lane would say. These guys had become my family, but I did miss my parents terribly. I would never admit it to anyone other than Blue. He understood completely.

Chapter 20

Trip Home

Holy terror, Ellie, are you a sight for sore eyes! What a terrible trip. I got jostled, bounced and knocked around, stuck in a dark, cool belly of the big bird next to other dogs, one of which would not shut up for the entire time we were there, then a few others started in, and I had to suffer through the worst canine choir on earth. How could you do this to me? So happy to see you. Where are we? This place smells familiar. Oh, I get to stretch my legs. Hang on. Where can I pee? Wait! What do you mean wait? Now. OK. Ah. Is that Dad and Mom? Oh, it is so good to smell you. Mom, you smell like soup, and Dad, you smell like diesel. Ellie, we are home.

"Ellie, you are a different person. You walk differently. You stand differently. You look so strong. Are you on steroids?" Mom asked.

"No, Mom, nothing we take is against the rules set out by the World Anti-Doping Agency. Dr. Chilton would never jeopardize our health or careers. It's not like that. We just train really, really hard mixed with days off. Everything is controlled. They can tell if I am overworked. That is why I am here, to rest a little more. I have a hundred-mile race in two weeks, remember?"

"Oh, Ellie. No matter what, we are proud of you. And it is so great to see our little buddy Blue," my dad chimed in. He scratched Blue's fur around his scruff and pushed his ears forward, egging Blue on to play with him. He had driven in to stay at the house, so we could all see each other together. I was so happy to be home with them. It seemed like a lifetime ago when I was trying to get away from them.

"Well, you are the talk of the town." Mom set plates heaped with food on the table. Nothing has passed the OK from EVT. I was sent with containers full of food, but I couldn't bear to tell her, as it would break her heart. I gave in to her delicious farm-fresh cooking. I reasoned she knows what she is cooking; she got me this far.

"Every time I go to town, someone asks about you, even complete strangers. Look what my friend Emily did for me." She pulled out a framed magazine cover of the EVT ultra team. We were in our running gear, sitting or standing on boulders with mountains in the background. The unusual detail about the photo was the huge fake mainframe computer with EVT letters boldly visible. It was set off to the side and slightly behind us. Each of us had a thick black cable linking each of us to the computer. The header said *Science and Human Endurance*.

I knew about the article that only hinted about the latest technology we were using and the studies being conducted. I thought it was more for academics and not lay people, so I was surprised to see my mother had a framed cover given to her by a friend.

"Do you have the article? I would like to read it. They didn't give me a copy. When did this come out?" I asked.

"Oh, I received this picture about a month ago. I think I asked you about it, but you were probably too preoccupied to remember. I do have the actual magazine here somewhere. I will find it for you," replied my mom. Without me there to tidy up, the house was a mess of stacks of magazines, boxes of jars, labels, scattered papers, and unopened mail.

I returned my eyes to examine the photo. We all have a determined expression on our face with no smiles. I relived the photograph session for my parents. "None of us could be serious that day. I think we just finished a tough training session on the track, and you know when you are too exhausted to care and someone says something silly, one person giggles, and then that starts a train reaction. Exhausted laughter. It was so difficult to get those straight sober faces, because the guys kept cracking jokes like, "Jake don't pee because you will give us all a shock." I laughed at the memory, but it was lost on my parents.

"None of these guys have a personal interest in you?" my mother blurted rather blatantly.

"No, Mom, not at all. We are too focused, too tired, and it is against the terms of our contract. We could get fired," I strongly clarified.

"Oh, thank God, Ellie," she sighed. "You look so beautiful in the photo. You stand out from the other two girls. They are lovely too. But you are so striking, and everyone has noticed."

I rolled my eyes in embarrassment, like she was making something out of nothing, but she was not one to give out compliments freely.

"I know I'm your mom, but I notice these things, and they have been pointed out to me as well. You have lots of admirers. Be careful, Ellie. Choose wisely."

My dad nodded in agreement, "Just lovely. You have changed Ellie. You have matured in only a few months and look like you are ready to go to battle. Keep your focus. No boyfriends until we can meet them."

"Oh, Dad," I whined, teasing him. "There are no boys who interest me. I am too busy training and sleeping. Blue is the only male in my life besides my coach, my trainer, Alex, the team and the mad scientists." With the mention of his name, Blue sat up to listen for his next command.

"Honestly, Dad. I can say I do feel exactly like a warrior. I have this mental thing going on. I have my Warrior Princess defeat my Pivotal Governor."

They both tilted their heads and furrowed their brows in confusion. "Never mind, it's hard to explain," I digressed.

The visit was entirely too short for two days, but I did get a chance to relax and catch up on local gossip. Soon Blue and I were on a flight back to Evotech headquarters for some mental training and then off to the race location. On the flight back, I took the opportunity to read the article that was full of scientific jargon, except one takeaway:

I was indeed a subject in a scientific study. Subject number eight. It never addressed any of us as individuals. They discussed us as objects identified by sex, race, competitions, heart rate, DNA, blood tests, and various other markers. Do they not care about the human inside? I had to let this thought go. This race was my first real test and no matter the stakes they had in the game, I had far more. I had set a record without them, now they were anxious to see how much better I was with the science, and I felt a lot of pressure to measure up. Thankfully, I could count on Blue to distract me. They needed to add how dogs help athletes stay calm into their scientific studies.

Blue came with me to all my races as part of my special contract with EVT, thanks to Dad's "two-bit" lawyer. I couldn't bear to leave him after all the training we did together. He was my emotional support when I needed it most.

Chapter 21

Meditation

I wait for the blender to stop making that obnoxious sound, and I check the floor for anything she dropped. A little blue ball rolls across the floor. I chase it down. Gone, down my throat. I come back sniffing for more and lick her ankle for good measure, which produces the giggle I love so much. She pours stuff into a glass, drinks it down quickly and off we go.

Ellie is different this time. There is a change in her. I sense she feels like I do when I dream of other lives. Her body is moving lightly like it is flowing. She moves like a breeze through the trees. We walk step by step together. I feel no need to smell anything. I am not curious about what lies outside this little world containing only the two of us. I am more intrigued by the vibrations coming from within her. Time seems to disappear. This is the same feeling I know so well—the incredible escape from this time and place when we feel like we are in a dream while wide awake.

She is talking to herself about her future. It feels strange to be from her past while she is discussing her future. Like Dad said about déjà vu — the paper that symbolizes time is folding over and over for an infinity and caught in the creases are memories of the past and glimpses of the future. Some parts of both I hate, but I have no choice. I cannot stop the future from happening. I must stay strong and readied for battle.

The team had spent a few days at headquarters meeting with a renowned meditation specialist, Dr. Norman Ross, who uses meditation to help people heal themselves from various medical issues from MS to depression and to help others, especially athletes, believe they can accomplish superhuman feats. I was skeptical, but after three days of learning his technique, I was demystified and able to make some personal breakthroughs, overcoming trying to control things and over analyzing everything. He measured our brainwaves while we were imagining and feeling ourselves as our future selves, with no connection to the present. We were all familiar with this line of thinking. Now we were fine tuning our thoughts. The meditations focused on all the elements we want in our future selves including emotional, physical and mental. It was not enough to merely think or envision it, but we had to feel the vibrations, smells the scents, see the sights, speak the words aloud and think the exact thoughts of our future selves. We had to talk to each other as if we were already living our future.

For part of the meditations, I had to create a mind movie of symbols and images as if I was living my future self, right now. Dr. Nathan wanted us to go deep into ourselves to focus on what we wanted and that meant sitting quietly for a few hours, alone. I was holding back by rationalizing my thoughts. But when I let go even a little, there started a feeling like a fire burning deep inside of me that traveled through my body from my fingertips and toes to the top of my head. It felt like I was transforming and moving away from any fears I had—this was all coming from so deep inside of me, like I was in another time and place. But yet I was fearful of this new sensation. Dr. Nathan assured me my true self was trying to make a breakthrough and not to try to think of it logically, but to let it happen. It was my future self being created.

"Stop holding on to what you perceive as reality is only the present, because Ellie, your reality is not this now. Allow your positive, capable future to come to you and pull you into itself. Do not combine your past with your present as that is not your life going forward. Magic happens when you create and experience your future vibrations as if it is already happening. You might call it a dream or a vision, but it must be thought of as your reality. You no longer have to suffer with past emotions when you experience the future of all you desire in yourself as if it is happening now. Trust me. You know how to positively visualize—that is just your success reaching back to you. Your brain doesn't know the difference between the past and the future—it only knows now. You can convince your brain that your future is now."

Dr. Nathan was talking with such conviction that I felt his energy, and he made my body shiver and the hair on my arms stand up. I tried to let go, but my fears kept hovering in place like smoke over a fire. I needed a good wind to blow them away.

Dr. Nathan said the goal was for us to practice this special meditation daily, sitting, walking, or running. As I walked with Blue, I created a movie screen all around us, like a 4D IMAX theater. We were walking through images symbolizing the future me, and I triggered all the emotions that went along with those images. I envisioned running strong, overcoming the pain and fatigue. I was standing on a podium collecting my first-place finisher's award. I could actually live it, feel it, hear the sounds of the crowd cheering for me. My parents with a look of pride, standing side by side, my mother grabbing on to my father with excitement.

As I walked with Blue, I became my alter ego, my warrior self. I felt superhuman and powerful. I did not see Blue as just a dog, but my fellow warrior. We were both on a mission hunting for our future successes and slaying what stood in our way. My meditation pulled him into this moving mind movie. I knew he felt it too. As I saw and walked into my true future self, I wondered while glancing down at my little buddy walking beside me, head up and forward like a lion king, who was Blue's future self?

Chapter 22

One-Hundred-Mile Triple Peaks

I flew up north to compete in a race called Triple Peaks 100, situated in the northern Rockies. The race organizers tried to cover the difficulty with a simple name that says it all. If you survived, you got a belt buckle with the three distinct mountain peaks we ascended and descended during the race. This race was a qualifier for my ultimate dream race, The Northern Lights 200, a two-hundred-mile race I would do later in the year. Triple Peaks was a difficult race with an elevation gain of over 30,600 feet over one hundred miles and forty-eight hours to complete it. The final leg of the course, we had to cross a large river called Hell's Gate, to reach the finish. I had to time my run to get to the small barge as it departed, every twenty minutes. If I missed it, I must wait at the aid station until the barge returns, losing precious time.

There would be an EVT support crew at each checkpoint to replenish supplies and offer support, including this checkpoint, so getting there with enough time to fuel up and rest was crucial. Jake would be running with me as my pacer for the last twenty miles, starting at the Hell's Gate checkpoint. There were no rules in this race about a dog running any of the legs so Blue would join Jake. We just had to get us all on the barge at the right time.

During the few days of tapering, I found little pains in different areas of my body, when I was supposed to feel fresh, and I had a headache that wouldn't go away. I was over stressing myself emotionally and reacting physically. I was starting to have doubts of my capabilities. As a result, EVT sent a package that was waiting in the hotel room. The label read somatostatin inhibitor, gamma butyric acid, magnesium, melatonin and valerian root and some other things to take before bedtime. I wondered how this formula would magically provide the courage I needed.

I knew the route by heart after studying the map and satellite videos provided to me plus information from Jake. He had won the race last year. It still didn't make me feel better. I felt like I was writing a final exam, and I didn't know any of the answers.

I turned to Jake, who simply reminded me, "Ellie you are at the point of no return. You will either do it, or regret not doing for the rest of your life. Fear is normal. You must trust in your training and have faith that all you have done is enough, because it is. You have no other option other than to give it all you got. You control only what you can and everything else will fall where it may."

I checked and rechecked my list of things I needed to take. I went through my meditation with my halo headset, which took me into a theta state of mind while listening to beats resonating at one thousand megahertz, as Dr. Ross instructed. I visualized my legs as powerful and full of energy, and my demeanor as calm and happy. All this had been part of my training for weeks. It was still not easy for me to slip into a Zen-like state in which I could picture the race going exactly as planned. I had spent a lot of time practicing this form of meditation, yet my body and mind still felt the prerace jitters.

I woke up at six, excited and feeling rested, thanks to the concoction they sent, ready to start in three hours. I had my rituals or habits. Everything had to be done in order with no deviations. No reason other than to tell my subconscious mind everything was going as planned. This strategy never let me down for a race and helped me get things done in everyday life.

EVT staff had prepared three boiled eggs, a whole avocado, oatmeal with berries with a special powder mixed in organic coconut milk. My race kit had been specially designed with fabric that measured practically everything possible going on in my body from simple things to advanced – measuring stress levels, blood oxygen levels and utilization, muscle fiber health and very importantly, how my body utilized energy such as fat and glycogen to let them know what I needed to eat and when, plus other data I would never truly understand. All this technology was built into my clothing worth thousands of dollars. There was a computer somewhere that knew more about me than I would ever care to know. They kept all the data to form an analyzed and condensed summary of all my biological functions, so for the next race, they could dial it all in to perfection. They probably knew not only how long I would last in this race at a certain pace but also how long I would live and the probability of what I would die from.

"Isn't this kind of cheating, Dr. Chilton?" I had asked when they first gave me the clothes and gadgets to wear.

"All we are doing is reading exactly the information your body supplies. If you need more electrolytes, we will know. If you need more sleep, we will know. If you need more water, a different shoe, a stronger core, relaxation techniques, a laxative, hey we will be reading what your body tells us and will fix anything we can. It is all legal. At least so far," he teasingly affirmed.

So here I was all decked out in the latest technology that kind of freaked me out. Could they read my mind as well? I took my watch off its charger and put it on. It immediately displayed I needed to hydrate. "Oh boy. Here we go, Blue. I am already in trouble."

Ellie has dressed with those strange noises coming from her body again. She hums and buzzes at a frequency only I can hear. They don't sound all the time, thankfully because that would drive me crazy. Oblivious to it all, she is a bundle of talking and singing this early morning before the sun lights the day. We arrive at a meeting place with other humans who are equally vibrating but not on her frequency, most vibrate with anticipation and nervousness. Alex and Jake are both here. I am sneezing nonstop because Alex's scent is overpowered

with spices. He is fawning over Ellie more than normal. There are other people here from Ellie's pack. They are giving her things and taking things away.

She bends down to give me a tight hug and lots of kisses so I give her a juicy lick across her mouth. She squeals, wipes her mouth, tells me she will see me soon, and turns to walk away. After some off-key singing from the crowd, which does not entice me to howl along, and a loud bang that does scare me into a sneezing and barking frenzy, we watch her and the pack of running humans take off with the sun only hinting at its existence behind the dark storm clouds. I know Ellie loves a turbulent sky, so this is a good sign. I don't see her again until waiting through the darkness and before light comes again.

We are waiting beside a wide and angry river. Jake is with me, talking to another person who has a box with lights, and they keep pointing to it. I think it is the box full of humans. Maybe Ellie is in there, but I can smell her coming from somewhere else. I try to tell them she is not in there. Soon enough Jake attaches my backpack filled with my treats to my back, and I cannot contain my excitement. There are loud cheers erupting all at once, and I hear Ellie's footsteps even though I cannot see her. She is only a bouncing light in the distance.

Here she is! She immediately sits and talks slowly and quietly. I smell her legs and take a lick of the salt and dirt. I can hear the blood flushing through her veins and her heart as it thumps, causing each flush. She sounds like the rushing river beside us. Jake talks calmly, almost in a whisper, and it slows down her heart. Ellie sits with her head back for a few minutes, slumped low in the folding cloth chair. I think she has gone to sleep, but comes back alive with a jolt. She eats something and tries to share a bit with me. I am too excited to eat. I want to get going. Time for us to run together like always.

She gets up a little unsteady, and we head for a boat that is violently yanking the ropes that secure it to shore. I struggle to hop on and Ellie has trouble keeping her balance and needs help. She finally gets on and sits with a heavy sigh. We make our way across the turbulent river. I try to balance on all four legs, shuffling constantly as I am tossed back and forth. Jake keeps me from falling over by tucking me tight in between his legs, while also holding on tightly to Ellie. When we get to the other side, she vomits all she has eaten previously. No problem, I eat it all up while she moans at me and wipes her mouth. What can I say? I am a scrounger.

We run much slower than normal. The sun is rising from behind the mountains in the distance and Ellie does not say a word. I can hear her labored breathing, but her pace is a nice rhythm I can match. We become one entity as we run close together, and I try to give her all my energy. After a while she sits down on the path and takes her shoes off to rub her feet. Jake gives me some water. I sense a deep emotion coming from her heart. I lick her toes. She giggles and lets me continue cleaning each toe on each foot, I taste blood. I do my best to help clean, and she takes out materials from her pack to put on her feet, puts on her socks and shoes, and we are off again.

I do not venture off to investigate the surrounding smells. I sense this is a desperate time for her. She trips and almost falls so I stay near offering my body should she need it, but Jake is stronger. His voice is calm when hers rises with emotion. He talks almost nonstop, telling stories and even singing, which makes Ellie laugh. I would try to sing but my tongue is practically dragging on the ground.

I smell traces of humans, but they are still a distance away. I start to lead a little quicker as she follows close behind. She tells me faster or to slow down, and I obey. I keep the same pace as her as I listen to her breathing and footsteps. Jake and I take turns leading the pace. There are some sharp descents and immediate ascents with rocks that cause her to shout out in pain. I feel an urgency to get to an end where she can stop this pain. I don't know where it is and how long this run will take so I do not complain. I am her General. I fear this is a battle we must fight until the last man is left standing.

After one more water stop, which takes her longer to get up while I encourage her with barking, we later approach an opening in the trees and a pathway that turns on to a road lined with small groups of people. They scream and jump as we pass by. Ellie's pace quickens, and I no longer lead but move back beside her with Jake on the other side. Off in the distance I can hear music and see a blur of humans moving *about. Ellie tries to quicken her step and moans with the effort but does not back off. We move steadily closer to a crowd held back by a fence surrounding a chute we run through to a pack of humans waiting for Ellie. They are clapping and howling, so I bark and howl to join in. A big bowl of water appears, and I lap it up quickly before returning to Ellie's side as she is led by Jake and sits gently in the chair provided. I pant and lay down to lick my paws. I get pets and belly rubs as I lay on the ground, exhausted. Everyone acknowledges my great accomplishment. That is the hardest run I ever done.*

Chapter 23

Podcast

"Find what you love to do, Ellie, and find a way to make money at it," my dad used to say. But why does it have to be such a tortured love? Running is a love-hate relationship. In the middle of it, I hate it. When I am finished, I am in ecstasy from relief. My mother used to say that about her sex life with my dad. I had no idea what she meant, only that she confused me completely.

Funny the random thoughts that come to my mind. They are even scarier out there, when I can barely put one foot in front of the other, too far from the beginning and not close enough to the end. Nowhere to go but forward. I keep going because I know it will all eventually end, and that feeling is like no other. The further the run, the harder the effort, the more joyous and satisfying is the end.

I never run with that purpose of setting a record. I run to learn how much my body can endure. As it happens that during Triple Peaks, I was able to endure just a bit more than the men and women who followed me. My efforts set a new course record that catapulted me into recognition, not only in the ultrarunning world but in the running and fitness world in general. All my social media accounts and the Evotech website had a record number of hits and increased my fan base by thousands.

The attention sat uneasy with me. I felt more uncomfortable with the media and fans than I felt at mile ninety-nine. I would run one hundred miles to avoid being interviewed, but I had obligations to Evotech to discuss my race. Thankfully, they supplied a PR person,

Agatha, who coached me on what to talk about and how to speak in public. I am comfortable with pain, but speaking to an audience was way outside my comfort zone.

Ellie drops a box to my ear and tells me to listen. I hear her voice, coming from the box! What? I cock my head one way, then the other, and she laughs. How can she be in the box and next to me at the same time? There is another voice in the box too. I look up. "Nice human trick," I tell her. Not fooled. The voice has the box people smell. I try to listen to this little box. There must be a reason she is showing me her voice.

It is like torturing myself in another way, hearing my voice struggling to say anything meaningful through a slur of ums, ahs, and hesitations. How do I explain to the podcast host how I ran so well over one hundred miles, when the real story is it took years to run this race, and I ran one hundred miles a week just to train for it? I tell him how I regularly ran with my horses and with my dog, Blue. I don't tell him I used to run as far away as possible from the sounds of my parents' arguing. I didn't want to go that deep.

Rick Roque was an experienced endurance runner himself, but he was also an astute interviewer. He asked me what I was running from. I laughed at the question because he saw right into my soul when I thought I was always running toward something, but as I sat and thought for a moment, while bringing dead air to a live show, I realized I was and probably still am running away from something. But what? He got me bamboozled. I told him I simply like to run. Period. We both surmised I would probably run into some self-discovery one day.

We discussed my upcoming race, the Northern Lights 200. There was a prize purse of $12,000 for both top male and female to attract top runners. We talked about gender equality in this sport. I didn't find any chauvinism at all. We respect each other equally. I did find most men, outside of running, who don't know who I am, have no idea what to make of me when they find out I run for a living. Rick laughed, making me relax.

I explained we picked this race because during that time of year there was about seven and a half hours of darkness, and even then, if we were lucky, the northern lights would be a beautiful distraction during the night. The race was known for the aurora borealis, the elevation climb, treacherous trail and the weather. There would likely be snow and high winds at the highest elevation.

"What time do you think it will take you to finish?"

"The cut off is one hundred hours. I would like to finish within that time," I proposed.

"As an endurance runner, I get that, but I am sure Evotech wants you to set a course record again. Do you feel pressure from them?"

"No, I don't. They don't put pressure on me. My coach might because he likes to push all boundaries out past logical limits—emotionally, psychologically, physically. Just to the edge of destruction, then pull back. But that has nothing to do with EVT, I don't think. They do all they can to repair me after he tries to destroy me. It is a teeter totter, back and forth, and I try to balance in the middle and not fall off either way."

"You have Lane Rogers as your coach. Oh boy, he was tough when he was coaching the Olympic marathon team. I heard he is a demanding, demon of a coach. Sounds like a lot of pressure for your age."

"You could say that. There is a huge trust factor on both sides. He puts in the time with us, goes above and beyond a normal coach, I think. I mean, everything is above and beyond anything I have ever experienced."

"Don't you feel like you are relinquishing control? Don't you feel like you are cheating by using all this technology?"

"I want to see how far I can push my body. Ultimately, it is only me who can go the distance. Sure, energy-releasing running shoes can help save some fatigue, but after one hundred miles the reward gets seriously diminished. At a certain point, it becomes mental strength that overrules the physical fatigue. It is not only training, technology, and nutrition – it is mental training. It is about desire. My coach focuses on how badly I want something. If I can't tap into how badly I want it, I probably won't perform to my ultimate ability. I will perform only within the margins my mental vision allows me. Genetically, I am all geared up, they tell me. I have the right genes. The devices they attach to me only collect data to help me train better and zero in."

"What kind of training do you do to help the mental fatigue?"

"This was the hardest part of my training, without a doubt. Umm, well, I run on a treadmill and stare at a blank wall for hours and hours. I sit and watch mundane objects on a computer screen until my brain is so tired I can't think straight; then directly after I take an exam that requires extreme focus. I do this over and over again. They have me training my brain for endurance, as much as they train my body."

"I had no idea they would go that far. What do you think about when you are staring at a wall?"

"I learn to daydream really well. I, ah, try to create movies in my head, or think about what I would say during an interview, envision the future as I want it to be, sing songs, that kind of thing. But I can tell you, the military and the CIA all want to learn from us, and Dr. Chilton is holding all the data locked up, hidden away. I don't see the results unless it will help me to prepare for a race."

"Do you have time for anything outside of training? Do you spend time on social media? Last I checked, you had almost half a million followers on Instagram. How do you handle that?"

"Oh gosh. That many? Ah, I wish I could say I am actively posting, but I don't because number one, I don't have time so someone posts for me, and number two, I don't like the distraction. It is advertisement for EVT, to be honest. They do not want me to be affected by the posts, good or bad. I was getting caught up in the haters, the baiters who want to start in with me about something. It was bothering me, and EVT could tell, so they cut me off. They could see the psychological damage it was causing me. I was taking it too seriously."

"Wow. I would agree. I get caught up in it too when I look at show ratings, but I have learned to let it go. I think I have, anyways. Don't you think you should be learning techniques to resist the emotions the negative comments create? Rather than ignoring them."

"Oh well. I have to put things in perspective. I guess I feel a lot better if I am not exposed to negativity at all, because those comments pop into my head when I least want them. I guess it goes hand in hand with all the positive comments too. I could let all those compliments go to my head. There are a lot more of those, but it's funny how one negative comment can ruin a day. I could use it to fuel my fire, to prove something, but in the end, a lot of those people don't care. They want to bring me down to the level closer to them. Oops, that should bring in a few negative comments." I laughed. "I am not judging. But why do people want to start stuff? Uh, I must let that stuff go, and as far as a social life, I have been so focused on my training for most of my life. Um, people are super nice when they meet me, but you know, I keep pretty much to myself. My dog Blue is the closest to me. He's with me morning, noon and night. See, he is at my feet wondering when to attack you. Just kidding. He probably is the only one who truly gets me because he doesn't care if I'm smart, fast, fat, thin, fit or sick. He would love me no matter what."

"Don't you wish humankind were more like dog kind," Rick added, more of a statement than a question.

I slipped into my own world for a moment thinking about my relationship with Blue and how he was closer to me than any living soul. I apologized for daydreaming, and he made a joke about how Evotech's mental training was apparently working to be able to easily daydream, even during an interview. He had no idea how true that statement was. He asked about future races, and we ended on that note. It wasn't such a bad interview after all, I told Blue as we finished our walk. I knew he was proud. It was written all over his face.

Chapter 24

Faith

"Blue has taken to chasing squirrels that ran along the telephone wires. He seems to think there is a way he can get to them if he keeps jumping up at them," I huffed out to Jake between breaths as we ran. Just another random thought came to my mind as usual. We are usually paired together, but Jake is always faster than me. He can't be paired with anyone because he is the fastest runner on the endurance team. He trains with the sprinters regularly.

"They say dogs don't know the difference in size, as a little dog will challenge a big dog, so I imagine the perspective of height is something Blue doesn't understand as well," replied Jake, hardly out of breath.

"It's either that or he refuses to lose the battle against the squirrel, even if the squirrel isn't there. If I somehow lose him on a run, sure enough he has gotten distracted and is jumping around a tree with the squirrel long gone. He has conditioned himself to start jumping around a tree even if there isn't a squirrel for miles. He just imagines it is still there. Sometimes I feel like Blue, jumping around poles for no reason, likes running these repeats. I feel like Blue, chasing squirrels I can't see."

I forced out the words between breaths while we were on our last recovery lap before finishing the last of our ten by sixteen-hundred-meter repeats. We hit the start line and Jake took off. I was beyond exhausted, but I tried to get in his draft. We were not allowed to slow down and Coach was yelling profanities at me again but as always,

I used it as motivation to keep up to Jake. We finished and dumped our bodies on the infield grass in complete exhaustion. I couldn't move a finger if I wanted to.

"I guess I can say you run like a girl if the girl can catch you in the end. Hey, Jake?" Coach Lane tried to tease Jake as he grabbed one of my legs to give it a stretch as I moaned in pain. "You guys need to run a few cool-down laps."

"Hey Coach, that is normally politically incorrect to say, you run like a girl, but in this case, I take it as a huge compliment," suggested Jake as he slowly stretched his legs and we moaned in unison. "I am not running anymore. Sorry coach. I couldn't get up if you paid me."

"Hurrumff. You are being paid, dumbass. How's the hamstring, Ellie? I saw your stride was off." Coach never called me by my first name. He always called me D'Angelo. I wondered who he was talking to at first.

"Ah. Um. It can be a little tight and sore, like right now when you do that!" I winced at the pain shooting down the back of my leg.

"I am going to do a little active release right now before you do your cool down run. Relax, deep breathe and don't fight it," he instructed me. He felt around the back of my leg with a little pressure until I jerked back with pain, pressed harder with his thumb on the most painful part, and repeated stretching and bending my leg, while pressing in various spots that hurt, then he rubbed the muscle to ease the pain.

"You'll have to go see Maria for some more treatment after this. They will strap on that new contraption for muscle therapy that will fix this in a day, I hear," he added. We dutifully got up and ran a few easy laps to shake the cramps loose, then dropped back to the ground and continued stretching for another twenty minutes until Jake rolled over to give me a quick peck on the cheek and got up to head home to his beautiful wife. He was such a lucky guy.

"Ellie, get ready for some peak training coming up before you taper for the two hundred. How do you feel mentally? Your fitness is where it should be, but we can't see inside your head," said Coach returning to me after talking to some other athletes, all of whom were slowly shuffling out of the stadium, equally exhausted.

161

"I feel almost ready, I guess. I have a few more weeks to go of training that should give me more confidence," I answered as he helped me up from the ground. We were now alone as the other runners had made their way back to their cars.

Coach stepped in closer toward me. I found myself staring at his chest, noticing how his muscles were straining the material of his T-shirt. He was a lot bigger than the guys on the team who were lean and sinewy. Coach was more like a boxer compared to them. His proximity ruffled me in a way I couldn't explain. He looked down at me and gently lifted my chin upward with his finger, so he could peer into my eyes. I felt like I had been caught ogling. I was sure he wanted the gesture to feel almost fatherly, but it didn't come across that way to me. I looked up and noticed the smile lines around his gray eyes. When we held eye contact, I was surprised by the fluttering in my stomach. He was standing too close to me. This must be how it felt just before someone kissed you. He moved his hand from my chin to the top of my shoulder and squeezed while letting out a deep sigh as he looked up over my head into the distance. His hand felt surprisingly heavy on my shoulder.

"You are going to go to war, D'Angelo. And you are so young. The youngest female to attempt this race. You are going to meet demons, angels, and maybe even God out there, in whatever form your mind invents. You need to be mentally ready to fight, not the course but yourself. I know you are capable of going the distance and competing against others, Ellie, but are you capable of competing against yourself?" He looked back down at me to study my reaction.

This question sent doubt searing through my veins that landed like a clunk at the bottom of my stomach. I dropped my gaze and kicked at the blades of grass with my foot and wondered if he didn't believe I could do this, how could I believe in myself?

He gently lifted my chin upward again and stared into my eyes, while shaking his head back and forth. "Joan of Arc was fifteen when she led armies to battle. All the power you want is only limited by what you believe in yourself, and having any doubts or fears is normal right now. You should have some fear, because then you will not take this lightly. Fear and doubt are great training tools. Overconfidence can blind you. Fear will switch to courage when the time comes."

"Joan of Arc had God on her side," I offered. "What if I can't find the courage?" I challenged while studying his face, waiting for the answer until I felt uncomfortable watching him think.

"Do you believe in a higher power, Ellie? Do you believe there is a greater force that exists outside of yourself? Maybe it is something you can't define, but you never feel you are alone, especially in your darkest moments," he asked while moving his hand from my chin to push a strand of hair away from my face.

I thought about the times I was alone and felt fear. I recalled a memory of when I was about ten years old and had gotten lost far from home, deep in the forest. A fierce wind picked up and lightning struck a tree near me with such force and loud boom, I screamed in shock and my body froze in fear. The tree lit up in flames, but the subsequent sheets of rain quickly turned the flames to smoke. I became disoriented, not knowing which direction was home. The darkness changed everything in my surroundings, and I recognized nothing. This was before I got Blue.

I remember shivering beyond control as I was quickly drenched in rain while the wind whipped at me. The memory came alive in me, forcing me to shiver in the warmth of the afternoon sun. I prayed for the first time in my life on that day. We never went to church or prayed at home. My parents weren't religious in any sense. My father always complained about the hypocrisy of the church. My mother only talked about the guidance of her ancestors. That was the closest she got to believing in something beyond herself.

In the midst of my fear, at that moment, in the middle of that fierce storm, I felt as if two hands were pushing me against my back to go in a particular direction. A voice in my head told me to trust it, and I wasn't alone. It was as if a higher power, or God was not only with me but in me. I had to let go of my fear and be open to trust my own instincts. I wasn't alone because there was no way I could have felt that kind of power by myself.

"I don't know what scared you, but I can see you drifted away from me for a moment. Did you have to trust in something you couldn't see?" he asked, studying my face as if the answer were written there.

"I guess, when I needed the courage, I found it from somewhere. Maybe it was a higher power?"

"Go home and reflect on all the times you found something in yourself to move past whatever adversity you faced. Know what you felt was real. When you can't believe in yourself, someone, or some greater power, does believe in you."

He let go of me and stepped back to study my reaction, then nodded toward the parking lot, then walked me to my car. The lesson was over in his mind, but I was still a little shaken by my memory. I was trying to make sense of the memory mixed with the feelings I had right then. I didn't want him to leave me; I wanted him to touch my face again. I was instantly embarrassed by this out-of-nowhere silly thought.

"See you in a couple of days, Ellie," he said as he deposited me at my car. "You've got a long run out in the mountains. Remember to take your largest water pack. Hey, before I forget, I want you to pack this as well." He reached around into his gym bag he had slung over his shoulder. I was surprised when he pulled out a hunting knife in a leather sheath about five inches long. He unsnapped the clasp that held it secured and slid the knife out slowly, holding it up for me to see.

"I want you to have this with you whenever you train alone. I know we have all kinds of bells, whistles, and tracking devices attached to you, but nothing can take the place of a good hunting knife to handle a quick emergency when you are alone. I am saying, in case you get caught in a situation where you might need backup immediately, like a cougar or bear. Who knows the reason? I would feel better if you had this with you. Sorry, I am a little old school when it comes to protecting oneself."

I stared at the knife as he admired it in the sunlight. I didn't like it one bit. "But I have pepper spray, and I have run in the mountains alone for years and have never had an issue," I protested. "Well, OK, maybe one cougar, but I stayed back until he left the area. And some rattlers." I started thinking of the wildlife and relented, accepting the knife as he handed it to me to examine. It was surprisingly light, with a clear handle, coming to a point at its tip that tempted me to test for its sharpness, but thought better of it. I hoped I wouldn't hurt myself with it.

I objected, "What if I fall on it?"

"Ooff girl, that is not going to happen because it can't poke through its casing. But don't fall." He laughed as he leaned up against my car with his arms crossed. I could feel him watch me as I handled the knife. "This is the strongest and lightest there is and easy to use if you are panicked. Just pull it out and thrust it in. Don't think. Just do it. I keep one on me most of the time when I am out. Or I have my gun," he said as he crossed one leg over the other.

"You carry a gun?" I was shocked a man with his strength would need a gun.

"I am licensed to carry one, so don't worry. I was in the military, but that is another story. You are always at the mercy of your surroundings, so you need to be prepared. I don't take any chances. Now, go to see Maria for therapy so you are ready. And get in the hyperbolic chamber every night." He pushed off away from my car and opened my door for me, then closed it after I eased into my seat slowly on my tired legs. I watched him walk away. Maybe the military made him so fit. The idea of him carrying a gun and being in the military gave me a different feeling about him that I couldn't explain. He wasn't a runner. He was a fighter. He didn't seem like he would need to run from anything.

Chapter 25

Running Cold and Hot

My heart was pounding so hard; my ribs felt broken. The vibrations were making bile come up from my stomach into my mouth. I knew my legs were still there, even though they felt like tree stumps. The pain was gone because my muscles had been replaced with cement, and they were incredibly heavy. It was pouring rain, and I was soaking wet and shivering down to the bone while my teeth were chattering uncontrollably. It was the final hill of what felt like a hundred, the last of which I was slipping on the mud more than making headway. I had reached my breaking point. I kept thinking about what Coach had said. "D'Angelo, it is always lonely when you go that extra mile because no one has the drive and courage to go there." So I kept pushing to that extra mile. My legs were done, but I was too afraid to stop because I thought I might drop and roll into a ditch, get covered in mud, and out of sight to anyone passing by. That is exactly what happened.

"Ellie! Ellie! Ellie!" I heard someone calling. I must have dozed off or was daydreaming. I didn't know how much time had passed as I lay at the side of the road.

"What the...! What are you doing? What happened? Did you fall? I have been looking all over for you. You didn't come back down after I thought you would be finished. You are soaking wet. Why didn't you call me on your cell to come get you when this rain started?" It was Coach Lane. He had been giving me new supplies every three hours. I was late for the pick-up.

My cell. I forgot. Coach helped me up off the ground, and I took off my pack, which was dripping in mud. I didn't think of trying to keep my cell dry even though it was my lifeline on all my runs. I felt stupid and disappointed in myself, and started apologizing, but because I was so exhausted, the words came out slurred.

"I could see on the GPS tracker that you stopped and didn't start back moving. God girl, I didn't intend for you to push yourself to this point." Coach sounded exacerbated. I quickly lost the strength in my legs and slipped in the mud. "I have you. It's OK. Don't worry. I have you." He changed his mood quickly consoling me as he picked me up off the ground. I sensed panic in his voice.

I was being lifted and carried, while I kept apologizing, and he kept telling me it was OK. He held me tight to his chest to keep me warm, so I rested my head on his shoulder. When we got to his truck, he placed me inside the passenger seat, returned with a blanket, and started the engine to blast the heat. He reached over to push the hair away from my face, wiped my eyes and face dry and rubbed my shoulders, back and legs, moving me as if I was a rag doll. I felt lethargic only sensing what was happening yet couldn't seem to form words to say anything as my teeth chattered noisily in my head. He picked me up, pulled the both of us inside on the passenger seat, placed me on his lap, hugging me, rubbing my body, wrapping me up tight as I was shaking uncontrollably. We sat there huddled together in the heat of his truck.

After a while he slid me off his lap, "You are OK now. You stopped shaking. Jeez, girl. What am I going to do with you?" I was starting to realize the situation I had put myself in. He went around to the driver side and started to drive. I was in a cloud, a haze, and even though he urged me to drink some water, I wasn't thirsty. My mind wasn't functioning.

When we got to my apartment, Coach helped me find my keys and carried me straight into my shower, turned the hot water on, stuck me in with my clothes still on. I assured him I was OK enough to undress. He left, and I slowly scraped the muddy clothes off my body, struggling to bend over to take my socks and shoes off. Oh, what a mess I had created. My legs and back were stiffening up, and I could hardly stand upright. I stayed so long Coach had to come back to the bathroom to check on me. I yelled through the rushing water to assure him I was OK. He was concerned because the whole drive home, he kept apologizing for not checking on me earlier. He went on and on, constantly reaching out toward me, rubbing my legs. Part of me wanted to be back in his truck being held by him, the same man I despised for putting me in this type of pain in the first place. I must have lost my brain out there.

I gingerly stepped out of shower because every muscle in my body shut down. It was a struggle to towel off. I realized there were no clean clothes, which meant I had to go out in the hallway wrapped in only a towel.

"Ellie, are you OK? It's been about thirty minutes. Do you need help? What can I get you?" he yelled through the door.

"I'm OK, but I don't have any clean clothes here. I am going to go to my bedroom. I'm fine now. You can go home if you want." I stammered, straining to talk through the door.

"I will wait until after you eat something. Go change. I have soup here for you," he yelled back.

"Soup?" I was motivated to move, clutched the towel tightly around my body, and opened the door, promptly tripped right over Blue who was lying against it, as usual. I fell forward taking clumsy strides, trying to stop myself from falling and landed squarely into the chest of my coach. His arms gripped tightly around me and held me close.

"Oh my God, Blue," I said, embarrassed, my head pressed into Coach's chest. Blue had scooted out to the side and was standing, staring with his head tilted to one side.

I got steady on my feet, squeezing the towel between mine and Coach's body, too nervous to step away fearing I would lose grip of the towel, yet also strangely wanting to feel his arms around me. Coach eventually inched away allowing me to get a firm grip on the towel. I stepped back awkwardly, avoiding eye contact. I quickly assured him I was OK, turned and tippy toed to my bedroom in pain as my muscles were waking up from the unplanned stumble. I entered my bedroom and closed the door. Blue barked and pawed the door. Oh, damn Blue, always so concerned about me.

I struggled to find my woolen sweatpants somewhere in the bottom of my closet, a fluffy zip-up sweatshirt, and some gray wool farmer socks—my tried-and-true comfort clothes. I opened the door to find Blue guarding it again, but I was smarter this time and stepped over him. He stood up and muscled his way in between my legs.

"Not now, Blue. I can hardly walk as it is, so please leave me alone right now." He stopped his maneuver, walked to the kitchen and plunked himself down with a deep sigh with his head between his front legs, apparently with some sort of bug in his butt.

I entered the kitchen to find a bowl of steaming soup sitting on the breakfast bar waiting for me, then I realized something. "Oh, Blue! I forgot to let him out. Coach, could you please let him out to pee? Open the door and say, 'Go pee.' And when he is finished, call him back in. He will come."

He called Blue to the door, but he wouldn't move. He kept his head down as he moved his eyes from me to Coach and back and blinked a few times.

"Really, Blue? What is up with you? OK, fine, I will take you."

He reluctantly moved when I opened the door, in a clear effort to demonstrate his mood. I waited in the cool air with the door open. I started shivering again. It was coming from deep within. I wasn't sure if it was the cold or something else. Blue came back quickly and stayed by my side as I went back to eat, but the spoon was shaking in my hand so badly I dropped it with a clink into the bowl. Coach got up and grabbed a blanket to wrap around me, and I held it securely under my chin with both hands. He didn't take his eyes off me, making me uncomfortable. I could feel the warmth from the bowl of soup but made no effort to eat it. I wanted him to say something rather than stare at me. One male was moping and ignoring me while the other was uncomfortably attentive.

He slid his chair closer to me, took the spoon, and started to feed me. I let him because at that moment, I lost control of who I was. He opened his mouth as I opened mine when the spoon came close to my lips, just as parents do with their baby. We stared into each other's eyes as he fed me. I noticed how the gray surrounding his pupils turned into a dark blue at the outer rim. He blinked, and I looked away. We finished the bowl, and he moved it aside to wipe my mouth with his thumb. It lingered a bit too long over my lips causing a different type of shiver to occur deep within me. I noticed the pupils in his eyes growing larger.

"Your lips are no longer blue," he said. Blue got up and put his head on my lap. I was conflicted with relief and desire when his hand dropped away from my face. This was too intimate a situation between us.

"My whole body feels blue," I replied.

"You are quite the trooper, Ellie," he sighed. "You amaze me," he continued as he reached around behind me to pull my chair in between his open legs. He rested his hands on the back of my chair, with his arms rubbing against mine while continuing to stare at me. I felt lightning race through my stomach followed by blood rushing to my face. I was sure he could hear my heart beating. I finally felt hot. I reached to pet Blue, nervous and confused at the feelings he was conjuring up inside of me.

He put his hand under my chin, and lifted it up and focused on my lips, then my eyes. I heard him take deep breaths in and out. I captured my own breaths deep inside, afraid to make a sound. I watched his eyes as he noticed a water droplet I could feel, trickle down from a wet strand of hair along my cheek. It trickled down, caught the top of my collarbone and rolled further down in between my breasts. My reflexes made me tremble.

I had to look down, afraid of what I would see in his eyes. I could feel his breath on my forehead. He made me feel something in my body in ways I had never felt before. His lips lightly touched my forehead. It sent a vibration down my spine I hoped he wouldn't notice. I wanted to feel his lips on my mouth but instead, it was a fatherly kiss.

"OK, Miss. Off to bed with you. Take this recovery drink with you," he said as he handed me a bottle, then wrapped his arms around me before lifting me from my chair. He carried me to my bed, sat me down, pulled back the covers, so I could get underneath, and covered me up. I became flustered with myself for feeling so strange toward him. I rationalized it was some sort of gratefulness for rescuing me and being so gentle with me. He tucked me in and turned toward Blue who was hovering protectively at the edge of the bed.

"Come on, boy. Let me find you something to eat. I got him looked after, Ellie. You get some sleep right now, OK? You are feeling better, right? Anything else I can do? I am going to stick around, if you don't mind. I feel guilty for doing this to you," he announced.

"Thank you. No, it was my fault. Don't worry. I am OK. It was a great lesson for me," I suggested.

He turned off the lights and closed the door behind him. My mind was whirling with questions and my heart was whirling with emotions. I kicked off the covers because I was heating up from the inside out.

OK he brings her in destroyed. He broke my Ellie. Why can't she walk? Why is she wet and dirty? The only difference is him. Her, alone, is normal. New male, and she is damaged. I am mad. What is going on? What do you mean get out? Who do you think you are, buddy? This is my girl. Not yours. OK. Fine. I will guard the door. Can you hear me, Ellie? Boom against the door—yep, that is me. I am here. I will wait right here ready to save you.

I opened my eyes and immediately became aware of a warm body next to me. The room was the usual EVT-mandated blackout. My stomach came alive with butterflies as I remembered the night before and being put to bed by Coach. I didn't want to reach my hand around to explore. I was afraid of what I would find. I ran through all the events in my head, from the day before. What was the last thing that happened? Nothing was coming to mind. Could it be him beside me? I listened for breathing. I didn't hear anything, but I definitely felt the warmth of a body up close against mine. I was sure I was going to wake him with my heart beating so loud. Would he have slept here to watch over me? Why not sleep on the couch? Was he that worried about me? Is there something going on between us? I laid there as quietly as possible, thinking on what to do next. I really had to pee. I couldn't wait any longer. I quietly slid off the bed and glowed my watch through the darkness to find the door. I left a crack open in the door and tiptoed to the bathroom.

I looked like crap when I saw my reflection. I yanked a brush through my matted hair a few times to try to look presentable. I went to the kitchen and made a pot of coffee rather than a cup. I heard some movement, a small thump, padding on the floor, and the shaking sound of Blue with the jingle of his collar and tags. He came sauntering into the kitchen and did his usual stretching routine, sat and swept the floor with the wag of his tail.

"Oh no, was that you beside me on the bed? Seriously? You know my rules. What is up with you?" Once again, I couldn't figure out what my mind or heart or something was conjuring up between Coach and me.

Blue opened his mouth to a big smile and panted. I smiled back with a huff, and he came toward me, wagging his body. I grabbed his leash, my coat, boots and cap, and took him outside. I felt tightness in my legs, but not as bad I thought it would be. The walking and fresh air made me feel so much better. We took a walk around the park, and I chastised myself for my delusionary thoughts. He wouldn't have slept over in my bed, you foolish girl. So why do I wish he had? "What is going on with me, Blue?" He was busy sniffing away, with a happy-go-lucky attitude. Much happier today than yesterday.

I returned to training after a couple of days off and a myriad of EVT recovery therapies as mandated by my bio-info EVT collected on all their devices. I was given extra supplements and spent time going in and out of treatments, special muscle wraps, and massage machines. I was exhausted recovering from the recovery treatments.

I was nervous about seeing Coach Lane, again. The memories of him touching my face and the embarrassment thinking he would stay over to watch me made me feel foolish. I did take extra time to put myself together in the morning, knowing full well what I was doing. He was my coach, and I had hated him so why was I so attracted to him? I couldn't focus. I couldn't train. I avoided him.

"D'Angelo wait up!" I was headed back to my car after a short training session when I heard Coach calling me. "You didn't talk to me. You didn't even look my way. Are you mad at me?" He ran up beside me.

"I'm fine." I tried to say the words as nonchalantly as possible to hide my absurd excitement at seeing him. "You know, I just wanted to be a good girl and do all my training. It's only two weeks away Coach. The big event," I tried to stay in control. I couldn't look at him for fear my feelings would jump out of my heart and leave me standing stripped bare. Please don't touch me.

He took me by the shoulders, and I stiffened up. Seeing this, he released me. "Ellie, please don't be mad. I don't know why you are, but honestly I want you to feel great. I mean, I know I was hard on you, and I don't want you to hate me. There has got to be trust between us." I studied the grass beneath my feet.

"Oh, Ellie," he whispered ever so smoothly, making my heart miss a few beats. When I glanced up at him, he cocked his head to the side and studied me, searching my eyes for something I was hiding. He thought I was mad at him, but I was afraid of the feelings he conjured up inside of me.

"Come on, let me take you for coffee, something warm." He put his arm on my back and turned me toward the parking lot.

I don't know what my body was thinking while walking beside him when my brain was saying this was not a good idea right now. I needed to stay away from him and focus on my race. These feelings were a distraction.

"No, I can't go. We are OK. Really, Coach, I need to focus. I feel distracted ... I ..." I trailed off as my mouth was about to betray my common sense.

"Am I a distraction to you, Ellie? How? Come on. We need to plan. Look, I'm sorry for pushing you so hard." He held up his arms, then dropped them to his side.

"No, Coach. No, I am OK. It is not you. I pushed myself. That is what I do. You know, especially. Everything is OK between us. Really. I should be talking to Jake, who will be pacing me." I nodded toward Jake who was walking toward us, and Coach Lane turned around.

"OK, Jake," he waved him over. "She is all yours. You two plan your course of action. I trust you. But if you need anything, Ellie, I mean anything, please let me know. I will be there for you." He reached toward me. I became angry that he had to touch me again. I could feel it linger on my arm when Jake walked up. Coach was looking at me with concern, his head tilted as if he discovered something. His eyes locked with mine, then quickly looked away.

"Hey!" said Jake as he sauntered up. "Strategy meeting here and now?"

There was a brief uncomfortable silence until Coach and I both glanced at each other again and then turned away as fast as possible. He knew. I knew he knew. And now I assumed Jake knew too. I felt like a neon light blinking "Ellie has a crush on Coach!"

"OK, this looks serious. Coach, I heard you tried to kill our dear Ellie, and she is mad, clearly. But, Ellie, girl, we got this. I will keep him away from you and put you on strict orders to start tapering." He stared at me misinterpreting my demeanor. "Whoa, she really is pissed at you," he said to Coach Lane.

"She is all yours, Jake, and she is in fine hands. I trust you both. Let me know if I can help. Yes, I tried to kill her, and she survived. Now she will survive anything life throws at her if she can survive me." With that, he threw me a sideways glance, turned, shoved his hands in his pockets, and headed toward his car.

"Oh, tension between coach and athlete. Hey, little sister, no worries. You are going to kick ass, and if not, I will kick your ass." He nudged me in a teasing way. "All OK?"

"Yes," I said clearly and stood up tall and pulled my shoulders back. "I am totally OK. There is nothing between us. It was the best thing that could have happened to me. I showed him, and I will show everyone what I am made of. I am no skinny weakling. I am made of something stronger than I even realize." I nodded, crossing my arms for added effect.

"You got this girl. This race is yours." Jake wrapped his arm over my shoulder and walked me to my car. "Tomorrow a strategy meeting. I have notes ready to share with you. Since it's your first two-hundred-miler, we need to strategize every detail. It will be fun," he said as he rubbed my back vigorously. I felt his excitement mix with my fear but tried to keep it at bay because I operated much better living in the moment, not thinking about the immensity of the task ahead. We would plan each detail for this race, but in the end, I must only consider one moment at a time, not over hours, but over days.

Chapter 26

Prerace

Sneeze, sneeze, and sneeze once more. I have gotten groomed by Hilda, the Swedish wrestler. There was no way I could get away from her. She tackles hard and fast. I was soaked, bubbled up, scrubbed and drowned again before being blow-dried by a noisy, whiny handgun from hell, then brushed by the pokey thing from heaven. Pleasure and pain coming from the largest paws I have ever seen on a human. Now I feel and look like one of those poofy fake bears Ellie had in her old bedroom. Never could understand why a human would create a fake animal. I think they like that they can squeeze them because I don't know about other animals, but I puke up a bit if someone squeezes me too tight.

All this smelly stuff she is putting on me, I'd rather be rolling in horse poop if you ask me. Why don't they have horse poop soap? That would be my preference. My teeth were also brushed. I gagged about ten times before she stopped. My claws were clipped and ears poked around in. I must admit I feel like new, but the scent of flowers and fruit following me everywhere I go is driving my nose crazy. It is distracting my scent detector. No amount of sneezing can make it stop.

I did not get shipped in a crate so I can wander freely in this smaller version of the big bird, which I now know is called a plane. I can rub up against anyone I chose, but mostly I sit next to Ellie. I couldn't see what she was showing me through the window. Apparently it was thrilling to her. We get out into a completely different location with new smells. The magic of traveling in the big bird. Time to mark new territory, right Ellie?

I know she has an enormous challenge ahead, and she is mentally preparing for it, because she is not talking. I've seen this before. It's always the same. She wants to be alone in her thoughts, kind of like me, but I am alone because I cannot talk. I can only sense. Too bad more humans do not have better sense, then they would stop talking.

Three days before my two hundred miles, EVT rented a beautiful A-frame cedar house for Jake, Coach Lane, Agatha, Anna the cook, Jerry the camera guy, Blue and me to share. My bedroom had its own deck with a stunning view of the mountains, and this is where I spent most of my time with only Blue by my side, trying to keep me calm. The view of the mountains I would run over filled me with excitement and impatience. I wanted to get it over with. I wanted to feel the finish line.

It is important to be introspective on the days leading up to any race. Time for me to tally up all my mental coping strategies. I reviewed my journal, where I kept track of all my training and race successes and failures and past mistakes. I also journaled about my fears and anxieties to get them off my mind and put somewhere else. I realized so many things are out of my control, including how I finish. I know it was important to count on Jake to get me through the last crucial miles, but my main focus was narrowed to only reaching each checkpoint. When times get tough, it might simply be going from ridge to ridge, tree to tree, or simply one step to the next step. Seeing the big picture of the daunting task ahead drained my energy and created doubt and fear. I already knew I must endure the same repetitive, relentless forward movement for hours on end, so I had to break things down to smaller attainable increments.

It was distracting to have my confusing feelings toward Coach mixed with prerace preparations. We only talked race strategy although I knew in my heart that he knew I was at odds with him. Thankfully he gave me my space. Everyone stayed away from me, except Blue. Glue Blue, we started to call him. Secretly I wondered if could survive this race without him – if I would come unglued.

Chapter 27

Northern Lights: Two Hundred Miles

"Where is he? Where is my team?" I yelled out to the volunteers at the aid station. They were cheering like crazy, and so I knew they only saw my mouth moving. It was fruitless. I heard my name in the mix of other words but didn't pay much attention because I was frantically scanning the faces looking for Jake. He was not there. He would have greeted me by now. I felt a chill run through my previously warm body. Something had happened. Tears burned the back of my eyes. I was looking forward to this 150-mile checkpoint celebration, but no one I knew was around and I suddenly felt so alone. This was the third last checkpoint and the point where a runner's pacer could join in for vital support in the final stretch.

The sun had begun to go behind the mountains making it difficult to focus my eyes. I knew I was early as I was expected to arrive here in the dark. I had lost track of how long I was running because my watch battery went dead. I didn't need to worry about my overall race time, because the EVT tech clothes tracked everything, but I needed to know the simple things like time of day and how far until the next aid station.

"Have any of you seen my support team from EVT and pacer, Jake Wellington?" I sounded desperate as I put my hands on the edge of a long table manned by a few tired-looking volunteers bundled up in jackets, caps, and scarves like they had been camping for weeks. They merely shook their heads and threw up their hands. The sky had been clear most of day with no clouds to trap the heat in closer to the earth. The air was chilly for those not moving much. They were bouncing up and down to keep warm after standing around all day waiting for runners to come in. I caused quite a stir to action.

They had radioed ahead, so the volunteers had my needs bag containing my supplies ready and waiting on the table. The race organizers recognized the possibility support crew would find it difficult to reach these checkpoints, so back up supply bags were encouraged. I grabbed mine and searched for a place to sit. Some volunteers and the medics were itching to ask questions. I sensed they were tentative, not knowing what kind of mood I was in since some runners at this point, who had not dropped out, were literally on their last legs and often struggled to talk and make any sense.

I made my way to a chair and struggled to get my legs to bend so I put one hand down to ease into it. There was a slight hesitation that if I finally got down, I wouldn't get back up again either physically, mentally or emotionally. Part of me wanted to cry, but if I started, I would not be able to stop. Up ahead lay the cold painful night. I didn't want to go it alone. Having a pacer also ensured the race organizers if we dropped out in the middle of a cold night, we were not alone and dying in a forest somewhere. I started to envision those thoughts, but quickly blocked them. That would be bad for business.

It took only a few seconds after sitting that they covered me in a warm blanket and started asking if I needed anything followed by the usual probing questions while they studied my reactions to see if they matched the responses given. They must hear a lot of insane words coming from runners who are at the proverbial death's door but say they are OK because they aren't thinking straight or are too stubborn to stop.

"I am good. Really. My pacer should be here." They sensed the urgency in my voice and responded as quickly.

"Oh, don't worry. He will be here I am sure," one of the volunteers spoke up. "The road is pretty muddy from the earlier snow. Trucks have created some ruts, which are causing some others to get stuck if they get off the track. Hopefully the trail won't be as muddy for you runners. Can we help you change your shoes or put on new mud gators?"

She was an older woman with a kind, glowing round face, and rosy cheeks surrounded by a granny knit soft pink cap and matching scarf that didn't match with her expensive high tech fiber jacket. She was a trail fashion oxymoron.

"Do you want a foot massage?" she asked as she patted the side of my leg gently. In truth, I would have loved one, but I was afraid if I took off my shoes, my toes would explode into swollen beans, and I would never lace them up properly again.

"Right now I feel no pain," I said as I shook out a no. Best not to take a chance she could find a trigger point. I couldn't help but take big bites from a salty mush and an energy bar of some sort, with ingredients that matched my DNA. I spat the concoction out. Same crap I had eaten for hours. I was sick of it. There was also a powder to add to hot water. The team would have provided added nutrition as the computer instructed them to. This mush was the backup. It tasted horrible, but it was all I had in my bag until I saw a Mountain Dew on the table next to me. I pointed with my mouth full of the EVT bar, but quickly changed my mind, then changed it back again, pointing like a belligerent three-year old. My stomach had become a separate entity all on its own, yelling out its demands with its own voice.

My body parts had been taking turns talking throughout this entire race. Some screamed, then shut up, and I didn't hear from them for miles while other body parts voiced their complaints. Eventually, they all took their turn getting mad at me. I had to ignore them. That was the main rule in this game, unless the pain was excruciating as if caused by an injury. I answered my stomach with gulps from the pop can. The bubbles made me burp and we all laughed. I was anxious to get going before the comfort of the chair made it impossible to get up.

"Sit a while more, Ellie. We have not seen any runners come through yet. We are very excited to see you," my little grandmother aide told me.

I knew this was supposed to be to my advantage, but it didn't register in my mind. I thought of who could be in front of me and counted this out on my fingers. She saw this and grabbed only one of my fingers and held it high for me to see. "This is you!" she showed me.

"Oh." I studied her as the message had not registered in my head. "OK, I will change my shoes. They are in my bag. I think I would like a hamburger," I said as I tossed the mush aside. I swore I smelled meat.

"Oh, let's see what we can scrounge up for you, my dear. Sit tight," she instructed while another lady gingerly took off my shoes and socks and brought out a fresh pair of each from my bag. She inspected my feet.

"Where are your blisters, Ellie? You must have some hot spots somewhere?" she asked. I pointed to my bra strap that had been annoying me. So much for EVT technological clothes. This one failed. It figured. It was probably designed by men.

"Oh yes. I see you have a blister from the strap. Let's see if we can fix this for the rest of the race." And she set to work padding my strap with bandages after she taped over my blister. My feet were a little swollen, so I didn't tighten the shoes as much as normal.

My hamburger request came in the form of a heated-up burrito, and I dug into it before I could stop myself. It tasted glorious. I hadn't had a burrito in years. The cheese melted down my fingers, and I licked it off every bit. As soon as it was down, I finished the Mountain Dew and followed that with a Snickers bar as a salute to Hans. I moved to get up, and they all moved in to help me. "I'm OK, really. Thanks, I'm OK." I told them. "How am I going to finish fifty miles if I need help to get up out of a chair?" Again, lots of boisterous laughter, much in part, I assumed, was to keep my spirits high.

I tried to get up and sat right back down. "Maybe I'll sit a while longer." I relented while they reached to help me down and nodded in agreement. They would do anything I asked.

I refilled my camelback with the bottles of concoction specially formulated for my biological needs, but I knew the Mountain Dew negated all that. I pulled out the other food in my special needs bag and packed it all away in my backpack. Jake was supposed to be with me to remind me to eat, to keep my mind in focus. I started to feel tears rolling, again. One of the medics gave me a well-rehearsed pep talk. She wiped away my tears, saying she knew I was well hydrated if I could cry. That made me laugh, but I still felt so alone.

A hot cup of chicken soup had shown up in front of my face. I mouthed a soft thank you. My sunglasses fogged up as I put the cup to my lips, so I lifted them off and the brightness of the sun before twilight hit my eyes, brightening my mood immediately. I wouldn't need them anymore, so I packed them away and if I was still running in the bright sun of the morning, I would punish Jake for his delay by using his sunglasses. I warmed both hands on the cup. The cool breeze was raising the hair off my exposed skin. I took a couple more sips, felt the heat travel down my throat and warm my stomach. I handed the cup back and grabbed a dry running top with long sleeves, a small vest, and a new buff that fit snugly around my neck, which I could pull up over my face in case there was a strong wind. I exchanged my running cap for a thick skullcap. I had to be prepared for the impending night. The needs bag was overprepared as usual, and I had to dig through all kinds of extra things to find what I needed. Hard lessons I learned on the trail and one of them was to be overprepared rather than be underprepared. While digging around, out popped a new fully charged watch I forgot I needed. I was so excited to put it on, it brought a new joy to get going. I noticed the time. My feet felt ready to go. Not too sure about my psyche at this point, but sitting and procrastinating was not doing me any good. I stood up to go.

"Come. We should weigh you now." The medic took my arm gently, helping me to stand up and escorted me to the scale. Down three pounds since the weigh in at one hundred miles. Eight and a half pounds so far. "You need to try to eat more, Ellie."

"OK, that is normal for me, but I will try to eat more." I knew the feast I had probably added two pounds to the scale. I needed to stay hydrated, even when the night air would reduce my sweating.

"I would eat if I could, but I am afraid it will end up in a pile of bile in a mile," I said, making my audience laugh again, boosting my false comedic skills. At least they thought I was of sound mind. The battle between my digestive system and my energy system was one thing, there was also the psychological battle. There was also the physical battle. Too many battles. What I wouldn't do to stop right there. But that would never happen.

"I am OK to go on now. Thank you everyone," I mustered a goodbye nod and reluctantly turned to the daunting trail ahead. I looked at my watch.

"Hey, Giselle! Did you know you are on record pace?" someone yelled as I passed the leader board without even noticing it. Usually it was the first place I stopped.

"Oh my God, really?" My stomach cramped up in response. I walked over to the board to confirm. I turned on my headlamp, so I could read it clearly. No names were on the board except mine. I had lost track of the number of runners I passed. "Where are the men?" I whispered to no one. I got a sudden urge to get moving faster than before. I didn't like being the one who was being chased; I'd rather be the one chasing. I tried not to let out any emotions, but the few people standing around were touching me gently on the back, and I couldn't help but smile and show gratitude. One more search for Jake, and I started back up again as all body parts started to yell in unison with the first steps stiff and awkward until some sort of haphazard rhythm kicked in.

I was lost in my incoherent thoughts for quite a long time when Jake pulled up next to me and if I had the energy, I would have slugged him. It felt like days that I was running on my own. Maybe it was.

"I didn't think you were coming and decided to leave me out here to finish on my own." I felt his presence without looking over. I struggled to keep it together as I felt the emotion of relief fold over in my heart.

"Hey now, I would never do that. Geez, we got stuck in the frickin' mud for over an hour. Then we had to four-wheel it to get as close to you as possible. I had to sprint to get here. Ellie, you are way ahead of your estimated pace. What the heck? You look so good. How do you feel?"

"No, I don't look good. Don't lie to me. How can I look good after running one hundred fifty miles—oops, no, one hundred fifty-eight miles? No one can look good except for maybe you," I scowled. I was still hurt they didn't give themselves enough time. I thought this was all about me.

"What are you talking about? You are running at a great pace. Still in the lead, Ellie, by miles. You know you could win this straight out, even beating the fastest guy. You can do this. I have no doubt." Silence. He hesitated. "Have you eaten?"

"Yes, I did, and I threw it all up back there. I needed you to hold my hair while I puked up my burrito." I wanted him to feel bad for me.

He responded in a typical Jake fashion. "Your hair is braided up." Pause. "You ate a burrito? Holy crap! No wonder. Your body is not used to that kind of food. Could you eat anything now? A little something? An EVT jellybean maybe? Did you sleep? You must have because I was able to catch you."

Silence for a few minutes. "I did sleep about twenty minutes. I fell down on the trail and slept. I couldn't help myself. Didn't care if some wild animal came and ate me up," I couldn't kick the anger. I wanted to use it to fuel me for a while. He was trying to appease me, which irritated me even more. He knew I heard his question about eating. I was racked with fear that anything solid would send my stomach into upheaval again.

"Can you eat, please?" he implored.

I eventually responded with a guttural sigh. It came out sort of like a growl. Feeling bad and not wanting Jake to think I was mad at him for the next forty miles, I gave in. "OK, a couple beans, then just keep talking. I don't care what you say. I am really struggling here. As long as you talk, but no singing, OK? You are a terrible singer. Just distract me and nothing more. That's all I ask." I breathed out a weak command. Then it struck me, "First. I am in first?" I asked while chewing, then thought to myself to not let this go to my head. I could fall, roll off the trail, and all my dreams would be gone. Be smart. Don't make any assumptions.

I could hear him breathing, and it started to irritate me, like when you can hear someone chewing. My irritation was building inside wanting to explode but that was dangerous. I had to change my mood. Taking my cue, Jake launched into the scenario of how they got stuck in the mud trying to pass a stuck truck. They stayed to help dig out the truck that was blocking traffic. All support crews would most likely be late for their runners.

"I never saw Coach so panicked to get here. We could see you had already arrived at the checkpoint," Jake explained.

The typical pang hit my stomach at the mention of Coach. Thoughts about the training run where he had to rescue me trickled into my mind, then embarrassment of my feelings hit my stomach, and I wanted to puke the jellybeans stuck in my throat.

Jake sensed I zoned out for a bit, so he tried to make the situation lighthearted and not a tragedy like it played it out to me, as I got mad again. "Left out here all alone for two hours because Coach Lane can't drive!" I hissed.

Quiet. Did he have any idea what this had cost me? I shouldered the entire burden on myself. Some pacer I had. Some coach I had. I kept the anger going inside of me. It was working. It had been fueling me for the last two hours. I wondered if I could stay mad for the rest of the race. Maybe Coach figured if I was mad I would run faster. That would be cruel if it were the truth, but it started to make sense to me. The madder I got, the faster I ran.

"Let's keep this pace right here. It's perfect." He was taking over control.

"OK," I relented as I matched his stride. "All I have to do is put one foot in front of the other. Right?" He grabbed my hand and placed a rice ball in my palm. "Wow. I love these." I stuck it in my mouth, savoring the bitter-sweet taste. My body felt like it did when I was eating my mom's comfort food. It hit the spot exactly. He knew my comfort triggers. My peripheral vision caught a smirk appear on his face.

No one passed us as the miles drew onward. We fell silent watching nature around us. Jake pointed out the shape of the clouds glowing in the moonlit sky as the sun had set hours ago. I didn't look up for fear of drawing my attention away from each footfall. Every step was a force of concentration. I wanted him to talk over the choir of screaming coming from all body parts. We set out conversation rules ahead of time on what we could discuss because I knew I could easily get irritated. Every feeling physically and emotionally had moved up a few notches on the drama scale. Extremes are dangerous areas.

I started a moan that went in time with my steps. "Uh, uh, uh, uh." Breathe. "Uh, uh, uh, uh." Jake joined in and together we carried on a few miles in a moaning rhythm. The sky had started to change colors, as the moon let go of its hold on the night and slipped behind the mountaintops. This was when I wished there were no mountains as it felt like we were running through a tunnel.

"Ellie, stop for a minute. Look at the northern lights!" Jake stopped dead in the pathway, and I slammed into the back of him pushing him forward a few steps. He turned around in time to catch me from falling. "Sorry, I didn't know you were so close behind me." He held me tight.

We turned off our headlamps and remained in a close embrace staring up at the sky showing us a brilliant display of lights moving to its own internal orchestra. It was true when the race organizers said we could be distracted by the aurora borealis. We were in jaw-dropping awe watching the waving ribbon of pulsating multicolored lights as it rippled and danced up, down, wide and narrow with a heavenly elegance. This was God's light show. I was breathing heavy and feeling emotional realizing there were much bigger and more immense events occurring in the universe that made our little lives on earth seem so insignificant. As we held our gaze upward, I imagined the northern lights were dramatic reflections of lively city lights on an upside-down black lake in a mythical magical world. There were so many dancing colors of blue, green, yellow, turquoise and violet reaching up to the universe overruling the beauty of the stars. The stars paled in comparison, as if they too were humbled. We didn't want to break the spell, but we knew this light show was distracting us from the job at hand, so we sighed with gratitude and made small steps to continue down the trail while still sneaking glances upward.

"Not yet. Let's enjoy the sky for a bit more," I pleaded after a few steps eyeing the direction we were headed. The blue, gray and black colors of the sky ahead were muted and opaque. I looked at the silhouetted mountain peaks so far away, knowing my headlamp would change my focus from this magnificent sky to only the drab gray and rocky trail ahead of us. I began to realize the magnitude of this journey. I had climbed up and over the tree line of those mountains through the snow and wind. It was hard to believe it happened on this same journey. It seemed like it was an entirely different race. The scrapes on my knees from falling on the crystallized abrasive snow were burning from the sharp cold wind, a sobering reminder of that leg of this journey.

An intense white-and-blue border outlined the mountaintops where the moon was last seen. The colors reaching out over the sky above our heads from the northern lights lost their intensity as we turned in the opposite direction. The clear spectrum of colors was gradually evolving from a soft baby blue to a dark blue, then into a deep black directly ahead of us allowing stars to appear far away from the northern lights behind us. We were staring into a dark blue screen covered with bright stars destroyed by a jagged cutting away of a mountain profile in the bottom half of this captivating canvas in front of us. I felt as if we were now running into a black abyss. We reluctantly turned on our headlamps and the scene disappeared. It was time to let go of this magical moment and finish this journey in the uncertainty of a dark and cold night.

Our world had been reduced from the universe to a couple of bouncing circles of gray light. If someone were claustrophobic, they might panic, but I felt right at home. I was more at home than in my living room. The darkness awoke senses. Now I had to rely on my sense of feeling with my feet and my perception of the dark space around me while seeing only what was illuminated ahead. This brought more life back into my steps. This darkness would bring me closer to the end—to when I could finally stop moving. I knew that getting excited too soon had destroyed others, and it could do the same to me. Tragedy could still strike. There were many hazards such as exposed tree roots that ran across the trail, rocks of varying shapes and sizes lay waiting to trip me up, and tree and bush branches that suddenly appeared to scratch me. I couldn't run passively and daydream my footsteps away. I had to sharpen my focus to the darkness when I was tired enough to drop at any moment.

After another couple of hours, I asked Jake to let us stop and turn off our lights for a few seconds. We walked cautiously in complete darkness and within a few moments, the sky came alive with stars in such multitudes, it looked as if it was going to burst open from the weight of all them. There existed enough starlight to add a faint glow to the trail. I immediately caught my toe on a root and stumbled forward a few steps but felt a strong hand grip my upper arm saving me from falling. We stopped completely, and breathing heavier I bent over placing my hands above my knees until the sharp electrical pains shooting through every muscle in my body finally subsided. My muscles went on high alert, expecting to fall. Now they were freaking out.

"That was close," I said in between breaths. Jake rubbed my back and helped me as I struggled to straighten up. He turned on his lamp and reached to turn on mine. "No, I can see. I will pick up my feet more. Please." I sounded too desperate. He turned off his lamp, and we walked for a bit, so we could take in the brilliance of the night sky. We heard nothing, only our footsteps and our breathing. The air was much cooler now, before the impending dawn. Sensing the sudden change, Jake took out my windjammer from my pack for me to wear, and I happily put it on, taking the chill off my body instantly. He also handed me a packet of pills from a pocket in my pack and reminded me to take one, despite the fact I didn't feel like putting anything in my mouth. I didn't have the energy to chew or swallow.

"Keep those pills in your front pocket and take them often, Ellie," he commanded. "There are so many in the bag. Have you not been taking them?" he asked.

Everything was all above board as far as legal substances. I was assured no illegal performance enhancing drugs were in these pills, but I still felt like I was cheating. Jake forced me to take a gulp from a tube of my gel made up of berries, seeds, amino acids, electrolytes, ginger powder and other stuff. It tasted so tangy, bringing saliva pouring into my mouth. I savored the tastes of bitter, sweet, salty and tangy. My mouth came alive and took my mind off my body. We turned our lights back on at Jake's insistence and started running, and I eventually lost track of time, mesmerized by the bouncing lights on the path ahead. Occasionally, I turned my light to the trees, but all I saw were clowns, tigers, alligators and the occasional monkey masquerading as tree trunks or rocks, or maybe it was the other way around. Sometimes it felt like we were climbing upward or downward, but I didn't know because the only place for the light was only a few feet in front of my footsteps.

I had no idea how long I had been running in total. The sun had started to rise bringing new colors to the trees from gray to dark green to neon green. The sun flickered through the trees creating patterns on the path like a kaleidoscope. I felt the warmth on my back. I could hear music in the distance. It was my tribe welcoming me home. But I was wrong. It was a circus instead. Loud music and people dressed in costumes parading around like monkeys. They invited me to sit, but I felt that if I sat for one second I would not be able to get back up, but the soles of my feet were burning so badly. The thought of soaking them in ice water was too hard to refuse. I sat and did nothing as everyone else took off my shoes and socks, and placed my feet in ice water. The upbeat music and volunteers dressed up in various costumes created a carnival atmosphere. Someone handed me salty, caramel-flavored popcorn, and I sunk down into my chair with my mouth tingling in orgasmic twitches. There was no place on earth I would rather be until Jake told me we are on pace to set a record. I ignored him. He had broken the spell of savoring the moment and swung me back into the task at hand. We left the music and sounds of the last human contact behind us. The faster men were catching up. I knew them all. They were primal mountain men on the long hunt too, who had grunted a hello at the start of this race to which I grunted back. No one had caught anything from this hunt yet, but I wondered if they saw the tiger too.

Jake and I continued our pattern of footsteps and rhythmic moaning. I had no idea where he was. His breathing had silenced. I did not hear or notice him beside me anymore. I was alone. I was an Indian, hunting, running so softly you could not hear my feet touch the ground. I felt the thump of my long braid against my back as I picked up the pace landing softly on my moccasins, feeling the strap of my quiver and the brush of the feather fetching against my head as I ran. I saw the eyes of animals in the forest watching me. They knew I was not after them. I was after something bigger. I was chasing whoever was chasing me, so I had to be completely aware of my surroundings. I picked up my pace even more. I could see more clearly now. I could see each leaf of each tree magnified against the blue sky when I looked up, but it was only for a second, as I didn't dare go off the track because when I did, the bushes and tree branches forced me to stay on the course. Focus. I took an arrow from my quiver, and I realized I must have dropped my bow, but it hurt my neck to look back. The arrow was now a spear. I ran with it hanging weightless in my fingertips. I could see my breath in the sunlight. The air was crisp, and its coolness made me shiver, but I kept going, lightly touching down on the path. I was climbing a ridge, forced to slow down and pick my way through the rocks. I heard someone approaching from behind. I quickly stepped to the side and struggled through the thicker brush to hide. Whomever I was hunting was now hunting me! Hide!

"Ellie! Where are you going? Stop!"

"Who are you?" I demanded.

A voice replied, but I did not know him. I was captured. I pushed him off and got up to run again but quickly tripped and fell. I scrambled away again, and he caught me, holding me close.

I looked into his eyes that were dark. A bright light was illuminating his cheek bones, but I couldn't see his eyes. They were dark holes. He must be dead. He was a zombie. I struggled to get loose.

"Ellie! Ellie! Snap out of it. It's Jake. It's Jake, your running buddy. Listen to me. You are almost finished, girl. You can do this. Do you understand me?" he was yelling at me, staring into my eyes while he held my face in both of his hands.

I finally understood. I felt a door open. I was running in my sleep, or sleeping in my run?

"Ellie," Jake said slowly, almost more of a question, "let's go back this way carefully and keep going. You are only five miles from the finish. Less than an hour. You are on track to set a record. A world record."

"I don't want a record. I want a shower." I felt tears well up in my eyes. "I want a chocolate sundae with a banana and whipping cream. And chocolate covered cherries. I want salty chips. Chocolate covered chips," I demanded.

"Come out here on this path. Take this chocolate I have for you." I thought I heard him eating without me.

"Hurry damn it," my belligerent three-year-old was speaking again. "I am going to die standing. I will turn to a skeleton before your eyes," I demanded.

"OK sister. Whatever you say," he replied. He turned me around and dug into my pack for some chocolate. I started to shiver as he stepped in front and shoved a large piece of salty chocolate into my mouth. I could feel the salt grains against my tongue. Then he forced me to drink, and it poured out the corners of my mouth before I could swallow, frustration growing like a demon deep inside.

"I am all muddy now." I moved the chocolate water across my face with my fingertips making war paint streaks across my cheeks.

"How does your stomach feel?" he asked.

"How should I know. You ask it!" I asked it instead. It had nothing to reply. "It is not talking to me right now. It's mad. Like I am mad at you! Damn stupid bear."

"If you are so mad at me, try to catch me, Ellie. Time to run, Ellie. We have to go. All you ever wanted is waiting for you, but you have to hurry." His eyes were alight with challenge, urgently searching into my eyes for a reply. The noise coming from his head was so loud. I narrowed my eyes and snarled at him. He half turned to go while still looking back at me, so I grabbed my spear and chased after him. I would catch him if it was the last thing I did. I kept my eyes focused on the back of his legs. At one time he was an alien in a space suit, smoking a cigarette and pulling me with a tether. We had to switch places because I hated the cigarette smoke. At least he was an amicable alien. Another time he was a gray horse with a raccoon on its back.

After some time, I broke out from the hallucinations I had allowed to take me out of my body, and I fell back to earth. It was a very painful landing.

"Oh, lady, you are a little too close." I don't mind the odd pet but when someone gets right into my face, I get a little nervous. She is grabbing my head trying to look into my eyes. I twist my head out of her hands and turn my nose to a familiar scent. I can smell her. Yes, that is definitely the scent of Ellie. OK, let me off this leash. I jump and try to break free. "Let me go!" I keep jumping for a few minutes. People telling me to calm down, but I can't. Someone yells out. If I could only break free of this leash. Finally, someone unhooks me, and I charge up the trail toward her. There she is! I slow down. I can see her silhouette illuminated against the sun. I cannot see her exactly, but I can smell her strong wild scent. I run toward a voice calling me. Soon I see her appear before me. She calls out my name with such emotion I cry in response. I sense her pain. She is running funny, without the usual rhythm she is so skilled at. Is she wounded? I smell dried blood, sweat, dirt, salt—a cornucopia of scents from mountains on the other side of my world. She reaches briefly toward me, then pulls back and starts to run quicker. I must pick up to a trot to keep up. Jake offers his greetings to me.

There are people everywhere along the side of the road. They are clapping, jumping and yelling. The air is alive with emotion and excitement. Jake reaches down and grabs my collar making me stop. He whispers in my ear that is it OK, and we must let Ellie pass the finish line on her own. There are many people and bright lights flashing. We wait and watch as people gather around her celebrating. After a few minutes we walk into the bright lights and hear Ellie call our names. We run over to her, and she falls to the ground as I jump up to greet her and cover her in kisses as I feel her small arms wrap tightly around me. I am so excited that I push her over on her back, and she giggles in her beautiful way. She holds me tight and buries her face in my neck, and we lie together like that for a long time. She whispers how much she loves me, sits up, and I move to lick her face. Oh, the smells and tastes have many stories. She has truly won a battle, and I am so full of love for her. She is the queen. Lights flash off and on. There are many people around her now. These are her loyal subjects. She has become who I have always known her to be.

Chapter 28

Magical Night

The repercussions of setting a new overall course record for this event meant I went sailing into the limelight. It was the first time a woman beat the men's field of competitors. My social media accounts were on fire and my numbers shot up again.

The next few days after arriving back home, I went through a battery of tests for the research department, while they put me into recovery therapy that involved a specialized hyperbaric chamber, a pulsing ice water bodysuit, float tank, massage, infrared and electromagnetic therapy, and various nutritional supplements. A few weeks later, after all the hype had died down, and I was mostly recovered, EVT hosted a celebratory dinner with Dr. Chilton, my parents, the key staff who were a part of my training, and athletes on the team who were available.

The night was magical and held in the same garden at the EVT headquarters as our first welcome dinner. It was odd to see my teammates out of their run gear, twisting, jerking and itching in suits and dresses. My baby giraffe walk in my heels contradicted the confidence I felt inside as I entered the event to applause.

The pride on my parents' faces filled me with a joy I never felt before. A few people stood up to give congratulatory toasts after they showed a short video of my training and racing from the past year. My mother had tears in her eyes. You would think I had won an Academy Award. I struggled to hold in my emotions while listening to Dr. Chilton recall the challenging year I had in training and adjusting to the EVT way of living. He said the EVT running shoes I wore during the race had been released and reached top three trail shoes in the world for sales. He said I would be getting a piece of the revenue as per my contract and joked I would soon be flying on my own private jet to my races. Of course, he was teasing, but I had no idea my bonus would be as lucrative as it was piling up to be. My parents had sat me down before dinner and forced me to agree to put it all away in savings for at least a year.

"We knew we were getting a superb runner, but we didn't know it was going to be two for the price of one." A collage of pictures of Blue and I running together appeared on the screen, including a picture of Blue proudly sitting with the Triple Peaks 100 medal around his neck. He added commentary. "We are now thinking of entering the dog food market, and I think we have our marketing spokes dog right here."

When Coach Lane stood up to give a toast, my mind wandered to how foolish he would think of me if he knew of the way I was feeling about him. I was conflicted with despising him as a coach to acquiescing to this crazy crush I had. If I could only erase my feelings and start over. I was roused out of my thoughts by Jake.

"Ya she became a powerful warrior," Jake was saying now as he took his turn to give me a toast sharing the crazy things I said during our running together. Everyone laughed. "She was even thankful to Coach Lane! Now that was the most frightening thing I had heard," he laughed and everyone joined in, but I sat wide-eyed and felt a flush raise up on my cheeks.

I rolled my eyes and shouted out, "Now you knew I was delirious by that time, didn't you Jake?" Coach held up his glass of wine to me and gave me a nod and a wink. I did my best not to melt through my dress onto the floor.

My parents said their tearful goodbyes to catch a late flight together. They warned me our hometown was ready to throw a party and name a street after me when I was able to make arrangements to visit. Dr. Chilton walked them out while I stayed to mingle with my teammates. I felt so comfortable with them because they did not see me as a superstar. Many of them had accomplished even bigger goals. Remy from the sprint team had recorded the first two-hour marathon in a sanctioned race. Olivia now held the world record for furthest distance run over twenty-four hours. Jake won the race series involving running across four deserts around the world, and Tim won Race Across the Andes, a twelve-hundred-mile bike race from Argentina to Chile. They also were given celebratory dinners.

I was in a room of superstars. It was only a matter of time before they each reached the goal they had set out to achieve when joining the team. Seeing our teammates succeed fueled each of us to work even harder. As long as we did exactly as EVT instructed, we would be injury free and eventually all be successful. In celebration, most of the team were well into a few beers, and I, too, was feeling a buzz from the champagne.

"Maybe ve should invite Coach Lane over here. He is looking fairly human tonight. Maybe a few beerz haff loosened him up," chuckled Hans.

"You don't have to worry, Hans. Here he comes. Brace yourselves for some push-ups everybody," joked Olivia.

"He looks like a human all dressed up. But do you think he really is human? I think he is a robot invented by EVT," piped in Rocky.

"Oh, come on, you guys," I responded.

"Oh, Ellie has a soft spot for Coach," I heard someone say, and I immediately felt my face heat up.

Jake fixed a stare at me looking a little too concerned. Immediately I wondered if I babbled something incoherently during our time running together. I gave him a sideways glance, then turned away. I could feel him studying me for a reaction.

Coach Lane came up and stood next to me, and my heart started beating like I was running. I inhaled deeply. He had on a white shirt with no tie and dark blue suit. He stood leaning on one leg with a drink in one his hand and the other loosely hitched in his pant pocket pulling his suit jacket back. I noticed how his shirt was opened at the neck showing his pectoral muscles below his collarbone. I expected to see running shoes, but he had on shiny dress shoes and all of it presented him differently. He appeared suave and urban, like he belonged on the cover of GQ Magazine. The rest of the group noticed too. This was the first dinner he could attend due to his coaching obligations, so we barely recognized him all dressed up.

"You clean up pretty good, man," remarked Boz. "I wouldn't have recognized you on the street. You look somewhat human." We chuckled but everyone did take notice as he was vastly different from the arrogant militaristic coach we were familiar with.

"I think I speak for all of us here when I say maybe we can appeal to your apparent human side we see here and announce none of us are training tomorrow in honor of Ellie. So you can blame her," Jeep said while stroking his goatee and tilting his chair back, precariously balancing on the back to legs that had become his signature position whenever in a chair of any kind. He was good at tilting off kilter, pushing the limits of balance, like he lived his life. He was training to set a new record for unaided crossing of Antarctica. He would be leaving in a few months.

We all cheered and clinked our glasses together at the center of the table. Even Olivia was having wine to celebrate. I wondered to myself if it actually was real wine or if EVT had concocted an alimental, no hangover, organic wine. I was sure they would hate to undo any training effects through alcohol, but we are all feeling something, I could tell.

"At ease, troops," he replied. "No worries. Day off to do what you want. Maybe get a haircut, Jack?"

"Oh no, sir. I have a photo shoot for *Mountain Man Magazine* coming up. I need to be as rugged as possible. I see you went through with hair and makeup before coming over," Wild Jack responded, leaning back in his chair, slinging his arm over the back of his chair while eyeing Coach up and down.

There was a collective set of "oooos" from the table. The banter between the two was normal and respectful. They would probably be great friends if Coach Lane ever broke the wall he had built around himself. He was motivating and tough, and he never crossed the line to being a friend. The only time I had seen him act human was the one night with me. My mind wandered there, thinking about how he touched me, until someone snapped me out by calling my name, "Ellie, Ellie. Geez, girl, you falling asleep on us? Give the girl a glass of champagne, and she starts to zone out."

"I think I will have another one," I responded, holding up my empty glass.

Jake yelled out, "A round for everyone on Coach's tab."

We all laughed. "Come on, Coach, join us. What's your poison?"

We didn't expect him to break his wall down, but he grabbed a chair and pulled up next to Wild Jack, who slapped him on the back, almost knocking him over. Our server came over, and Coach ordered a round of tequila for everyone. A few of us declined, but the shots arrived in front of us anyways. Steamboat Annie downed hers first, and everyone howled in shock. They offered one to Olivia, who shook her head in disagreement, as she had to study in the morning. We all admired the sacrifices she made to study medicine and train at the same time, so we let her off the hook. They looked at me, and I said no. Crazy to think there would be peer pressure to drink coming from some of the fittest people on the planet.

"Ellie, I am sure there will be some sort of antidote in our water tonight to combat the side effects," said Rocky, looking more like a businessman than runner in his suit. "Don't worry. It will help with the inflammation."

"Or zis vill be another shtudy about zee effects of alcohol. Be prepared to pee in a bottle, and poked vith a needle in zee morning, ya," added Hans.

It was my first tequila ever, and I feared this was not going to go well. I glanced around and couldn't see Dr. Chilton. I didn't want to disappoint him. Jake showed me how to take the lime and salt before downing the shot, then I stared right at Coach Lane, held up my shot glass in a toast, and he held up his, looking me directly in the eyes as we downed ours together. I promptly keeled pretending to be sick. Coach, who was close by, rushed to check if I was OK, but I sat up, holding my stomach from laughing so hard, and everyone settled back down, relieved. Coach gave me a smirk, squinted his eyes, and nodded his head side to side.

"Ooooff, she is human after all," remarked Hans, sitting back in his chair, stretching out his long legs. "Another round, and bring me a beer to chase it," he yelled. Wild Jack slapped him on the chest. Olivia and Annie got up to leave, claiming it was a game they couldn't play. We hugged our goodbyes as I wanted to stay to watch and listen to this group of jovial men exchange entertaining gibes. Another glass of champagne showed up in front of me.

"Don't worry, Ellie, its organic." Boz winked at me. He had his own celebration dinner for winning the Extreme Triathlon Championship title in Norway while I was competing. He was well into a few tequilas as he was in his off-season and heading home for a break.

The night went on with the guys sharing their race goals and experiences, and I was humbled by their magnitude. The alcohol had opened us up to relax and share stories. I ordered a pitcher of water and drink almost all, while the guys continued to drink and banter teasingly back and forth. They let me in for a short visit into their notorious boy's club. They were quick and experienced at teasing each other. Coach Lane held his own against the razzing from the others. He threw back some verbal punches that never hurt but were cunning and amusing.

As the night drew on and some started to leave, I got up to personally thank each of them with a tight hug. They were like family, my older brothers. I was honored when they referred to me as their little sister. I felt my face flush when they complimented me in my dress, but tried to act nonchalant. I wanted to be like one of the guys.

With a few of us left at the table, I found a couple shots of tequila in front of me again. "Ellie, champagne will kill you in the morning. No more for you," announced Jake.

"How do you know, Jake? Are you a closet champagne drinker?" teased Boz. With that, the banter started back up, and I spent the next half hour with a sore abdomen from laughing so hard. My running accomplishment and being here with them made me feel I had passed a very special and unique initiation into an exclusive club.

As the hour drew past midnight, everyone agreed they had enough and decided to run back to the condos to try to sober up even though they were wearing their dress shoes, and it was at least thirty miles. I knew someone from EVT would rescue them on the road back if they did start the insane journey. They invited me but noticed the heels and tight dress. The joking started back up again as they teased me about how much they would like to run behind me. The idea sounded like fun, but Coach piped up and offered to rescue me. They each gave me one last congratulatory hug and set off leaving us alone at the table.

My thoughts were on the connection I solidified with the guys tonight, and the special attention I received, smiling to myself as I thought of some of the quips. I collected my purse and headed to the bathroom one last time before I met Coach at his car.

The car was an Audi S5. My father always dreamed of owning one. He opened the door for me, which felt strange to be treated so properly, and I clumsily plopped my body, which was stuffed into a tight dress, ungracefully into his car, wishing he wasn't watching me. He hopped around, got in and pushed a button so the rooftop slid back as we started to drive. We didn't say too much to each other as I reflected on the night. I couldn't wipe the smile from my face. The night air was fresh, helping to relieve the buzz I felt from the alcohol. We yelled out to the guys as we passed them on the road, laughing and backslapping as they went along.

"No room!" yelled Coach as they tried to hitch a ride.

I tilted my head back in the headrest and studied the constellations in the sky, recognizing and pointing out a couple. "Don't look! Keep your eyes on the road," I cautioned, while scanning the night sky.

"You are enough of a distraction," he yelled over the music.

The music was classic rock and loud. I felt exhilarated as the wind whipped my hair into mayhem, and sat back to enjoy the ride. I realized we were taking the long way home. I could feel Coach Lane glancing at me occasionally. He could see how much I was enjoying the drive, and he settled back into the groove as well. The Police song "Bring on the Night" started to play, and when the chorus began I sang along, almost shouting, "Bring on the night. I couldn't stand another hour of daylight." My body started to move instinctively to the music feeling blissful and alive. I stuck out my lower my lip when the song was over, and he laughed. We anticipated the next song and cheered when it was one we knew some of the words to, and laughed when we messed them up. I lost all track of time, so caught up in the moment, until I realized he was not taking me back to my condo. We were gradually climbing a hill until we came to the top of a lookout.

"Come on, Ellie, you've got to check out this view," he insisted as he rolled the car to a quiet stop.

I tried to get out on my own, but fell back in the seat as I struggled to adjust my dress while balancing on my heels. He jumped around the car to quickly offer his hand. I stood up and we met almost eye to eye until I slipped off my shoes, so I could stand without falling over. The earth felt cool to my toes sending a shiver up my legs. He left the music playing and "To Turn You On" by Roxy Music came up next. I knew this song, too, because eighties music was all my parents ever listened to. At that moment, it felt like a drug.

My hair was a mess of tangles. I tugged at sections trying to pull them apart until Coach started to help, lightly tugging here and there, so I gave up trying to untangle it myself, freeing my hands to hold me steady against the car. He gently untangled a few strands and as I watched him, we locked eyes. We held the stare for too long, enough time for me to notice his breathing and how his lips parted a little and his eyebrows knit together as if he was trying to figure something out. He tugged at my hair playfully, took a deep breath and let go. He took my hand in his and put his other around my waist and led me gingerly, as he watched my steps, to a bluff overlooking our little town. There was a fallen tree perfectly positioned back from the edge. He straddled it as I sat and tossed both legs over the log and let my feet tangle loosely feeling the rough bark against the back of my legs.

"Damn it these dresses are so inconvenient," I struggled to get everything adjusted until I looked up in awe to see the view. "I didn't know this place existed," I whispered.

In the distance, lay the tiny gold lights of the town. Behind the town was the black jagged edge of the mountaintops pointing upward to the sky that was lit with millions of tiny diamonds—some in clusters with different hues of white, while others were bright and domineering.

I searched the entire night sky and found the moon behind us peeking through the treetops. I became dizzy trying to take it all in.

"I found it running one day," he explained. "I am surprised you haven't discovered it." He was staring at me while I kept my gaze on the stars.

"You can run?" I teased, and he gently poked his elbow into my side in response. "This is clear on the other side of town from where the condos are. Do you live in the condos too?" I investigated, since he was a complete mystery to all of us.

"No, I prefer to keep my distance from the team. That is your place to hang out," he answered.

"Oh," was all I could think to say. The music coming from the car started to play "Can't Find My Way Home" by Alison Krauss. I moved to the guitar and hummed, then started singing softly to myself. "Well, I'm near the end, and I just ain't got the time. Well, I'm wasted, and I can't find my way home." I giggled at the truth of the words and closed my eyes, inhaling the fresh air scented with pine and moss. I finished the song as if singing to the world laid out before me. I don't think I ever felt more connected to the earth, the sky and to life. I turned to see Coach shaking his head in amusement. I bent over with giggles and a little embarrassment, returning the smile. I could feel his eyes watching me, causing a zap of electricity to move from my feet to the tip of my head. He kept staring over at me with dark eyes.

"You never fail to amaze me. You are one incredible human being, Miss Giselle D'Angelo, let alone the most beautiful woman I have ever laid eyes on." His voice was deep and soft.

I never heard those words from a man before. I wanted to deny them instantly. I could hear my mother's words of telling me to always accept a compliment with a thank you, but I felt conflicted between fear, nervousness, and excitement of what he truly meant by telling me this. I kept my eyes forward searching in the view for an answer to how I was feeling. He was opening a door. I had to choose whether I walked through it or not. I didn't want time to move one second. I needed a pause so I could think this through, but he got down off the log and stood in front, looking at me. I looked down at my feet to avoid his gaze and gripped the bark with my fingertips, breaking it away in pieces. I placed my chin on my shoulder to avoid looking at him until he reached over to pull a stray hair away from my face and put it behind my ear, and gently dragged his fingertips along my cheek and jaw, and let his thumb caress my cheek bone. I turned to look up at him. He moved his thumb down to touch my lips. Again, he took a deep sigh. I felt weak, hardly able to hold my balance on the log. I wanted him to kiss me. I was going to walk through the door.

Ironically, "Knocking on Heaven's Door" by Bob Dylan came on. I was knocking on heaven's door for a different reason. He dropped his hand away and turned around to lean up against the log beside me. I felt his shirtsleeve graze my arm causing chill bumps. We stayed silent enjoying the night sky with a few heavy sighs. When Bob finished the song, I spoke, "I have to stand up. This log is painful." I was ready to jump down but unsure of where to place my bare feet. He noticed my apprehension and turned toward me again. "Shine" by Collective Soul started to play.

"Here, let me help you. Place your feet on top of my shoes," he said. I did as I was told, and he pulled me close in an embrace, and I put my arms around his waist to hold my balance. He moved us slowly to the music. I put my head up against his chest as he held me tight enough to hear him breathing and his heart beating. The song made me want to cry.

"Heaven let your light shine down," I sang.

His hips pressed against my stomach, and I felt heat coming up between us. He pulled me tight and rested his head on top of mine and caressed my back with his fingers. We moved that way until the song picked up its beat, then I slipped off the top of his shoes. The earth was cool under my feet. A strong contrast to the heat between us. I stood still making space between us, curling my toes in the dirt while catching my breath, then shook my head wildly and danced to the music as it picked up its beat. I wanted to shout with happiness. I stopped and sang to him, "Give me a word. Give me a sign. Show me where to look. Tell me what I will find. Lay me on the ground. Fly me in the sky. Show me where to look. Tell me what will I find." I danced and sang until the song ended and stood staring up at him.

"Oh, Ellie." He laughed, then took my hands in his and studied them, rubbed my fingers, looking down at me with dark eyes. "What am I going to do with you?" he whispered while staring intently at me, glancing from one eye to the other. His eyes were completely different from the coach that would peer at me with intensity, demanding, scolding, praising. His eyes never looked like this. I knew what I found attractive about him. It was his mystery, his strength, his authority. I wanted him to take control. He opened the door into a different world, and I walked through, but he had to show me where to go next.

The Dandy Warhols started next, singing "You Were the Last High." I took a deep breath and swayed gently.

I was startled back to reality as Coach lifted me back up on the log, so my face was closer to his as he leaned toward me with his hands resting tight beside my thighs. I shifted my eyes around because the intensity of eye contact was too much. We looked at each other again. I noticed things about his face I had never seen before, his gentle lips, his strong jaw, his eyebrows as he lifted them with thoughts I suspected he had, because I had them too.

"What do you want to do?" I felt the words slip over my lips out of my control.

"Be careful what you ask, Ellie," he whispered. He moved his head down toward me, placing his hand under my chin lifting my face to his.

As "Secret Garden" by Bruce Springsteen started to play, I had my first kiss. My first real kiss. His hand moved along the side of my face. His lips were smooth, moist and warm in contrast to the cool breeze that took my hair in flight. He started gently with small, soft kisses, then with an urgency as the kisses became harder. His hand moved to the back of my head, and the other embraced me tighter. Then he stopped. He pulled back, stepping away, and took a deep inhale filling his chest. He tilted his head to the side, scratching his forehead. "Oh, Ellie. This shouldn't happen." He glanced away quickly and back to me. "I'm so sorry. This is wrong." We stared at each other.

I realized it was wrong. He was my coach. He was older than me. We were breaking the EVT contracts about getting involved with each other. I knew there were lots of reasons, but driven by alcohol, the moment, the constellations, the scent of the forest, and the music, I asked anyways: "Why not?"

He breathed out strongly again and raised his hands to cradle my face. "I shouldn't," he whispered as he bent down to kiss me again with more passion and intensity. I kissed back and this uncontrollable feeling of wanting to feel his body on top of mine took over my logic. I wanted to feel the weight and strength of him on top of me. I pulled on his shoulders and kissed back with passion. I wanted him to know it was OK.

"Secret Garden" ended and The Clash started up with, "Darling you got to let me know, should I stay or should I go" and we both started to smile through the kisses. We pulled apart and the spell was broken for a short while until his face turned serious again. I could see him staring at my lips. His lips were parted, ready to kiss me again, but he pulled back slightly and looked intently at me for quite a while, then looked past me as if deep in thought. I thought I saw conflict written on his face. His eyes were slightly squinted, and his brow was slightly furrowed. His irises were black in the moonlight when he turned back to me, and his eyes softened, his eyelids heavy. My hands felt his chest breathing heavy against wide shoulders and straining his shirt buttons. His concentrated breathing overpowered the sound of the breeze that carried a few stray hairs across my face. He took a stray hair the wind moved gently in his fingertips and pulled it and me closer to him, and we kissed again.

I always fantasized what this would be like. As a young girl, I watched enough love scenes nervous about what I was supposed to do. They were orchestrated so perfectly. How did the actors make it look so perfect? I had no idea things would happen instinctively. I didn't need to read a book or watch a movie to know what to do when a man's hand moved across my body and touched me in places provoking an animalistic response. We reached a point of urgent passion, and he stopped. We both needed to feel cool air. I felt thoroughly wrecked as I watched him run to his car to bring out a couple blankets from the trunk and spread them on the grass back a few feet from the edge of the bluff. He came back to gather me in his arms and carry me there without saying a word.

All words used to describe my feelings that night are entirely too cliché, but I will never forget them for as long as I live. I had felt them all before, buried back in time. Something deep inside of me responded knowingly to the sensations of fingertips moving across my skin, causing chill bumps and shivering only to be heated back up by breath, lips and sweat. I knew how to move to the vibrations, tingles and rhythms of touch and passion. I knew intuitively how to invoke those feelings of painful desire. With the power of breath, touch, force, hesitation, and movement, however slight, gentle, or rough, together we teased each other until it was unbearable.

The universe witnessed what was happening as I took a trip outside of my body. I didn't want to return. I saw the stars moving, flashing back and forth, streaks of light up and down and side to side. I was on their trajectory and squinted my eyes to see the stars blend and melt together. Then I shut them out. I lost myself in my other senses, each one newly discovered, rolling over my body, making it move like it was possessed. I felt primal with the earth under me, the scents of musk and sweet spices floating on the breeze caressing my skin. I opened my eyes to watch his shoulders muscles tensing and glistening in sync with his movements while my body moved in rhythm to his. It was frightening and amazing at the same time. The heavens disappeared as the intoxication within my body blinded me. The music played through from "Wicked Game" to Joni Mitchell's "This Flight Tonight" to Neil Young's "Helpless" and Bruce Hornsby's "Mandolin Rain." I will remember every song, every lyric. They will trigger this memory over and over again. Something I grew to hate.

We lay breathing in synchronicity to the postclimactic shivers of our bodies. I squeezed his hand tightly, and he rolled me in close and covered us in the blanket to watch the colors on the horizon start to turn from black to dark blue. I think I fell asleep for a bit, lying there in his arms. I didn't want to. I wanted to keep listening to his heartbeat. I wanted to hold that moment forever with no thought for what it started.

"Ellie, we have to go before the sun comes up. I don't think it is a good idea for me to be seen dropping you off at dawn," he said as he kissed my forehead and started to get up. He wrapped me tightly in one blanket and gathered up the other, picked me up and carried me to the car and placed me in the seat. He picked up my shoes and handed them to me with a wink. He got in and we started back down the road. Anyone could see us driving together, if they cared to notice. Maybe I was being paranoid. He closed the top of the car and held my hand tightly. I realized the ramifications of our actions. We had feelings for each other but couldn't show them in public. If EVT found out we have crossed the line in our professional relationship, we would both be fired, and for him, the repercussions could be worse.

I ventured out a desperate question, "What is going to happen now?"

"I don't know what to do, Ellie, but I want you to know this was not me getting caught up in the moment. Please don't think that ever." He pulled the car over to the side, turned to me taking my hands in his and brought them to his lips to kiss. His face changed to match the tone in his voice.

"You have no idea the demons I have been fighting ever since I saw you that day on the track. I watched you the entire time you were there. I watched you run so gracefully. I knew who you were. Working next to you has not been easy, Ellie. I had to tell myself a million times, 'You can't let this girl get to you.' And then that day. You know the day. I wanted," he paused briefly, "I have never felt that way with anyone before. And I couldn't figure it out why I couldn't keep my distance from you. I have worked with young beautiful girls before and was never aroused or tempted. I know there is a line, and we crossed it tonight. I crossed it. And even though I loved every minute of it, I feel incredible guilt. I feel I have jeopardized your career and mine as well, but mostly I am worried for you." He caressed my face with his hand and drew in to give me a kiss. I said nothing and closed my eyes imagining how all I have could be taken away if we got caught together.

"Look, drop me off somewhere, and I will walk back."

"Ellie, I don't mean for it to be this way. And the worst of it is, I want to see you again. Oh my God, it's like I am caught in a spell. Ever since I first laid eyes on you."

I stared at him with understanding and a little sadness. I was feeling the same way.

"Why her?" he asked himself aloud as he held my hands and continued to talk. "I realized your beauty is everything about you—the way you move, the way you talk, say things, see things. The way you think. The way you run. Oh my God, the way you run, walk, dance. Everything is mesmerizing to me. And I am breaking rules. Rules on so many levels. I have done everything in my power to stay away from you. I acted out in opposition to my true feelings, yelling at you, demanding of you, trying to make you hate me so it would be easier. But you didn't. You kept taking all my crap." He let go of my hands and brought a hand to his forehead and rubbed it intently, looking straight ahead, as if his explanation lay there. "I am stronger than this, but you reduce me to," he took another deep sigh, "nothing. You've melted me down."

I didn't expect this. I didn't think I was that much of distraction for him. The tension between us, what I was feeling, was also real for him.

"We can't deny these feelings. This is real between us. In a way that it is so wrong makes it kind of exciting," he continued.

Did he mean to say that or was he thinking out loud? I found it exciting and fearful. Was this all because I was a risk taker in love with the danger this encounter offered? Now that we got together, was I questioning where this was headed? I was beginning to wonder if he should have known better. I was so confused by my feelings. I wanted to see him again alone, not because it was wrong but because he made me feel good, but undeniable turmoil was building in my mind.

"We are one sloppy melted blob of mush, aren't we," I said as he held my face with one hand pulling me in for a kiss. It was hard, almost angry, then he sighed, pulled away, and started the car. The music started up. Manchester Orchestra, "I Know How to Speak." Perfect timing. I wanted to cry.

He dropped me off—apologetically, with no goodbye kiss—at a park near the condos. I watched him drive away and checked if anyone had noticed, but it was quiet except for the birds as they started to chirp in a new day. The sun was announcing its arrival, replacing the secrets of the night. I took my shoes in my hands and walked home feeling an incredible mix of feelings settling heavy in my stomach. What was I going to do now?

She is near. It has been a long lonely night of waiting and every sound from the outside had sparked my anticipation of her return, but this time she is at the door. Where have you been? I sniff her legs and take a step back as she drops her shoes, leans back against the door and slides to the floor. I go to her and squeeze in between her outstretched legs and rest my head on her lap with a sigh. I know the smell. Humans and their strange potpourri of scents. I should let her be with other males. I knew it was a matter of time when I would smell the pheromones, but it still pains me. She is young and beautiful, as I remember her. The vision has never left my heart from so many lifetimes ago, as glimpses in foggy dreams of touching, smelling, tasting her. And here she is very real. We are together, and I don't care how. Ellie, I missed hearing your breathing tonight.

We get up, and she lets me outside, but I am quick to return. I don't want to leave her alone. I sense more than I am willing to accept, that she has changed. We move to the bathroom, where she stares at herself for a long while in the mirror, then she discards her clothes and steps into the shower for too long. I fall asleep. I awake when she moves to the bedroom and drops into her bed. I listen to her toss and turn with dark dreams that never have an end because our past life haunts her now as it has for me for centuries. I jump up on the bed. I know it is not allowed but as I lay beside her to calm her down, she snuggles in close as the darkness of her subconscious lets go to a different dream. I hear my name and feel reassured I am her one true love. No human can take that from me.

Chapter 29

Communication Breakdown

A few months after winning Northern Lights, I won Pacific Rim, a one-hundred and fifty kilometer race, and set a new women's course record. EVT paid me great bonuses, and my social media accounts kept growing along with the sales of my trail shoe. The only thing I didn't seem to have control of was my relationship with Lane, no longer Coach Lane. Going away to train and race were the only times he and I could be alone together beside late night rendezvous. We couldn't meet at his house because he said there were eyes everywhere. I had told him numerous times how I felt like a mistress, and we were both married to EVT. He laughed it off but offered no solution and always focused on caution.

I found the situation ridiculous and wanted to confess to Dr. Chilton, but Lane was adamant against it. My fear was getting caught, and I was getting tired of hiding, taking long drives to other towns to spend time together or having Lane sneak into my condo, but despite the inconvenience and guilt, I found myself falling in love.

I couldn't help thinking Jake knew something was up between Lane and I when he had commented I looked like I was in love but admitted he couldn't figure out with whom. He wouldn't accept my continuous denial. It was unbearably difficult to keep my feelings toward Lane neutral while in public. To cope, I found it easier to act like I hated him when we were around others, and it so worked well as a cover-up. Dr. Chilton even asked if I was still OK with Coach Lane. He could hire another coach for me, but I assured him it was my way to get more resilient with running—to act tough around everyone, including my coach. He bought the story, but the deception toward him and everyone else weighed me down deeply. The only thing or person I had to confide in was Blue. Sadly, I couldn't share with anyone about being in love.

I don't like what is going on. I love Ellie, but I don't like change, and things are changing fast around here. Emotions are moving faster than my mind can keep up. Mindless emotions. Irrational emotions.

Coach Lane has been making his bed with Ellie. He thinks he is the alpha male in our pack now, but I tried to set him straight. I can't go up and bite him. I tried that and Ellie got very upset with me. I would like to rip him to shreds, but I am more dignified and civil than that. I don't like him sniffing around here, in our den and leaving his scent everywhere. I tried to remark his scent at the big watering bowl and got into trouble for that too. Ellie! Come on! This is my den. Our den.

I don't take my eyes off him the entire time he is here. In fact, I don't sleep. I sit at the side of the bed and stare at him. I don't like him in bed with Ellie. I sit there until she puts me outside on the small deck. I stare at him through the window. She closes the curtains, so I bark incessantly. I get in trouble, but it works. She tells me I don't listen well when he is here. That is what I say about her. She is not listening to me. The coach has clouded up our communication line.

Don't you remember, Ellie? True love is not supposed to cost more than one is willing to pay yet it must be indulgent. Real love feels like the whole purpose and meaning of life is held within its embrace. How can you embrace a secret or a lie?

Chapter 30

Fanatic

Since winning again, I had done a few interviews for magazines, podcasts, TV, and newspapers. *Ultra-Athlete Magazine* and EVT had teamed up for a magazine signing and shoe promotion tour. Despite the notoriety of having a shoe named after me, I was more fixated that Lane planned to sneak into a few of the promotional tours, so we could spend some time alone together.

My first engagement was at our local coffee house, and I was surprised how packed it was when I arrived for the presentation. Alex was there with me as well as my social media liaison, Agatha. I insisted Blue come as well because he became a social media hit as, Endurance Dog, and was drawing a following of his own.

The fans of ultrarunners are a humble, laid-back bunch. I call them the granola people—earthy, healthy, and just a little sweet and crunchy. They dressed like trail runners almost all the time. A typical ensemble was worn trail shoes or recovery sandals, khaki-colored hiking shorts, and T-shirt from a monumental race. They took pride in being identified as a trail runner and not a jogger. I loved this crowd. They were my tribe.

Blue and I drew immediately attention when we arrived and impromptu applause picked up as we walked through the coffee house. It was a perfect location for a meet and greet with a balcony overlooking an open area and a stage on one end, where we headed to sit down. A large crowd assembled all the way up the stairs to the second floor overlooking the open area. The place was packed. I took my seat and was immediately taken aback by a large banner strung across the back wall displaying my picture, name and photo of the new trail shoe, Ellie, along with my record finish times printed out in a list. I was told people drove for hours to see me. Standing in this fishbowl, I smiled at everyone and gave a humble wave of my hand to cheers, applause and shouts of, "We love you, Ellie!"

I took my seat behind a table stacked with boxes of my shoes on the side. After we all settled, the coffee house owner introduced a representative from *Ultra-Athlete Magazine*, who in turn lauded my accomplishments while introducing me. I was expected to stand and give a small talk about my races, which I had rehearsed numerous times with Blue as my ever-attentive audience. I thought I was well prepared, yet my stomach was doing flip turns. I pressed a smile onto my face and tried not to make direct eye contact with anyone. I remembered the words I read somewhere to picture everyone in their underwear. It wasn't working. I felt like I was the one in my underwear. I stepped up to a podium and clutched onto it as if it were a life preserver, and the crowd let go a welcoming cheer. The smiles and looks of genuine admiration set me at ease a bit, but I was definitely not in my comfort zone. I would pick the last ten miles of a two-hundred-mile race any day over public speaking.

I explained how much credit I owed to Jake and to my coach. Lane was at the back of the room and threw out a nod of customary recognition. I mentioned how I wished Jake were here with me to pace me through this and it got a chuckle, with an especially loud guffaw coming from a man standing at the back of the crowd. A few people turned to look at him, but the guy kept his eyes on me.

My nervousness showed as I began talking with my hands. They flew around out of control, knocking things off the podium while the front row reached out to catch them then handed my papers back with big smiles. I eventually started to enjoy myself while dramatizing my stories of endurance and I finished by asking for questions. They came easy and predictable, and I had no problem answering and even getting a few laughs. I was really enjoying the attention until The Loud Laugher from the back of the room shot up his hand and while my intuition made me reluctant, I couldn't be rude.

"I think you are the most amazing thing to happen to this sport," he began with more passion than I thought necessary. Everyone turned to his direction.

I put a small smile on my face, nodded and replied, "Thank you very much." After an awkward silence I added, "Do you have a question?"

"Oh yes, I do. I was momentarily mesmerized by how good-looking you are in person," he replied, leaning up against the back wall with his arms crossed. He was only a few feet away from Lane, who looked ready to pounce. The crowd quickly turned from him to me, anticipating my response. My face started heating up, and I slumped a little trying to disappear behind the podium.

"Thank you again, but how I look doesn't have much to do with how I run," I managed to say. People nodded in support.

"Yeah, but hey, that is how you sell yourself all over social media, isn't it? Lots of sexy pictures and all," he shouted back waiting for my reaction.

Agatha jumped up to the podium, "Excuse me. I am the one who posts on Ellie's accounts. EVT decides what gets posted. Ellie doesn't have the time to approve every picture on her account. They are all tastefully taken." The crowd nodded in agreement and turned back at him. It became a tennis match of comments lobbing back and forth.

"They are fake accounts and those comments and motivational speeches aren't written by you, aren't your words? What a farce," he sneered.

"Hey, buddy, uncalled for," barked a guy in the crowd as he turned to face him.

Loud Laugher ignored this man and continued, "No, man, I thought you were genuine, Ellie, but you are only a bought, sold, manipulated, and vain athlete."

"I am simply an athlete," I interjected and stepped in front of Agatha to take control of the mic. I had to show my strength and defend myself. "You are right: I should be more accountable for what is posted about me. Yes, I agree some pictures," glancing sideways at Agatha, "are maybe too sexy for my liking, but unfortunately that gets the numbers up, and numbers sell shoes. I have a great relationship with EVT. They have supported me in all my needs, and I trust their decisions. They allow me to focus one hundred percent on my training to become the best athlete I can be, and I am thankful for that. Any other questions? Anyone?" I desperately wanted to change the subject, and his comment calling me vain hurt me deeply and I was positive my face was beet red. I was too distracted by Lane to check these posts as I had promised to do, nor was I responding to inquiries from fans as I needed to.

"Well, you have the whole running world cherishing the ground you run on, following your every move, giving you thousands of likes, so your ego must love it," the guy in the back snapped back.

I didn't know how to react. He put me down after complimenting me. I felt a little bullied, but before I could respond, he continued, "I mean, you are like, twenty years old and have lots of money, fame, and your picture everywhere. There are guys, even here, who don't care about your running—they just want to fantasize about you," he jeered.

The crowd turned in my direction for my reaction. There were a few boos. His words impacted me. Was I not seen simply for my athleticism? Was I being objectified? I looked at Lane but before I could read his reaction, Agatha approached me and reached toward the mic. I gave her a nod no, as I had to learn to deal with the public, and I could not let someone else fight my battles for me. I might be an introvert, but I was not a wimp. My alter ego came on strong, ready for a fight. I wanted to send a message to Lane as well.

"I think you are just baiting me, like a lot of people do on social media, and I actually applaud you for not hiding faceless behind a text, but let me explain something very clearly: I run because I love it. It is my passion. Honestly, I don't care about how I look or about attention or being sexy. If you saw my race pictures after running two hundred miles, I was far from sexy—more frighteningly ugly than anything, but I didn't care." The crowd nodded in agreement, giving me strength to continue.

"Although you may not believe this, I don't care too much for the attention either. I am the happiest running alone in the mountains. That is my passion. I will never be a prize or notch in a belt for anyone, even EVT. I will only be a prize for myself, and my reward is the ability to run well. This fame and sponsorship," I said as I pointed to the banner at the back, "is not why I run." The room went quiet as I continued my pontification.

"I can see why you would be concerned. We ultrarunners are an elite group of individuals who, and I think I speak for many of us when I say, we are an example of pursuing something against all odds - the mental and physical challenges including what nature throws at us. It takes an extraordinary amount of dedication, training, solitude, determination, consistency, and willingness to endure suffering. We must be passionate about running to be successful, and fame and money are *not* why we do it. In fact, it is a distraction. I run for the intrinsic reward. It is never on my mind about what I will win, or how many fans I will get as a result, or who will love or hate me. I run for the satisfaction of finishing. In fact, I compete because I love the training, if that makes any sense to you. The competition is a test of how well I run. And if I finish well, *that* is my prize to myself." I stopped and waited for a reaction.

The crowd broke out into whoops, whistles and enthusiastic applause. I could see Lane clapping slowly, accentuating each clap. I heard the comments and saw heads nodding in approval. Yet the guy was not satisfied, "We shall see. I will still be following your every move, Ellie. Remember I am your biggest fan and you are only just beginning."

"I sure hope it is not the end," I replied, refusing to let him have the last word, followed by more cheers from the crowd. He nodded his head, turned to leave, brushing past Lane with a slight bump. Lane looked at me and shrugged his shoulders. As I watched him shuffle out, with Alex tailing behind, there was a slight air of familiarity about him I couldn't place. He wore a backpack weighed down heavy on his shoulders over an oversized hunting jacket. His baggy pants hung below hips and dragged on the floor. He looked vaguely familiar, but he was too far to get a good look.

I gladly fielded a few less confrontational questions and concluded by thanking the crowd for their support. When I walked away from the podium, many people wanted to shake my hand and take pictures with me and Blue. I was happy to oblige but the words of the confrontation held prominent in my mind. I was itching to get away from the attention and be with the one who always brought me peace of mind and comfort, and he was patiently waiting, wagging his tail, staring up at me.

Chapter 31

Social Media

I decided to pay more attention and logged in to my social media accounts only to find my followers had doubled since the last time I looked, after the Northern Lights race. I had been too distracted with Lane to focus on anything other than him and training. There were an incredible number of posts advertising my Evotech running shoes and clothing. There are the same pictures they have used in the magazine and internet advertising I approved of, but I also saw some that made me feel objectified. I chastised myself for not paying more attention to this. I let Agatha run with it. I decided to give her a call.

"Agatha, honestly, can you remove some of these pictures of me? I am so uncomfortable with all the comments that do not talk about what I accomplished."

"Ellie, look at the numbers. It is a sick world out there but the shots of you showing more skin are getting the most attention and the great thing about it, that sets you apart is, most are not staged or posed. You are in a natural state of movement and we, well, we singled out the photos that are a little sexier. And you approved of the 'hair and makeup' photos, as you called them. Ellie, look at the numbers. You are the most popular female endurance runner in the world. In the world," she repeated. "This puts money in the bank for you. Your shoe sales are up by sixty percent, big bucks to you, all nicely tucked away in a trust account because, Ellie, the photos sell."

"I have some haters too," I complained. I was heartbroken and shocked by how mean people were.

"They are trolls, Ellie. This happens to everyone who has large number of followers on social media. The secret is to not read the comments and never engage. They are baiting you and others for all kinds of reasons, mostly they are jealous, bored and insecure. Think about it. Anyone who feels good about themselves would only support and encourage you. If they are jealous, they want to attack. You have no time for those kinds of people."

I didn't feel very reassured. There were quite a few replies to a seedy comment. Everyone was sticking up for me, but I couldn't help feel violated. I hadn't done anything to be hated by anyone. "If he can say such vile things about me, what is to stop him from finding me at my races and doing what he says he wants to do? Seriously, this freaks me out!"

"Ellie, these people talk a lot to scare you and get reactions. It's a numbers game. One percent of people out there are evil. So out of one hundred followers, one person will be malicious. Now multiply that by the number of followers you have. We have Alex as security following you around, even though you don't know it. That is another reason why Coach Lane mentioned he wants to be at your races. He also wants to protect you. He is aware you might have a possible stalker. I am not saying that you have one. I mean, we are being careful, and we don't want to upset your frame of mind when training. Coach doesn't want that. Dr. Chilton doesn't want that. But we will stop posting any picture without your approval. You have been so busy with training, we didn't want to have to contact you for approval all the time. We need to keep posting daily, and we only have so many opportunities to photograph you. You are always out training in the wilderness." Agatha argued.

I did like most of the pictures they had of me. But I couldn't help but think of how all this was evolving. Agatha mentioned the word, stalker, but no one told me. Lane was quick to use this opportunity for us to be together, but was he worried about needing to protect me? I felt like I was starting to lose control of my life.

I spent a few hours going into everyone else's accounts to check what Evotech had posted on their sites. I could see how people wasted time when I should have been packing for a training camp with Lane.

I wondered how he arranged for us to sneak off only the two of us to a mountain cabin and no one questioned it. Now I knew it was the stalker excuse. He must have told Alex that he would handle my security.

These camps usually involved a lot of running over three days on the race routes coming up. This weekend was for my next race called, Nine Lives in the Cattail Mountains. It consisted of nine loops on a very unforgiving track with incredible elevation climbs and drops for a total of ninety-nine miles, eleven miles per loop. I questioned the sanity of the race organizer. It was a true test of endurance and determination. Hans and Wilde were coming as well, the only others crazy enough besides me to challenge a course with a less than 50 percent finish rate.

Lane had arranged for us to stay in the nearest town, while the guys were staying in a cabin closer to the course. He also told me no dogs were allowed. It was part of my contract to be able to take Blue with me wherever I went, but I knew how much Blue hated Lane. Of course, it was jealousy, but I didn't want to have to be in the middle of them growling at each other all night. I cried a little when I left Blue with Alex. His sorrowful demeanor nearly made me cancel the whole trip.

I had packed and unpacked three times. I loved the anticipation knowing I would get to spend more time with Lane alone. I thought about him day and night, and felt light-headed and spaced out most of the time. Was this what being in love felt like? The effort of running disappeared when I thought about our times together or imagined what it would be like to be with him later at night, after all the post training meetings were done, and we could stop faking animosity toward each other. We had our routine down pat. We bickered, snickered and complained about each other when everyone else was present, then we were all over each other when we were alone.

The results on my body physiologically were registering through the devices and recorded. I was embarrassed that my feelings could filter through to me physically and Evotech could see the difference. Would they be able to know I was in love? I had remembered one of Dr. Chilton's video lectures in which he explained that our positive feelings such as joy, happiness, and love affected us in a way that was directly related to quantum theory. The first principle of quantum theory is consciousness creates a life experience. My consciousness controlled the chemistry from my brain, which in turn controlled my behavior, my genetics, and my overall health. Whatever information I put into my brain, it transferred, and since I felt love, happiness, and joy, it was directly affecting my capabilities. This was how my body behaved depending on how I perceived my life, and my perception was influenced by my emotions. Dr. Chilton said that we could even affect our body by thinking about being happy, like Coach told me before: "Fake it until you make it."

Dr. Chilton explained that at the same time if we are depressed and sad that would also affect performance. But to see it work in the opposite form is how we should feel all the time. We should be in love all the time. As we discussed Dr. Chilton's lectures, I asked Lane, "So tell me, were you instructed to have me fall in love with you so my performance would reach a new level?" I teased him as we lay together in bed after the first day's camp. I would have preferred to stay in bed all day. I didn't feel the energy to train. I felt drained. I figured it must be love.

"Oh, of course, Ellie. Yes, that was Evotech's mission all along. To have you fall in love with me," he replied, a little too sarcastically for my comfort.

His flippant reaction, although very much in his nature, had me confused. I knew what I felt was real. Yet, Lane hadn't told me he loved me, and I was OK with that, but I couldn't help but wonder what a fabulous experiment it would be to take it that much further. If I was happier and performing better, then sales go up. I was a happy, moneymaking, running machine.

Chapter 32

This Changes Everything

Ever since Ellie has come from the bathroom, she sits quietly with her eyes moving back and forth, closing, opening while she takes deep breaths. I think she is sick, but a small smile comes to her face and quickly disappears. She gets up and paces back and forth. I follow. She pauses. I pause. She sits and touches her stomach, sighs, then holds her head. She looks at something in her hand and stands up, hops up and down a little, and does a few turns. She drops the thing on the floor, and I go to sniff it. She pulls it away before I can investigate the scent further. She pierces her lips and gives me a quick, "No, silly dog." I hear ringing and soon we are racing out the door.

I soon realize we are heading for the track. Run at the track time! I love surprises. My whole life is full of surprises. We pull up to the track but do not get out of the car. We sit inside and watch the runners. I whine. She stops me. What are we doing here, if not to run? She still has that little thing in her hand. She has kept the paper in her hand the whole drive. The scent is strong to me, and somehow different. I sense it makes her feel different.

She is not watching the runners as much as I am. I typically am not allowed, so when she comes home with the track smell, I don't feel so bad for not going along, because I know she will either tie me up or put me in the SUV, which is too painful to watch others have fun. So why do we sit and watch others play? I stare at her and the people. She stares at the people and at the paper.

We are out of the SUV and walk fast toward Coach Lane. I stand closer to guard her. We all know how I feel about him, and it never disappears. The fur goes up on my neck every time he is around. He knows I know about him. It has been many times now I have tried to explain it to Ellie, but I must accept what I cannot change.

Let's run! We sit in the bleachers. OK. I'll wait. There are words. High and low sounds. They are talking closely together. She has given him the marking paper. He turns his head and feel the emotion growing inside of him. I must watch him closely. He brings his hand to his hair but does not touch her. She does not look anywhere but at him. I watch the runners, but I soon hear deeper sounds and smell tears. Their voices are lower and faster. There are moments of quiet, but the air is full of noise from their bodies. She drops the paper. I finally get to sniff it, but choose not to.

"Oh my God, Ellie, how could you let this happen? You said you were on birth control. How many weeks?" Lane's voice was a harsh antipathetic whisper taking me completely by surprise. There was no emotion in it. He was mechanical.

"I am, or I mean I was on birth control. I think only a couple of months. It can't be longer," I searched his face to get a better read of his reaction, but he wouldn't look at me. He was staring blank-faced out at the track. He was doing a good job of keeping emotionless in case someone took notice.

"I wasn't getting my period for over a year and the doctor told me amenorrhea can be normal when a woman runs like I do. Evotech doesn't like it when I use birth control. When they asked if I was sexually active, I said no. I didn't want them to suspect anything. I thought, *Well, if I don't have birth control, what will it matter? I am not ovulating anyways.* I know it was stupid, in hindsight but maybe it is not such a bad thing. I mean. I'm ready. I could have a baby. We could have this baby. Women still train when they are pregnant and after the birth, they are much stronger athletes. You even coached some of those Olympic women. We could tell Dr. Chilton. Come clean and make this relationship legit. I mean. What better way? I think everyone would be happy for us. He would understand. It is not like they don't suspect something is going on between us."

This made him finally turn to me, but I was shocked by the anger in his eyes. His face was tense and mean. "Hold on. Stop, Giselle." Lane grabbed my hands, immediately dropped them down, and glanced around. He never called me Giselle. "You don't understand. I can't do this." He couldn't hold my eyes. He was breathing deeply and rubbing his hands back and forth on his knees. I knew I was about to hate him.

"Go ahead, tell me." I stared at him. His eyes were everywhere but where they should be. He rubbed them with his fingers and thumb, put his hand through his hair and finally looked back to me. Tears burned the back of my eyes. I couldn't stop them, and I hated myself for being vulnerable. I dropped the paper along with all my hope. He was going to choose his job over our relationship and having our baby, having a family. How could a job overrule all that?

"Ellie, I don't want this baby. You don't understand. Why did you have to let this happen?" He stared passed me and hissed the words through gritted teeth. "I will deny it is mine if you decide to keep it." His eyes shifted to me. They were on fire, squinting between pinched eyebrows. He forced me to pull back and wrap my arms around myself to feel some sort of protection against him without getting up and running away.

He snapped, "If you decide to keep this baby, it will ruin your career, and it is too big a secret to keep. They will find out it's mine, and all I worked for will be gone. I have not built my career as the top coach in the world, written books, hired by Evotech to have it ruined by you. I can't let you keep this baby." He looked away. I followed his gaze, watching the team out on the track. "You need to go have an abortion," he said to the team. He couldn't face me.

I struggled to force the lump that came up from my heart into my throat out of the way in order to whisper, "Lane why are you saying this to me? Why are you being so mean to me?" I couldn't catch my breath. I couldn't just simply erase a little human being.

"You can't keep running and have a baby? Are you crazy? Evotech would fire you so fast. And me. It would destroy me. You are making a huge mistake if you keep this baby. I won't have anything to do it with it. What's worse, they have DNA testing to find out its mine. Damn it, Elllie! You will not keep it."

We were far enough away from the athletes on the track, but I couldn't help feel the whole world could hear. I felt embarrassed this man I thought loved me, even just a little, suddenly resented me. It didn't feel real. This was not the reaction I was anticipating. Why was I so stupid?

"Ellie, take care of it. It isn't a child right now. It is just cells dividing. This is my whole career, everything I have worked for, damn it. People are reading my books. I am getting paid more than I ever dreamed. I am living my fantasy and you would ruin it all. I will find a place and take you."

He placed his elbows on his thighs and held his hands together in a fist, continually wringing them together. I couldn't stand watching him. He was sitting there on the bleacher like it was another spat with an athlete. Now I was starting to feel anger creep upward from my gut. I deserved more than this. His words burned reality into my heart.

"Why did you let this whole romance happen between us? Was I the notch in your belt?" He gave me no reply. I was so angry I thought I was going to punch him, but I kept my composure beyond what I thought I was capable of. I swallowed hard and words I wanted to yell at him landed hard in my gut, churning away. I tried one last time because as an endurance athlete, I never gave up. I kept beating myself up repeatedly, so why not do it in every other aspect of my life?

"Lane, we will be honest with Evotech. Tell them we fell in love. They can't stop people from falling in love. I won't abort any child. That is so far away from my core beliefs. This is a new life and all life is precious to me. That is who I am." I threw it out there hoping he would respond with some compassion, but he shot back hard.

"Ellie, damn you. We broke the rules. There is no coming back from this. It is game over for both of us. And my having an affair with an athlete, oh my God, the repercussions would never end. Listen, I don't want to be mean to you. I thought I felt something for you—I really did." He looked at me and took a softer tone as if I were a small child, trying to placate me but turned away again and continued without consideration for my feelings, "I don't love you enough to throw away everything I ever worked for."

He had no emotion in his voice. It was simply a statement, while my head was spinning as the reality of his words hit me. His words mixed with my blood as it rushed from my head into my stomach like a waterfall. Wham. I felt sick and couldn't bear to be sitting there one second longer. I had to get out. I rubbed the pain from my forehead up through my untidy hair. I had an unimaginable need to run away. I would never be able to come here again without thinking about this moment. Everything was over. Everything I knew and loved was gone. What was I going to do now?

"I'm sorry, Ellie. I had to be honest with you." He glanced at me and then looked around. I started to get up, but he grabbed my arm and pulled me back down.

"This was all just a fling for you so you could screw the young, hot star on the team." I was so angry and hurt and didn't know what else to say. I felt foolish and empty. I tried to resist his grip to get up, but his fingers dug into my forearm in a warning. I immediately thought of my father when I told him about Mom, the expression on his face. I was the one getting the shock of reality this time. My whole world felt like it had drained completely away leaving my legs trembling and leaden with shame and dread.

He sat with a blank face looking around to see who took notice of us. Anger rose from my stomach bringing vomit along with it. I had to leave at that very moment and pushed hard against his grip to stand. He stood up right in front of me and grabbed my hand to pull me along with him as he directed me out of the bleachers.

"Ellie, let's go somewhere to talk. I want this to be more private, not here with the team on the track. Let's go." He grabbed my arm forcefully and pulled me while yelling at the team to finish their sets, cool down, and stretch, that I had a little emergency. Everyone stopped in their tracks and yelled out their concerns.

"It's nothing serious, you guys," he yelled out. "I'll be back!"

"Nothing serious? How can you say that? This is pretty damn serious!" I let everything explode out of me as he pulled me along toward his car, opened the door, and indicated to get inside, shutting the door behind me.

"Let's both calm down and sit here a little while," he huffed.

I turned and saw Blue jumping up against the door.

"Damn dog. Get down," he yelled at Blue through the closed window. I got out and calmly called Blue to come with me as Lane watched, and I put Blue inside my SUV. I thought about walking back to him, but something deep inside asked why? Why did I need to listen to his reasons for hurting me? I didn't want to subject myself to his condescending rant. So, like I did when I was a child, I ran. I got myself into the driver's side, locked the doors, started it up, and quickly reversed the SUV back and wheeled around shooting gravel from my tires as I sped out of the parking lot. The dust flew up and adumbrated Lane as he stood beside his car. I got a pang of regret but quickly stopped it, chastising myself for thinking that way. I didn't owe him anything. I didn't know where I was going but like I did as a child, I needed to get away from the source of the pain. I needed to run.

I drove out of the town toward the country. I was surprisingly focused despite an heavy pain in my chest, breathing hard, whimpering every third gulping breath, my hands tight on the steering wheel. Thoughts came running nonstop like a ticker tape. I had to quit the team. I would lose my contract. I would have to pay back EVT. They won't sell my shoes anymore. I will be a disgrace. We were deceitful. Oh my God, the media will crucify me. Who cares? I won't have any money. I would have to move back with my mom. I would have to raise this baby by myself. OK that is OK. I could handle it. Abortion was absolutely not an option. I don't need anyone. Oh my God, living with my mother. Oh God. Maybe she would change. Maybe I can afford to live on my own. How will I support myself and this child? And Blue?

Oh God, Ellie! That is one of the bravest things I have seen you do! A puppy! You are carrying a puppy? That runt is the father? He doesn't want to be with you? I felt a warning about him deep within from the very start. There was an overwhelming feeling that something in your relationship was stalking and ready to pounce. That is fate's way of beating us in a fair fight. It gives us warnings that we hear but we never pay heed. I tried to tell you. Ellie, I know you want to run from him, but you can't bury him like an old bone. The smell will find its way back to you someday heavy with regret. You must find the courage to deal with this.

I was startled out of my thoughts by a honking horn and my cell ringing at the same time. It was Lane calling. Of course it would be. I looked in the rearview mirror and there he was tailgating me, so I decided to pull over. I couldn't drive away forever, however much I wanted to. I pulled over to the side off the road and got out, leaving Blue inside for fear he would attack Lane. I should have let him out.

Lane rushed toward me, grabbed me in his arms and held me tight, pressing me close to his chest trying to hold me secure. I fought him at first, but my body responded without my head. I wanted to be held so badly. I wanted to be wanted. But as he started to kiss the top of my head like my father used to do, in an instant, I hated him more. It was a pathetic attempt to sooth me with insincere actions what his words destroyed. My heart was breaking, yet I wanted him to tell me everything would be OK, but his lack of words spoke volumes. I hated, but I still loved him.

"Sssh, Ellie, please. God, I could lose my job if anyone found out about us this way."

"Lose your job!" I swallowed hard. "This is what you are thinking about? Your job? What about me?" I struggled to pull away, but I could see he didn't want to take a chance anyone to see us like this. He was searching around for spies from EVT. He was telling me to be calm. I pulled away and stared at him. I hated the look in his stupid little eyes. It was always about not letting the team see us, but I realized it was more. This relationship was a lie. Everything was coming together for me. I needed to throw up desperately, so I broke away from his grip and ran into the forest to vomit.

I felt Lane's hand reach to rub my back. I stood up and asked before I could brace myself for the answer, "Do you have children?"

"I have a son."

He had a whole other life. I wanted to fold up and fall to the ground, but I feared I would break into a thousand different pieces and never be able to put myself together.

"I am going to tell you the truth. You must believe me. My wife and I are separated, and I don't love her anymore. I was falling in love with you. But I am still stuck in a delicate situation because I don't want to hurt my son. I don't want him to have divorced parents. I have seen what that does to people."

"You were falling in love with me, and now you are not?" I zeroed in on his admission, whether he meant it or not. "And you think I am screwed up because of my parents? Well, maybe I am, but I am a survivor. I did pretty good. They made me strong by being real—by being honest." I realized there were lies and deceit, too, but didn't want to admit that to him.

"I am a good person. I don't hate them, if that is what you are worried about, that your son will hate you. That is a pretty selfish reason because he is going to hate you more for raising him in a fake relationship. What a thing to teach him—how to be deceptive. And you know what? You are pretty damn good at faking things, being deceitful, lying, manipulating. Are you going to teach him those traits? Well, I can assure you this child of mine will not have a father like you." I wanted him to hurt as deeply as I did in that moment.

I brushed by him and back to my SUV where Blue was sitting up watching through the window. I felt numb. I couldn't feel anything even if I wanted to. Lane did not follow me. As I got in my SUV, I glanced back to see him still standing where I left him. My heart wanted so badly for him to fight for me, but my head was logical and yelling to leave him, to run. I turned over the engine and a song started, as if as a premonition, *Hey Little Girl* by Icehouse. I kept it playing, forcing the pain of my situation to burrow deeper into my heart through the lyrics of the song.

She is really crying now. I stand up on the back seat and put my head on her shoulder as she is driving. Normally I would be buckled in, or she would be commanding me to lie down, but she is not. I soon figure out where we are going, and I am a little excited. I jump out and wait as she changes into her running shoes. It won't be a long run because we don't take water with us. We head up the trail, and she starts to run. She is more excited than I am. She doesn't wait for me when I sniff around. She keeps going at a faster pace than normal. I have to work to keep up. I hear her sniffling and breathing hard. No water. It will be a short run.

We make it back to the SUV after dark. We had run for so long I can hardly move my legs. My paws hurt, and I am so thirsty. I was able to take water at a creek and a few muddy pools along the way, but she took no water at all. She had only washed her face and sat for a few minutes staring out at the dark silhouette of the mountains, as the late afternoon sun weighed heavy in the sky. I lay in the water to cool myself then I got up and tried to nuzzle her to encourage her to tell me something. She only put her arms around my neck and rested her head against mine with heavy breaths. She had a very heavy smell of salt, and I licked her face. A glimpse of a smile touches her lips, then quickly disappeared.

When we returned, she had to help me into the SUV and I fell onto the seat unable to move until we got home. I felt her hand apologizing for my exhaustion. Once in the house, I slowly walked to the big water bowl, knowing it would be full and cold. After I left, she went in and closed the door. I threw myself against it and slid to the floor with a moan. I will wait all night if I had to. I would never leave her side. I would never be able to watch her go without chasing after her. I think that is why she is so sad. He didn't chase her.

I eventually fall asleep waiting for her and dream about being a cat. Ellie is calling for me. I try to move, but I can't. My paws and legs are burning. I can't save her. I wake up with a jolt and a realization that I was living my pathetic life over and over again trying to rescue her. I heard her crying behind the door. I found her, but I can't save her from her pain.

Chapter 33

Nowhere Else to Go

After the situation with Lane, I packed up a bunch of things and left the next day to go home. I drove with Blue, and it took unbearably long. I had to stop so many times to get sick. My legs were so cramped up and sore when we arrived. I had never been this sore before, even after the two hundred miles.

Mom wasn't expecting us. My appearance and demeanor must have shocked her from asking a barrage of questions. She knew something was very wrong. She had changed the house around and made my room into an office. I felt like I was intruding, but I didn't know where else to turn. I was so afraid to tell her, but I was moved by her compassion for me. She did everything she could to make me feel at home, and she didn't lecture me. I looked around for my real mother. She must be hiding in here somewhere.

She took out all her wrath on Lane. She was ready to press charges. For what? I was a consenting adult. She called him a predator. She wanted to call Dr. Chilton. I pleaded with her that I needed time, and she reluctantly agreed. She convinced me it was the right thing that I left. We would raise this baby together. She tried to say all the things I needed to hear, and it worked for the most part. I started to see a future with this baby. I was getting excited to have her all to myself, to raise her in truth and love. My mother called my father, and they were both excited about a grandchild. They didn't care how or what it would do to my career with EVT. We made plans for us to go together to meet with Dr. Chilton and tell him the truth. Then she made an appointment for me to see a doctor for a checkup.

There was no communication from Lane. Secretly I was hoping he would try, but there were no calls or messages registered on my cell phone or to the house. I called Jake to let him know I was taking some time away in case EVT came looking for me. I needed time to put my head together, and I was feeling physically tired as well. I knew he sensed something was terribly wrong but thankfully didn't pry.

"You will tell me when you are ready, Ellie. But know I am here for you. I will not judge you." Jake had such a sweet way of telling me things. I wished he were Lane, or Lane were him. This was not how I envisioned my life. Everything was so perfect: I was in love, making money, top endurance runner in the world. That chapter was over. I would be a parent and the thought of holding a baby, raising her to become an awesome human changed my perspective. I had to be positive for her. My parents were going to help, and planning for this new little life was bringing us closer together. Blue must have known what was going on with me because he would not, for any reason, leave my side. He would lay with his head on my stomach as if listening for the sound of life. I had to move past the resentment, hurt and enmity for Lane as each day passed. I had to be, was going to be OK. This child would save my broken heart.

Oh, Ellie. With my deepest regret, I know you have lost this battle in this part of your life. I can smell something that will terrify you. Your sorrows are only beginning. How can I prepare you for this? How can I hold you up when I know you are going to fall apart?

"Ellie, it was nothing that you did, honey. This wasn't your anger or that run or your sorrow. Sometimes these things happen. Your body is simply not ready for a baby. It had a glitch. But you absolutely did not do this to yourself. OK? Do you understand? I am serious. Do you understand?"

I heard the words from our small town doctor, but they weren't registering. I didn't believe her. I told her about the long run without water. When she asked how far, I could only guess it was about twenty miles. But she hopelessly tried to convince me it wasn't my fault and offered me some pills to take, so I could calm down and rest. In my own selfishness, I did this to a precious little child. I was blaming Lane for being selfish, but I was the one who was selfish. I felt the life go out of me—this child's and my own. My mother collected me at the doctor's office. I guess I blanked. I don't remember much of anything. She told me she was taking me home. But I no longer felt like I deserved a home. My child didn't have one.

I felt like I was drowning in sorrow. Tears boiled up inside of me and came in waves as relentless as an incoming tide slapping against a sea wall. All this sorrow was more than my heart could hold. What had I done to deserve this? I never hurt anyone. I was a good person. Why was this life so cruel? I needed to feel Lane's arms around me, comforting me. I missed him terribly, and I hated myself for it. I wanted to break down and call him but knew nothing good could come from a relationship built on lies. Mom pussyfooted around me, afraid of showing too much emotion in case it would set me off again. Dad was in shock and without words to console me for the first time in his life. His Dean Martin didn't know how to handle tragedy.

I felt the spirit of the child when it left her body. She stopped to smile at me. It was not her time, but she will be back. She was not prepared enough for her rebirth. I have seen it many times. The soul is wanting but not yet ready. The desire to return to a life is so great sometimes the soul slips into a new life without understanding the ramifications. Sometimes they make it through with memories of a past life so strong it affects the new family because the new life doesn't know how to handle the memories of the old one, kind of like Ellie and her bad dreams. Sometimes they catch them and stop the soul from rebirth. I don't know who "they" are, but it feels like a collaboration of beings who can move back and forth through time. They have evolved

further than the rest of us who are still heading back for some form of redemption in the next life.

Some of us, such as me, need to go back repeatedly to learn more lessons about life, to eventually atone for our sins, not just in one life, but in many. Spirits learning from another human experience. I lost count of my lives. That is the real hell. Then when we finally make sense of our true spirit, give in to our purpose, recover the essences of our true soul and make amends, only then can we move forward. Being with Ellie is my last attempt to forgive myself. They allowed it. I was ready. Her child was not.

My sorrow for Ellie amplified when she spoke of her latest dream. She told me was with child when she is in the fire that haunts her reoccurring nightmare. My sorrow for her grew a million-fold. I didn't know it was two lives I couldn't save in that fire so many lives ago. They knew this was going to be hard for me, but I had no idea it was going to be this difficult. How can I ever be worthy enough, rise above my powerlessness, to save her from this intense pain and sorrow?

Ellie, please don't give up or give in to sorrow and guilt. You don't want to be me. I refuse to let you go down the same never-ending path I took. That is an endurance race that might never end.

Chapter 34

Jake's Visit

"Ellie, honey, someone is here to see you. It's Jake." My mom knocked gently as she spoke through my closed door. She was treading softly around me. I knew she was afraid for me. It had been a couple weeks at home, and I hadn't made any attempt to see or talk to anyone. She had been taking calls and making excuses to the team. I heard the desperation in her voice getting stronger, but I had no energy to respond to anything. I felt black and empty.

I didn't want to see anyone, but I knew Jake came a long way, so I did my best to look as good as possible and threw my slimy hair into a ponytail. I couldn't remember the last time I washed it. I put on a clean shirt and headed out to the living room. I smelled cinnamon buns in the air. For a smell that should have made me hungry, I felt sicker.

"Hi Jake," I tried to sound excited.

He looked up from a fresh cinnamon bun with icing on his lips. Mom fed him while he waited for me to get ready. He dropped the bun on the plate and rushed over while wiping his mouth with the back of his hand. "Oh, Ellie. My God, Ellie. What is going on? What's happened? Are you sick?" His eyes opened wide in shock and mouth agape as he grabbed my shoulders and stood back while inspecting me up and down.

"Do I really look that bad?" I asked as I turned to regretfully compare myself to Jake in the large mirror hung on our living room wall. I was so much thinner when we used to be the same size.

"Ellie, girl!" He grabbed me. It felt so good to be hugged tightly. "You have lost so much weight, I can feel your bones," he stuttered with an honest ignorance of my true condition.

We sat together on the couch, and I ignored a cinnamon bun my mom placed in front of me while I felt Jake's eyes burn holes in my head. I turned to face him, "What? Don't look at me that way. You must know the whole story by now," I turned away from his stare toward my hands instead. I hid my fingernails I had bitten to the quick.

"Ellie, all I know is you and Coach Lane had a big disagreement and you took off. That is what he told us anyways. The team hopes you come back, but I didn't know you are sick. What is going on? You won't answer my calls, emails, texts. You shut down completely. When I called here, your mom said to come. So here I am. Surprise!" He leaned back and waved both hands in the air beside his face.

I attempted a smile, then looked down at my hands again.

"What can I do, Ellie? Tell me." He folded me into his chest and rubbed the back of my head as I released convulsions of tears. After I could breathe again, we both sat up and laughed at the large wet mark I left on his shirt. I experienced my first real smile in a long time, and it felt foreign on my face. He grabbed me in a hug again and whispered in my ear, "Tell me. I am here to listen. I am here for you."

I told him the whole story. He went through a myriad of emotions, and I led the way.

"Coach Lane did take some time off from the team. We thought it was a holiday. Now I know. Ellie, you need to come clean with Dr. Chilton. Coach crossed the ethical barrier and though you say it takes two, he was in a position of superiority, and he shouldn't have taken advantage of you." Jake's advice was nothing I hadn't already heard from my parents.

"I don't want to go back because the memories are too painful. I went from being on top of the world to the bottom of the trash heap. I can't seem to pull myself out of it. My mom tries, and even Blue tries. I feel like I am swimming out in the middle of a deep lake. I am sinking and can't reach the surface for air. My body is worn out, but worse, my heart and spirit are gone. They all left with the baby. The baby I killed with my anger. Don't tell me otherwise. It is what I feel. I keep having nightmares. The same ones I used to get all the time, but they went away. Now they are back and are worse. It isn't only me dying in a fire; there is the child I am carrying too. I can't get the image out of my brain."

Jake watched me. I could sense he didn't know what to do, so he rubbed my back and tried to console me, but I interrupted him.

"Here's what I want you to do for me, Jake. Go back and talk to Dr. Chilton. I don't have the courage at this point. I would be a mess of emotions. Tell him I know I am fired from the team," I paused to take a breath. "He can decide what happens to Lane. I don't care, but I hope he is fired and never finds another job. I can't hold on to this anger toward him. I have to let this go, but I am struggling," I paused. "The good thing is no more stupid social media posts about me."

"Ah, you haven't looked at that stuff? They keep posting old photos of you training and saying you are enjoying a much-needed R and R. They got everything covered." He continued, "I think you should tell Dr. Chilton yourself, Ellie. I am sure he won't let you go. He will let Coach go, but not you. They have invested a lot in you, and they'll get you counseling. They probably have a supplement to help with depression. Who knows, Ellie? They won't drop you. They aren't like that."

"But Jake, I don't want to go back. I don't want all that publicity and pressure. I don't want the spacesuits and technology, and special foods, pills, contraptions and devices talking in my ear to run faster or slower or breathe deeper. Sorry. I know you like that stuff but for me, not anymore. It doesn't fit. They want to prove we need technology to make us better than who we are naturally. I have been thinking, Jake. Not only about my mistakes but about the whole thing. It feels like a scam, like I have been set up. My popularity on social media, this stupid relationship with Coach—all of it was some weird setup for them to make money off me. For all their efforts to reduce toxicity in our lives, I feel it gave me more. Don't get me wrong: There is a place for all that technology. I know it helps people. I deeply admire Dr. Chilton. His heart is in the right place. But they took away my love for running. It became a job. Maybe I am the only one. Maybe this thing with Lane messed me up. I don't know, but I feel used. I hate everything right now, including me."

"Oh, Ellie, you are just confused and don't know where to turn," Jake lamented. He tilted his head to the side and a look of pity crossed his face. "I guess you are in the best place being here. But I know you are not capable of hating anyone, even Coach."

I huffed out a half laugh. "Well, I know Blue hates Lane, that's for sure." I quickly changed the subject. "I can be myself at home. I don't have to be a superstar or perfect, so please don't feel sorry for me," I spoke louder so Mom could hear me clearly, even though I knew she had been eavesdropping our entire conversation.

"Well, everyone loves you, Ellie, more than you know. You have your parents and Blue for support. I have never seen a more loyal dog. He's Glue Blue, remember?" With that, Blue laid his head on Jake's lap and sighed, making us both smile.

Jake brought a little light into my life, but the darkness all came pouring back in when he left. I was deep in it, but what was worse, I could see I was sucking my mom and Blue in with me. I could see the sadness on their faces. I wanted to cheer them up, but I didn't have the energy.

She wouldn't come out of her room when I heard Coach Lane's voice. I barked loudly. Mom was angry. She was shouting. They were both shouting. Ellie didn't move from her bed until it quieted down, and she got up to look out her window. Then she went back to her bed and started crying again. I feel so hopeless. I nudge her and lick her. Mom tries to feed her, but Ellie gives it to me. I can't eat it. I knew it isn't right. I want her to live. She is a sick pup, so I keep lying beside her to keep her warm. I refuse to lose her again. That will not happen under my watch, but I desperately need help.

Chapter 35

The Letters

"Ellie, I have something I want to share with you." My mom opened the curtains in my room to let in what was left of the daylight, and I instantly hated her for it. I was used to my hovel of darkness. She brought with her a small yet heavy box, larger than a hatbox, and dropped it on my bed beside me so that I could feel the impact of its weight as it landed.

"I have debated whether to do this for a while now," she said as she turned the desk chair around to face me and sat on it with a heavy sigh. It used to be her office until I made it into my cave of self-pity.

"I had made a pact with myself I would never show you this, but I think I have no choice." She sat waiting for me to sit up. It was early evening, and I had already started to nestle in for the night. I sat up and stared at an old worn box, the kind with a lid that flips over the top. It was tied with a thick ribbon attached at the bottom.

"Ellie, I know you and I don't always see eye to eye. I know you are disappointed in me as your mother. I made mistakes, was selfish, and had my priorities wrong. When I should have been loving you and spending time with you, I was giving attention away to others," she paused to swallow, "to men." She continued, unable to make eye contact with me and focused on playing with a tissue in her hand.

"I guess I was looking for a way to validate my existence. I don't know. I never felt worthy of anything. I never felt good enough at anything. The only thing I felt I had was my looks, and in the end that didn't even matter. I had no self-respect, no respect for your father nor you.

I have deep shame for that. I am so sorry I was not there for you when you needed me, and I forced you to run and hide from me. I can see you are still doing that." She was crying and dabbing her eyes with her tissue she had twisted up into a rope.

"I don't expect you to change, but I had a lot to do with who you are today." She glanced up at me for a reaction. I sat quietly and stared at her.

"And when we are together, we relive those feelings whenever they get triggered by a word, or situation. You are someone I am both so proud of yet, also afraid of because you are so much better a person than I am. I am a little envious of the success you have. I am envious of you because you made yourself into someone, when I struggled and still struggle to find out who I am."

I butted in, "Mom. Look at the business you run. You are so successful. Everyone loves your products. You are wrong when you think I made myself into someone. I don't know who I am," I confessed a new realization. "I defined myself as a runner. But that is not who I am—that is what I do. I thought being a mother would give who I am supposed to be, but now I don't even know about that either."

"Ellie, it's not entirely your fault. It was hard to raise a human being to be all I hoped she could be when I struggled with who I was as a human being. Oh gosh, honey, it is so hard. I made so many mistakes. I sent you out into the forest, then into the world, hoping you would find your way. And you did. You turned your struggles into something great. You turned it into a success. But I see it doesn't mean anything if you lose something or someone you love. You are not alone, Ellie. Others have suffered and made their way back, and I wish the same for you. As I see you suffer and know I cannot heal you because we have a wall between us and if we broke down that wall, there would still be rubble we would stumble over. I am certainly not an expert, and I understand why you don't want to go for counseling, because it didn't help you in the past."

I nodded in agreement at the same time as I shrugged. I didn't think it was hopeless. I loved her no matter what kind of obstacles were in our path to making amends. Maybe I was too much to handle.

She had broken her tissue rope in half. Twisted it until it tore and was now staring at the two pieces in her hands as if she didn't know what to do with them.

"I do know someone who can help you, Ellie." She nodded toward the box. "He is in that box. And as you read, keep in mind there are two versions to every story. Don't pass judgment until you talk to me. But I will let you hear his story first."

And with that she got up, held a kiss for a long time on the top of my head, turned and walked out the door, closing it gently. She left her torn tissue on my bed. Blue jumped up and sniffed at the box. I opened it and shuffled through the stacks tied together and pulled out one letter that was sitting alone. I smelled a hint of sage or grass. I couldn't quite place it. It opened easily.

Dear Giselle,

I assume you will be reading this letter at an age when you can understand what it means. I write this on the day you are born into this life. From the ashes you rise again. I held you today and felt your spirit, as strong as a wolf pup and a howl to match. You are a survivor, a warrior like no other. You are still wearing your armor and your greatest fault will be not knowing when to take it off and when to put it back on.

You are my first grandchild. I may have others. I have had many lovers. I am not a man to comply with traditions of this society, tribe or family. I have never felt a true attachment to this time, in this world. I feel an attachment to different way of life because for some reason it pierced my soul and spun me around in a trance I don't know how to get out of. I have a past life that keeps hanging on in shadows and dreams. But time, as we know it, does not exist. We are all timeless souls. Birth and death are the same thing.

I am not welcome around your mother, and that is why I was allowed to hold you only once and that one time was the greatest gift I have ever received. I pray that day will come when I can hold you again. Because of my beliefs, your mother has decided you should not be influenced by me, and I cannot blame her. I was not there for her life and because of that she does not know me. She believes I would influence yours negatively, but she couldn't be further from the truth.

The world I know is one of freedom. I believe your mother is afraid of freedom. I love my daughter dearly, but she is a river stone, and I am a bird. Perhaps some would say I am a hippie, but I am not. Some would say I am into free love, but all love comes with a cost. When there is love, there is also heartache. That is how I know your mother loves me. I couldn't break the heart of someone who did not love me. To experience the positive, you must also know the negative. To see the light, you must also know the darkness. You cannot know one without the other.

When you love, the pain of loss is harsh, so why love, you will ask? This will be your first lesson in life. You will feel pain, my Giselle. You will love intensely because it is in your soul. You will also be guarded and that is wrong. Guarding one's heart is like living in a cage. You, my dear Giselle, are meant to be free. Right now, before you can form words or let this world influence your spirit, you are free. Finally, you are reborn. You are never to be caged but a past life will haunt you and make you guarded. You search for solitude, which is where you will feel safe. It will bring joy, but it will bring loneliness, and in loneliness you will lose your judgment. Be open to trust. Know that all the heartache will pass, but only if you open the door for it to leave. Know that through the open door will also blow in new love. It always does, if you keep the door open. A house without love is a closed house, a cave, dark, lonely, and damp with tears.

When I am needed, call me because I can provide balance when the waters of life are swirling around, and you feel like you are drowning. I know who you are, Giselle. When you feel like you are lost, I will help you find your way again.

With the greatest of love, your grandfather,

Toko

How did he know that much about who I am today back on the day I was born? There are letters in bundles according to years. There was at least one every two months. I opened another from the middle of a bundle. It was Toko talking about going to Peru and learning about natural healing. Another letter had a newspaper clipping of my first high school x-country race. He noted he bought two papers, one for him and one for me, in case my mother forgot. She did. I remember that race. It was my first win and a very special moment for me. Other parents were there to watch, but I had to ride back to school on the bus with my coach, and then he drove me home, when I couldn't get a hold of her. I came home to an empty house. It is funny how something so good could also have something so sad attached to it.

Another letter near the bottom was dated last month. He wrote he was worried about me. He had seen no new reports on social media, in which he purposely bought a "stupid radiation device" to keep track of me. He was very concerned and prayed for my heart, and ended this letter with, "May you be healthy and happy. Sending all my love to you, Toko."

As I read through a few of the letters, I found a powerful message I could take from each one. He summed up each letter with a lesson. I couldn't help but wish I could have seen these letters sooner. Each letter carried an underlying theme of some sort, based on a lesson he had learned, either to forgive, to let go of painful thoughts because they will cloud vision, or to not be distracted by symbols and status. He explained how each of his life experiences, the good and the bad, helped to fill a tool kit he used to grow spiritually, and he was sharing those lessons with me.

For the first time in a while, I felt like doing something. I found a couple of old binders from high school in the back of the closet and a hole punch, and organized each letter in order into the binders. I kept the envelopes in the original box. There were return addresses to places in the United States, Canada, Bolivia, Columbia, Peru, Chile, Australia, and Mexico was the postmark from the last few years.

Blue pawed at me to go outside. Through my window the sky was black. The sun had long set. Poor Blue. I had neglected him for the last few weeks. His head hung low most of the time, and he slumped along with me wherever I went. He wasn't eating either. My mood was contagious. I am sure mom felt it as well.

I opened my bedroom door and found the house dark except for a spotlight from the lamp, under which Mom was sitting knitting, with a steaming tea on a table nearby.

"Is everything OK?" she asked hesitantly as her face contorted into a grimace as if she was waiting for a blow to the face.

"Oh, Mom, please don't worry. I am not angry with you. I mean, I was briefly, but I get why you kept those letters from me. You did what you thought was the right thing to do. You didn't know this man. I know he didn't expect a response from me, so I am amazed he kept writing month after month. He was writing a journal of his life and sharing it in hopes that someday, you would share it with me and you did. That is all that matters now."

She put down her knitting, tilted her head to the side and brought a smile to her face that lit up her eyes and released the tight wrinkles she had grown since my arrival. She brought a hand to her chest. "Oh, Ellie, I am so relieved to hear you say that. I have been sitting here on pins and needles—excuse the pun—waiting for you." We both smiled.

"I can explain why I kept him out of your life, if you want to hear my side," she said. I nodded back a reply and went to curl up in the couch across from her, tucking my knees into my overstretched sweatshirt as she continued. "I felt if you read all his letters about his travels you would leave me to go find him, or at least go on your own adventure because you are so much like him," she paused, looking down at her knitting needles. "You would leave me, like he did. You were that little free bird, who he wrote about. It scared me. And when I saw the person you were becoming, growing up to be, all I could see in you was him. I see his face in yours. I see his spirit in you. He would run, just like you. He would come home to my mother and then take off running. He could never stay in one spot. He always had to be moving."

"That's for sure," I responded, and we both shared a laugh again. "But Mom, you ended up marrying a man who did the same thing to you."

"You are right, Ellie. You are absolutely right. I have thought about that. You know how they say little girls want to grow up and marry a man like their father—at least they used to say that. Now I don't know so much anymore."

"Hey, I am not judging you Mom. I am the last person who should do that," I replied and turned to go into the kitchen to feed Blue and opened the back door a crack for him to go out when he was ready. He headed out right away to bark and howl into the night. Mom had joined me, and we both stood at the door to watch and listened as coyotes responded. "How strange. I have never seen him do that before," I said.

"Me neither."

As she prepared a plate of food for me, she continued, "Ellie, I feel all the losses I have had in my life are now your losses. I have lost my mother to death, my husband to my dishonesty, and my father to my stubbornness. To shut someone out with such finality, as I did to him, I feel I can never get him back. Those letters are the only lifeline—the only tie I have to him—and I didn't want to share him with you. I read all the letters, to let you know, but sealed them again, so you wouldn't notice since they were addressed to you. I couldn't help myself. They were the only connection I had to him. I also knew he wrote them in hopes I would read them too. I didn't know when I would give them to you. But with this last letter from him, I knew it was time. Please forgive me."

She stood like a diminutive little child in the middle of the kitchen, holding her hands together above her apron, scratching her fingers in anticipation of my response.

I met her eyes as she struggled to read my reaction. I felt like I was seeing her for the first time. She was a young girl at one time too – full of hope and crushed by disappointment. But I could see the hope of that girl in the eyes of an older woman. All we both wanted for ourselves was to be loved. For withholding the letters, something that should have driven us apart, the letters and her honesty brought us closer together. I stepped forward and folded into her chest as she welcomed me with open arms. She held me tighter than I thought she was capable. As I pulled away, we paused our breaths to listen to Blue howl and then further in the distance, the coyotes responded.

Chapter 36

Finally, We Meet

Reading Toko's letters didn't change how I felt about myself. I was still feeling a deep sense of loss, like a part of me was cut out. I wasn't whole any longer. One saving grace was Blue. He was a crutch for me to lean on, a teddy bear, a tissue, and a good listener. I was using him as a pillow lying outside watching the clouds pass by, when a shadow covered my face. I squinted to make out the figure of my mom towering over me with her hands on her hips.

"Ellie, I know where Toko is living. I tracked him down after I saw how the letters impacted you. I thought you might like to talk to him. Maybe go and visit?" She sat down on a nearby tree stump before continuing.

"I was able to get a phone number, and he actually answered the phone. I was shaking and full of butterflies when I heard his voice. It was awkward at first, and I can't say I know how I feel about him overall, but I do feel an incredible relief in talking to him. I had to tell him about you, and he wants you—and Blue, of course—to go and visit him."

Blue lifted his head when he heard his name, which blocked my clear view of her face, so I sat up. I was very intrigued.

"He thinks it would do you good to get a change in scenery. He assured me of that. And Ellie, I believe him. I believe you need to do something. You can't sit here and waste away. I know it has been hard, but honey, this might really help you to move forward." She squeezed her hands in between her legs and leaned forward, anticipating a response. Blue got up and came around and dumped his head on my cross-legged lap staring up directly at me, raising his dog eyebrows as if in anticipation of my response.

"At least do it for Blue! Look at him, Ellie. He is as depressed as you are."

"Yep, Mom, you are right. I should do it for Blue, and for me. I will go." I surprised myself with my quick answer. I didn't think about it. It came from nowhere and the words flew out of my mouth as if someone else put them there.

"Did I hear you correctly? You said you would actually go," she extended the word 'go' into a musical note.

I held my hand to my mouth. "I guess I did, didn't I? You are right. What have I got to lose? I feel like I need a change. No offense, Mom, but there are a lot of memories, good and bad, here. I wouldn't mind taking a break from all them. I need to make new memories."

"Oh, Ellie, I am so proud of you. Let's go make the arrangements. You are off to Cabo San Lucas, Mexico! He said you could come anytime. He is waiting for you." She got up and reached out a hand to help me up. I moved to push Blue off me, but he already sensed the change in mood, stood up, sneezed, shook himself and trotted along leading the way back to the house.

Chapter 37

Toko

It feels like Mom opened the door of the oven, but no smells of food, only strange new scents. I was put back in the magical crate and the big bird delivered me someplace new. The bird opens to the outside world and I am birthed out onto a ramp then placed on a cart and rolled over heatwaves coming up through the pavement, until I am pushed into a large area into a rush of cool air. I see Ellie running toward me, and she lets me out immediately to cover me with kisses. She picks up the bag that smells like ours, and we fall in behind a long line of humans excitedly talking and waving papers in their faces. Eventually, after a man stares at us while inspecting our papers, we are back out to the sun and oven heat. What is happening here, Ellie?

From the distance, I see a tall shadow of a man moving toward us. He moves in a way that is somehow familiar triggering a feeling filed away in the deepest crevices of my mind. As he walks closer, his scent brings a dream of a past encounter that is fuzzy and vague. I know him but can't remember him. He walks toward us like a warrior, tall, straight and strong, taking long strides with determination. I see some people move out of his way. Now I can sense him clearly. In my head, I hear a voice. "Hello, my old friend." I cock my head to the side as smudged memories pull me into the past. I shook myself back into the present moment, shuffling back and forth on my front paws in anticipation of greeting this human.

My grandfather stood out like a cowboy at a disco. I knew it was him. I thought maybe it was the way he walked or held his body that was familiar, but I saw my mother in his face. There were no other tall, dark men wearing jeans, a cowboy hat with two long braids hanging below, so I didn't need any detective skills to know I might be related to him. He moved with a cowboy swagger through the crowd of taxi drivers and excited tourists in their sundresses, and Tommy Bahama shirts and golf shorts. They seemed to think he was someone important and my heart filled with pride as he strode directly up to me. He didn't look his sixty-odd years I figured him to be. He was strong, fit, rugged, and tough, the Indian version of the Marlboro man without the cigarette. He wore a braided leather rope around his neck with a striking silver rimmed stone pendant of carved turquoise. There were silver and turquoise bracelets on each wrist along with leather ropes and beadwork. The sleeves of his shirt were rolled up to show the muscular striations in his forearms. A faded blue bandana was tied loosely around his neck.

When he came up to greet me and removed his aviator-style sunglasses, I was mesmerized by his eyes, inspecting me from under his thick eyebrows. They were ink black, but the pupils reflected the light from behind me and appeared white like they could see right through me. My mother and I have his straight slightly broad nose and high cheekbones, but we didn't have his strong square cleft chin. His lips were straight but with a perfect cupid's bow. I knew he could both charm and intimidate. His weathered face looked like it had seen its share of history but when he smiled, the lines around his eyes broke the spell of his mystical gaze and softened the imprint of his well-worn adventures.

"I hope you are as excited to see me as I am to see you, Little Cub," he said in a deep yet soothing voice. I melted when he drawled out my moniker, as his letters addressed me. "I see you are much more beautiful than a little cub. You are a true princess. A warrior princess. I will have to change your name."

I was mystified he picked my running alter ego to describe me. I wanted to say I felt like a warrior who had lost the battle but didn't want to break the spell of our first meeting by being gloomy. I reached out my hand to shake his, but he refused it and instead pulled me into a deep embrace that left me wanting more when he let go to inspect me. He said nothing, only tilted his head and clicked his tongue with approval.

I was surprised at Blue's reaction. He acted like Toko was an old friend, which he only does with people he loves and hasn't seen in a long time. Toko bent down and whispered something in Blue's ear and Blue licked him on the cheek. With a light laugh, he stood up. "Come on, Princess, we have a long drive to my place, and we can get acquainted along the way. The quicker we get away from here, the better it'll be for all of us." And with that, he picked up my bag and headed off to a big clean but older truck. "I got it washed for you," he yelled back to me as I struggled to keep up with his long strides.

To avoid any discussion about me, I spent the drive asking about him. I learned my grandfather moved down to Baja about five years ago to work on a commissioned sculpture. I missed the letters that mentioned him being a big-time artist, so I was very surprised he was doing commissioned work.

"You don't appear the artist type, if you don't mind me saying. You look too," I paused not knowing how to describe him respectfully, but Toko finished my sentence for me.

"Too macho?" he asked and then laughed. "It took me a while to stop denying my passion. I was born with a talent but not until about fifteen years ago did I let it flourish."

"You never talked much about your art in your letters. Well, you only really grazed the surface of your life." I took in the scenery of the small mountain range. I wasn't expecting to see mountains, and they made me feel more at home.

Toko took his time, pausing after each sentence. It seemed like he was not the type to rush through anything. "Well, I spent my childhood secretly carving and drawing. I grew up on an Indian reserve that was in the business of raising drunks first, sorry to say. The second business was ranching and oil. I escaped that life as early as I could but wasn't raised to see being an artist as masculine enough, you could say. I was raised to ride horses, but I didn't have a happy childhood. No point going there. I don't go into the past unless it brings a smile to my face." Toko kept one hand on the steering wheel and another on Blue, who was sitting in the middle of the bench seat.

He was mostly Native Indian with a mix of French from somewhere down the line, he figured, but his family lived on a reserve for many generations. He met my grandmother while working at a museum, and secretly taking art classes. I could see why my grandmother would fall in love with him. He had movie star quality looks. I could imagine him wearing a tight T-shirt and jeans, with cowboy boots and artist paint on his hands. I only knew snippets of his life from his letters. Mom told me my grandmother was a college student working on a summer internship at the same museum. They met, fell in love and got pregnant by accident. Toko was an absentee father. She later died of cancer before I was born. Mom only talked of fond memories of her mother. She never wanted to talk about Toko. He filled in the missing history of his life as we drove along.

My grandmother was about a white as white gets, he told me. She was Irish with black hair, white skin and green eyes. His face took on a glow with a gentle distant gleam in his eye when he described her.

"Evelyn was a beauty. I begged her to pose for my art class project," he recalled. "I was studying metals at the time, not even painting. I didn't need a model. I lied to her just to be able to spend hours staring at her. Hours of talking while I painted only to give the painting to her as a gift. We fell in love like it was out of our control. Her parents were so against it because I was more Indian than white," he shook his head disgusted. It still pained him to talk about it.

"When Evelyn became pregnant, we were both scared. We knew it would be so difficult for us to be as a family, but we were determined to make it work. We moved to a new area because I got a job breaking horses on a ranch while Evelyn worked in the ranch house until the baby was born—until your mother was born. Evelyn wanted to have her baby, even if it meant putting her studies on hold. In those days, her field of Native American History was quite new even though our history is older than this country. She knew more about my heritage than I did. I think she secretly wanted to be Native American," he smiled to himself.

"I was a young and impetuous son of a bitch. I didn't want the responsibilities that went along with having a child. I never knew what it meant to have a father, let alone be a father. So, after a few years of feeling stuck and struggling to make ends meet, I told Evelyn it was best she took Mariella and go back to live with her parents while I searched for a better-paying job." Toko took off his cowboy hat, held it between two fingers as he scratched his head between his braids, then put it back on.

"I told her I was coming back, but I didn't for three years. Kept making up excuses. I was a lousy piece of crud for what I did. When I came back, I tried to fit into their life, but it wasn't easy. Mariella didn't know me. She was more afraid of me. Who wouldn't be when they see a dark-skinned, hair-braided cowboy walk into a middle-class white neighborhood and say he was her father? I got that kid so confused. I left and came back every few years. We were never married, Ellie. We simply disconnected our love. What do they say now? Uncoupled." He snickered. "I couldn't keep breaking their hearts every time I came and went. Evelyn never hated me for it. She just let me go. That takes incredible bravery. The hell she must have gone through."

"I tried to stay in touch. But you know I lost my way and had to go looking for it. I was a complete mess. I came to a point in my life when I realized that I was trying to be someone I wasn't. I had to sit for a long time on my own, in my own personal asylum and keep asking myself who I was and what I was supposed to do with my life. I love animals, but I was tired of breaking horses when I wanted them to be free. I am curious. What did Mariella tell you about her mother?" He turned his head toward me. I knew he was desperate to know.

"I was only told she died before I was born, from breast cancer. I never learned too much about her because it was painful for Mom to talk about her. They were close, and she needed her guidance when I was born, but she had no one to ask questions or get help," I finished. I didn't want to get into how she thought of him.

Toko continued to fill me in as I took in the beauty of mountains on the right with glimpses of the blue ocean on the left. Being the free spirit he was, he could not stay in one place for long unless he felt a connection to it, so he traveled. He eventually succumbed to his passion for art. Each new place offered him new opportunities to learn more about himself, study, connect with other artists and learn different techniques to create paintings, pottery, jewelry from the elements of the surrounding area. He never set up a gallery or promoted his work. His pieces were so unique that word of mouth made him famous. People sought him out. He would not *sell* a piece of his art. The buyer had to agree not to be an owner but only to be a caretaker of the art and pay him rent for the benefit. And as the creator, he never owned the art; the art owned him. It was a painful thing for him to let go of something he had created. He said it was like letting go of a child, and it felt like a knife twisted in his heart each time. Letting go of his art, was like letting go of Evelyn and Mariella. It pained me to hear him say that. I wish my mom could have heard him.

He refused to let his art go to some people. Plastic people, he called them. They had lost their soul or never had one to start with. "They do not know their spirit," he said. "Doesn't matter how much money they offer me; it holds no value. Their money had suffocated their spirit."

As we drove along, Toko pointed out the direction of places that were hidden way up in the mountains, far off the main freeway. We turned off toward Toko's casita, which sat on the top of one of the many ridges that tapered toward the ocean from the peaks along the Pacific side of the Sierra Laguna Mountains. On the west side of the Baja Peninsula, bordering the Pacific from Todo Santos to San Lucas, there is a geographical exchange of flat desert arroyos, or dry riverbeds, and smaller mountain ridges that reach out like fingers toward the ocean, then cut off sharply at the shoreline. From a small community called, El Migriño southward, there was not much flat land. The mountains rolled sharply to the coastline allowing occasional stretches of sand beaches or smaller hidden coves, but mostly a rough sharp drop to the water's edge. It was on one of these ridges Toko lived in a small compound owned by one of the largest landowners on that side of the peninsula. The living accommodations were included in the commission for a life-size sculpture of a Mexican cowboy, or caballero, to greet visitors at the entrance of an estate hidden further up in the mountains. Toko was given an opportunity to set up a studio to work and have the solitude he needed to make the statue. When he and his benefactor grew a deep friendship, he allowed him to stay for as long as he wanted.

Don Javier's family dated back hundreds of years in Baja as caballeros and ranchers. Rarely seen in the cities of San Lucas or San Jose, these caballeros are tall, strong and not the same stock as indigenous natives from the mainland. Juan respected my grandfather. They were about the same age. My grandfather's wisdom helped guide Juan's decisions about not selling part of his land to developers, even though his advice was never given outright. Toko would hint at what he thought was the right path, leaving Javier with the full responsibility and reward for making a wise decision for his family heritage. I imagined Toko was a man of silent dominance. Most men probably yielded to him without realizing what was happening. Toko shared that Javier was an expert horseman, but he was far superior and that respect among caballeros was held in the highest regard.

The turn off to the house was unmarked and anyone could miss it unless you knew of the landmark of a giant cardon cactus about one hundred meters up from the entrance. The road was steep, lined with agave and was not graded, so the occasional pothole shook us in our seats, and Blue nearly fell off until Toko held him tightly. I was speechless as we came over a rise and opened before me was a wall of blue, one third of it the dark blue sparkling, moving ocean, and the other two-thirds was the lighter solid blue sky. Not a cloud was in sight. The surreal beauty took my breath away.

The road turned and dipped further to change the scene from the wall of blue into a lush green oasis hiding a periwinkle blue two-story house with a terracotta-tiled roof in the distance. A beautiful array of metal and some terracotta clay sculptures of reptiles and various animals and birds hung on the outside walls around the house. Tall date and coconut palms surrounded the grounds, along with a few blooming plumeria and fruit trees close to the house, various sizes and types of cacti, and various smaller palms and agave creating a lush desert garden. I rolled down the window to smell the tropical mix of flowers and seawater carried in on the hot outside air.

Off to the side we passed a corral of horses that started to run beside the truck. Blue clambered over me to bark excitedly. We pulled up close to a smaller violet colored one-story casita and all jumped out to stretch. The afternoon heat hit hard in contrast to the air-chilled truck.

Toko took my bag from the back of the truck and opened the door to the little casita. "Welcome home, Ellie."

It was a simple, charming and inviting casita with a very small kitchen to the left with a small breakfast bar, and to the right was an open area with a couch, chair, coffee table facing a small clay fireplace. A mix of traditional patchwork quilts folded over the couch and chair. The walls were filled with various abstract paintings that hinted at being a landscape or a person, but that was up to the imagination of the observer. The kitchen was painted muted yellow and the walls of the living area were calming seafoam green. The bedroom door was open showing a simple bed with a bright Mexican-style blanket. All the furniture was made from beautifully carved wood.

"Toko, did you do these paintings? Everything is so beautiful, so peaceful and happy," I commented, excited with my new surroundings.

He took his hat off and brushed a few loose strands of hair away from his face. "I did indeed paint those. I wish I could take credit for the rest, but I had help. Glad you like it. Do you need to freshen up or would you like to see the main house?"

I smiled and headed out the door before him and behind Blue who immediately took off running toward the horses. I was excited to see more, but we had to stop at the horses who were anxious to see Toko or maybe it was Blue as I found him right under their noses in the corral, like it was home. He has always known how to speak their language. Toko and I watched with amusement and thought we'd leave him as we headed to the main house, but he was right behind us when Toko unlocked the beautiful dark mahogany door. It was about three feet wide and eight feet tall with trees, rivers, flowers, birds, animals and the sun intricately carved into it. I decided I would examine it in detail later.

Toko's main house had a small entrance leading into an expansive open area with a kitchen off to the side separated by a colorfully tiled breakfast bar. The furniture was simple yet very elegant with darker more masculine colors that did not fight for attention with the art hung on the sand-colored walls. Despite the ocean expanse beyond the wall of glass sliders, my eyes were stolen away by the many works of art hung indiscriminately about the house. There was more art than wall. I was amazed how they fit together like a puzzle. Nothing was hung in an organized manner. To an organized mind, it was chaos—sensory overload. Paintings and shapes all shouting out for attention, "Look at me! No, look at me!" The ocean offered the eyes much-needed tranquility.

"I know. It is a lot to look at, but you develop selective vision. I think you need to if you want to be an artist. How else do you see the tree from the forest? It takes a while to get used to all of it. I don't see individual paintings or sculptures anymore. I see music. And the more chaos there is, the livelier the music," he said as he slid along on his tile floor moving to the rhythm of his paintings, dancing with an imaginary partner. I imagined her with fiery red hair for some reason. Blue joined in the dance. He knew what Toko was doing, feeling the joy of his granddaughter's arrival. Toko grabbed my hand and pulled me into a waltz. Blue barked, sharing his joy of the moment.

"Toko, you are amazing. You are so very talented. It's unbelievable." I let my eyes roll over each piece as I saw scene after scene come alive. He danced me closer, so I could see what looked to be abstract art, but as I examined them closely, I saw geometric shapes and recognizable objects—animals or other things—mixed together, barely detectable. I couldn't keep my eyes away, captured as if in a dream I couldn't wake from.

"Each piece of art has a different story, of course. A story mostly about a time, person, or experience in my life. They all hold cherished memories. For example, this one is of your mother."

He walked me over to the corner of the room to the left of the sliding doors, which filled most of the wall. The painting showed the shape and features of the face of a woman with an uncanny resemblance to my mother. The woman's expression was almost detectable, yet one got the impression she was melancholy or sad, but her green eyes were striking. Her face was surrounded by mysterious shapes and swirls of various shades of blue.

"I can't explain it to you. You have to see the message for yourself." He leaned back, folded his arms, reaching with one finger to tap his lips while watching me down the end of his nose. "I think you get it." I bobbed my head slowly, mesmerized by her similitude.

"I will show you my studio." Toko broke the spell of her image.

We headed upstairs. As soon as I entered, I was taken aback by the unobstructed open view of the dark blue ocean, which made me feel like I was hovering over it ready to jump right in with one big leap. In the middle of the room was a sculpture in progress. The back wall was full of shelving with supplies and smaller sculptures. The tops of the palms surrounded the sides offering some shade, plus shutters lined the windows to close off the outside when the sun got too hot. Toko explained a constant breeze from the ocean kept things fairly cool. There were also larger stronger hurricane shutters installed on the outside should another hurricane hit like it did in 2014. He had lost a sculpture in progress from the vibrations that shook the house even though Toko was well prepared ahead of time. He told me he knew before NOAH confirmed the impending hit.

"The birds and animals were heading to the mountains to hide, a few days before the winds started. It became a ghost town. No sound at all. The calm before was an eerie predictor of the storm to come. I wanted to let the horses go, but I didn't take the chance and brought them into the little casita for safety from the strong winds. It was terrible," he explained. "We had a lot of rebuilding to do around here." He paused and kicked a loose piece of plaster from the sculptor. I had a feeling there was more to the story but didn't pursue.

Eventually we made our way down and outside to let Blue wander around and for me to unpack, while Toko prepared dinner. While I laid out my clothes, I realized for the first time in a long time I was not thinking about myself and my troubles. I was grateful for this new experience. Mom was right. Despite her feelings toward her father, she felt I needed him and that was a very courageous thing for her to do.

Chapter 38

Blue's Dream

Toko and I walk early every morning while Ellie sleeps. He comes to the casita, opens the door for me, and I am already waiting for him. It is very dark and the sky is full of incredible lights even I can see with my dog eyes. I look up at their brilliance. For some reason I know they go on in layers for eternity because I have been out there among them.

"That is where we are from, Blue. All of us. We are all connected as if time did not exist, and you know this better than anyone. You and I both. We are caught in an open portal of time. Space has put us here for now, but time has us in other places too. How ironic my spirit friend, we are here together again. You were called through the space-time continuum to save a soul, weren't you? To teach something, perhaps? To learn something, as always. You and I both still have much to learn. That is why we are here and not up there with the stars. Can you feel the flow of energy here? It is immense. It is powerful. We are all one, connected to all that surrounds us. You and I. The earth and the sky. Such connectivity creates a vibration you can hear and feel."

Toko and I are sitting on a ridge staring outward. He explains what he sees. "Between us and the edge of this earth is the chaotic movement of silver lights twinkling on a mass of deep dark black water. At the edge of the earth is the starting line from which the universe opens up all around and above us. This is our earthly and watery home, my friend."

Toko is barefoot, sitting cross-legged. He is sitting still and begins humming a deep-throated rhythm that vibrates into my head I have laid on his knee. The wind picks up my fur and puts it down again. I fall asleep and dream. He and I are walking through a field of tall grass. I can see over the grass, so I am no longer a dog. But I can't see myself, so I don't know for sure. We come to the edge of the grass and below us are the tops of trees. We step away from the edge and fly over the trees, brushing against them with our bellies. We dip and swirl, climb and dive until we see the smoke, and stop midflight, holding ourselves in the air, watching the smoke grow taller, spiraling upward to the sky, and then I wake up.

Toko opens the door enough to let me back inside to be with Ellie. I pad my way to her bed, and she stirs awake and invites me on top, then lays her head on my back as I pull in close to her warmth.

"Blue, you smell like the ocean, and you are cold. Where have you been?" she asks.

To everywhere and nowhere, Ellie. Now it is your time to cover yourself with the scents of different places, away from the smell of yourself.

Chapter 39

Spirit Animal

I stood and stared at the front door, thinking whether to walk in or knock. Toko was never late to feed the horses and clean the corral, a chore I looked forward to doing with him each morning. It had been a couple of weeks, and I was beginning to feel a little like myself again, but mostly because I was not thinking about anything, except at night before I fell asleep when my mind woke up and immediately went to my memories. If I chose to go there, they kept me awake all night, but I was learning to let go by thinking of what was planned for the next day. I used my imagination to distract me from myself like I used to do when running, which seemed a lifetime ago, when running was my whole life. I was good at punishing myself by holding back doing the thing I loved. I felt I didn't deserve to run. But maybe I would later today. And then again, maybe not.

I ran my fingertips over the images carved into the mahogany door, feeling all the different shapes. There was a totem pole, a bird, other animals, several trees, mountains, exploding volcanoes, and rivers. What was this little creature swimming in between them? It had doglike face and a long, thick tail like Falkor in *The NeverEnding Story*. Everything was intricately carved with such detail. Toko must have carved this door.

I let my fingers explore the carvings while thinking Toko had not asked me to explain anything. He knew the basics but hadn't pried for details. We barely knew each other, but sometimes a stranger is the best person to share things with. But this stranger had quickly become familiar enough. I feared his judgment, even though I was certain he wouldn't judge me. Maybe he was just giving me time.

In the first few days of getting to know each other, he had no problem sharing more of his life with me. What intrigued me most was how he found his spirit guide as a teenager during a discovery journey. According to tradition in his tribe, when the medicine man was still alive and the chief was still upholding traditions, he had to live in the elements of nature, on a sacred ground, without shelter or food, walking and praying until his spirit guide, usually in the form of an animal or reptile, appeared to him. When he told me about the experience, I felt an incredible calling to go to this sacred ground and find my own spirit animal.

He, along with many other young males generations before him, walked the same ridge for miles either searching for or waiting to be found by their spirit guide. He had to endure the elements as a way of purifying his soul or his essence to be able to be united with his soul spirit. He told me that the body must be raw and open to receive. There must be no regrets, sins, or enemies left inside. The walk could take weeks if you had a difficult time letting go of the demons you had built up inside. You may have to stay until the elements overwhelm you and you are close to death before your body relents, releases and opens its heart to the spirit. The spirit that appeared would be his guide for life. Toko explained his tribe called this *poha-nymy-pya*. The term "animal spirit" came from the Latin *spiritus animalis*: "the breath that awakens the human mind."

He walked for ten days and by this time he had no food and had ripped off his clothing to get closer to Mother Earth, to feel her breath on him. He left shrouds of clothing next to clothing of generations who has passed before him. Their clothes remained blowing in the wind as sun-bleached threads.

On one particular day there was no sun but only white light, like the sky before a snowfall. He noticed a wild dog watching him. He thought the dog might have been following him for days, waiting for my grandfather to drop dead, so he could have a meal of his remains. A tame dog would have eventually come up to him, but this dog only watched him and never came when he was beckoned. He never thought the dog was his guide. He wished a bear or eagle, something more romantic and stronger, would be his spirit guide. A dog is just a dog. Everyone had one. He pressed on searching and walking until the weather turned for the worse, and he fell to the ground frozen in exhaustion. "If I am to die here, so be it."

He woke before dusk with the dog lying beside and almost on top of him. It was the smell that woke him. It was the smell of smoke, which to him meant fire, warmth, food and people, and he was craving all of it so intensely that it was all he dreamt of. But there was no fire and no one but the dog. When he struggled to move, the dog sat up and stared at him directly in the eyes. He looked back and forth from eye to eye. And then the dog pierced his lips and blew at him.

"But dogs can't do that," I responded.

"But nor can they do what he did next."

He had become paralyzed and could not look away from the world unfolding within the dog's eyes. The deeper he looked into his eyes, the more multicolored layers appeared, and the depths of the earth's mantle began to unfold. Within the deep, rich, red-brown mantle were rivers of gold streaming toward the pupil of the earth. In the eyes of the dog was a reflection of himself as the Mother Earth saw him: brave, strong, loyal, gentle, and compassionate. What the human world saw was selfishness, arrogance, and laziness.

Bursts of fearless flames rose up from the endless depths of the pupils and shot rivers of colors back through the irises. The colors blended and swirled into a deep purple lava. It was but a blink in time yet lasted since the first dawn of earth and Toko understood this vision was the most ancient and sacred. This was the soul of the earth that was gifted to him. His body felt the shock of ice water running through his veins while his skin felt on fire. He felt the rumble of the waves hitting faraway shores and the weakness of the forest in his knees during a heavy rain. He felt the floods racing over a dry desert floor cover his chest. Slowly his body transformed into earth, away from his flawed human self, and the dog led him to the universe where he watched the evolution of his being, changing through time.

He became excited, fearful and sad all at the same time when he realized the truth of earth's existence from the past and into the future. He saw through time as it was nothing but a tool for travel.

He saw the earth melded through time into one soul—one collective soul that was then broken into a trillion pieces. Toko could not glance away from the dog's eyes. He felt that if he did, the pieces would spill all over the ground never to be recovered. He began to feel responsible for keeping the earth together. The enormity of this insight weighed him down like a rolling mountain boulder finally settling on the sand. He drifted from the depths of the universe back to earth, feeling the warmth of its dirt surrounding him with a sense of peace, and he fell asleep with his head resting on the belly of the dog moving up and down with each breath.

My mouth was agape in wonder of the images he created in my head. "The dog is your spirit animal," I said half as a statement and half as a question.

He nodded. "The dog was my teacher. When a person gets stuck, they need someone or something to teach them the skills to overcome. I was stuck at that time. We all need spiritual teachers. And they come to us in different entities, even ones you least expect, but we are often so wrapped up in our own self we cannot open our eyes to see. I was wrapped up in my sorrow from the childhood I had on the reserve. I felt my life wasn't fair. I was full of blame, anger and loss. When I went on my spirit journey, I had to be stripped down and desperate. When I was ready, the elders had sent a dog to teach me.

"What did the dog teach you?"

"It is difficult to summarize those lessons, but I can say that this master teacher told me we are eternal souls living a human experience. Your spirit animal is your soul, what breathes life into you. It is the breath that awakens the human mind. I saw not only my life in the eyes of that dog but all lives. He broke my soul wide open. He opened my eyes to see with compassion, empathy, forgiveness, honesty. When I woke up, he was gone. That was when I found an eagle on the pathway staring at me, tilting its head from side to side. He made a high-pitched piping sound at me repeatedly, as if it were a lecture from a parent for my misbehavior. I could hear him tell me that I could fly. Why was I so stupid to only walk when the whole world was there for me to see? So I opened my wings, and I flew. I flew all the way home."

"Oh, Toko, really?"

"Really."

I now recognized the eagle hovering over the large sun that was centered on the door. There was the dog. There was Mother Earth. The door was the story of his spirit journey. As I stood engulfed by the images on the door, I felt a vibration under my feet, growing in intensity. The brass knocker on the front door began to vibrate and tapped rapidly against its base. Pebbles on the stone steps under my feet started to dance ever so lightly. I heard thunder coming from inside the house. I turned around and realized the thunder had echoed off the house and was coming from behind me. Racing through a cloud of dust was my grandfather sitting tall with his long hair flying behind him, part of it trapped under a cowboy hat that was hanging off his neck by a chinstrap. He was riding a grand, shimmering velvet brown stallion. Toko was leading another horse behind him. It was like a scene out of a western movie where the hero gallops up on a great steed with its mane flying in the wind, tail high, and body muscular and regal. But this vision was real. Blue was running beside, in his element.

He jumped off his horse before it came to a stop and walked up to greet me with what had become our morning ritual. He reached out to grab my shoulders with his arms extended and studied my face. When his eyes reached mine, he pressed his forehead into mine, and we stayed like this for as long as it took. I am not sure what dictated the time. This moment was broken by the scuff of one of the horses, scratching at the ground. Toko let me go and turned toward the horses and laughed, "This beautiful creature is Troy, and your lovely ride is named, Bella.

"What? My.. my ride? A horse?" I stuttered.

"The last I checked she was a horse and a magnificent one, she is. I have been working with her. She is looking forward to meeting you. I have been telling her all about you. They have both been with Don Javier at his ranchero. Come meet them both."

Both horses stood proud and bold as I inspected them. Their bridles were a rainbow of colors of yarns and not leather as would be expected. They both had small charro saddles made with a beautiful light tan leather. Troy's was a magnificent blue and Bella's was red. As I reached to admire Bella's coat, I saw a large ugly scar on her hind quarter. It looked like she was tortured.

"Toko, what is this?"

"During the hurricane, her fright brought on premature labor. She had broken loose from the coral before we could move her to safety and look after her. When we found her the next day, she was on the ground, cut up from flying debris, and the struggle she obviously had with the birth, and God knows what else. It is amazing that she survived. She wouldn't leave her baby, that was stillborn."

This hit me like a punch to the gut and took my breath away. Toko knew this horse would trigger emotion in me. Why would he show me this poor horse, making me feel this way?

"I c ... can't ride her," I struggled to say the words.

"You are the only one who can understand her pain, Ellie. She is scarred but still so very beautiful. So very strong, isn't she?"

I looked her in the eyes. They were soft yet noble, and she blinked as if to say it was ok, but the story of her loss and her pain hit me hard. I struggled to hold in my tears. "Toko, I can't ride. I, I just ... I can't."

You are never the only one in this world who has suffered loss, Ellie. Can't you see? We all know how it feels to lose someone you love and feel pain. It was so complex for Ellie—to lose a child but to have its father, a gilipollas, a new word I learned from Toko. I know she will never fully repair the wounds left from the loss of her child, but they are not meant to heal over without leaving a scar. The pain will slowly go away but the scar is a mark left to touch and remind ourselves of how precious loving someone is. I know. I have a deep scar I keep touching. It is not an ugly scar, Ellie. It is a beautiful scar.

Suddenly Ellie drops head into Bella's neck and she cries softly to herself.

"She is far worse than I thought," Toko says to me when I turn to look up at him. I pad over to Ellie and stick my nose in between her knees. She bends down to me, and we lock foreheads.

"I'm sorry, you guys. I can't. I just can't do this. I used to run to solve my problems and help me think. Now I can't run at all. I can't ride. I can't do anything. I feel like I am trapped," she struggled to say between gasps for breath as she sat down on the ground and buried her head in my neck.

I press into her chest. I have so much I want to tell her. Oh Ellie, our very existence - our purpose and the impact we make is influenced by the community we keep and our own awareness. There are souls who walk amongst us – souls with no nation, no race, no prejudices, no alliances, no needs. These are our teachers. They walk amongst us, they come to us in dreams, they come from places we don't bother to search. Just as miracles happen every day that go unseen or unacknowledged, our lessons exist everywhere and anywhere – in the efforts of a hummingbird, the secret of an old lady, a bead of sweat, a stranger's smile, a luxuriant garden, the scent of a memory's perfume, or in the scar on a survivor's backside. The awareness of each of these brings the human closer to the spirit.

Toko looked down on her from his position beside Troy and said, "Ellie, when the wound does not heal, and when you have lost your passion in life, it is time to take drastic measures. It is time to ask our ancestors for help."

Chapter 40

The Sweat

I stirred in my bed, awakened by the sound of waves hitting the rocks. I kept still and listened. They reminded me of the sound of a car racing down the highway close to our farm. The big roar as it approached our farm, then the swish as the car disappeared down the road. I was amazed at how loud and furious the waves could sound. It was like Mother Nature was telling me to pay attention.

I pulled out from under the warmth of my blanket and slid my legs over the bed and my toes found the soft fur of Blue's back. I curled my toes and kneaded his back. He rolled over, so I could also scratch his belly. He no longer slept in his bed but had somehow felt it better to sleep on a mat next to me.

I found the floor with my feet, grabbed my robe, and slipped on my sandals to head to the main house. There was no way I could fall back to sleep. I knew full well of this latest insomniac habit. No sense fighting it. I paused in the pathway to look up and absorb the twilight sky. Somnolence continued to affect my balance. I focused on the brilliant stars toward the west, then followed the arch of the sky toward the east, which presented me with a tinge of purple peeking over the ridge to my left. A memory suddenly warmed me. I remembered this time of morning when I was running with Jake, finishing off that long two-hundred-miler. It seemed a lifetime ago. I couldn't run ten feet now. I remembered standing with Jake, admiring the majesty of the sky and feeling so privileged to exist at that place in time. The feelings of gratefulness mixed with exhaustion came back to me. I missed them.

I quietly opened the door to Toko's house. He wouldn't be up this early I thought, until the strong aroma of freshly brewed coffee tickled my nostrils. The sky failed to wake me compared to this delicious scent. Blue woke me further with a loud sneeze.

"Ah, look what the universe has brought to me before the rising sun," a shadow yelled from outside on the deck.

Careful not to stub a toe while stumbling along in the predawn darkness inside the dark house, I balanced my full cup of java in both hands to find Toko leaning his weight against the balcony ledge already with a steaming cup sitting next to him. The sun was hinting its presence beyond the ridge bordering the coastline. He pushed out from leaning, stretched his lanky body and took a deep breath. I stepped up to give Toko a morning kiss on the cheek and then our customary forehead tap, which always made me giggle.

"How does the world find Miss Giselle this morning?" he asked, stretching his arms above his head.

"I couldn't sleep, as usual. But this view is certainly worth getting up for," I replied, as I watched the hint of a new sun's rays flickering off and on with the waves. Blue left my side to position himself in between Toko's legs as he stretched. I acknowledged their special connection, but I couldn't help feeling a little jealous. I thought he was all mine.

"Ellie, I know you have come a long way to be here, but there was a reason. Little Princess, the time has come for you to do a sweat. I have been told by my ancestors: it is time."

"You were told? What is a sweat?"

Toko always spoke slowly and deliberately. This has taken me some getting used to. Now I waited patiently for him to fully explain his thoughts. There was no point in interrupting him. He would simply ignore me.

"I was actually chastised for not moving forward sooner because I felt you were making progress on your own. You were starting to express yourself in some painting, helping me with jewelry-making, cooking, working with the horses, but I now realize these were merely ways of distracting yourself from dealing with the bigger matter tearing at your soul. I knew it is going to take time until you allowed yourself to heal, but Ellie, you have put a stubborn foot down and are standing your ground holding your pain like armor. You have built a wall around yourself and nothing good comes from building a fortress because, my love, you have no enemies."

"I have a huge enemy in myself, I guess," I sighed.

"That is profound awareness right there, but you must realize what you are doing is extremely self-destructive, self-punishing, and it has to stop. It is OK to mourn, Ellie. That is part of the process, but to punish yourself is not. The soul of your child cannot rest, knowing you are so unhappy. A restless soul gets stuck. Your own soul might be stuck not for what has happened in this life, but perhaps you have unfinished business from a past life."

"What do you mean, a past life?"

"Our native ancestors believed everything is alive and related to everything else. All that exists on earth is connected through an endless time."

"Including the rocks and earth, things that aren't alive and breathing?" I was confused.

"Yes. Very much so. When we die, our bodies feed the earth. We go to be with Mother Earth and our spirits go to Father Sky to be nearer to the great Creator and our ancestors, Grandfather Sun and Grandmother Moon. When Father Sky cries upon the earth, his tears in the form of rain or snow mix with the earth, Mother Earth. Mother Earth then builds rocks from our ashes and the rain. She molds them into beautiful rocks with her fire. Look around you. The mountains are made from different elements, all mixed from ashes of living things. These rocks are our ancestors. They hold our history and talk to us, if we want to listen. If you cannot connect with Mother Earth to be healed, then you ask for help from your ancestors who live in the rocks. We bring them back to life. You will see. It is in the Sweat Lodge that you will meet your ancestors. I know you will see. And when you do, then Mother Earth will help you to heal."

Blue moved from between Toko's legs, sat and stared up at me. For a strange moment, fleeting and mystical, I thought it was Blue who was the one talking to me, and not Toko. He tilted his head to one side and then another. Then he circled around and sat back down, staring at me. I surmised, "This is a conspiracy between you two, isn't it?"

"It was not my idea, Ellie. I was conspired upon by our ancestors. I am only the messenger for those who cannot speak." Toko nodded at Blue and clapped his hands together. "Let's prepare. Shall we."

Toko spent the rest of the day pulling the supplies together we needed to take with us. He told me to pack for a couple of nights of camping, and then to go quietly reflect on what my intentions would be to ask of our ancestors. I was to ask for help to heal but to set very specific intentions.

I wanted to stop feeling guilt over this baby. I wanted to understand why I lost her. I wanted to know why I still loved Lane, or did I just miss my past life? How would I ever find my strength and courage? I wanted to understand why I couldn't forgive my mother. Would I ever find my love of running again? The more I thought about all my issues, the more I felt like I was a lost cause.

Blue was in and out of my casita all day. He knew we were preparing to go somewhere. He would saunter in sniff out everything I put in my pack, come over to lick my leg or arm and then saunter out again. Mom and I called them Blue's drive-by kisses. I reassured him he would not be left behind. He brought me his leash just to reinforce my words. "I don't think we will need this Blue." Then he'd saunter out again. It was during one of these processions I noticed Toko put a new collar on him.

"Sit back Blue. What is this?" He sat regally, showing the pride the collar gave him. It looked more like a necklace, the way it hung and came to a large V in the center of his chest. I inspected it closer. It was heavy and made with a strong leather backing. The leather strap had inlaid of an intricate embroidery in the pattern of light blue, red, and white triangles meeting together at their tip and then arrow fetching coming out from the where the triangle tips met. It was a continuous pattern all the way around until meeting up to the center V, which held an aquamarine stone, rough and raw, circled by gray-white thin leather rope. I was astonished at its elaborate detail. The pattern and colors must mean something.

A shadow darkened the doorway. "We will leave before sunup tomorrow. We'll walk and take Sammy the burro to carry our gear. Lana, my housekeeper, will be joining us. You haven't met her yet. You will love her, I'm sure. She has done many a sweat with me. She has a natural calmness to her, and you will need that. It will be about an eight-hour hike, Ellie. We will follow a trail and then veer off into the brush, so make sure you bring long sleeves, pants, hat and everything you need to protect against the elements. Pack a bathing suit for the sweat. I will pack everything else we need. I am not joining you for dinner tonight, but you can fix yourself something. Sleep well, Ellie. I love you." He turned and left before I had a chance to mention Blue's necklace.

"OK, Blue." I looked back at his collar, then met his eyes, bluer than I had ever seen and through the blue I could see white flakes like in the bubble of a shaken snowdome. He did not look away. Nor did I. I got lost in his eyes.

Chapter 41

The Vision

Toko woke me in the middle of the night and told me to load up in the truck. Sam the burro and our supplies were secured in the back of the pickup already. Toko introduced me to Lana before we got in. She greeted me with a broken English, "Good morning," and I replied with my awkward, "Buenos dias," and we both giggled. She and I were around the same age. She was a clear foot shorter than me, not reaching five feet, but stocky and strong with delicate hands and feet, a round pleasant face and button nose. Her eyes were the most striking, a bright hazel brown, gentle and kind with thick long eyelashes nearly reaching her full rounded eyebrows. She had her long thick black hair pulled back into a ponytail that fanned out halfway down her back. Her high cheekbones popped with a rosy glow when she smiled, making her whole face light up. She looked like a little doll to me, and it took everything to stop from squeezing all her cuteness in a tight embrace.

We hopped in the truck, the four of us and snuggled in with Blue on the floor of the passenger side. He circled and fell asleep with a deep sigh. Every time I turned toward Lana, she had a smile on her face. I wondered what she thought about, to be smiling all the time? After a few minutes, I fell asleep as well.

I had no idea how long we had been driving as the truck came to a jerking stop and woke me up from an incredible deep sleep full of dreams that faded quickly. We all slid out and stretched with a chorus of yawns and smiles. We were deep in a valley with mountains on both sides so close I could almost stretch my arms out to touch them. The sun was peeking over the mountain ridge bringing light to a forest thick with lush, green vegetation, a sharp contrast to the area around Toko's home. Blue jumped out and shook himself and stretched proudly wearing his new collar. It fit him perfectly, not getting in the way when he bent down to sniff.

We loaded up Sam, took our own packs and started off down the trail. We walked mostly in silence. Toko was not making conversation. Lana's face was lit up into a continuous smile, like she had a secret she was delighted to hold. Toko explained earlier she had no family in the area, as she had come here with her boyfriend from the mainland, but he left her for another woman after a few months of arriving. She was already working for Toko, cooking and cleaning, and with no other means of money and not able to afford rent, he arranged for her to stay with an older woman who needed help with her basic needs. Lana cared for her and then came by horseback to clean and assist Toko with various chores. Toko made sure both women were well taken care of with food, medicine and supplies.

The pathway along an arroyo, or dry riverbed, was sandy and rocky with various low-lying bushes and cacti. I learned the Spanish names of some of the vegetation such as the Torote Blanco or Elephant tree we encountered off to the side of the trail. It had a trunk the size of a table for eight with roots snaking around the rock outcropping, grasping onto whatever was in its way. There were pitaya trees whose white trunks and branches grew in a drunken manner—out, around, and back in every direction. The trail grew steep in sections as we continued to climb higher in elevation where the trees became much taller and fuller. They must have been hundreds of years old.

We worked our way through enormous Cretaceous granite boulders or "canto rodado," as Lana called them, which collected together like marbles in a crevice. Some were the size of a small car. Toko only broke his silence to answer my questions of how these boulders came to rest here. All this was the result of plate tectonics and fault blocks. Mainland Mexico sits on the North American tectonic plate, which in turn sits on the Farallon Plate. Millions of years ago as the Farallon plate was pulled further deeper under the North American Plate and mountains formed from compression and uplift, at the same time there was a great amount of volcanic action along the west coast of what is now Mainland Mexico.

The Pacific Plate eventually pulled completely away from the Farallon Plate while taking part of the North American plate mountains along with it. This continuous pull eventually created a trough, shallow at first, but growing deeper over millions of years eventually creating the Gulf of California. All of Baja was once underwater. Giant megalodon sharks' teeth could still be found, along with other marine fossils high in the Sierra Lagunas. The North American plate containing Mainland Mexico was separated along the various faults and rifts, which run down the center of the gulf.

The climb was laborious and made me realize how much of my fitness I lost, yet I was better off than Lana. Toko lifted her on to the burro for a rest from walking on more than one occasion. I noticed her swollen ankles and immediately felt badly for her. It was hard for me to believe Toko's virility. He kept a tough pace. We stopped briefly to refuel, but I noticed Toko only took a small sip of water. He hadn't eaten the night before and now nothing today creating a very solemn nature to this parade. He had a purpose I would learn later.

Eventually, we reached a lookout in which we could see the Sea of Cortez—or Gulf of California, as some of the locals would prefer so as not to reference the tyranny of Spanish conquistador Hernán Cortéz, as he was responsible for the destruction of the Aztec Empire. We continued a little further off the beaten path. I reveled at the scenery, as it took me completely by surprise at almost every turn, reminding me of the setting of the movie *Jurassic Park*, with green tropically forested mountains and palm tree oases towering over small creeks and waterfalls.

We eventually came to a bit of a clearing after crossing a small creek that opened into a clear water pond and then continued further through a small grove of conifers. The small pool of water was next to the base of a mammoth erratic rock. There was no reason for it to be there, looming over the smaller rock piles scattered in and around the fresh flowing creek. It was as if a giant dropped his marble. This was where we would set up camp. Toko explained that he had found this small oasis during a solo hunting trip and spent a few days alone engulfed in its metaphysical energy. He explained it was a sacred location, very protected from the wind. It did have an eerie stillness to the area with not a breeze enough to move a leaf.

Toko gave me two tents to set up, and he went to work clearing the area of debris and Lana helped, knowing what to do. She found a branch and using its leaves to sweep the area clean.

"Look," I whispered as quietly as possible. A small deer stepped gracefully to the creek for a drink about fifty meters upwind from us. We all stopped what we were doing to admire it. We were slightly hidden by our lower elevation and the trees surrounding us. It turned and loped off as quietly as it came.

"This is a very good sign," said Toko.

No sooner had he spoken, a rabbit hopped over to the stream as well. He was oblivious to us. It was a quick pause for him, as he lifted his head to scout out the direction of his journey showing us his long translucent ears, half the size of his body, glowing red as the sunlight shone through them.

"Another very good sign," Toko decreed.

Blue was dog napping in the shade at the base of a Mexican Piñon or pine tree, oblivious to the visitors. He didn't acknowledge even a hint of their scent.

"We have only a couple of hours of sunlight, so I want to finish setting up camp, but first Ellie, come. I want to show you something."

He led the way, following the creek upward as it meandered down the mountain ravine off to the side of our camp and then took a sharp turn to a rock overhang I would not have seen from our campsite. As we come closer, the outcropping revealed a small cave. The surrounding area was completely swept clean of debris. Lana must have been here cleaning too. I peered inside wondering if something was going to jump out at me. It was big enough for about six people to sit around a rock-filled fire pit in the center. Outside, was another fire pit very close to the entrance. Beside it was a mound of dirt that was dug out from both pits.

"This was an extraordinary discovery for me, Ellie. Normally our people would build Sweat Lodges with branches from willow trees, and we would cover it with animal skins to resemble something like a small teepee. Finding this cave brings a deeper connection with Mother Earth."

Toko swept away any debris Lana missed, making the cave and area pristine. "This process of cleaning out the cave shows our ancestors reverence and honor. Help me to pick some rocks from the stream that will be placed in the fire when it gets hot. Pick the ones that speak to you."

As we each gathered up an armful, Toko continued his explanation. "The cave symbolizes the womb of Mother Earth. When we go inside, it is like we go back through the birth canal to her belly where we are fed. We are fed different messages that will give us the nourishment we are lacking. It also provides for us a natural process of elimination of all our personal garbage we carry inside. This garbage weighs us down and becomes toxic to our well-being. Through the ceremony we open ourselves to letting go, cleansing our inner selves so we can be open to communication with the Creator. Through this process, we can connect with the Sacred Divine Energies surrounding us here on earth."

We brought our rocks a little bigger than softballs and made a neat pile beside the mount of dirt at the cave entrance.

"I was made aware of this cave in a dream. At one time in my life, I denied my gift of seeing, but during my travels to Peru I met a shaman by chance, so I thought, and he allowed me to see my path in life through an ayahuasca ceremony. That story is for another time, but now I am wide open to receive messages from our ancestors, and they often come to me in my dreams."

"Toko, there is so much I don't know about you. You went to Peru and met a shaman? You have dreams that tell you things? How do you know they are not just dreams?" My curiosity was overflowing with questions.

"They are different, very different. Sometimes my ancestors talk to me without dreaming. If you listen, Ellie, you too, will hear their voices. Maybe you already have but didn't recognize it. Have you ever felt you were getting messages coming to you through signs or coincidences?"

"I wouldn't know, Toko. I guess, when I am running, maybe. I have heard voices and seen things when I have run long distances. My brain sort of checks out, I guess, and then I start to see things. I assumed they were hallucinations caused from exhaustion and as a way for my brain to stop registering the pain. It was kind of strange. But I don't think it's the same thing."

"Ellie, I have always believed your running was a form of a spirit quest. Each time you ran those insane distances, you went deeper into discovering yourself. Those moments when you were most raw and depraved, you were closer to yourself, the universe and all that was around you. It seems very similar to what I went through in my spirit quest."

I thought of those times he was referring to. They happened many times and each time, I was kind of excited to experience something new. I have had spiritual experiences while running long distances, there was no doubt. It was like some sort of awakening, because I always discovered something new about myself.

Out in the forest, my imagination used to kick in a lot when I was a kid. I saw and heard things when I was out with Blue, playing around. I would hear a voice and think Blue was talking to me. We would cuddle together my back up against a tree and watch the tall pines dance back and forth to the tune of the wind, hearing it whispering its secrets through their branches. Those places were sacred for me, in touch with nature, lying with Blue pressed against me, protecting me and keeping me warm were some of my most cherished memories. Being in nature was always my happy place. My mind started to wander as Toko drew me back in.

"Ellie do you feel the vortex here?" Toko stopped piling the rocks and stood up to look directly at me, breaking me from my memories. After a moment, he raised his arms, then licked his finger and held it up to the air.

"Ellie, look at those trees on each side of us. Watch them move in the breeze. But feel right here. Do you hear or feel anything at all?"

He was right. I heard not a bird, an insect or a rustle of a leaf. It was dead silent. There was no breeze reaching the cave entrance where I could see it waving the palm fronds in the distance. It had its own atmosphere by this cave. It invoked a solemn realization

I was going to take part in something that might change my life. It was like the kind of realization that stops you in your tracks when you remember, out of the blue, where you left something you had thought was lost.

"This is a sacred place. That is why the ancestors presented it to me. You saw the animals. They know as well. We will have the ceremony tonight, with Lana."

"Why did we bring Lana along? It seems like a big effort for her to walk this far. She doesn't speak very much English. Does she understand what is going on?"

"She understands far more than we can imagine. She has a very strong spiritual connection to Mother Earth. Her heritage is full of traditions such as this. There is a union of esoteric traditions among aboriginal people around the world. It is not a religion but a fundamental wisdom that has existed since the beginning of time. We don't need to know *how* she knows, but we know *that* she knows. You don't know what you know, until you know you know." Toko let out a loud, hearty laugh. "When a person knows, then they need to say nothing. You can simply tell by their reaction. They don't question things. They acknowledge things."

I sat and thought about his words and how blessed I was to have him in my life. Mom would have gained so much knowledge from her father if she gave him a chance, but there was too much water under that bridge. But deep inside I thought maybe I could build a stronger bridge.

We went back to camp to change out of our clothes into bathing suits and shorts and went to the river to wash the dirt off our bodies. I noticed how Lana was wearing a baggy shirt and shorts, covering her modesty. We all trudged along the path back to the cave wrapped in towels, carrying jugs of water, with Blue following close by my side. He was the only one allowed to eat before the ceremony, yet he hadn't eaten much at all for a dog who walked all day.

We watched Toko build a fire at the entrance of the cave.

"We will give it time to breathe. Now we will take this sage roll and smudge our bodies to purify them. It is a symbolic washing of the body.

My fasting is also a symbolic cleansing so that I can act as your guide through this ceremony. As we do this cleanse, please set your intentions of what you wish to overcome. Verbalize them softly to yourself, or if you want, shout them to the mountains."

As Toko took the sage wrapped in a thick bundle and waved it around us, letting the thick pungent smoke engulf our bodies, I whispered to myself that I wanted to be free of the pain in my heart, to know my child was at peace, and have the courage to forgive, to let go and find my strength again. I couldn't think what else to say. Those things were more daunting than I could handle. I wasn't sure things would be so simple. I would have to see for myself if there was magic in those stones.

As Toko waved a fire stick, I sneezed a few times. I can feel an incredible vibration within the air. I didn't think the humans could. There is a strong sense of stillness here, but it is filled with heavy vibrations coming from the earth. It reminded me of how I would feel before returning to another life on earth. I was rarely in limbo. The gods sent me fairly quickly back to life on earth because it was my requested punishment, and it was their education for me. The transition from one life form to another was always heavy, full of vibrations so intense they were painful. They were accompanied by images of the past but also images of the future, short glimpses of what will be. I tried with all my might to remember a flash of what it was to give me hope. I knew I was caught in a vortex between time and my soul deciding which direction I was going, from punishing myself repeatedly or choosing forgiveness and moving forward. Now I see Ellie is going through the same thing in her own way. She is stuck in self-punishment, like I was. While I am trying to make amends for my sins against her, is her soul holding on to a past life of being a victim?

I only know of one continuum of my inner soul, my essence, and it will never leave me. In this body as a dog, over all the other creatures I have been, is the closest I have come to feeling full of love and devotion. I give Ellie my devotion, and I would give her my life.

I start to sneeze again when they smoke tobacco from a pipe. Lana reaches down to sooth me. Ellie looks like she is going to choke but holds back. Toko bends down to blow some tobacco in my face. I hold it in as much as possible before I sneeze. I know of its symbolism.

Toko takes some rocks piled near the cave and drops in them into the fire pit. Ellie and Lana do the same. They hold hands and Toko says a few slow words while Lana hums. I stand in between Ellie's legs. When they are finished, I follow Toko in and out of the cave as he uses a small rack of horns to take the hot rocks and place them in the pit in the cave. When he is finished, he calls the girls to go inside, and he closes the opening with a heavy blanket hanging down from the top of a rock ledge at the entrance. Toko tells me to stay outside near the entrance, so I lay down and wait. I want to stay awake and guard the entrance, but I can't keep my eyes open as I listen to Toko's deep and slow descanting.

"We are here in the belly of our Great Mother humbly asking for her to share her wisdom through those who have gone before us since the first man walked this earth. There is incredible wisdom gathered in our earth. Time changes and yet does not move. We are open to the wisdom of our ancestors and wish to thank them for their guidance. We offer a small gift of this pouch of tobacco. We offer these flags of color. We also offer this water filled with herbs from the earth." Toko poured a small amount of water on the glowing red rocks, which hissed a release of steam. "This steam from the rocks is a door. We ask our Spirit Guides to lead us through." He then poured herb water over the rock three more times, explaining the symbolism of each pour. "We are asking for help from our ancestors. Hear our call."

He went on, but slowly I was losing my concentration on what he was saying. It was completely dark in the cave, except for a slight glow from the hot rocks. I started to feel pressure in my chest like I couldn't breathe. It came upon me quickly. I was trying to inhale but the air was going nowhere. I knew I was sitting, but I had no connection to the ground. My body started to tighten, my fingers tingled, and then I couldn't feel my body breathing at all. The glowing rocks started to fade. My fingers started to curl in a ridged form, tight and locked. The skin on my face pushed back away from my lips and my jaw grew tight and clenched. My heart started pounding through my chest. I couldn't move even though I was desperately trying. I was dying. My life was leaving me, and death had me in its grips. I couldn't speak or move my lips. The only sound I could make were grunts, so I grunted as loud as I could to save my life.

The flap opened, light and fresh air rushed in. Blue came up to me and licked the sweat off my legs while Toko helped me to stand up and stagger outside.

"What happened to me Toko? I felt like I was dying." I started to shake as the cooler air of the night hit my body laced in sweat. I inhaled deep breaths of the clean cool air.

"Ellie, before you are reborn, you must die."

I didn't believe him. That experience was crazy. I didn't want to go back inside. Why did this happen only me? Toko and Lana were fine.

"Blue will sit outside the flap so you can feel him touching you and Lana will hold your hand."

After I recovered, we went back inside, and I sat near the small opening and could feel Blue's fur up against my lower back. Lana gently took my hand in both of hers and rubbed it soothingly. I could see her mouth curled into a smile, and her eyes lit up as they reflected the lights off the glowing pile of rocks that radiated a thick heat. Toko sat down cross-legged and tall. He gave shakers to Lana and me and placed a drum between his legs. The red rocks reflected on the wood inlays on the sides of the drum creating a mesmerizing dance of light.

"Ancestors see the troubled children who sit here. Yellow Moon who protects and guides our moods, fill us with courage to continue our journeys. To God, the Greatest Creator of all the universe, we accept your wisdom. Lana, por favor, canta para nosotros ahora."

Toko threw more herb water on the rocks and steam hissed upward. He sprinkled dried herbs on the rocks and the cave filled with the smell of incense, sweet like sage but heavy like cinnamon. I started to feel calm and relaxed. I could feel Blue give out a heavy sigh against my body. I reached behind me and scratched his back, then drew the flap a little smaller.

Lana started to sing with the most lovely and peaceful voice. It was deeper than I expected from such a small woman. She held my hand tightly and started to shake her rattle with her other hand as her body moved ever so slightly to the rhythm of the song. The cave was getting hotter. Toko started to drum lightly and threw more water on the rocks, which hissed and steamed. The cave filled with steam and Toko became a ghostly image across the glowing rocks from me. Sweat rolled off my face and dripped on to my legs. I followed the thick smoke coming off the burning herbs traveling upward toward a slight crack in the cave above our heads.

I was deeply moved by Lana's singing. The song sounded like "The Lord's Prayer." I recognized the words *Cristo* and *Nuestro Padre*. The heat was opening every pore releasing rivers of water down my body. I reached to take a drink from the bottle hidden behind me. I was mesmerized by the images I started to see in the smoke. After Lana finished singing, the drumming continued. I felt like I was in a trance. Toko began to speak in a slow and methodical voice.

"Matter is energy that has slowed down, so we can touch it. Matter and energy are interchangeable. We are matter and yet we are energy. We are beings of energy vibrating at different frequencies. This vibration is a way of communicating not only with each other but with the universe. Those who learn to tap into their sacred vibrations, to see with their third eye, communicate with the ancestors, or use their vibrational influence to change their world for the better, recognize this as gifts from the Great Creator. Gifts open to all humankind. Our vibrations through our actions, songs, and prayer connect us to the divine. This important connection is like a lightning rod attracting answers, solutions and directions when we listen closely. Man must learn to use his ability to listen.

"Tell me what you see in the smoke, Ellie."

"I see faces. Lots of faces."

"Whose faces? Describe them."

"They are old faces. There is an old woman with lots of wrinkles and an old man. They are looking directly at me. Their lips are moving, but I cannot hear them."

"Ellie, try to listen to what they are telling you. Go deep inside of yourself. You have had to trust your intuition in the past. It is the same here. Trust your feelings. Listen to them."

We sat quietly and Lana started to chant again, a low guttural chant coming from deep within her throat. Toko began to drum very quietly and deeply causing the beads of sweat to bounce on my skin. I stared at the smoke wondering what it was I was supposed to hear. Hiss. Toko threw more herb water on the rocks. He got up and took Lana with him to fetch hotter rocks from the fire outside. I heard him talking to Lana and Blue. I heard Blue talking back to him in plain English. I don't know how I heard him, but a voice resonated deep inside of me. He was responding to every question.

I closed my eyes and was lost in their conversation.

She must let go of the person she used to be. It is one thing to forgive others, but it is another to forgive yourself. That can only happen through unconditional self-love and acceptance, in this moment. The past can never change. In the universe, on the time continuum, our small sufferings are singular and minute, but seem immense in our own little world – in the universe we create within ourselves. Eventually we must see them for what they are in the big picture of our existence. That is nearly impossible to do until you have perspective. The ancestors help us. They can see forward and backward in time. They try to tell us our soul will be forever happy, if you are able to forgive and let go of things that are connected to time. When you accept this, then you do not live that

past memory repeatedly. When tragedy strikes us, we relive it to punish ourselves while looking at an empty future. But here we can learn from religions that teach that we should offer our suffering as penance. We suffer so that others do not. It is the honorable thing to do. Of course, we do not know it at the time. But when the pain subsides, when you have suffered enough, when the memories and feelings of guilt or emptiness fade, then you realize how you have grown from hard lessons learned. It is exactly the same in the universe. It is part of nature, for planets, suns, and earth to shake, move, shatter, destroy, die, only to grow back stronger somewhere else. When a volcano explodes, it kills but also creates life. Pain is a part of our self-evolution. It is part of birth and part of a rebirth. All death brings life. All pain will eventually bring happiness.

After Ellie finishes a very difficult race, she always talks about the hardest parts, wearing the suffering like a badge of honor, of survival. It reminds her of how strong she is. She must recognize this suffering as bringing her into a new life, stronger from her loss and stronger from her suffering. It doesn't mean we forget; we just let go. Just as I must do—as we all must do.

I heard these words as clearly as if Blue were human. His voice was one that was familiar to me, and I was not frightened by this. I felt comforted. I didn't turn to look out through the blanket; I didn't want to break the spell. I looked to the glowing rocks instead. I saw myself in the pulsing colors of red and orange. I saw the pain and torture I put myself through. And then I saw myself stand strong and turn to run up through the smoke and through the crack in the cave. I felt the relief of having finished the run. I felt joy, relief, a sense of completion, the ending of the suffering, just as I had in my endurance races. I felt the pain lift off my body. I wanted to feel the pain gone from my heart, but at the same time I didn't want to let go. The hard parts of life make me who I am. I wanted to love myself, scars and all.

Toko came back into the cave and sat close to me. "Ellie—" he began, but I cut him off.

"Yes, I know, Grandfather. I know what I must do. I have to break free of the shell of pain I have encased myself in. I keep wanting the way my life was before. Before I lost her. Before I was living a life that was not true to who I am. It was full of plastic things and a plastic person. Then I was running in the same circle of sorrow, never finding a way out. Running the same race never letting myself get to the finish line. This became comfortable to me—my new comfort zone. I didn't know what it would feel like to let go of the pain. It is like running; I feel comfort in the pain. But when I finally stop running, it feels so much better, almost like heaven to finally stop, knowing I have arrived and there is no more pain. Right now, I must trust myself that I have arrived. It is time to stop running, to stop suffering."

Toko had guided me to purge my sorrow and through sweat and tears. I let out all my emotions, anger, resentment. He left me to let my volcano explode. I told my ancestors about my parents, Lane, about my childhood. I asked for forgiveness and compassion. I sat with my ancestors, listening to them tell me I was not alone, that we all share suffering, but we also share love. Toko came back and picked up his drum and chanted. We continued to drink water to sweat and cleanse our bodies while gazing upon the red rocks glowing inside of a trance filled with emotion, chanting, drumming and breathing. After five hours in the sweat lodge, I was spent.

Lana had left much earlier but Blue was lying faithfully by the entrance. When Toko and I stepped out into the cool night air it felt like a rebirth to me. I felt emotions boil up through my core into my throat. All the emotions came to the precipice. I rushed behind the nearest bush to empty my stomach. I had felt all kinds of emotions flow out of my body. I stayed until I was dry retching with Blue and Toko not far away watching me. When I finally stopped, my head felt too heavy to lift, and I felt a flu-like feeling throughout my entire body. Toko told me purging was a natural way of letting the negativity go. It was part of the path of healing. We dug a hole and buried my emotions and left them on the side of the mountain. Afterward, I felt lighter and freer. Now I knew what people meant when they said, a weight was lifted off their shoulders. I purged more than my losses of my baby, Lane, and my perfect career. I also let go of the wanting a perfect life.

I realized running was a kind of metaphor for my life. I set out such big challenges for myself, accepting some guidance, but ultimately responsible for my own race full of valleys, peaks, muddy and rocky trails and beautiful scenery. It had been a beautiful journey so far even with all the falls, scrapes and bruises. They make me the warrior that I am. A survivor.

When we returned to camp, Lana was already fast asleep, but she left us some food for dinner. Toko and I sat around the fire, and we shared some tortillas, chicken, salsa, avocados and cheese. We didn't talk much as my head was trying to get a grasp of what I had learned about myself. I didn't eat too much before dropping into the tent with exhaustion and Blue curled up at my side.

We spent the next day swimming in a small lagoon, taking short hikes over the boulders and napping in the shade. Toko set up a hammock between two trees, and we took turns enjoying its comforts. Lana made a wonderful meal of tamales, chorizo sausage, and bowls of pozole she had surprised us with already prepared for the trip. She also brought fresh tortillas we fried over the grill and folded up with slices of avocado. For dessert, she had homemade churro chips. Even Blue had his share of special treats.

We finished the night listening to Lana sing a myriad of traditional songs with her continuous sonrisa, or smile. Toko brought a little mezcal to warm us before heading to our beds for the night.

The second night I decided to sleep under the stars in the hammock with Blue tucked in beside me for warmth. I lay awake for hours watching the brilliance of the night sky full of shooting stars, bright planets, and moving satellites. The universe gave me a light show I never experienced before and will never forget.

We rose with the sun to break camp and start the long day's hike back to the truck. I noticed Blue seemed different. He was more distant. I don't know if the voice I heard was his, but I felt it in my heart. He appeared deep in his own thoughts. Lana smiled more, if that was even possible. Through my peripheral vision, I saw her glance toward me, then quickly turn away, nodding her head slightly and humming while looking at the views across the valley.

We all walked silently, contemplating the events of the last couple of nights, but often stopped to marvel at the views surrounding us. While we walked in a gallery forest of cedars, evergreens and old oak trees, across the valley it was gray and brown, full of short desert shrubs and cacti with boulders and rock slabs jutting out from the terrain. We were heading in that direction, out from the cover of the lush forest. As we passed along the trail, we saw the Tecote Cypress and the tall white willow or Huerivo towering over everything else in the middle of the river bend gorge or arroyo. We saw young glowing-red smooth-barked eucalyptus, tall old pine trees, and wild plum. We stopped to admire an elephant tree's roots wrapped around a rock and the Torote Colorado with its red trunk. Lana had made tea for me from its branches in the morning after the sweat lodge to calm my stomach. There was so much beauty I was seeing for the first time.

After arriving back at dusk, Toko and I unpacked and showered while Lana made soup. We still didn't talk much. We were tired from the long hike and full of our own thoughts. I said my good nights with a strong hug and kiss for Lana. Despite the language barrier, I couldn't help but feel as close to her as a sister.

In the casita, I wrote in my journal for a few hours. I had to get it all out—the entire experience. There was so much to remember. I laid back, exhausted and relieved, when I noticed Blue was nowhere in sight. I called for him but nothing. How could I not notice him gone? I opened the door and called continuously. In a few minutes, Lana came running with Blue at her heels.

"Lo siento mucho, señorita Ellie. Estaba en el estudio de arte conmigo. Quizás estaba preocupado por mí. No lo sé. Lo siento mucho. Aquí está él. Seguro. Sin preocupaciones," Lana said without taking a breath.

I had a slim idea what she was saying from her body language – Blue was with her, "Please Lana, everything is OK." I wished I could invite her in and have a girl-to-girl talk as I desperately needed one. I gave her a deep hug. She gave me a warm kiss on the cheek and turned to leave with a percipient smile.

I followed Blue back into my casita. I suddenly missed my mom. It had been over three weeks. I knew she would rub my back or brush my hair as we chatted. I forgot about those times when she was a mother to me. I needed to remember them more. Why was I always focusing on the negative aspects of our relationship? I decided to go back to my journal and write a list of all the great qualities of our relationship.

I jumped up on the bed and thought to invite Blue to sleep on the bed with me just this one time. He cocked his head to the side when I called him, as if questioning this unique privilege. "Yes Blue, come up here with me." I hadn't finished my sentence before he leaped up, landed in the middle of the bed, plunked himself down, rolled on his side and dropped his head onto a pillow with a deep sigh.

"Well, OK, then. Feel right at home mister," I teased him while giving him a belly rub. His fur was so soft and fine on his belly. Then I ran my fingers through the fur around his neck and noticed for the first time that he was wearing two necklaces. He lifted his head as I inspected the new one. It was a stunning, thick round silver pendant about two inches in diameter hanging from a thick silver chain. Inside the circle was a silhouette of a girl running, with a dog running beside her. They were encircled by flowing waves.

"Oh my God, Blue, what is this? Where did you ..." Of course, it had to have been Toko. It was lovely. I slipped it over Blue's head and jumped off the bed to check it out in the mirror. I unlatched it and wrapped it around my neck, admiring it as it sat just below my collarbone. It was absolutely perfect. I skipped back to Blue and jumped in next to him. "Why do I feel this actually is a gift from you?"

Blue tilted his head and blinked his eyes. He glanced from one eye to the other eye like humans do, reading my reaction. We held a stare. His eyes were a soft baby blue tonight. He looked tired almost as if he had wrinkles around his eyes. I had the privilege of his life with me for about nine years. I was closer to him and have spent more time with him than any other living creature. He was my soul mate, if that was possible. My thoughts of this brought tears to my eyes. Could it be possible to have a dog as a soul mate? What will happen to me when he is gone? What would I do?

"Please don't ever leave me, Blue. I love you so much. What would I do without you?" I nuzzled my head in his neck thick with soft fur. He placed his head on mine and let out a heavy sigh. "You understand me more than anyone, don't you?" I looked at him, and he stared back, eye to eye, started to pant, then threw his head back on the pillow and pawed at my arm. "OK, I will pet you. Then let's go to sleep, my friend."

Chapter 42

Starting Back

"Ellie, there is a race here in Baja in four weeks. It is a small race called Cabo Mountain Marathon. I think you should enter it," suggested Toko over dinner a few nights after returning. "It would be good for you to have a goal. Do you think you could pick up where you left off and go enjoy the race?"

I hadn't thought of competing. I only thought of running again briefly during our hike when I realized I would have run the trails we were hiking in a fraction of the time it took us to walk them. I had started back running and exploring cow trails with Blue. It intrigued me and sparked a little excitement in me so without giving it too much thought, I said yes.

"Fantastic Ellie! Running is in your genes. It is part of your blueprint. I am proud of you for taking the first step in the rest of your life. Or maybe it is the second or third step." He winked at me.

The sweat lodge made me discover or rediscover a few things. In the last few days, that followed, I felt the weight of my sorrow lift. Then I realized there was no clear definition of who I was anymore. I decided I was who I defined myself at the time but running was where I felt harmony between my mind and body and denying that did not help with my emotional stability. If I did not find harmony again, I wouldn't feel whole. I didn't want to lose part of me out of my own self-pity. If I were injured, then I would have to come to terms with it, but taking away a passion in order to self-punish was insane.

I was reminded of quantum theory Dr. Chilton taught me, that my consciousness created my life experience, but now I must put my conscious back into action to heal myself. I felt like I have been under anesthetic and lost track of my reality. I regained the courage to feel that I deserved to treat myself better and expect better than what I had been doing. I had the control to change my life.

Running was a space I occupied alone on the trail. It was an incredible feeling to have a mixture of effort, solitude and a deep sense of connection with nature. I didn't realize how much I missed it, but I clearly didn't miss all the bells and whistles of the Evotech technology. With no beeps, buzzes and vibrations, I was out in nature free of technology. I wondered if others have felt this way. Maybe a fisherman at sea, an artist at his easel, a musician with her instrument, or farmers working their fields. People connecting to what they love with no outside interference.

I didn't lose all my fitness in the two months I took off from running. The race was a struggle, but I didn't feel a need to push into the pain cave, like Lane always wanted me to do. I wanted to enjoy the effort and the company of fellow runners in this small, charming local event, and I was surprised to be called to the podium to take second place. It was then that someone in the group recognized my name. Most of the participants were Mexicans, and I felt relieved when I arrived that I could go unnoticed, but unfortunately that was not the case. It was Blue who was recognized with me. I eased into the questions about my year and Evotech. Soon more people gathered when they learned of my accomplishments. I took a few photos with people, which later showed up on Instagram, and that was when all hell broke loose.

Chapter 43

Breaking Loose

Social media came alive, and so did the emails I had irresponsibly avoided for nearly three months. Running away and avoidance were my coping mechanisms. There were hundreds of unanswered emails demanding contact. Mom called to tell me Jake called first, then Dr. Chilton, and they wanted me to call them back immediately. I had no idea one little race would cause this much panic.

"Toko, I have to go back to face the music, and I am afraid."

"Ellie, tell me what the race was you did in your past that scared you the most and why?"

"It was Northern Lights 200 because it was so long. I had never gone that far before, and I didn't know if I could finish."

"But you not only finished it—you led the entire way. How? Tell me in detail what made you so successful. You were not just a little successful. You set a record, correct?"

"I see where you are going with this. OK. I prepared for it. I trained relentlessly, visualized my success, had a plan, and when that fell apart, I had to improvise. I had to listen to my gut feeling or my instincts on what to do, believe in myself, have faith. I trained for pain and how to handle it. I rehearsed my mantras. I forced myself to do things I didn't want to do because I knew it would prepare me for the worst-case scenario, and even then I wasn't sure. I forced myself to feel pain—to run in the dark, wind, and rain. I remember how this race scared the crap out of me and somehow I got myself to the start line, despite all my fears. Mostly because I was excited to see how far I could push myself. There, how was that for a plan? But Toko, this is different!"

"How is it different Ellie? You are facing your fears. Tell me what you are afraid of."

"I'm afraid of disappointing Dr. Chilton when he learns the truth. I, I mean, we deceived him. I am afraid of seeing Lane again and how I am going to feel. What about my teammates? What about those people who admired and respected me?"

"OK. Let's really think about this. When you started to doubt finishing a race, you said your mantras. I imagine if you let the negative feelings and fears take over, you would give up or give in, but you overpowered them with positive words, mantras, visualizations. You never visualized yourself tripping and falling and rolling over a cliff, did you?"

"Very funny, of course not. Nothing negative was allowed. I planned for things just in case. I had bandages with me." I laughed out loud. "I always saw myself running through the finish line. That is all I thought about, getting all the way to the end and how gratifying it would feel."

"Ellie, the fears you believe you face are only in your imagination. If you keep focusing on them like you are, then you are creating a reality that is sure to happen. You are building your anxiety by focusing on a negative outcome. Yes, you are to blame for breaking company rules, and you will face the consequences. At first, you were hurt, angry and now you don't want to face Lane from fear of all the emotions you will have. You need to face him with your head held high and your eyes on your future, not your past. Do not feed on your resentment because it will turn you into someone destructive. Confront your emotions by speaking from your heart and don't overthink it. You would never slump at a start line. Take your superman pose and when the gun goes off – when you see all these people - charge ahead like a warrior. And if Giselle cannot do it, then it is time to dust off your alter ego and put on that warrior suit."

I grabbed my journal and went outside to contemplate a plan of action while watching the calming motion of the ocean defy the action that lay within its depths below its surface. I appreciated the metaphor it presented me. I stopped to watch Blue rolling around in the dirt, enjoying the simplest of pleasures. I took a seat and leaned back into the palm tree, distracted by the blessing of my surroundings. I didn't want to leave. I didn't want to face my future. I could stay there for the rest of my life.

Aarrhh, this feels good to scratch my back. Maybe a little extra on my butt. Yeah. Let me just check it out. Yep, the pecker is still there. I smell healthy. Up and shake. Oh, that feels better. Hey, Ellie! You smell soapy. Sneeze. Where are you going? Can I come? My favorite spot under the palm. Ah, the book and the pen. This might take a while. While you are scribbling away, here is what you should consider—what I have learned from being a dog: 1) If you are on a scent trail, follow it to the end – that is where your reward is. 2) Be loyal to those who treat you well. 3) Dogs don't know how to lie, but as a human at least know when not to tell the truth. 4) Don't care what other people think. Be your own self. 5) Avoid nattering squirrels who just like to get you jumping and chasing. 6) Go leave your mark on the trail so people know you were there. 7) Listen. Carefully. 8) There is usually something you can learn by watching. 9) Trust your sense of smell or your gut feeling about something. 10) Defend your loved ones. There, write that and hurry, because I am getting hungry.

Chapter 44

Time to Move Forward

"Ellie, it was a blessing your mother had suggested you come to me. Keep that in your heart when you see her. I know you feel she is stubborn in her ways, and no one truly knows that more than you and I. She saw past her anger toward me, to see hope for you. Be gentle with her. Be grateful for her." Toko whispered in my hair as he held me in a tight embrace. I was dreading the day we would have to say good-bye, but I knew in my heart I would see him again.

I had watched Toko take Blue for a walk before we packed him in his crate for the trip home. It was odd that it seemed to me they were having a two-way conversation, the way they were looking back and forth at each other. Lana was teary eyed as we said our good-byes. I wished I could have offered for them to come to see me, but we all knew that was not a possibility.

As I ascended the escalator to the airport security, I turned to yell out, "I forgot to thank you for the beautiful necklace, Toko. You are so amazing. I will miss you!"

"I will miss you too, but what necklace are you talking about Ellie?" he shouted back at me over the crowd lined up below me as I ascended.

"This necklace!" I held it up for him to see, but he shook his head, threw up his shoulders, and held his hands open as if he didn't know what I said. I saw Lana standing so small and demure beside him give a small wave. I blew her a kiss, and her face lit up even brighter than I thought possible. I suddenly felt a pang of heartache watching the two of them. When I first arrived, I had no idea how powerful this experience was going to be.

Mom was waiting at the airport when Blue and I arrived. The green of her eyes magnified like droplets on a green leaf, when she pulled away from our deep hug. She clearly missed me. Blue created an audience of onlookers with his huge production of stretching, shaking, waging and crying when I let him out of his kennel. On the drive home we had lots of time to discuss what I experienced. Completely out of character, Mom didn't interrogate me, made no judgments or criticism. She was curious about Lana, more so than about Toko. I think that was her way of indirectly searching for information. I sensed she wanted to learn more about her father but was too stubborn to ask.

I scheduled a meeting with Dr. Chilton and packed Blue up for our drive back to my place. I had been away for over three months, so I was certain they would have given my apartment away to someone new. The long drive was filled with reliving the sweat experience and preparing for the deluge of memories that lay waiting to be released upon my return. I questioned whether I was brave enough to face everyone, let alone Dr. Chilton. I thought purging my pain, regrets, and losses after the sweat was hard, but I knew I was not done yet. I kept thinking, what was the worst thing that could happen?

I was anticipating a mixed feeling of dread and relief stepping back into my condo. The images of romantic times with Lane haunted my memories. I would be arriving after a late gym session and walk in to see Lane had sneaked in and was waiting for me. I half expected that when I opened the door.

I felt anxiety churn in my stomach as I opened the door. My key worked; they hadn't locked me out. Blue nudged it open with his nose before I stepped forward, then I dropped my bags and quickly closed the door behind me. Was this my condo? I had to catch my breath. Before me was a room full of vases filled with dead, dried-up red roses. It looked like a sick joke or a bad scene from a B-grade zombie movie—death all around. There were vases on the countertops, the coffee table and my desk. I stepped over my bags tentative to look further. Lane's memory followed me through the house like a ghost waiting to jump out. There were vases in my bathroom and in my bedroom. It had a sick irony to the scene. He had hoped these roses would be a symbol of his love, but now they were a symbol of mine. I found a card on top of my bed next to a single dead rose. A burning sick feeling crept into my stomach making its way up my throat as I opened the envelope. What lies would he have scribbled?

Giselle,

Please don't run away. I know you hate me right now, but I never got a chance to fully explain. I do want to be with you. I made a mistake by blaming you. I am part of the blame. We need each other. We can try to make this work. We will talk to Chilton—make him understand. Just talk to me. Don't ignore me. That is not fair. Everyone is looking to me for answers. They saw us talking at the track. We need to fix this. Lane.

My hands went numb, and I dropped the card. I was holding my breath. Breathe. Maybe he didn't know I lost the baby. My head was a whirl with thoughts. I wanted to call Toko. But what would he tell me? "Listen to your heart, Ellie," and my heart wanted so badly to have things like they were and that this was all just a really bad dream. I needed to think this through. I became afraid of making things too complicated when I had already resolved to live my own life.

"Look Ellie, you have to do what is right for you." I talked aloud as I gathered the roses from all over the house into a big garbage bag. I stopped to catch my reflection in the bathroom mirror. My hair was in a messy bun and my eyes tired and sad not like the young excited girl who first arrived at this condo a few years ago. How things changed so drastically. I knew this was manipulation. He wanted to keep his job. Be strong. Think. No, don't think. Feel. This letter cannot change anything. Let it go. I gave myself a confident determined blink to the image staring back at me. I was so much better than the reflection of me holding a garbage bag of fake love.

I put the garbage bag in my car and drove as if on automatic pilot over to the track. I glanced around and could see no one. Blue lopped off to sniff the familiar territory. It was dusk when the colors of everything started to dim and wash out into gray and brown like an old photo. The colors matched my mood adeptly. Lane had a small office adjacent to the track where he kept a computer, water, towels and fridge always stocked with Evotech foods. He used the computer to track how our bodies were reacting to the training. What would it report about me right now? Unwelcome feelings of melancholy crept over me as I remembered the intimate moments we stole away in his office. Clips of memories rolled through my mind of him taking my hand as he closed the office door behind him, assuring me no one was looking, and then his touch would quickly turn heated and passionately aggressive as his hands and mouth moved over my body. I had responded equally animalistic, which now made my stomach turn, filled with regret and shame. I forced those memories to vanish and left them with the bag of roses at the base of his door.

Chapter 45

Team and Chilton

"Ellie, over here," Jake yelled out when I walked in the door to the team's favorite coffee hangout. The endurance squad was sitting in their usual spots, like time had not moved. Each of them got up to give me a hug and welcome me back.

"OK, vat is going on, Ellie? No-von vill tell us anyzing. You just got up and left us. My God, ve ver all so vorried. Jake told us to be patient. So here ve are. Shpill ze beans. Vat is going on?"

Hans still had his abrupt way of getting to the point. Nothing had changed with this group I had come to love so much. Everyone focused on me with concerned looks on their faces leaning forward over their coffees, unnerving me. Olivia handed me a coffee, rubbed my back, then straddled her chair, leaning forward, staring at me intently like everyone else. I started in slowly, hesitating often, coming clean with everything about the affair, the miscarriage, going to Mexico and meeting my grandfather. I begged them to keep it to themselves and not to confront Lane. I was scheduled to talk to Dr. Chilton the next day. There was a flood of condolences from around the table that sparked tears, but I refused to let them flow. I had done enough of that for a lifetime.

Rocky pushed up his glasses on his nose, sat up straight and balled up his fists. "I am so freakin' mad, I would like to grab that jerk by his whistle and strangle him. You are almost like a daughter to me, Ellie. And that frickin' dirty old man is older than me."

I never thought of it that way. His strong opinion of Lane took me by surprise. I guess Lane was almost twice my age. That is what excited me about him; he was so worldly and experienced. Now I felt naive and stupid. I had to stop berating myself. That was enough.

The group was steaming up with emotion throwing comments in at me from all directions on the course of action I should take.

"Look, you guys, I appreciate your caring and all this advice. I am going to talk to Dr. Chilton. I must confess I was debating about it. I thought of simply quitting the team and walking away from all this. It would be so much easier to do, but as you mentioned, this is kind of a "#metoo" thing. I must do the right thing. I have to be honest and take responsibility for my part. I am an adult. I did fall in love. It takes two people you know. I was in it one hundred percent. And then in the end, he wasn't there for me." I trailed off as all the thoughts I had previously gone over a million times in my head came flooding back, and I didn't want to talk about them one more time.

"Ellie, you fell in love under false pretenses," Jake added. He was sitting close to me and rubbed my leg in support because he knew how difficult this was for me.

"We are behind you in whatever you decide to do," said Tim. He was playing with one of his leather bracelets, turning it around and around on his wrist, elbows firmly planted on his knees leaning forward. While looking down, unable to meet my eyes he said, "I like Rogers, but Ellie, his ass needs to be fired." He glanced up at me and said, "If you want me to go with you, wait while you talk to Doc, Sister, I am there for you."

"I really appreciate it, but I can do this alone. Hey, if I can run two hundred miles, I can do this," I stated, then huffed out a chuckle, straightening up my back, faking confidence.

"I was there for that two hundred, so I will go with you, Ellie." Jake took my hand in his. "That is what a pacer is for, to see you through the most difficult stretch."

I stared at my hand in his as he squeezed it. I didn't dare look up at the others for fear of losing all control over what I was barely holding on to. I wanted to let the tears flow but like most endurance runners, once you lose control and that is a very difficult thing to gain back. I had to stay for the course. This was going to be my most difficult event yet.

I hung around to hear about their latest news. Jeep was still freezing his way to the South Pole pulling his own sled, trying to set a new world record. Boz did not finish the Nine Lives of the Cattail Mountains, but Wild Jack did. I was envious and sad that all the training I did for that race got thrown away with a broken heart. The three months I was gone, I was out in orbit off this endurance team planet, but they brought me down to earth for a short time reliving their training and racing, and usual banter back and forth. I would miss this terribly.

After everyone shared their new goals, I told them I was making no plans. They told me to keep posting on social media, so they could see how I was doing. But I confessed I would probably close all the accounts. The couple of haters were still out there antagonizing me, and I couldn't deal with that right now.

"Shcrew ze haters, I say. Ellie, do vat makes you happy. Ve luff you and vill see you at zee next race, as you burn past me unt leave me in zee dust." Hans pulled me in for a deep hug as did the rest of the team. I vowed to chase them all down on the trails soon. It was a difficult thing to say goodbye, but it was the end of that chapter of my life. Next page, Dr. Chilton.

The next day, walking through the building with Jake lit up fond memories of excitement and hope from the first time I visited. There were many subsequent times, coming to the labs, seeing the latest in biohackery the scientists were anxious to show us and test. I attended many lectures on nutrition, training principles and science, but it felt like it was another version of me, many lifetimes ago. Evotech, in all its science and gadgetry, was just a high-tech company claiming to be able make life better, faster, easier, healthier, and less stressful. But in the end, no amount of technology or biohacking could repair what was once broken in me.

Dr. Chilton's office overlooked the mountains, which took my mind off the task ahead for a couple of seconds when I walked in. I would do anything to be out there rather than in here. He gave me a quick embrace and let go with a little squeeze on my shoulders, then invited me to sit down across from his massive desk. One side had three computer screens while the other side was clear except for a couple of clean pieces of paper and an elegant pen. Water in an Evotech monogrammed glass sat on a bamboo coaster in front of me. He walked around behind his desk and sat forward with his hands on his desk clasped together in anticipation. Doc was like a father figure to me, despite his attempts at conversation were at times strained. He wasn't one for small talk, so he got right to the point, which I appreciated. He was concerned, yet clearly disappointed I had not contacted him about my absence.

"Ellie it is completely unprofessional what you did. You left with no warning. No communication. When you did not reply to our calls, when your mother said you were not well and with no real explanation, we had no idea what to think. Lane had nothing to add. He said he didn't have a clue why you left. We asked Jake. Ellie you left your teammate and your coach in a compromised position because we knew they were keeping secrets for you. I can understand a couple of weeks, but three months! What is going on?"

Dr. Chilton sat back in his chair bringing his hands up to his lips in a prayer position, his bushy eyebrows furrowed together darkening his blue eyes. I knew he had a million other projects on the go and taking time to address me personally meant this was an extreme situation for him. For me to invoke his disappointment, when he believed so deeply in me, filled me with despair.

With Toko's encouraging words swirling in my head giving me a backbone, I stared Dr. Chilton in the eyes and admitted what I did was completely wrong. I explained to him running away was the only way I knew how to handle my situation. I ran home to my comfort zone. My parents were the only ones who could provide the space for me to mourn. I spoke from my heart. I told him about my lost child. I told him about Toko. He listened intently, shaking his head in sympathy, but did not speak until I was finished.

"Ellie, thank you for sharing all this. It takes great courage, and now I feel remorse for having judged you." He cast his eyes down as if asking for forgiveness, then up at me directly. "The unfortunate part of being human is we cannot read minds—at least not yet. I am grateful you shared this with me. I am pained you had to go through this. I am also upset we made the unfortunate decision to hire Lane Rogers and you have been hurt as a result of his unethical choices. I will question him and hear his side of the story, of course, and then we will proceed. Right now, he will be notified not to have contact with you."

I didn't need to hear more, but he went on to say that since I broke the contract, this was the end. I told him I had already accepted the consequences.

"You will be taken care of Ellie. You still have your trail shoe. It will forever be yours," were his final words. Jake walked me out, and I gave him the deepest hug I could. I didn't want to let go of him.

He squeezed my shoulders as he looked deeply into my eyes and said, "You are on a new path, Ellie. I can see a massive change in you. You have become much stronger, mentally, even stronger than you were for the two hundred miles. I know you will achieve great things going forward because you are a survivor. This is not goodbye because I will see you again. Happy trails, my dear friend."

Chapter 46

Nine Lives of the Cattails

I was back to running the trails around home with my buddy, pushing myself to the edge of my limits, resting, and eating well with my mother's cooking, and sleeping in my old nontechnical, uncomfortable bed. I felt such immense relief at being set free from the control of Evotech. No one telling me what to eat, wear, how much to rest, or measuring the waste my body expelled through sweat and crap. There were no gadgets, no high-tech devices to measure every vital sign. Running felt more organic and freer. I made my own steam room out of willow sticks and plastic tarp and placed hot rocks from a fire inside so I could sweat, then get out and ran to the little creek, back and forth for my invigorating recovery. Back at home, I rolled out my aches with a tennis ball and rolling pin, then fell into bed exhausted for ten hours of sleep with no expensive temperature-controlled magnetic, earth-grounding massage mattress.

I wanted to prove I could run the same challenges without EVT. When I announced my decision to leave Evotech but would keep posting Blue and me running on my mother's business media sites, I had close to three hundred thousand followers transfer over to her. They wanted to see if I could do it too.

All those tears I cried made me more resilient, and I could feel my strength returning even stronger. I wanted to test this strength by attempting the last race I was training for with Evotech: Nine Lives in the Cattail Mountains.

Nine times around an eleven-mile loop with over fifteen thousand meters in elevation gain was enough to defeat most of the runners who dared to enter. If I finished, I would be only one of a handful of women to complete the entire course. There were different colored faux cat tails pinned onto the back of each runner symbolizing the completion of each loop. I had such a fierce desire to collect all nine; it became an obsession that filled every hour of each day.

I repeatedly visualized the course in my mind. I planned the composition and timing of my nutrition and fluids with numerous back up plans. Mom and I concocted variations of nutrient rich energy bars and fluids that would convert quickly into fuel for my muscles while helping them rebuild from the wear and tear. I researched how best to meet my body's needs and tested it all during training. I had my plan dialed in, rehearsed and ready to execute. I was ready to go to battle wearing low-tech clothing and a simple watch to track my pace. I needed nothing more.

My parents both agreed to support me at the eleven-mile loop checkpoint. I wanted no hype and no publicity, so I never announced my entry, but as word spread, the crowd got noisier with each loop I finished.

We are hiding from the weather as Ellie left us off to hunt again. There is an electricity of excitement and anticipation building in everyone here who has watched her come and go. We all can see the determination that propels her to chase some elusive clowder of cats out in the forest. Nine of them. She has hunted seven different ones so far, and she is wearing their tails like a badge of honor, bouncing off her backside. She is now after number eight. I was never this type of cat she is hunting. I was flippant, moody, unpredictable, and affectionate on my terms, but harmless. Mom is kind of like that, especially right now as she complains about standing in the cold, which has lasted over two suns and two moons that can't be seen through the damp, foggy air. Ellie has not complained. She wouldn't dare. This is the beginning of the third sun. I am waiting for her. I am allowed to hunt the last cat with her. She promised me.

Ellie has settled into her life with a stronger spirit. I feel as if I have made amends to her for a past she was forced to relive in her dreams. Now those dreams have stopped completely. I haven't felt her suffering. Is my job here with her done? Have I helped her move forward in this life as a stronger woman? Is this race the final test? For the two times we have been blessed to be with one another, the gods had taken her from me, and they will eventually take me from her, so I am going to enjoy every moment with her, as I have done. That is all I have. It is all I own on this earth—moments shared in time passed.

Here she comes down the soggy track looking like she rolled in mud from head to toe. She arrives, and they cheer and put another tail on her back. She refuses to sit like she had done the last time we saw her. Something about not getting back up. She quickly changes her jacket to a dry one, but keeps on her muddy pants, and exchanges her water pack. She takes some food and commands me to follow. Dad has put a raincoat on me to protect me. I am slightly embarrassed by this. A general doesn't need such amenities.

I quickly lose my footing in the mud, but I have four of them. Ellie has sticks in her hands to help her keep her balance making up for her lack of legs. I follow as she leads us alone down a well-worn trail that soon turns to exposed tree roots, then rocks, then patted down heavy, wet, slippery grass. It changes to a steep climb as she pulls herself upward using nearby trees. I dig my claws into the ground to get traction. I don't smell any cats anywhere.

She is walking now, and I can pull up beside her to listen to her as she talks. Nothing makes sense, but I remember soldiers who would go to battle and after days of no rest, would talk nonsense to no one standing anywhere within earshot. The exhaustion took over their mind, just as it has with Ellie. I don't want her to mistake me as a cat and be one of those tails hanging from her backside.

Our continuous pressing forward through this dark forest reminds me of being a human at war. I feel like my human ghost is running with us and my other lives are shadows hiding deep in the forest watching my every move, judging my efforts. I pull out in front of her, and she praises me for my efforts. I will find that cat, Ellie. Leave it to me.

The track is narrow and gives way to a steep slope off to the right. We are on the side of a mountain with nowhere to turn. Walking is treacherous. Soon the path levels and opens to a large field of grass with different tracks in various directions. I expect to find a dead soldier lying in the path. Dead from exhaustion of running around in a circle, lost. Ellie leads the way. The wind has picked up, and I am grateful for the jacket. I have no need for water when Ellie offers it. We march onward, pulling our heads down against the wind like two drenched and battle-weary soldiers. When we get back into the forest, Ellie drops to the ground with her legs spread out in front, leaning against a tree. I fear she will not get up. I go between her legs, mustering my strength to stand tall with my head up.

"Ellie, come with me. We must go. Please. This way. Follow me," I say to her. She looks at me through wet lashes and war paint of mud across her face. She closes her eyes. She drops into a sleep filled with heavy breathing. I go off to sniff for this notorious cat. Nothing. I keep my ears on Ellie. When I come back, I wake her with my tongue against her cheek. She whimpers and wipes her mouth, struggling to get up. "If we stay here, we will die," I tell her.

I woke up from a crazy vivid dream to find Blue staring at me. I heard him talking to me, but no one would believe me if I told them. I was probably delusional. I distinctly heard him telling me to keep fighting, that I was a soldier, a warrior. He told me to prove everyone wrong. "Show them that running comes from the heart. 'Get up, Ellie!'"

A lot of the last loop was in a fog outside and inside my body. The forest was distorted with black tall thick sticks engulfed in a thick dark cloud. It smelled damp and musty. The ground squeaked and sloshed at every step. I started to shiver deep inside my bones. My hands and feet were dumb. I had to push through on what felt like stumps for legs. I followed Blue's paws and spots of bright green jacket peeking through the cakes of mud with a steady step, step, breathe, step, step, breathe rhythm that lasted for a couple hours. Time disappeared into a trance of sounds coming from the creaking trees moving in the wind, and the rain hitting the path in torrents, then easing back to a pitter pat. All of it making music for a horror movie. I wouldn't let my mind go there, seeing beings in the misty forest was dangerous. All I focused on was Blue.

I came out of my trance to the sounds of bells ringing. I didn't know where I was. Streams of light filtered through the trees before us. We had arrived and as emotion pulled up from the soles of my aching feet to my eyes like a wave in a tsunami, I was caught by a group of kind people, my parents among them, both with tears streaming down their faces. I was carried to cot in a warm tent and wrapped in foil as I shivered uncontrollably. I finished with only four minutes to spare before they closed the course. It was over. They handed me my ninth very long, pink and striped cat tail. The other tails were muddy, wet and heavy, and I removed the belt that held them and let it drop to the ground. I pulled Blue under the covers with me and fell asleep with him whispering in my ear that he was delighted that I found the cat, because he couldn't.

Chapter 47

Redemption

"Is it time for us to go for a run? Take a little jaunt before we drive back to the farm?" I slapped my hands to my thighs and got Blue crying with excitement as he tapped his front legs back and forth in anticipation. We were driving home and close to our favorite trail. I thought it would be a great idea to stretch our legs on a short run before the celebration feast waiting for us. Dad was arriving later after delivering a large shipment to a grocery chain warehouse. My parents were working together for my mother's growing company. I had now accumulated over five hundred thousand followers on social media, which increased sales for my mother's products, and we couldn't keep up with demand, so Dad had to step in to help with the logistics.

Today, I had posted pictures of Blue with me at the signing of a lucrative deal to set up larger production for Mom's natural products. We would be hiring about thirty workers from our town, which was big news in our area. This made local online headlines, and with my posting, was spreading across the country. All the exposure was great for business.

"It would be good to work up an appetite before stuffing our faces, wouldn't it?" Blue put on a smiling pant in reply followed by a quick woof. Ever since the Sweat Lodge, I have an even deeper connection to Blue. We seem to be able to read each other's minds more so than ever before. I took the turn off to our favorite trail. It was late afternoon, so we could go for an hour and then arrive home in time to help set the table.

Being one of five women to ever finish the Nine Lives of the Cattail Mountains course blew my publicity out of the water into a tidal wave of endorsement offers, magazine articles, podcast interviews and offers to appear at charity events over the last month. I reunited with my old Evotech teammates for a celebratory coffee before meeting with Dr. Chilton about his curiosity on my mother's natural products. No one mentioned Lane other than to say no one had heard from him or his whereabouts. Now I was back on rested legs, starting back slowly and planning my training for my next event in Europe.

Two cars were in the parking lot and another turned in not far behind me. It would be great to have the trail to ourselves. I pulled up and turned off my semi-new SUV that I proudly bought myself. I pulled out a warm jacket but decided to leave Blue's leash, with not many people around. He never disobeyed me, always staying close. If we encountered a bear, he knew to be quiet, back track, then head in the opposite direction. I was sure he would follow me if that happened. We walked up to the trailhead, and I sat down on a stump to double tie my laces. Blue came and sat on my feet.

"Look, buddy, how can I tie my shoes if you are sitting on my feet?" I wrapped my arms around his neck and gave him a big kiss on the top of his head. His fur was getting thicker in preparation for winter. I grabbed his face in my hands and kissed him again on his wet nose. He narrowed his eyes in pleasure, looked at me and focused eye to eye. His eyes were a darker blue than I had ever seen them. Is it possible as he aged, his eyes would change color? I stared into them and was swept away in the swirls and waves of tiny white lines that mapped like meandering creeks through his irises. I could see my own spirit journey reflected in his eyes.

"We sure have been through a lot, my friend. All the running we have done. All the trails we have covered together. I wouldn't be surprised if you were the only dog in the world to have run as far as you have. Thank you for all of that. Thank you for being there for me at every crossroad, when I took the wrong turn, or when I fell. You helped me to get back up every time. Again and again. I never had to ask you. You were always at my side. You are my dearest and best friend. There is no one on this earth like you," For some reason, my eyes welled up with tears. He licked my mouth.

"Yuck. Blue. OK, I will allow you to get away with one dog kiss." I grabbed his face, pierced my lips tight, and planted a kiss right on his black, wet lips. He licked me again before I could pull away fast enough, and I laughed, wiping my mouth on the side of his head. "OK, enough of that, my friend. Let's go enjoy nature. Let's see what there is to find." He turned on his hind legs and trotted off a few steps ahead, starting in on his routine sniff and mark reconnaissance.

I broke into a slow easy run over the amber and brown leaves that covered the path. The air was thick with the smell of damp tree bark and fermented berries hanging low on the bushes. It was a good sign they were not eaten, which meant the bears had not come down from higher elevations to feed. Must be plenty of berries up higher. The crisp air of the beginning of winter was tickling us with its presence. It hinted the air would be chillier in the days to come. The sun was still bright enough to take the chill off, but the temperature was cooler nearer the ground. Blue ventured down a side deer trail, then switched back toward me at my command. He could easily get caught on a scent of a rabbit or fox, but I wanted him close beside me.

We got to our turnaround point, a clearing in the forest overlooking the valley below. He jumped up to sit beside me as I looked out on the view. His eyes closed into slits as I could see him enjoying the sun on his face. In the past, I ran by this point either because we had a longer run planned and stopping to enjoy every view would be too much of a distraction, but here and now, with no pressure to train, we fully enjoyed the moment. Blue leaned up against me, and I wrapped my arm around him. Even though I know dogs don't see distances very well, nor colors, he appeared to take in the view along with me.

"This is our territory, Blue. This is all ours. Remember how we went camping for the first time and Mom and Dad were freaked to let us go out on our own. The only reason they let us go was because you were with me. I have to laugh. They trusted you more than me. Oh, buddy, I have to admit I was scared that night." I took a deep sigh at the memory. "I held you so tight, you poor thing. I knew you were hot, stuffed in the sleeping bag with me. Finally, you couldn't stand it any longer and got up to sleep near the tent opening. We will have more of those camping trips. We better get one in before it snows."

We sat there for a few more minutes enjoying the peace, not a sound in the air except for the wind blowing the tops of the pine trees in small infinity circles way above our heads. I grew melancholy. Wind in the trees always made me feel alone, even in a crowd. "Well, let's go, boy."

I started back down our route with thoughts of how good it would be to sit down together for a family meal. Mom said she and Dad were working well together. He would reach out to her, and they were able to have long chats via Bluetooth, she at work in her kitchen while he was driving along a highway. In the years of their marriage, that was not possible unless she had a radio. They were talking more now, and I was looking forward to this special dinner as a family.

The sun was dipping behind the clouds, and it cooled faster than on a summer's day, so I started to pick up my pace until Blue stopped dead, right in front of me in the middle of the path almost sending me tumbling downward. I scrambled to prevent myself from falling over him for what was usually an enticing scent or deer poop he couldn't resist. Ready to scold him, I turned around and saw him staring past me. I turned to see what he was looking at, and I caught a glimpse of a shadow move out from behind a tree. Instinctively I felt was an animal. If it were a bear, we would have to run in the opposite direction as fast as we could. I was unnerved and my heart started racing. It could just be a deer, but Blue's reaction was not to chase as his instincts always drove him to do. He had stopped dead. It had to be a bear, but the shadow didn't move. Maybe we were upwind, and it couldn't smell us yet.

I took quiet steps backward and whispered for Blue to follow me, but he stood his ground. I reached down to pull at his collar, but he dug in and refused to move. He started a growl from deep in his throat. I felt it vibrate against my hand. "Come on, Blue, "I whispered harshly through gritted teeth. "Move!"

He dug in harder and then started to bark wildly. I looked up to see a man approaching us. I debated turning and running. But I was frozen, gripping on to a dog with his teeth bared, giving warning barks, and digging in pulling me forward toward the figure approaching us. My heart started to pound into my ears. Blue was in a fright, scared into an instinctive reaction. I yelled out, "Hey, identify yourself or say something. My dog is going nuts here."

There was silence, only the sound of leaves crunching under footsteps before Blue started barking again.

"Do you want to chance a dog attack? Stop where you are and tell me who you are," I demanded although my voice cracked on the last word. My mouth felt thick and dry, and my body instantly heated up.

"It's OK. Ellie. It's me," said a voice from the shadow.

"Who?" My ears were buzzing from the blood rushing through my head and Blue's deafening barking.

The figure came forward out of the shadows at the same time as the realization came to my mind the shape of this person was familiar. I started to feel a little more at ease because he knew my name but then quickly the shock of who he was struck me with a slap of reality.

"L ... L ... Lane?" I stammered out in disbelief, still holding Blue tightly as he wouldn't stop his barking and growling.

"Hey, Blue. Don't worry, buddy. It's me," he said in an attempt to sound amiable, but it came out as desperate as he walked cautiously a few steps closer, then stopped abruptly about ten feet from Blue's bared teeth. "Ellie, do something with your stupid dog," he commanded, completely changing his tone.

"What on earth are you doing here? Were you following me?" I snapped at him in confusion, my mouth left open in question, puzzled beyond comprehension, then my stomach started to feel hot and burning. My hands started to sweat as I held Blue back. He had to be stalking me. Or was this the wildest coincidence? I had to consciously stop myself from trying to rationalize his bizarre sudden appearance, but the truth seemed a lot scarier.

"Ellie, I know this seems strange." He made a move to walk toward us but thought twice as Blue started growling a warning. He stopped and took his cap off to run his fingers through his hair that was much longer than normal and put it back on. He dove his hands deep in his jacket pockets leaning over one leg, took a deep breath in through his nose and blew it out forcefully through pierced lips. He kicked a stone down the path in our direction. It bounced and rolled, stopping a couple feet from where I was crouched next to Blue. I watched the rock but Blue never took his eyes away from Lane.

"I was driving out to see you. I knew you were headed to your mother's after that press conference. And, well, I saw your SUV turn up here. I know this must be the place you told me about. Your favorite place to run. How ironic to confront you here. Time to have a talk."

"We don't need to talk about anything. That would be fruitless. Everything between us is over, and I have moved on. If you need closure, that is all I can give you. Now turn around and walk away. Please."

"Ellie, listen to me. Yes, I was angry. It was a shock to me, but you tricked me by getting pregnant. Then you take off back to Mommy. Just leave. I tried to see you there. Drove all the way out, and you refused. No one would talk to me, tell me anything, until I get pulled into Chilton's office and interrogated like a criminal. Of course, they don't listen to my side of the story. You see, Ellie, you can't just dump flowers and leave. That wasn't very nice, you know." His voice grew angrier. He was moving in closer to me and with each step, aggravating Blue more. "Can't you shut that dog up?" he demanded.

Blue's growling turned to barking again. I tried to calm him down. I wish I had his leash. I felt if I let him go, he would charge at Lane. My anxiety was fueling his tension. His body was taut and ready to bolt. He licked his lips, stood up, then sat back down at my insistence. I wanted to stand, but it would have put me at a disadvantage holding Blue awkwardly. Lane stepped in closer, and I felt incredibly vulnerable.

"Look, I think it's best that you just stay back. You are freaking out Blue. Please just stay back," I pleaded. Every ounce of me knew this was all wrong. No one with a sane mind followed someone halfway across a country unless he was desperate. My mind backed into a dark cave of awareness of the truth. I wanted this to be an illusion. I prayed it wasn't real, but I soon realized there appeared before me another reality, beyond what I could see with my eyes. Blue had felt it. It was thick in the air that separated us. There was more to reality than what we see with our own eyes. There is the reality we feel. This man whom

I used to love was now a complete stranger to me and there was no connection between us other than the one he held in his head.

"Lane. You did explain. I sat there with you and you told me exactly how you felt. You didn't want us to have a child together. You wanted me to get rid of it. You were pretty clear about what you wanted then." I felt a need to placate him. If he followed me all the way here, he was determined to get something from me. I tried to judge his reaction, thinking I better tread softly.

"Ellie. You didn't let me explain. It was a shock to me. I didn't know what to think or do. I want you to come back to me. Everyone will see I wasn't to blame for this."

He wasn't making sense to me. "It's over, Lane. Can't you see I have moved on? It's been months now. I had to move on. You need to do the same."

"Well, I can't Ellie. You see, when you told Dr. Chilton all about what happened, he blamed me. He said I took advantage of you being a subordinate. When you and I both know it was you, Ellie. You seduced me. You wanted a relationship so you could have me with you all the time. So you could win every race. You know it was me who told you what to do. Without me you would be nothing. I told you how to train, how to race, how to think. You were nothing but a little girl. Then you grew too big. All those fans on social media. I made you who you are. I made that team famous. And you think you can just take that away from me? You think you can waltz into Chilton's office and lie about me and have me lose everything? Everything I have worked my whole life for. I am blackballed because of you."

Lane's eyes narrowed, and his face had turned red with fury. He couldn't look me in the eyes as he continued to rant. I sat crouched next to Blue thinking of words I could say to calm him. I felt whatever I said or did, even with the best of intentions, would interfere with the mission he had made in his mind. I didn't want to risk a disaster of my own making because if I said something that would backfire, I could trigger a reaction in him that wouldn't have happened in the first place. He had worked himself into finally releasing all the anger he had built up. He continued, as if it were a planned speech he had practiced, wanting to say each calculated word with an intention of swaying me to agree this was all my fault.

"He fired me and now no one wants to work with me. You took that all away from me. Do you know how infuriating that is? Do you know you destroyed me?" He stood evenly weighted now, swinging his open hands in various directions when he spoke accentuating words by pointing his finger at me. "But really, what do you care? You care more about your stupid dog than anyone, ever."

I racked my brain trying to think of words to pacify him but there was a fear amplifying through my brain stopping me from thinking clearly. "Of course I loved you, Lane," was all I could mumble out from my lips, and they fell on the dirt and rolled away without feeling.

"Really Ellie? I don't believe you. Show me," he urged as he stepped closer, reaching toward me with one hand held open.

I stared at his open hand. "What do you want, Lane?" I asked without moving forward.

"Come on, Ellie, take my hand. Let me hold you like I used to. Let's make love in the wild like we did that first time. Remember how easy it was for you?" His demeanor changed so abruptly I felt like he was toying with me, testing my emotional stability. Was I looking at my fate in his outstretched hand? The word *kismet* came to mind and a quote I had heard once: "What chance do we have against destiny? Fate cannot control our freewill, and fate cannot lie." No typical forlorn lover follows his lost love into a forest to make amends, if only to himself. He had nothing to lose he hadn't lost already. He continued to lie to me and worse, to himself.

I looked at my surroundings. For being in the forest, I felt I had nowhere to run. I shifted from my crouched position next to Blue, releasing the tension building up in my legs. I put one knee in the dirt on the path and the other up next to Blue, his body taut with tension. He wasn't letting up. I didn't like the disadvantage of being lower than Lane. I wanted to stand up, but Blue was still pulling against his collar. He had stopped barking, but I could feel growling vibrating deep in his core.

I remembered Dr. Chilton's words of advice, when I started off on my first ultrarace. He said, "It is human nature that our best qualities are called up quickly while in a crisis but are often very hard to find in the ordinary calm. The discovery of our virtues is found in adversity." Here I was, facing my adversity in the form of someone I never thought would threaten me, who always said he wanted to protect me.

"We can't have what we had before. It's not possible. Let's just move on. OK? Let's just walk back together. We can talk along the way. We can sort this out." I tried my best to mollify him.

I watched him as he slowly adjusted the pack on his back. It was the first time I noticed he had one. He put his hands on his hips and glared down at me through narrow eyes.

"Ellie that is not going to happen. You don't get it do you. You destroyed my life, and you have to make amends. You are the only one. You have to tell them it was you who seduced me," he jabbed a pointed finger at me. I could tell Blue wanted to bite it off.

"You are going to call Chilton and tell him you made the whole thing up to get attention. You did it because you wanted your fans to feel sorry for you. Call him!" he commanded, his face contorting with a newfound anger I had never seen in him before.

This didn't make any sense to me, but I responded, "OK, yes, I will, if this will make things better for you." I talked softly believing I had a way out of this situation. "There is better coverage in the parking lot. Let's walk back. I'll call." This didn't have the effect I thought it would. He stood taller, looking down at me, shaking his head, hands on his hips.

"I'm not stupid, Ellie. It is not that simple. Don't you see that? You are not going to get away scot-free. You are going to have to pay a price for ruining me, Ellie. Why should you be so successful, have all those fans when I am ruined? How is that fair? It will never be the same for me, and you know it."

He was close enough I could feel his spit hit my face. His cap was shading his eyes, but I could feel them sear into me. He straightened and turned as if to walk away, whipping his cap off his head to run his fingers through his unruly hair, but he aggressively paced taking two long, forceful strides to one side before turning abruptly to retrace his steps, back and forth. He was contemplating his next move. I watched his hand go to a resting spot on top of something he had attached to his belt. It was the knife he always carried. The same one he had given to me to carry when running. My stomach dropped and my legs went numb. I couldn't take my eyes off his hand.

I immediately envisioned the worst-case scenario. My mind had leapt to a dark, irrational place. He kept talking, but his words became muffled to my ears. For some reason, I couldn't understand what he was saying. I could see spit flying from his mouth as he got louder and closer to me. They say fear can be paralyzing. I think the reason is that all the blood rushes from all parts of the body directly to the stomach where it turns to acid and ignites a fire, burning, putting pressure on the lungs, making it difficult to breathe, and then the rest of the body simply goes numb.

When they say things happen so fast they become a blur, is it because the brain doesn't want the details. It only needs limited information before acting on impulse and pure adrenaline. The whole time, all I could think was, "This isn't happening. This isn't happening. Why?"

In a flash of a few seconds what is burned into me forever is the complete disbelief of actions all gone completely wrong. All the actions of which I had no control over. The one secure thing that kept me from falling over suddenly disappeared. It wasn't so much what I saw that shook my core, but what I heard. It was the sound of kicking. It was the sound of yelling, screaming and growling coming from everywhere, echoing throughout the trees. It was the rush of wind not from nature but from movement that felt imagined and not possible. The screams turned from human to dog and back. The screams turned from female to male and back. The word "no" screamed over and over again until it was just a whisper.

If only time could unwind, rewind, start back at the beginning, so we could have one time to do it over, and change the outcome. If we could only play God, one time. Why can't we have only one time that

God says, "OK, you get a do-over. You get to rewind the tape of life, just this once. I will give you a few seconds to change fate." But He doesn't. There is no bargaining with God. There is no bargaining with fate. There is no bargaining with time.

After my screams of denial, I realized he left me there all alone. For that I was grateful. I crawled, dragging my heavy body toward my whimpering friend. The realization of what happened still hadn't reached my brain, but it reached my heart. How ironic the knife was still lying there, covered in blood. Was it my blood, from my heart? Blue lay on his side, breathing heavy and calling to me through his whimpering. I crawled around to face him, trying to find out where the blood was coming from and how I could stop it, but from the warmth and wetness of his fur I knew there was nothing I could do. He was gasping for air, and I only had seconds to tell him what he did for me. I lay my head down facing his, for fear if I moved him, I would cause him more pain. I pressed my nose against his, and we looked at each other eye to eye. He blinked like he always does.

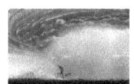

We held our eyes, while all the parallel universes, all the parallel lives that might have been, would never be, and waited yet to be, whirled around us. I saw my past and my future reflected in her eyes as I floated weightless through a warm, deep and silent water. I felt no pain, no regrets and no remorse. I felt free. My love, I am breaking your heart, but in a valiant way. The cost of knowing love is often greater than any of us can imagine paying, and it is well worth it. It will be OK. Trust me.

I kissed his nose, his face, and rubbed my fingers gently across his face as I cradled his head in my hands and told him a million times how much I loved him. I watched the life leave from his eyes. It was there, and then it was gone. He was staring into another world I couldn't see.

It is amazing the strength we can pretend to have when we need it and how quickly it disappears when we don't. I had nothing. I had no breath, no strength, no life left in me. That is how they found me. That is how I wanted to remain.

I will always be with you, Ellie.

Chapter 48

Deeper Sorrow

"You know I would be there for you if I could."

There was a deep sigh on the other end of the phone. We were both sobbing, between trying to take a breath. Mom was standing behind me with her hands gently squeezing my shoulders, listening closely as I talked to her father. She had been a solid brace on which I had been leaning since they brought me to her. I couldn't drive. She came to get me, bringing blankets to wrap Blue. I held him as we drove home. She was the one who dug a hole under a tree where he and I used to sit together. She was the one who took him from my arms, removed his collar, gave it to me and laid him gently in the ground and then buried him. She was the one who sang an old prayer song from her childhood. She was the one who told me he was not dead, that he would never die in in our hearts. I didn't want to not believe. Despite the feeling of emptiness, she did her best to fill it in with understanding and love that I never felt this deeply from her before. I needed her more now than ever, because I couldn't breathe without help.

"Ellie, you know how very sorry I am for Blue. I deeply feel your pain." Toko was barely audible through the phone. His sorrow was deep and seemed to surpass even mine.

"Toko, I can come to you. Let me come to help you."

When I finally had the courage and the voice to call Toko, I found he had only recently come back from the hospital. Lana had been pregnant when I was there, but they didn't want to tell me because of my grieving. She had gone into premature labor and by the time Toko could get to her and take her to the hospital it was too late, and she died during childbirth. Toko was still in shock.

The combination of losing Blue and Lana brought such incredible sorrow. It completely engulfed my body in a way I didn't know was possible, even after my miscarriage. I couldn't believe life could be so cruel. God had taken two beautiful creatures from this earth on the same day. Sorrow brought me to my knees.

"Ellie, I need you. I don't know what to do with this child. There is only Marta and I to care for her. She is an old woman. Lana had no family. She never talked about anyone. The father was some random guy. No idea who because he never came around to see her. She never talked to anyone about her family." His voice trailed off.

I heard the desperation in his voice. Lana had passed as a result of complications. I didn't ask for details. I didn't need to do that to Toko. Because they were not able to locate any next of kin, Toko decided to take the baby rather than give it up for adoption. There was no foster care in the area. He had no idea what they were going to do with the baby so he told them he was family, and they simply believed him and gave her to him.

The memory of Lana's smile covering her entire face tore at my heart. She was always smiling. I remembered her bringing Blue to me that one night wearing my special necklace. I am sure now she was the one who had made it. I grasped the pendant in my hand and lost control of my emotions. Mom took the phone from me to talk to her father.

I sat down on the floor as an image of the two of them, Lana and Blue, came to my mind. I pictured them together and the thought gave me a fleeting sense of peace. I held on desperately to that vision as it got me through each tortuous minute. I had wanted to get strength from Toko, but he had nothing to give. His wise words were hidden in his own sorrow. We were both lost for consolation.

"No matter how you both feel right now, there is a little baby girl who has no mother. Justice will be served to Lane. Leave it to the authorities. There was a witness who saw him. Some guy in a black diesel truck who said he knew you. Go be where you are needed. This child is a light for the darkness you both feel right now." Mom knelt in front of me, taking my hands in hers. She handed the phone back to me.

"You should see her, Ellie. There is something about her. Can you help me, please? I don't know what to do." Toko's sorrow was unbearable to hear coming from such a strong man.

I knew he was right. I had to find the energy to go. I was so incredibly empty inside, like part of me was missing, never to be replaced. It was impossible to erase the horrible images flashing in and out of my head. I was angry, then inconsolable. There couldn't possibly ever be a light to this darkness I felt. No matter where I turned, I was drowning in reminders of Blue's existence.

Chapter 49

Through the Eyes of Blue

I don't know how it is for anyone else. I don't know how this life thing is supposed to work. All I know is I was born, I was raised in goodness and in turmoil, and I met a dog who changed my life. He was the one who gave me courage. He was so much a part of me. I could not take a step without him following. I spent a lot of time looking into his eyes, and he into mine. I got lost in those eyes. Now they visited me in my dreams.

I never questioned how an animal could dig in so deep into my heart. It felt natural. It felt like human nature. He depended on me for love, for food, for his life, and I depended on him for my courage and my strength.

Now holding this helpless child in my arms brought a realization to me that sometimes animals, and people, come into your life to save you. They give you what you need if you are open to it. But you must be open to letting some things go, by holding on tightly to others. I held on to this little one sleeping so peacefully in my arms. I watched her with an odd sense of familiarity. It felt like a complex bond traveled through time, twisting, turning, yet incredibly strong had pulled me to her. She opened her eyes, yawned, and blinked at me. She looked at me, remarkably, from one eye to the other through a newborn's focus. She looked at me through her cloudy blue eyes, then reached her little hand toward my mouth. I swear I saw her tilt her head to the side and smile.

Toko named her Azul. Welcome to this world, Azul. I love you.

www.ingramcontent.com/pod-product-compliance
Lightning Source LLC
Chambersburg PA
BHW050519110726